The Collecting Point

K.E.Crawford

To Ann
With best wishes
Kathleen

Labrador

L

First Published in Great Britain 2003
By Labrador
PO Box 38250
LONDON NW3 7YT
Email – Labrador.k@btopenworld.com

This novel is a work of fiction, though it includes references to actual people and events – these references are used only to enhance the story in its historical context. All other characters are fictitious and any resemblance to persons living or dead is entirely coincidental.

A catalogue record for this book is available from the British Library

ISBN 0-9544018-0-8

In memory of my son Neil, whose fortitude and dedication to his specialist subject, Bullying in the Workplace, inspired and sustained me during the writing of this novel.

THE COLLECTING POINT

VIENNA

1

In Austria, the word *please* is a command, not a polite form of consent. This became apparent at my first meeting with Professor Wilhelm Frohmann in his office in Vienna. 'Please' he said with a sweeping gesture, as he held the back of an old green leather chair. I felt his eyes running across my dress, seeing only a young presumptuous art curator about to suggest some implausible idea for his approval. I sat on the edge of the chair, aware that my proposal could well appear to be calculated lunacy.

I had expected a more sophisticated interior, in keeping with his celebrity. Instead, a massive dark oak desk, stacked with papers and slides, was cramped into an untidy room with floor-to-ceiling bookshelves spilling volumes on to the flagstone floor. A long narrow medieval window was the only source of natural light. Frohmann was cordial but aloof, making sure I appreciated his time was valuable, looking at text on his desk, not giving me his undivided attention. 'Professor, I shall be as brief as I can. I have already discussed the project with Dr. Anton Hempf in London and it has his full approval and support.' The Professor looked up sharply, and smiled.

'Ah - Dr.Hempf - it must be almost thirty years since we met. A lot has happened since then.'

'I'm sure it has,' I agreed, 'but may I explain the project to you: perhaps we can discuss how to make it practicable,' implying his involvement would be without question.

'I want to mount an exhibition in London of paintings, stolen during World War 11. I know that since reparation began many works of art have been returned to their owners. But many have not. The list of major works still unaccounted for is immense.' I said. 'What I want to do is to find them, exhibit them, and hopefully establish right of possession.'

Professor Frohmann sat back in his chair. A taut smile flicked across his face. He rested his chin on his collar and looked at me over the top of his spectacles.

'And why, Miss Edan, do you think I can help you achieve such an exhibition?'

'Because, your participation would give credence to any project. And I've been told you can be very persuasive. Your involvement, Herr Professor, would be invaluable.'

The Professor spoke slowly, lighting a cigarette at the same time. 'Well, I think the idea is a good one, but it's too late. If you had started fifteen, even ten years ago, it might have been possible,' he said dismissively. 'But so many records were lost during the occupation, it would be impossible to research.'

'I'm not sure I understand. Which occupation?' I asked.

'The British and the American,' he said.

'But Professor, those records exist - they were removed by the allies in 1945, not destroyed.'

'Even so, Miss Edan, to locate such material after twenty-five years, considering the circumstances of their loss, would be unrealistic. I am sure you know that details of all the paintings held in protective custody during the war, were widely circulated: the time limit has elapsed. No one would be able to prove ownership. As much as I would like to see you succeed, I am not able to help.'

I had not expected Professor Frohmann to respond enthusiastically to my proposal. From any Austrian viewpoint, it was a sensitive subject. But I knew an exhibition would give museums and galeries a chance to legitimise stolen loot and works with false documentation. The owners were dead. The Professor knew that. If looted works of art were exhibited, and some were recognised and claimed by descendants, the number would be small: unclaimed orphan pictures could then be offered legitimately on the open market.

He leant across his desk and handed me his card. 'Please' he said, 'give my regards to Dr.Hempf, when you return to London.'

I took the card and put in my briefcase. 'Professor, would you think about the proposal? Perhaps we can meet at the same time tomorrow?'

He nodded. 'If you insist. But you are wasting your time.'

My impression of Professor Wilhelm Frohmann was as I had expected: an academic with a media persona, a charismatic personality, and a gentleman of breeding. I had been told he was the most respected Art Historian in Austria, with influential friends in politics and the arts. He thrived on exposure, his face appearing regularly in Die Presse and Die Salzburger

Nachrichten, often in the company of elegant women. I looked forward to knowing more about this cross between Errol Flynn and Sigmund Freud. I had time to think it over. I walked the streets, drank coffee, and looked at cold nude stone statues with icicles trickling from penises and breasts.

The following morning the Kartnerstrasse, Vienna's main thoroughfare was gearing itself for a day's work. Shutters of elegant boutiques were being raised, coffee houses beginning to fill. I turned into Dorotheergasse. It was a narrow street, cobble stoned, with old six storey buildings and small galeries selling antique furnishings, antiquarian books, religious artefacts and paintings. I went through a double-arched door similar to the front of a Romanesque church, into the Galerie Frohmann. Inside, a small bookstand displayed exhibition catalogues and artists' postcards. A young man dusting a bookshelf moved quickly forward.

'Guten Morgen,' he said. I asked for Professor Frohmann.

'Your name, bitte?'

'Katrina Edan,' I replied.

'Moment, bitte.'

He went to a very old-fashioned wall phone and wound the handle. Turning to me, he said, 'please'. He opened a side door leading into a cobble-stoned courtyard. To the rear was the long low building where the Professor had his office. Maybe it was converted from an old wine cellar, as the arched ribbed ceilings were low and the stone stairs pockmarked by time. There was no daylight in the stairwell, no handrail, and the narrow steps curved up one flight. The young man opened a heavy wooden door into a small vestibule crammed with books, leading into an office, occupied by a woman in a black dress. Her desk just fitted into the space. 'Frau Stolz, this is Miss Edan. She has a meeting with Herr Professor.'

'Danke,' she replied. She did not move, only raised her eyes to establish approval or disapproval. Anything resembling a smile would have been an intrusion on her face. Her desk was littered with cuttings and papers, no semblance of order. A naked light bulb in a green metal shade hung close to her work. The room was claustrophobic. Opposite her desk was a pair of double carved doors. Professor Frohmann emerged. 'Guten Morgen Miss Edan, please,' he said and waved me into his office.

In spite of Professor Frohmann's dismissal of my idea, I had formulated a programme for his perusal, in the event that he had changed his mind. Before I could divulge my plan he spoke.
'Miss Edan, I have decided to help you set up an exhibition.' He did not clarify why and his reason was unimportant to me anyway. He placed a cigarette in an ivory holder, took a gold lighter from his waistcoat pocket and held it to the tip, his eyes on me at the same time.
'But I must warn you, Miss Edan. There are some very ruthless leftovers from the war years, repressed feelings enraged by loss and resentment, and given an opportunity, explode. Some people will take extreme measures to protect what they have acquired. I can persuade some owners to loan, but I cannot and I must repeat cannot, have any involvement concerning the return of art works, indiscriminately to expatriates. They could use your exposition as a means to make money.'
'I don't understand your choice of word, Herr Professor. These "expatriates", who lost and left everything, except the skin they stood in, were subjected to the lowest depth of degradation, then, in most cases, the final solution. Are you suggesting that Jews, whose possessions were stolen, might falsify documents, for gain?'
'Miss Edan, you misinterpret my meaning. We are talking about masterpieces, which on the open market would demand millions.'
'Excuse me, Herr Professor, but dignity and self-respect, cannot be bought with money. You know, and I know, these masterpieces must not become the currency of illicit trading, nor can they remain hidden. Complicated circumstances maybe, but paintings must be flushed out now, while these "expatriates" are still alive to certify them.'

At the same time as I was trying to convince the Professor, I was also convincing myself. I went on. 'All it takes to get this project started is expertise, guile and blatent chutzpah. You, Professor, have the expertise, I have the latter.'
He chuckled. 'We don't speak the same language, Miss Edan.'

The intonation on the word language was weighted with meaning.
'We do,' I replied. 'Our language is art - it's only our motives which differ.'

The Professor picked up the phone. 'Firstly,' he said to me, as he was dialling, 'I think you should meet Gerhard Hofer. He is a colleague of mine and he owns a galerie; he may be able to help you.'
'Gerhard,' he said, 'here is Wilhelm. I have Miss Edan from London in my office. I think you should meet'. The Professor was listening. 'Gut, I shall ask.'
He looked at me. 'To-night?' I nodded.
Conversation continued in German, too fast and too complicated for me to understand. When he put the phone down, he said to me 'Gerhard will meet you in the Cafe Mozart at nine, and you will learn that Vienna is a village, a very difficult place to keep secrets.'

At that moment I had none, but I wondered if the Professor had.

I was surprised when Wilhelm Frohmann suggested we go to a coffee house. We walked along the Graben, past Hapsburger Gasse into the Kohlmarkt. It was an elegant street, frequented by advantaged overdressed ladies in furs and ridiculous hats, men swathed in Loden coats and trilby hats with feathers stuck in ribbon bands. Some wore the tails of pheasants or wild duck, which hovered high above the crown of their hats, giving them exaggerated height and a haughty presence. Men and women were trying to upstage each other, the men feeding on their vanity and pride, the women on sexual innuendo. They were both in the grip of a past, long gone, out-moded epoch.

From what I had seen so far, Vienna is a city, which leaves little to the imagination. Grandeur on a massive scale was overwhelmingly abundant. Created by Franz Josef, the last Emperor, the sham Gothic and Imperial Baroque buildings within the inner city were testimony to a past age, culminating in the building of the Ringstrasse, a street, not just to enclose the city, but to represent all that was important to a dying Empire. The Ringstrasse epitomized the past. It became a social parade ground for the demimonde. Lifestyles alternated between opulence and decadence. While the Empire was in decline, the Viennese wrapped their apprehension in a display of outward frivolity that eventually, through its shallowness, became transparent. Mozart, Haydn and Strauss were played in all the salons and concert halls throughout the world. The Viennese thrived on reflected glory, and when the Anschluss took place in 1938, annexing Austria to Germany, it was welcomed by the bourgeoisie as a chance for renewal and a return to the past greatness of a lost Holy Roman Empire.

Between 1939 and 1945 when war raged in Europe, I was a child. Not till later did I learn that Vienna and Salzburg, the two centres of cultural eminence, were the nesting grounds for citizens to show solidarity with Germany. They collaborated with the Gestapo and SS. and perpetrated unprecedented crimes against humanity.

Professor Frohmann stopped just before reaching the end of the Kohlmarkt opposite the Winter Palace and the Spanish Riding School, at the Café Demel. Lace curtains covered ornately cut frosted-glass windows set into deep wooden frames. I wondered why he couldn't have told me in his office. Perhaps it was a hangover from the war, I thought, when no one knew who was friend or enemy. Mostly they were both. I had read, that during the Nazi regime, everything and everyone was for sale, even among families, brother betrayed brother.

Inside the revolving door a hostess greeted the Professor.

'Herr Professor' she said, 'Guten Tag . . . a table for two?'

We were seated in a quiet corner, by the side of the entrance, reserved I presumed, for regular clients. The interior was luxurious Empire decor. The wall panelling, tables and chairs, were so highly polished they looked like glass. The work of myriad flunkeys had created this everlasting effect. Professor Frohmann grinned as he lowered his voice.

'This café is famous for . . . assignations.' His eyes scanned the room like a mischievous schoolboy, knowing other suspicious eyes were watching us. 'That is not why we are here.' The Professor looked up, as a woman acknowledged him - smiled - a knowing smile - an affectionate smile - a don't-forget-me-smile; before going through the revolving door: another lady removed her glove, before shaking the Professor's hand and exiting with a sweep of her fox fur coat.

The Professor was totally at ease. 'Try the Linzertorte,' he said 'it is the best in Vienna.' I stirred my coffee, swirling a mass of whipped cream around the cup.

'I think you should know something about Gerhard Hofer before you meet, as you might find him somewhat, aggressive. Firstly, he volunteered to serve in the German Army following his service in the Hitler youth movement and his dedicated belief in Adolf Hitler. He was convinced that the Austro-German pact of 1938 would be the salvation for Europe. He became Captain, and was wounded in France. He spent the rest of the war as an "internal" officer.'

I looked up from my pastry. 'What was the role of an "internal" officer?'

Frohmann answered abruptly. 'I cannot answer that question. I was not in the army. But I can tell you, he has built-in prejudices: no gaps - no room for reasoning. Hofer admits nothing, gives nothing, and bleeds people. Since the end of the war he has lived on his wits, and he has more than survived. I am telling you this, Miss Edan, so you can be on your guard. Do not mis-interpret my meaning. I am sure you are in safe keeping with yourself. Just be careful.'

***

Swinging my handbag in tune with the Harry Lime theme, I hummed my way to the Cafe Mozart. I remembered the moment in the classic film "The Third Man" when Josef Cotton saw the face of Orson Wells (Harry Lime) in a doorway, when he emerged from the sewers of Vienna and I wondered if Anton Karas was still playing the zither: any apprehension at meeting Gerhard Hofer faded.

The menu at Café Mozart was an eclectic mix of Kaiser platters favoured by Kings: Hungarian Goulash soup and the proverbial Wiener schnitzel mit sauerkraut. Lace covered lamps hung above each table, and the red chequered tablecloths were more reminiscent of a French bistro than a cafe this far into Eastern Europe. Waitresses with white aprons the size of a doyley sticking out over their moneybags, hustled about. There is something ridiculous about these stomach pouches, especially when they raise the apron and fish around for change! They wore laced ankle boots to keep the famous Viennese ankle trim: a remnant of Empire, when to show a little ankle was the most titillation a man could expect.

I ordered a glass of wine and watched the entrance. A man limped heavily on a clubfoot towards my table. Every cliché, that has ever been quoted about mystery and subterfuge manifested in his appearance. He was short, sloppy, fat, wore a black leather coat and a black beret and he was chewing a cigar. He sat.

'You are Katrina Edan. Gerhard Hofer.'

He didn't offer his hand. He spoke in a very precise tone, ejecting words at me, using German when he could not think of the English, or more likely didn't want to.

'Frohmann has told me you are here to do the impossible, I tink.'

I didn't respond.

'You vant to dig up the past and come out with everything nicely filtered. I can tell you now, forget it. No one will assist you in perpetrating crimes against innocent people who have rights. Yes, rights. Ve von our rights.'

Good start I thought. But I didn't like the script. Could Professor Frohmann have prompted it? He went on.

'I do not know who sent you, or who is paying you. My advice is, you are vasting your time here. Ve have laws, rules. Ve respect our independence. Ve are not answerable to any outside interference.'

This sermon was long enough. I had no intention of being lectured by this ex-German soldier and made it clear to Hofer.

'Your information, Herr Hofer, is second-hand and I am not intimidated by words, in any language. Firstly, I am not being paid. Secondly, you lost a war others lost everything. I represent the others. Also, Herr Hofer, if Austria does not participate in this project, it will only confirm what is already known. Larceny on a grand scale.'

Hofer re-lit his cigar while still chewing on the soggy end.

'Herr Hofer, I will make sure that every outlet for the sale of works of art will close to Austrian dealers who attempt to trade in looted art.'

A confident grin crossed Hofer's face, as his nodding head allayed any fear that I could be a threat.

'Go on' he said, almost laughing.

'I will release information to the press that will put curators worldwide in doubt as to the authenticity of works purchased from here. Your borders are small, Herr Hofer. Since the communists built the Berlin wall, you're blocked to the East. The Germans are courting confidence from the West, and Italy has no money. Where will you trade? My exhibition could be the turning point for Austro-European confidence. Goodwill has to be earned. You could be part of that renaissance.'

'Another vine?' Hofer asked, looking at my empty glass. I was tired, but accepted.

I had deduced from what the Professor told me that in no way was Hofer altruistically motivated: he was a prowler, an opportunist. Money made him tick. So, knowing the ingredients, I offered him something to suck on.

'Herr Hofer,' I asked. 'Do you have anything important to sell?'

His beady eyes did not move. He just stared directly at me.

'Fraulein Edan, it is late. I vill be in my galerie at Am Hof tomorrow morning.' He handed me a card, touched his beret, and limped to the door.

The intimidation thrown at me by Gerhard Hofer only fuelled my confidence. While his support for the exhibition would be useful, it was not essential and I could cause considerable embarrassment to his pocket.

I returned to the Hotel Sacher on the Philharmonikerstrasse: a grand hotel, which still retains rooms at the rear where Emperor Franz Josef entertained his mistress. The concierge handed me my key and an envelope. It was a note from Professor Wilhelm Frohmann. 'Please' it said, would you come to my home for dinner tomorrow night. Guests will arrive at seven.

This invitation astonished me. My intuition had led me to believe that Professor Wilhelm Frohmann was motivated by art history. Or did he have ulterior motives?

Finding the Poltnergasse was not easy. Tucked away in a small courtyard behind the Am Hof, the old market square was a group of renovated buildings. A dark green, newly painted door was prominent, with a nameplate in brass set into the wooden frame. Gerhard Hofer - Erste stock. I went to the first floor.

The entrance was ultra modern with glass doors and a bell push. A young girl answered and took me to Hofer's galerie, which was surprisingly large - more like a mini ballroom - with highly polished light wood floors. Bright directional lamps spotlighted contempory paintings. Another door led to a smaller galerie where a single painting rested against the wall. It was a full-length portrait of a dark haired woman, wearing a white flouncing chiffon dress with a feather boa at her neck.

'It is the Portrait of Hermine Gallia painted by Gustav Klimt between 1904 and 1906, one of his great vorks.'
'Who owns the painting, Herr Hofer?'
'I do, natürlich,' he said, as if the question should not have been asked. Having been warned by Professor Frohmann, I felt my question mandatory. I pressed a little further.
'With provenance?' I questioned.
'Certainly, mit provenance, Fraulein. Vy all dese questions?'

The blood was rising in Hofer's face as he tapped his cane on the floor. 'Is it for sale?' I asked.
'Ja, it is for sale, zie price ist half a million in sterling.'
'How long has it been on the market?'
'It has not been on zie market.'
'But have you offered it privately? I'm asking these questions as I can't access its potential for sale until I have all the facts.'
'It has been illustrated in books. But it has never been offered for sale.' I wondered why.
'You must understand, Fraulein Edan, zie market vas not ready. I knew it could take many years before Klimt vould be recognised, so I vaited.'
'What do you expect from me Herr Hofer?'
'I vant zie painting sold by private treaty in Britain or zie United States and not on zie open market. You, I believe, have zie contacts.'

Curious, I thought. Where did that information come from?

A business deal "on trust", is the fast route to litigation. So I politely asked. 'What are the terms of sale?'
Curtly, he told me. 'One per cent.'

Gerhard Hofer and Professor Frohmann could have arrived from different planets. On the one hand the sophisticate, on the other an impaired survivor. Both had their uses, both their needs. Frohmann the historian was dedicated to stimulating interest in great art, his charisma a means to an end. Hofer, on the other hand, was a demonic, embittered reactionary. Both were the sum total of their backgrounds, but Frohmann respected the living and the dead, while Hofer could dispense with both.

***

My room on the first floor of the Hotel Sacher overlooked the Ringstrasse. I took a wool dress with long sleeves from the wardrobe. The black top fitted closely into the waist, then flared into a short peplum: the finely pleated skirt of a multi-coloured oriental pattern dropped just above my ankles. My ample breasts gave a good curve into a small waistline. I stepped back from the mirror feeling confident. I took the Professor's card from my briefcase.

I waited a few minutes for a taxi, my red hair blowing in the wind. The lights of the city twinkled like ground stars, and then disappeared as the taxi climbed the snaky road into the Vienna woods above the city.

A maid in Tyrolean dress answered the door. She was slim, blonde and about fifteen. I heard laughter coming from the interior. The hallway was impressive with hunting trophies staring down from the walls: a deer's head, a boar's head, a stuffed duck, and on the floor a massive bear skin, transformed into a rug. I was taken to the salon.

Professor Frohmann rose from his chair and with outstretched hand took mine, bowed, raised my hand to his lips and said, 'Miss Edan. Come; let me introduce you to my wife. Gerda, this is Katrina Edan.' We shook hands. Then in turn he introduced me to the other guests.

'This is Helmut Wingler, the director of Austrian television,' an over-sized puffy-faced man, with a sticky palm. Then, 'Luigi Preizmeir - he's a good painter but he's lazy.'

The young man grimaced and nodded in agreement. The Professor chuckled. 'Maria Proll from the Opera House and Frau and Herr Weisskoff from the United States.' I shook hands and smiled.

The maid was holding a small tray with a single glass and a decanter. The Professor poured.

'You'll like this. It's an Austrian speciality, a very fine old plum schnapps.' He watched as I sipped. 'Gut?' asked the Professor.

Gerda Frohmann, a short compact woman in her mid-fifties, well covered, without fat, moved gracefully, speaking to her guests individually as though no one else was there. Her hair was dyed a light shade of brown that complemented her tawny brown eyes. But her most redeeming feature was a milky white skin, slightly rouged, which gave her face a doll like fragility.

She moved slowly to speak with the maid before turning to her husband. 'Dinner will be served in ten minutes, Wilhelm.'
'Fine, my dear,' he responded, with artificial formality.

The pictures decorating the salon walls were of incalculable value, but before I could get closer, we moved into another room. It had a grand piano at one end, the dining table at the other, with a chaise longue and Victorian high-backed armchairs grouped in the centre. The round dining table was covered with an antique lace tablecloth. Fine silver and crystal were in place. I noticed each setting had its own tiny condiment set for salt and pepper. I was seated between the Professor and Helmut Wingler.
Gerda Frohmann asked. 'Do you speak German Miss Edan?'
I said 'no, but I understand a little.'
'Well I'm sure we can all manage in English,' she said, while the maid liberally filled our glasses with a white Spatzlinger from the Kloster Neuburg.

To bring me into the conversation Wilhelm Frohmann asked if I had visited the English Theatre on the Josefgasse. I hadn't, but I had heard that performances were well attended and the Viennese liked British humour. 'Do you know,' Frohmann said, 'it's the first English speaking theatre outside of Britain: it opened in 1963. It's a wonderful way for us to keep in touch with the language.'

Yet no one asked me what brought me to Vienna nor mentioned my profession. The conversation tripped over the evening like a duck with ducklings following, crossing a main road, not looking left or right and certainly not including me. I had the feeling they knew why I was in Vienna, but chose to ignore the purpose of my visit as though I was involved in socially unacceptable conduct. Even Mrs.Weisskoff from New York was desultory. 'Love the English countryside' she said 'so green and fresh,' leaving nothing to add.

By the end of the main course, the conversation became more animated.

Helmut Wingler's voice echoed round the room, speaking German at increasing speed. 'Haben Sie eine rotwein, Marta?' he said to the maid. She hastily appeared with a flagon of red wine. Helmut waved his arm, 'don't take it away, my dear. Put it under my chair.'

Neither the host nor hostess commented so I presumed that this was his normal behaviour and I wondered, when Helmut's hand rested on my leg, if that was normal behaviour too. He told a lewd joke in German with illustrative gestures, which he attempted to translate for my benefit. His arms were flying in all directions, returning to rest, periodically, on my knee. I shuffled uncomfortably.

At this point, Wilhelm Frohmann asserted his role as host and said, 'Shall we take coffee?'

I selected a high backed individual chair next to an inlaid mother of pearl table. Luigi Preizmeir sat next to me and said in a pedantic lilt, 'I understand from the Professor that you're searching for lost works of art.'

'Not exactly lost Herr Preizmeir, more likely stolen.'

Surprised by my forthright judgement he said, 'I wish you luck, Miss Edan, you will certainly need it.'

The Professor sat opposite me, so I was able to observe him more acutely. He is a tall man, even when seated, with an abundant amount of greying hair, smoothed back with no parting, which reached to the edge of his collar. His forehead wide, his eyes playful, hiding behind thick black rimmed glasses, darting pools of grey, which smiled as the taut skin at their corners allowed them to reveal - nothing. A neatly trimmed Victorian moustache shadowed generous lips. He was expensively dressed in a dark pin striped suit and waistcoat complemented by a silk cravat held in place by a pearl pin. The charm was unmistakeable: gentility at its most polished. Yet something in the demeanour of the Professor put me on edge.

After thanking him and his wife I had the misfortune to share a taxi with the drunken television director, who expected me to join him in his apartment. His behaviour was outrageous as he pushed his bulk close to me, but he was disadvantaged by alcohol as my elbow pressed into his ribs, producing a loud burp. I left the taxi without saying thank you.

***

The following day I met Otto Prantl, director of the Prantl Galerie. His galerie occupied the corner of Singerstrasse and Kartnerstrasse, and was showing modern paintings in one window and period pieces in the other. Pictures were standing on easels near the entrance, none I might add of particular merit. I introduced myself to the dyed blonde sitting at a high fronted desk. 'Please will you take a seat,' she said, and pointed to an upright chair. She dialled Herr Prantl.

A tall, extremely thin, dark, sleek-haired man in his fifties moved quickly from a door at the end of the galerie. We shook hands.' Shall we go to my office?'

We went to a small room with catalogues neatly arranged on shelves, an antique desk with a silver inkstand and an old brass telephone. Prantl sat at the desk, his hands locked together by his thin nervous fingers.

'I understand from Professor Frohmann you are trying to collect paintings for an exhibition.'

His English was clipped, but very clear and precise.

'That's correct, Herr Prantl. But I want to find stolen paintings, those mis-appropriated works of art which found their way into Austrian homes.' I hesitated before adding, 'for safe keeping.'

Prantl was studying me like a hawk: an impudent impostor into his sanctuary, where the past was only history and not for regurgitated consumption.

'I am unable to see what my galerie can do for you, Miss Edan.'

It would have been counter-productive for me to tell Prantl the strategy I intended to use. This information he would have already received from Professor Frohmann. So I tried a different approach.

'I have substantial backing for this project. Finance has been promised from three banks,' I exaggerated. 'Your Galerie will get vast exposure to a worldwide audience at no cost, and the gratitude of innumerable people.'

'How much money have you raised, Miss Edan?'

'Whatever it takes,' I said confidently, although not exactly true.

He stroked his chin. A large diamond, set in heavy gold, sparkled from his little finger.

'I said politely, 'would you agree to look for any paintings being sold on the Austrian or German markets without provenance? That would be an invaluable start.'

'It may take some time, Miss Edan.'

'I have three years, till 1973, Herr Prantl.'

To flush out recalcitrant keepers of looted art, Prantl's trading since the end of the war in 1945 would be invaluable. He

regularly attended auctions in Berne, Hamburg and Vienna: trading posts for selling war time loot. I gave him my telephone number in London and said. 'I believe you were at university with Dr.Hempf.' His thin frame stiffened, his head grew on its neck before it dropped into an abrupt nod.
'Correct.'
'He sends regards to you, from London,' I said.

I left the galerie with the tension following me. If Prantl held illicit paintings, it would be in his interest to collaborate with me, rather than be exposed by me. I suspected that both Otto Prantl and Wilhelm Frohmann had acquired paintings by corrupt means. Gerhard Hofer was obviously a serious contender. But Frohmann and Prantl were more sophisticated and additionally more cunning.

I wandered into a wine cellar, ordered a jug of wine and ruminated on my day in Vienna.

At my final meeting with Professor Frohmann before leaving for London, a number of issues had to be put in place. I was encouraged when the Professor said to me.
'Professor Gutman Holbeck, the director of the Albertina, is prepared to support the exhibition.'

I had not expected The Albertina to respond so quickly. The museum owns the largest collection of Graphic works in Europe, second only to the British Museum. Any involvement from them could set a precedent for other museums to follow.
'How many works do you expect to exhibit?' asked Frohmann.
'It's more a question, Professor, of how many we are able to find.'

He relaxed in his large leather chair, his arms draped over the armrests. I noticed his slim hands, long tapering artistic fingers, buffed nails and pale delicate skin. In spite of the importance of the meeting, I couldn't resist thinking, would I enjoy those hands touching me? I hoped my lapse of concentration had gone unnoticed. I wasn't sure.
'Professor, I shall have a contract written in London and sent to you for approval. Specific clauses covering venue, insurance and the final date will be left open till later. How long will we need?'
He replied 'what is the English expression, about string? How long?'

'Professor Frohmann, two years, three, four?'
'Miss Edan, I suggest we allow three years, with a review after eighteen months.' He continued. 'One other clause must be included in the contract. Provenance on all the works collected, must be researched by you.'
'Any more amendments?'
'Not exactly,' he replied ambiguously, as he crushed a cigarette end into an ashtray. 'But I am preparing a definitive assessment on the works of Rembrandt. Dr.Hempf is an authority on Rembrandt's works. I would like you to ask him if he would be prepared to edit my book.' The Professor lit another cigarette. 'As we have not been in contact since 1939 - almost thirty one years, I am apprehensive that he may not consent.'

I thought carefully before I answered.
'I can only be your messenger. I have Dr.Hempf's ear, but not his voice. When I return to Austria next month, hopefully, I'll be able to answer your question.'

It was cold and dark when I arrived at Vienna airport. On the flight home, I fell fast asleep. February is not the kindest month to be flying north, but I was flying home.

LONDON

2

The task facing me was gargantuan. Flushed with the excitement of the exhibition, I had fallen headlong into territory beyond the usual boundaries of a curator. I was committed to exposing wartime crimes, which could not and would not be tried. I searched my conscience for a reason for following this route. I had to justify to myself that three or four years of my life would result in something worthwhile on many levels.

Artistically, the exhibit had to be innovative. Politically, it had to be neutral. Financially, it had to be viable. But most importantly, it had to be morally explosive.

I arrived in my office in Inverness Street, Camden Town, at noon. My assistant, Sue, had the coffee percolating and handed me a china mug.

'Did you have a good trip, Katrina?'

'I'm not sure yet. Any messages?'

'Dr.Hempf phoned. He will call later. He wants a meeting as soon as you've surfaced. Desmond Hegarty invited you for lunch. Barbara Murkin would like you to review the Manet exhibition. And guess what? Your article on the merits of soft sculpture was panned to buggery, just as you had hoped. That'll stir up some nice sweet controversy.'

We laughed. It was good to be home.

Sue Hepple had worked with me for five years. She almost wrote a book once. The talent's there but not the application. She liked company and the pace that builds with a project. She liked her job. I liked her.

Sue was a good fencer. She kept the sharks out and the Inland Revenue too. She also knew when I was out but in, and to whom to give the heave - ho. Her telephone manner was discreetly lethal.

I looked at the pile of papers on my desk and decided that my first priority was to find financial backing for the exhibition. Sponsorship for the arts was not a priority for companies or banks: advertising from football, cricket, athletics and cigarettes paid the right dividends: kept the shareholders happy and the directors in situ. Vast sums were ploughed into the pockets of high profile agents J.Walter Thompson and Saatchi & Saatchi, to promote companies' products to such an extent, that any funds left for altruistic causes, went to established charities.

I decided to write to Bernard Anderson, the manager of Samuel Hall Bank, briefly outlining my proposal, in the hope he might consider sponsorship. I had met him a few times at exhibition previews and I knew he had an interest in paintings. We had what one colloquially calls a nodding acquaintance.

***

The telephone rang. My eyelids felt like gritting machines scraping relentlessly over my pupils, refusing to open. One eye managed to focus on the wall clock. Eight. On-the-dot-eight. Who the hell dares I thought, as I picked up the phone.

'Good morning, Katrina, its Sue.'

I knew I was lucky to have a secretary who opened the office at eight but unlucky when she expected me to follow suit.

'There's a message in this morning's post from Bernard Anderson's secretary,' Sue said. 'He'll see you at 9.30.'

'Which day?' I asked

'Today.'

'Don't play games Sue.'

'Katrina, that's the message. I suggest you jump into some battle gear and get there poste haste: we need some money, remember?'

By 9.25 I was in the foyer of the Samuel Hall Bank in St.James's Square, a private bank where clients have to be introduced, like joining an exclusive club: unlike a High Street bank who will open an account for one pound, here the minimum is £10.000. Not that they don't want your money, they are just fussy about who's money it is and how much of the stuff you have.

A liveried doorman asked my name before pushing a revolving glass door for me to enter. Once past his scrutinizing smile I was in the open plan marbled ground floor. There was nothing to indicate this was a bank trading in millions: no grilles, counters or offices. My reflection cast shadows on the shining marble and the heels of my shoes echoed as I walked across a vast empty space towards two smartly dressed women waiting

behind enormous teak desks. They were not receptionists, I later discovered. They were there to discreetly take in or hand out any negotiable currency.
'Miss Edan, Mr.Anderson will only be a few minutes,' the smiling middle-aged lady said to me. I settled on a black leather couch facing a glass-plated coffee table with The Times, the Investor's Chronicle and the Financial Times, neatly placed in a contrived fan shape, which I did not disturb. Five minutes later I was escorted to the first floor via a wide curving glass sided staircase and along a carpeted corridor, hung with impressionist oil paintings.

Bernard Anderson was a slightly plump man in his early fifties, with a round face, and dark receding hair. I assessed he had become a manager through graft and good mathematics: certainly not by way of the old school tie.
'I read your letter Miss Edan,' Anderson said. 'Would you tell me more precisely what you hope to achieve?'

I explained to Bernard Anderson my proposal for the exhibition and the contacts I had already made with the help of Dr. Anton Hempf. Anyone with a hint of interest in the arts would know of Dr.Hempf. He was the leading scholar on the works of Rembrandt and the most published writer on art history in the English language.
'Anton Hempf is assisting me with introductions to past associates in Austria, who might know of the whereabouts of looted works of art.' To substantiate this added.
'I have already met Professor Wilhelm Frohmann, Otto Prantl and Gerhard Hofer, in Vienna.'
Mr.Anderson didn't waste time. 'Tell me, Miss Edan how much money are you looking for?'
'In the region of £1,500,000.'
'That's a hefty sum,' he said as he put his pen down.
'It is, I know, but if that amount could be split between four sponsors, it would reduce liability.'
'And what are the risks?'
'None. In fact you don't even part with the money. What I propose is that a sum, let's say £375,000, is deposited in an account by your bank, for a period of four years and the interest only is paid into an exhibition account, to fund the research and

expenses. With the interest rate at 12% to-day and going up, this represents £45,000 a year, at no cost and no risk to the bank's capital.'
'So, you're calculating an input of £180,000 over four years. With four banks that gives you a working capital of £720,000. Could it take longer?'
'That, unfortunately, I am unable to answer at this stage. In normal circumstances it should take three years, hopefully I can keep within that schedule.'
'What would the bank gain from being £375,000 short on investment capital?' he asked.
'Nothing, Mr.Anderson. This exhibition is not about gain: it's about loss. What I can suggest is that any orphan pictures which I uncover that are not claimed during the exhibition, are offered first to the sponsors at the market price, and those submitted by museums and galleries are returned when the exhibition closes.'
'Miss Edan, I appreciate all you're telling me, and personally think the cause is worthy, but decisions on finance must go before the board of directors: it's for them to decide if funds can be made available.'
'Are you on the board, Mr.Anderson?'
'Yes I am, but I can't anticipate what response the board will give. Send me a written proposal, so I have all the facts and figures for the next board meeting?'

I reckoned my time was running out so I pressed my cause.
'One last point I should like to make for your consideration. If the bank gets the opportunity to buy any of the exhibits, the investment could produce upwards of 300%. The Art Market is rising, and I can predict it will outstrip any other investment. I am not talking about pictures Mr.Anderson; I'm talking masterpieces. There is only ever one of a kind, and that one, is irreplaceable.'

I shook Mr. Anderson's hand, thanked him for his time, and hoped that Samuel Hall would be part of the consortium.

***

As I left the bank, a taxi rounded the corner. 'Inverness Street, Camden Town,' I told the driver. Within fifteen minutes I was in

my office. Sue's desk and I settled myself on Sue's visitor's chair. Her wide eyes, always questioning, turned to face me.
'Good news or bad?' she asked.
'Neither' I replied.
'What does that mean?'
'It means, my dear Sue, that you get your fingers on the typewriter and tap out a proposal for Bernard Anderson, with the commas and colons in the right place, and absolutely no postscripts of your own divine intervention.'
'O.K. boss lady, fire me the text.'
I gave her the details of my conversation with Anderson.
'I like it, she said. 'Did he buy?'
'Don't know. It'll be a committee decision. I think I've convinced him, but I'm not sure where he stands in the pecking order. We've been down this route before, Sue. I hate chance. Shouldn't be in the English language. To chance even sounds ridiculous. If I have to knobble the Chairman, I will.'

I went into my office and pressed the inter-com button. 'Sue, when you've finished the proposal, I want a search on Broderick McKenny. He's the Chairman of Samuel Hall Investments. I need everything. Who he sleeps and eats with, where he does both, what his hobbies are, or better still, who they are. Where he lives, what time he leaves and when he returns, and what happens in between.'

It is really unnecessary to tell Sue Hepple how to beaver a body. She has a nose like a bloodhound. But I like to keep the dialogue close when we're working on a project. I want her to know every detail of what happens outside the office, so she is prepared for any eventuality. Also, she has lips like a fish. She breathes through her ears, and only opens her mouth to eat.

***

My address book has edges like the fringe on a Persian carpet: frayed to bits. I bought it at Gucci's store on Michigan Avenue, Chicago. It is a double book, one side for home, and the other foreign: so simple, so sensible. I have never seen another like it. I flicked through the foreign section to the R's, and then dialled Paris.
'Bonjour, Madame Corinne de Rothschild, s'il vous plait.'

'Votre nom?' came the response. 'Katrina Edan.' Then I heard the familiar voice of Corinne.
'Katrina, ma Cherie, comment allez-vous?'
'Bien, Corinne, I'm very well. Et tu?'
'Oh, so-so, too much work, not enough play, you know how it is.'
'How long will you be in Paris, Corinne?'
'Till the end of this month. I leave for New York early April.'
'Wonderful, I have an exciting project which I think will interest you, but it's not for the phone wires. I could take the early bird any day this week and give you a complete synopsis.'
'Moment Katrina,' I heard the ruffling of papers. 'Jeudi, can you manage Thursday? We could have lunch at Le Soufflé. Let my secretary know the flight time and Jacques will be at Charles de Gaulle.'
'Bien, et Merci, Corinne.'

I looked at my watch, it was 2.30 and I hadn't eaten. I went to Sue's office and asked what was in the fridge.
A bacon butty with or without mustard, or a stale Danish.'
'Sue Hepple, what would you do if there was a flood, a hurricane, a nerve gas attack, and you were trapped in this office?'
'I'd drink scotch, boss lady!'

I took the bacon butty, poured some coffee, and wrote the flight details for Sue to make the reservation.

My involvement with the Rothschilds goes back five years to the time when they were starting to produce wine for the mass market. To keep expensive quality vintages, separate and identifiable they had to highlight the difference. In the early sixties wine drinking became fashionable, and the British, nurtured on beer and spirits, were virtually selecting their wines by label.

The proposal I made to the Rothschilds was to create 'Famous Labels' to identify distinctive wines. This involved negotiating with living artists or their descendents. While the Rothschild name was well known enough to attract the mass market, connoisseurs spending upwards of £10 a bottle not only bought superb wine but also the added attraction of a label by a famous painter. Chagall, Picasso, Max Ernst, Cézanne and others were represented. This satisfied two dimensions, the palate and the other essential ingredient – snobbery. Corinne Rothschild signed the contract on the initial presentation. The venture proved an unrivalled success, most vintages selling out worldwide, on first tasting.

***

The BEA flight was on time. By 9.45 I was in Corinne's Mercedes en route to the Bois de Boulougne. Her office was on the top floor of her home, overlooking the famous woods, indelibly recorded by the impressionists and never really changing over the centuries. It was, by any criteria, romantic, and I must admit that Paris is one of the few cities in the world, which commands that you think of love. I have tried to define why, many times, always concluding with a different reason.

Historically, Paris conjures thoughts of existentialism: Jean Paul Sartre's 'Modern Times,' Simone de Beauvoir's 'The Second Sex,' François Sagan's 'Bonjour Tristesse'. An index of discard, where free thinkers broke all known conventions on unprecedented levels, and masterpieces, as yet unrecognised, rested on easels in grovelly studios in Montmartre, and Edith Piaf sang 'Je ne regrette rein.' Collective abandonment released great creativity, liberated inhibitions, and free love thrived in this permissive eclectic society. Picasso said, "There are only two types of women, goddesses and doormats." He should know he sampled so many!

I think, if I put Aristotle Onassis and Pablo Picasso, two small men, both lacking classical contours, side by side, I wouldn't know which one to choose. Both had the fatal ingredient for love: charisma.

The familiar sight of the Rothschild mansion swept into view as we passed a magnolia tree in full bloom on the carriage driveway. The façade had bay windows on either side of double doors, supported by pillars with ornate capitals: an impressive example of symmetric rococo architecture. Since 1784, the Rothschild family had owned the house, each successive generation changing the decor. The ballroom was now the salon, decorated in blues and gold. Priceless examples of Louis X1V furniture nestled in groups, and huge floor to ceiling mirrors magnified the scene. I took the lift to the fourth floor. Corinne was waiting, chic in a yellow tailored suit with a royal blue silk scarf knotted at her neck, and yellow high heeled shoes to gain a few inches on her own 5ft 3ins.

Over the years we have worked together, we had become friends and confidantes. Not because of the venture's success but for the simple reason that we understood each other. We settled into tapestry chairs in the curved bay window.

'Shall I give you the details of my proposal first?' I said. 'Then we'll be free to gossip over lunch.'

I continued to outline the same proposition I had offered to Samuel Hall Bank, with one exception. I suggested the deposit of £375,000 or the equivalent in French francs might be split between two banks, one in France and one in Switzerland, so the interest accruing yearly would be available in two currencies. Corinne said. 'I'm listening, ma Cherie.'

I sat forward in my chair. 'If I have to pay for information to find looted property, no one will risk exposure by receiving payment through normal channels. It would be an admission of guilt either by connection or to actual theft. But, if a bribe is in cash, it's not so easy to trace. This gives me leverage and negotiating potential.'

Corinne seemed agitated. She walked to her cabriole desk, took a notebook from a drawer and wrote while I was speaking. She looked up at me over half rimmed spectacles.

'I don't understand how you'll find paintings in France when your source of information is Austria?'

'Ah - you have anticipated my next request.'

'Don't tell me you want more than money?'

'Corinne, I'd like you to look for looted pictures.' She reacted acidly.

'Non! Absolutment, non!'

From past experience I know Corinne can divorce business from pleasure and no one should assume her beauty affects the agility of her brain. Educated at Roedean, which she hated, her nonchalant French manner belies an astute defensive mentality, culled from public school in England, where attitude is equal to intelligence, and more important often, than knowledge. Her marriage to the Baron in 1935, when she was eighteen, dashed the hopes of many French mothers, whose coquettish offspring had been waiting in the wings for the Baronetcy. Paris and the haute monde were stunned by the liaison, but title is everything. When she wafted into society like a cygnet from Swan Lake her radiant personality and the love and support of the Baron, eventually dispatched the aristocratic chill.

From 1940 the Germans occupied Paris and by 1942 with the exception of Vichy, the whole of France. Corinne was always on the run eventually being hidden in a hayloft on a farm near Aix-en-Provence, and in constant fear of exposure, until the liberation of Paris is 1944. She was one of the lucky Jews. The Baron suffered considerably with lengthy stays in work camps while his cellars and home were pillaged by the Germans. The elegant mansion in the Bois de Boulougne became the headquarters for the SS. the Schutzstaffel, Hitler's' elite guard since 1925 and during the war the controlling apparatus for the concentration camps.

'Forgetting any request for money, what do you think of the project?' I asked Corinne.

'Katrina, it's dynamite. Do you realize the implications? You could have the KGB, Stasis, Mossad, and the Austrian neo-Nazis, interfering in your life. Is the risk worth the result? But, ma Cherie, that's for you to decide. Regarding the capital amount, I must discuss the details with the Baron, and, if I understand correctly, you only have access to the interest. Seems reasonable enough, but what concerns me is the Rothschild reputation.'

'What exactly do you mean?' I inquired.

'We are not bankers. Our family are, but we are wine producers. We contribute to the French economy and employ many people.'

'Are you really saying, the subject is too explosive?'

'Not exactly. Sensitive, yes, et dangereux.' She repeated 'tres dangereux.'

I tried to be more convincing. 'May I put it another way? I think ethics will be obsolete once the publicity gets into motion. The exposure of paintings will attract every area of news media. Publicity will be enormous. Credit will come to the sponsors beyond charity, beyond redeeming art for posterity: it will be a humanitarian gesture regardless of its political or ethnic overtones. Any event that breaks new ground is branded with the cliché 'sensitive', Corinne. Please, give the project serious consideration.'

Jacques drove us to Le Soufflé, on the Rue du Mont-Thabor. I could see the familiar door of the restaurant tucked between a lingerie boutique and a jeweller. Once inside the vestibule, one feels like a wandering peasant who has landed by design on an epicurean planet. The waiter bowed and escorted us to a table with wing armchairs, a pale yellow tablecloth and space enough to keep our conversation private.

Confronted with my usual dilemma, I didn't know which soufflé to choose, my usual problem. The selection was endless: wild strawberry, blueberry, fresh vanilla, black chocolate: cheese, oyster, lobster. I could picture each one, in a soufflé dish, having risen uniformly above the rim, never wobbling, nor sinking.

'I'll make a suggestion,' said Corinne, 'start with a langoustine mayonnaise, and follow with a soufflé Grand Marnier.'

'Perfect,' I said. 'I'm still suffering withdrawal symptoms from a bacon roll in my office.'

Corinne is a pretty woman, (defying her fifty three years) with blonde hair, swept into a chignon and a sense of chic that only French women have. I never try to compete it's useless. I reckon my own classic style, albeit British, suits my lifestyle and my figure.

'Katrina, I'm worried about you.' She hesitated as the white-gloved waiter placed finger bowls on our table.' Why aren't you in love?'

'I just haven't found time.'

'Time,' she exclaimed 'is for Greenwich. You're thirty-one, attractive, sexy, and in nine years you'll be forty. Surely it's time you found time?'

'I know you're right, but with this project about to start, I don't want to get emotionally involved. And I must be careful that someone isn't planted just to mislead me. They will be out there gunning for me I know.' . . . I sighed. 'It's the wrong time for love!'

Corinne tapped my hand to emphasise her words. 'There's never a right time, Cherie, only opportunity.'

'I'll take your advice and I'll fall passionately and ravenously in love if you will make an exchange.'
She looked at me suspiciously. 'What are you plotting now?'
'You know the French openly traded with the Germans. You won't have to be a sleuth, just keep your eyes and ears open. Any leads I will discreetly follow myself.'
'Your order book is very demanding, Katrina. I'll have to think about what we have discussed, I'll speak to you in London. Maybe we shall be hand-in-glove again or more likely for me, hand-in-pocket!'

The seven o'clock night bird brought me to Heathrow both exhilarated and apprehensive. Confirmation from the banks was what I needed to progress.

LONDON

3

Friday is loose ends day. Work is consolidated and preparations made for a racing start on Monday. Sue always had the agenda in place and told me my meeting with Dr.Anton Hempf at his home near St.John's Wood, had been confirmed. I took a taxi to this leafy part of North London between Regents Park and Primrose Hill.

I had been in awe of Dr Hempf since I had attended his lectures at university, always arriving early to get a seat near the front, so as not to miss a word or an inflection. He was passionate about Venetian painters especially Titian but it was his love of the Dutch school and Rembrandt that quietly convinced the students, including me, that historically we were looking at some of the greatest paintings ever; even in the 20th century Van Gogh's genius, Dr Hempf told us, must be accredited to his Dutch origins.

I met Anton Hempf for the first time at the home of Anna Frishman, an Austrian refugee, after we had discussed my idea for the exhibition. She was convinced that if Anton Hempf agreed, he would be an invaluable source of information. During subsequent conversations with him, he suggested I contact Professor Wilhelm Frohmann and Otto Prantl. But I had never visited his home.

I pushed a brass bell by the side of the door. A woman in a white apron, whom I presumed was the housekeeper, opened the door. She took me to Dr.Hempf's study. Bookcases lined three sides of the room with sections on art, psychology, history, and music. Leather bound editions on art and architecture mostly written by Anton Hempf looked impressive in beautiful antique colours, including translations in many languages; Japanese, Spanish, Italian and German: a lifetime's achievement in scholarship, which he only acknowledged reluctantly.

Anton Hempf was the youngest of three brothers, born in 1914 in Hungary. His parents owned an established commercial bank started by his grandfather. Anton was five when the family moved to Vienna. His childhood was happy and secure. Being the youngest of three children, his choice of studies was eclectic, but his aptitude was towards the arts. His two elder brothers were apprentices in the bank, with the intention that one would manage the Budapest branch, the other, Vienna. At sixteen Anton applied for admission to the Academy of Fine Arts to study Drawing, Painting and Art History. He was accepted and within three years received his first degree. He was a brilliant student, his contemporaries mostly two or three years older. These included Wilhelm Frohmann, Otto Prantl, and Gerhard Hofer.

Kristallnacht shattered the hopes of Anton Hempf. Under a decree by the Reich Chancellor, Jews were no longer allowed to study. All rights of entry to schools, libraries, and universities, were forbidden. The family home on the Prinz Eugen Strasse was not raided, but interrogations followed. All possessions had to be listed. Every knife, fork, and plate, silver, jewellery, works of art and antiques. It became a criminal offence to omit any item, especially money. All investments had to be declared. For Julius Hempf, Anton's father, this was a nightmare of inestimable proportions. His two elder sons helped, leaving Anton free to pass the time at home by studying, but he had to rely on friends to loan him books. He would linger outside the university until late when it was nearing dusk, and wait for someone in his group to slip a book to him from under their coat. The most consistent source of supply for Anton was Wilhelm Frohmann. Sometimes, there was a short note slipped between the pages, warning Anton not to trust anyone. Many of his class were ardent members of the Hitler Youth movement and recruited younger students within the University.

The horrifying crisis of the Holocaust was not only a tragedy for Anton as a Jew, but an indictment of civilization in our own time. History proved that Adolf Hitler conceived two concurrent wars: one personal the other territorial. The territorial war propelled his armies into Poland, Czechoslovakia, Hungary and the Soviet Union. Hitler's personal war was to purify Europe and create an Aryan master race, and to rid the world of the decadence perpetrated by art, science and literature. Books by Einstein, Sigmund Freud, Emil Zola, Thomas Mann, were burnt. Paintings by Picasso, Matisse, Cézanne, Chagall, were seized. Decadence took on a new meaning for suppressing creativity. Not since the Dominican Savonarola burned the works of

Botticelli in the streets of Florence in the 15th century, had such a scourge been perpetrated.

It is impossible to analyse a mind so virulently warped, except to trace its beginnings in Mein Kampf. Hitler was born in Austria in 1889, and went to Vienna when he was seventeen. He was rejected by the Academy of Fine Arts in the same year the young and talented sixteen-year-old Egon Schiele, was admitted.

It would have been a compelling twist to history, had Hitler been accepted. Hitler later wrote:

"To me Vienna, the city which to many is the epitome of innocent pleasure, a festive playground for merry-makers, represents, I am sorry to say, merely the living memory of the saddest period of my life. Even to-day this city can arouse in me nothing but dismal thoughts. For me the name of this city represents five years of misery, in which I was forced to earn a living, first as a day labourer, then as a house painter. A truly meagre existence, which never sufficed to appease even my daily hunger."

In 1938 when Hitler annexed Austria to Germany, he had his revenge. Kristallnacht, the night of the Broken Glass organized throughout Germany and Austria, was the beginning of his reign of terror, and for the next six years Europe was gripped in the horrors of war and genocide.

Dr.Hempf's slim figure came into the room carrying an armful of books, which he put on his desk. He wore a neat grey suit, a conservative tie and black shoes. Everything about him appeared quiet and constrained. He sat in a leather armchair, his legs crossed, his delicate small hands resting in his lap. I sat opposite.

Living in England for twenty-seven years had not produced an Englishman in any sense of the word. He was reserved, but this I attributed to his self-contained lifestyle rather than reticence. He married Herta, a German refugee in 1954, when he was forty. Ten years later, she died. His marriage had been happy and very private. They never appeared on the burgeoning art scene in London.

I wondered if he was lonely in this large Edwardian house, If so, he wouldn't have told me. In fact emotions of any extreme appeared alien to Dr.Anton Hempf, as if something in his soul had been numbed.

While sipping coffee in the study, I recounted my meetings with Professor Frohmann and Otto Prantl in Vienna. As I was describing the Café Demel, I could see he was hanging onto every word and no doubt I was projecting pictures into his head that he preferred to forget.

During the morning Dr.Hempf and I discussed the raising of funds. To date I had not had a response from either Samuel Hall or Rothschilds in Paris. I was hoping the approval of Dr.Hempf, would facilitate introductions, both in London and abroad, to organisations, which might otherwise slam the door in my face.

'I must confess,' I said, 'I feel I'm on the road to nowhere.'

'You shouldn't, it's early days. Give yourself time. What did Wilhelm Frohmann suggest?'

'On the money front, nothing, but he did suggest I contact Gerhard Hofer, someone I'd never heard of. Do you know him?'

Anton Hempf's face stilled into immobility. He sat erect in his chair, his hands on the leather arms. He leant forward.

'And what did Herr Hofer have to say?

'He told me I'd fail. "No one in Austria" he said, "would contravene their well-earned rights, and giving paintings to Jews was not part of their peace agreement."

'Their peace agreement!', Dr.Hempf exclaimed. 'They lost a war, the allies made the peace.'

'I do agree, but I need as many worms in my can as I can get, and he's a fat one. I don't trust him, but I need contacts. I already have some bargaining power. He wants me to sell the Klimt portrait of Hermine Gallia, which he says he owns. I haven't checked the provenance.'

Anton Hempf rose from his chair, walked to the fireplace, and stared into the empty grate. It was some minutes before he turned to face me. His cheeks were red; his lips tight, the knuckles on his hands were white like alabaster. Tears were clouding his eyes. In a barely audible voice he said.

'It's mine . . . It's mine.'

We sat in silence until Anton Hempf regained his composure, then he explained: 'After Kristallnacht, my father went to the immigration office, and queued daily for a visa. Each time it was refused. He asked to speak with the commandant Adolf Eichmann but was refused. No explanation was given except, "Nein." Weeks passed. The situation became acute. Jews were taken from places all over the city. No one knew what would happen next. They presumed they would be interrogated and released. A reaction, I suppose, to wishful thinking. Shortly after the sequence of interrogations, I received a telephone call from Gerhard Hofer, asking me to meet him on the outskirts of Vienna, near Schunbrunn Park, and to come alone. I told my parents who warned me to watch carefully, and go quickly. They knew Gerhard: he had been to my home many times. It was dark when I slipped through the silent streets. I wore a black running suit. Gerhard was waiting at the gate where we had met many times before. We shook hands. Gerhard spoke first.' Anton Hempf paused and coughed to clear his crackling throat.

'I can tell you his words exactly. He said: "I understand your father is applying for an exit visa." I asked him: how do you know? I received the stock phrase "You know, Vienna is a village." This simile served as an antidote to counteract suspicion but I was, I must admit, afraid. "I know how to get a visa for you immediately," Hofer said. Hempf's eyes were downcast, his hands clasped. 'This is what Hofer wanted. "Your father must bring the Gustav Klimt portrait of Hermine Gallia to this address", he handed me a piece of paper, "I will bring you an exit visa." I stuffed the paper in my pocket quickly. When I returned home and looked at the address for delivery, it was to Gerhard Hofer, Währingerstrasse 9. Vienna.'

Anton Hempf pulled on the cuffs of his white shirt and said to me, 'You look confused.'

'I am. I can't understand why Hofer said he owned the painting, knowing he'd stolen it, and then offering it to me, for sale. Yes, I am totally confused.'

'Because by his reckoning and the decrees at that time Miss Edan, he bought it legally. He paid my father 720 Austrian Schilling, the equivalent of £10 to-day. It will be documented as sold by the Hempf family and the date.'

'But you were blackmailed for a visa. Surely that is also documented?'

'There is no record Miss Edan, because Gerhard Hofer did not deliver the visa!'

Looking back had no lasting memories for Dr.Anton Hempf, except those of death and destruction. I felt guilty for bringing the past so cruelly back into the present.

The war years also starved the British of culture. In 1947, paintings stored in the Menod Slate Quarry in Wales were restored to the walls of the National Gallery, and mile long queues stretched around Trafalgar Square to view them. Anton Hempf told me he had been in that queue.

In the ruins of Germany, Austria, and the Soviet Union, masterpieces remained hidden in barricaded castles, in museum vaults and in underground caves. And I was going to find them.

***

I was totally deflated by the time I arrived at the office. God help Sue Hepple, I thought, as I walked through the door. She looked at my face and knew, had she said even one word, she would have been selected for the second crucifixion. I hurried into my office, closed the door, and cried.

Sometimes it's good to cry, even if the reason isn't absolutely clear. Usually it's a combination of events and self-pity: loss, deprivation, rejection, and failure. I cried from helplessness. The past was nothing one could change, only something on which to build: at this particular moment I had lost the foresight to take me forward.

I shuffled through some papers, and realizing my concentration was haywire, I rang Desmond. 'I have to see you,' I said hastily, 'Can we meet to-day? It's important.'

'For you, kiddo, I have a lifetime. Camden Brasserie, give me half an hour.' I walked past Sue's desk, turned and said 'don't leave, I'll be back.'

Desmond Hegarty is an architect, in the broadest sense of the word - he encloses space. We have worked together on two exhibitions, and he is an astute professional and a reliable back up. His plans are always clear and accurate, and he directs the public around an exhibition avoiding bottlenecks, so viewing is effortless. Lighting is always exceptional and noticeable for its distinctive style. Subtle placing of spotlights draw the viewer's eye into focal points of a painting: unsuspected by the onlooker, they are being led around a picture by Desmond. Of course, the artist made it clear first, but it takes an expert to enhance the original concept.

I have known Desmond for six years, and though I've never been involved with him romantically, I had fallen into bed with him once, after two bottles of champagne, when he was celebrating the ousting of the President of the Architectural Alliance. It was sex under the influence of alcohol, never discussed nor referred to. Anything said would have been totally redundant.

The Camden Brasserie is near my office and close enough to Gower Street for Desmond. We arrived at the same time and I felt a bear hug and saw his broad smile.

'Katrina, it's good to see you . . .' He stood back and eyed me from head to foot. 'Still in one piece,' he said.

Desmond is taller than me, around six foot something, thin frame, aesthetic rather than athletic and in spite of his forty-five years, his mousy hair isn't receding. In fact, sometimes, it falls across his eyes in a foppish way. Conversation with Desmond is easy; we are honest with each other, although sometimes we squabble. It is difficult to hoist emotions onto Desmond: he's too grounded. He can be sympathetic but never sentimental, and combined with his sense of humour, self-confidence exudes without conceit.

He didn't look at the menu, just looked at me and said. 'Spaghetti?' I nodded.

'So what happened in Vienna, Katrina?'

'It wasn't easy. I made a few suggestions for them if they didn't co-operate. You know, blackmail with saccharine. Not on a personal level, more political.'

'What was the response?'

'Professor Frohmann was the most co-operative, but there's a rider to his involvement, that makes me responsible for returning paintings if they're unclaimed.'

'Not unreasonable,' Desmond responded.

The waitress put two plates of spaghetti, French bread and a carafe of red wine on our table. 'Otto Prantl will also participate, for a price,' I said. 'I offered him a golden spoon. He licked it: free advertising for his Galerie. Not much of an incentive, so my guess is, he's got access to loot he wants koshered; he's certainly hiding something.'

'Aren't they all?' Desmond said.
'Yes, but he's sinister. I can't gauge him. He's smooth, slippery. He's going to use me for his own ends. Trouble is, I don't know what those ends are.'
'Katrina, you're good at cat and mouse. Leave him to make mistakes. You have plenty of time. What about the other leads?'
'Gerhard Hofer's an anachronism. He's a crook, with a proven Nazi pedigree. His glory days are over. Now, he's a small fish in a big pond and only getting the flotsam. Not a big player, but a card I need in my pack. He wants to sell a Gustav Klimt painting and use me as the negotiator.' A lump came into my throat as I thought of the emotional complications this sale could engender.
'Who owns it?' Desmond asked. I explained Anton Hempf's reaction when I named the painting. 'He actually said: "It's mine." '

Desmond is a concerned listener. He knew this was an assignment extraordinaire: to find hidden art, I would have to uncover hidden truths: make people vulnerable to their own emotions. Harbouring guilt is not easy. At some point the burden has to be released. I would trigger that moment.
'What's happening on the home front?' I inquired.
'Everything,' Desmond replied. 'My plans for the Festival Hall have been accepted. I've already started on the foyer. I have a great plan for an interior one way system.'
'Like the underground,' I commented.
'Katrina, you haven't any imagination. Have you seen the raging swarms trying to get to their seats for a concert? Or heard the constant ding-dong bell, as men rush from the loo struggling to release their trapped dicks from the zipper, then racing to a crammed staircase? The first twenty minutes of any performance is lost because the audience isn't ready. They've just come from a battle ground and they repeat it in the interval.'

Desmond set my imagination alight.
'You could create an interior spaghetti junction,' I said, as I chased some spaghetti round the plate, 'with a series of coloured plastic tubes, red, blue and yellow. Then, you funnel them to their seats, all wearing electronically controlled stickers, so blue people only go down a blue tube.'
'Katrina, you mock my integrity. You know I hate blue.'

Desmond was mopping up dark red tomato sauce with a piece of French bread.

'That was good, I was hungry.' he said.

'Are you listening, Desmond?'

He grimaced into an artificial grin, and then broke into a laugh. 'Katrina, my love, I always hear what you say, but sometimes you're serious about the wrong issues.'

'I don't understand.' I said, 'What issues?'

'Well, think about your priorities and look ahead. Your main thrust now must be money.'

'What the hell do you think I'm trying to do?'

'You're inclined to get side-tracked.'

'Desmond, you've forgotten the issue', I countered. 'On one hand I'm dealing with people who have been dispossessed: refugees, who have made something from nothing. On the other hand I am dealing with a backlog of deception and avoidance. I'm bound to get side-tracked, it's called being human.'

Desmond stayed on course. 'I'm not denying the human tragedy; I'm urging you to get some finance. Assets, Katrina, remember; they come in two forms, solid and paper, and they're both called liquid.'

I got as close to Desmond's face as possible without touching his nose and whispered: 'I write the script Desmond, you write the background music.' I defiantly sat back in the chair and finished my wine. Desmond looked around the restaurant. To attenuate my demeaning remark, I said sulkily.

'I'm upset Desmond.'

'I knew that when you called sounding like Judas Iscariot.'

'Well, I had a good reason. I only knew this morning that Dr.Hempf had been cheated by Gerhard Hofer. I had already concluded that Hofer was a serial offender but I don't understand why he wants me to sell the Klimt painting, when I'm trying to restore stolen works to their rightful owners. It doesn't make sense.'

'Maybe he's tried through other channels and not found a buyer, or found a buyer, but not for the right price. More likely he's desperate.'

'Could be, but knowing I'm working with Anton Hempf it seems bizarre.'

'It is bizarre, but you must remember thirty years have elapsed. A large slice of life! A lot has happened that neither you nor I could anticipate.' He poured the last of the wine, and said.
'I have some hot gossip to cheer you up. Samuel Hall Bank is going into the investment art market, to the tune of several millions, fronted by Broderick McKenny, the Chairman. Also, pin your ears back, take a deep breath, and listen with your life. British Rail pensions fund is about to launch an investment portfolio of art to the value of, are you listening, thirty million pounds.'
'That's not hot news. Desmond, it's been on the wires for the last six months.'
'Maybe, but Samuel Hall and Rothschilds London are now holding the lolly. You can bet your frilly knickers that's not been broadcast.'

Desmond collected the bill and once outside hailed a cab.
'Jump in,' he said. 'I'll show you my new plans.'

Desmond's office was a tip. For someone producing plans for visitors to the Festival Hall and numerous exhibitions, I wondered how he managed to find his way around his own space. A 3ft square model, set on plywood had a sticker: Foyer, Fest.Hall project. Matchsticks were glued in place forming a grand curving staircase, polystyrene pillars two inches high supported canopies of balsa wood, which he'd cut with a scalpel. Clear plastic stretched across the top of the stairwell, imitating a glass roof.
'Fascinating' I said, stabbing a matchstick into some bread-crumbs. 'What's this for?'
'Ducks' he replied.
Off guard, I said 'You're putting ducks in the foyer?'

Desmond turned on his swivel chair.
'Of course, and bags on coat hangers for stale bread!' he said in amazement.
'By the way, did you tell Dr. Hempf you hadn't any money?' said Desmond, as he moved a bead, a brown duck, on the foyer's lake, a fragment of broken mirror.
'Of course: I intend to tell him everything.'
Desmond looked sheepishly at me.
'Everything?' he said.

***

Sue was sulking. I managed a strained smile and sat in front of her desk. 'I've just had lunch with Desmond Hegarty.'
'That's great.' she said. 'Let me introduce myself. I'm the under privileged, unappreciated, underfed secretary of a boss with the moral superiority of a monkey and a degree from the university of arseholes.'
'Any other messages?' I inquired.
'Yes, I've got the low-down on Broderick McKenny. He's about to spread some millions of bank money on the investment market. The most I could discover about his personal life was so boring it's not even noteworthy. He goes home every night - by that I mean the evening - and leaves the following morning. His hobby must be his wife. Not one piece of disarranged shit anywhere in his lifestyle. Bur twinkle your toes, they haven't appointed a consultant to spend the millions. And for the record, British Rail is on the move.'

Sue, I realized, was suffering from diminished worth, so I feigned ignorance of what she told me.
'That's a smart piece of detective work!' I said.
'Cut the crap, Katrina, its been on the block for months, we both know that. The only piece of information I've unveiled is that Samuel Hall's chairman sleeps with his wife. How sodding ordinary. Not even a quickie on the billiards table, in the executive playroom.'

The ice had cracked, I felt relieved and grateful. For Sue, challenge was paramount. She had to balance the impossible with the extraordinary. For her, in between doesn't exist. It's not so much that life is black and white: it's just that grey is so bloody non-committal: everything and everybody, caught within its confines, is reduced to impassivity. This is the cross of suburbia, relentless repetition, and why someone like Sue can rise above the obvious.

Her desk had bundles of papers tied neatly with different coloured ribbons, except legal pink. 'Never use pink,' she said, 'it's a direct line to the law courts.'

I scanned the desk, and selected the file with royal blue ribbon.
'What's your system this time, Sue?'
'Starting on a black to white scale it goes from morbid to exhilaration. No greys. Hot warm colours, citron, orange, red,

are careful to bloody dangerous. All the greens are the go files and all the blues, failing fast.'

I pulled on the thin royal blue satin ribbon and the file spilled open showing blank pages. 'Nothing to report, no failures, no refusals. Try the citron.' Sue pointed to the yellow file.

'What sort of game is this? I have a desk full of bills to be paid, and deadlines.' I opened the yellow file. Inside was a note with Professor Frohmann's telephone number in Salzburg.

Sue had forgotten our altercation, her face was more animated, more relaxed, and her eyes crinkled before settling into the wide spaces in her otherwise rather flat face. It is a face short on contours, big and open, an outdoor face, slightly ruddy, a legacy from her Cornish upbringing. Her most redeeming feature, her eyes, are fringed with long fair lashes, never touched by make-up and, regretfully, never fluttered. Her build is wide without flab, big without superfluity. Cuddly perhaps, except for the apparatus she keeps in her mouth for occasional annihilation. She read to me from her notebook keeping as scant as a newsreader's headlines.

'Professor Frohmann has booked an hotel in Salzburg. I've made a temporary reservation on Austrian Airlines. One snag, the flights are weekly. The alternative is a three hour hop by train from Vienna.'

'Book the weekly return - I'll need all of one week to get started. Has Dr.Hempf called?'

'Yes' Sue said. 'Tea at his place at four.'

My admiration for Anton was crowned with superlatives. Any hurt I could divert from this retiring man, I would divert, and any retribution I could enact, I would enact too. It was a sunny day and shafts of light reflected in the highly polished mahogany table.

Anton spoke first as he removed a tea cosy from the pot. 'Miss Edan would you please call me Anton, I'd feel more comfortable?' He poured two cups of tea. 'Would you like milk or lemon?' A gentle smile moved across his face. 'I hear you're going to Salzburg. I think you'll be very surprised.'

'Really. What will surprise me?'

'It's like a Chocolate Box, almost too perfect to be real; a tinted etching, dominated by a medieval castle overlooking the river

Salzach. Snow-capped mountains are the horizon: narrow cobbled streets connect vaulted alleyways and massive towering baroque churches overpower everything.' Anton spoke with passion. 'When the bells toll in Salzburg, their vibrations, shake the roots of one's soul: the invasion is inescapable. You'll go back to the time when salt was traded and burghers ruled the city. Salzburg can't change. There's nowhere for it to go. Nature has confined the perimeter, man cannot move them.'

The picture was vivid in Anton's mind, but it was dated in his childhood and whatever it is like now, I had no intention of changing that image. But, lingering with reminiscences would have satisfied me for the rest of the day but priorities had to come first. I sipped my tea, helped myself to a piece of cherry strudel and ventured the important question. 'Professor Frohmann wants you to edit his book on Rembrandt. He knows, any book on Dutch 17th century art, especially Rembrandt, would be enhanced by your scholarship.' I was nervous of stirring personal traumas again but sensed by Anton's reaction that he was in control.

'You can tell Wilhelm Frohmann I will edit his book but I will not write a foreword and only agree if you will be responsible for delivering the text.'

'I will be crossing the Alps for the next three years, Dr.Hempf, I'll make sure not one word slips into a ravine.'

Anton walked to the French doors, overlooking the garden. The first buds of spring were promising another spectacular display of mauve and white lilac.

In a strong voice he said to me. 'I should like to tell you a little more about Professor Frohmann before you leave. I hope it won't deter your efforts: frankly I don't believe it should. What I'm going to tell you, I'd rather you heard from me, than by accident or malicious design. In 1938, after the Anschluss, my father was forced to sell the bank and all allied interests. When I say, "sell" I really mean he made an exchange for our lives. The Laufenbankgeschaft of Vienna became the new traders. Our bank building on the Graben, the investment offices on the Ringstrasse, our home, were all part of the transaction. Wilhelm Frohmann's father was a Director of the Laufenbankgeschaft. I suggest you ask Wilhelm Frohmann for an introduction to the investment department in their Salzburg

office. A twinkle invaded his usually sad eyes: 'they may give you some money!'
'I'll do that and I'll give them regards from you.' I added with a hint of irony.

WENDOVER

4

The romantic idea of a fairytale castle, with prince charming waiting to transport me on his charger, had been a recurring dream when I was a child, in Wendover Buckinghamshire. My reality came from books where rules were made and broken by magic and I would become a character in a story, even imagining I was an animal; the horse in Beautiful Joe, the Cheshire cat in Alice in Wonderland.

The Second World War interrupted my childhood and I learned that what appeared normal, most often was not. By the time I was old enough to read, posters told us "Walls have Ears" "Is your journey really necessary" and the one that confused me most "Keep Mum".

During the war my mother, Cynthia Edan worked in the hospital wing at Halton Royal Air Force camp, not far from our home. My father major Richard Edan travelled daily to The War Office in London. At the time I wanted him to be the King of England, but of course he wasn't. My father's work or his nature, more likely a combination of the two, made him both secretive and retiring, while my mother on the other hand was more social. She arranged jam-making sessions or knitting events, when all the local villagers brought old woollen jumpers and vests and they would undo the garments, make them into skeins and back into balls. Everyone knitted for the forces. I knitted mittens at school but sometimes there were more holes than the five needed for the fingers. I watched my mother knit socks that grew into long sausages turning at the heel then go in a different direction till she reached the toes. I watched excitedly every time, until she slipped the needle away and tied a knot in the wool at the toe and that sock was ready to go to war.

When my mother took me shopping she would hold my hand. I can still feel the grip, as my small hand nestled in hers and hearing the voice in my head, saying, I love you mummy. I think she loved me too, but it was a love of possession rather than a nurturing love. Sometimes I felt unwanted but in hindsight it was my mother's way of making me independent: forcing me to work things out, saying, "Try again Katrina". . .Something I heard again and again.

Pippa Rawlings, my friend, was more fortunate, or so I thought. Her father was in the Navy and she had all her mother's attention. They made cakes together, with powdered eggs, and had bets with chocolate pieces on whether or not the cakes would rise. Sometimes when I went for tea we had to eat the failures.

Her father, Captain Peter Rawlings, visited my father when he was on leave. They sat in the garden and talked. Pippa and I couldn't understand why grown-ups only talked, never actually doing anything.

We had a thatched summerhouse at the end of our garden with spaces for windows without any glass. "It's the way it's been designed" my mother told me, "so the sun and air and butterflies can visit in the summer". Our old wooden kitchen table had been painted green and an assortment of chairs, which didn't match, were inside. An electric light socket served the kettle and the hot plate, so we would eat outside but inside.

I had a secret hiding place between the summerhouse and our orchard, which bordered the Wyman Farm. Cows would put their heads over our hedge and look around the garden: they didn't come in, because I had told them they couldn't. Sometimes a prickly gooseberry bush spiked me as I climbed into my secret place: it was worth it as I had secret friends waiting: worms and ants and toads.

We had rhubarb and red currants and black currants, and all sorts of apples. Mother put them in bottles with clip on lids, which I helped to fill, and then stood them on shelves in the garage, for fruit pies all winter.

Pippa and I went to the village school in Butler's Cross on the Upper Icknield Way, the old Roman Road. We started at the same time, in 1943, when we were four. There were only fourteen boys and girls and Mrs. Williams, our teacher. I liked Mrs Williams: she had blue eyes and brown hair, which was cropped quite short. She made us laugh, especially when she told us stories. She quacked like a duck, and roared like a lion and even croaked like a toad. When the air-raid siren sounded, its high pitched whine going on and on, we all became mice and went to our hole, a dug-out Anderson shelter made of corrugated iron, where we sat in two rows, seven on each side. Head mouse, a boy named Elvin, then counted all the mice, to make sure none had escaped. Mrs.Williams opened her big bag, and said; "now children, we shall continue."

Sometimes I had tea at Pippa's house in Little Kimble or we would visit her grandma in Princes Risborough. Her grandma was very funny. She rode a horse sidesaddle in her youth, and we teased and said she walked sideways like a dressage routine. But she made lovely meringues: big golden brown crusts with marsh mallow inside. Sometimes she even managed to find cream: no one asked any questions about the supplier.

Captain Peter Rawlings had been at sea for over a year when he came home on leave. Pippa and her mother Ann were at my house after school. We were playing in the garden when Ann called us inside. She explained to Pippa: "Your father and I are going to spend the week-end in an hotel. It will be a nice change for Daddy as he has been away for so long. Would you like to come with us, or would you like to stay here with Katrina?" Our mischievous eyes met. Pippa was already visualizing a daring weekend of monumental naughtiness, reserved only for six year olds.

"Would Daddy be unhappy if I stayed with Katrina?" Pippa asked.

"Of course not, if that's what you'd like: anyway he'll be home all next week, so you can be together."

Captain Rawlings was very handsome and his uniform was more exotic than the khaki of the army, with gold braid on the sleeves and the peak of his cap. He was tall and slim, and together, he and Ann were a very attractive couple. She was blond, with her hair twisted and curled on top of her head. Pippa was mousy blonde but she was quite tall for six and when we played film stars, she was Lana Turner and I was Rita Hayworth because I had a mop of flame red hair, which gave me the nickname of "carrots".

My father had a small petrol allowance, which he conserved by walking to the railway and walking home. His petrol coupons then allowed us the occasional outing. He was home the weekend that Pippa stayed and he took us to a duck farm near Aylesbury. Clucking ducks were everywhere, even in Farmer Belton's house. They jostled around our feet for the stale bread crusts that we had saved. Daddy had a drink with Farmer Belton, and we roamed the farm, looking at the baby ducklings being fattened possibly for someone's Christmas dinner. On the way home, we stopped and spent some sweet coupons. I had a penny's worth of liquorice allsorts, and Pippa had a penny Nestles chocolate bar, which we shared. That night we had duck for dinner and made secret plans for a midnight feast. Unfortunately the air-raid siren sounded as we were about to raid the larder, so we had to go to the cellar. Why did Hitler always mess up our plans?

In the morning we picked fruit from the trees. We had a long ladder that stood against the tree trunks. My father held the base and we took turns to go to the top rung. We were small enough to get between the boughs and get the really big apples from the top. I never understood why nature made it so difficult by keeping the best so inaccessible. Pippa and I were good climbers and soon the baskets were full of Bramleys and Coxes.

I was almost at the top of a big sprawling old apple tree when my father called me down. Mother had called him to the phone and it was a rule that treetops were only allowed when he was there. My father returned to the garden holding a whiskey glass. Mother followed also holding a whiskey. Not unusual, except it was 10.30 on Sunday morning.

They sat together in the summerhouse. We collected fruit, which had fallen from the trees into the rough grass. Sometime later a car came along our drive driven by Pippa's grandma, with her Aunt Mary and Uncle Joe. They went into the house with my parents.

"Oh dear, "Pippa said, "it looks like I'll have to leave early."

We both waved from the end of the garden, then my father came and took both our hands and led us into the house.

The grown-ups were sitting in the drawing room. There was a haunting silence. We sat on the sofa between my mother and Pippa's grandma. My father stood in front of the fireplace.

He said, "Pippa, I want you to try and understand what I am going to tell you. It is going to be very difficult but you are a big girl, and I hope a brave one." He was very direct.

"A bomb fell last night on the hotel where your mother and father were staying."

Pippa stared at him . . ."A bomb!" She repeated. "A bomb!" She turned to her grandma. "Are they hurt, Grandma?"

"My darling" she said, choking back tears, "they are dead."

Neither of us understood what dead really meant. Of course, we knew things died, but that was different. Animals were killed for food, and sometimes we trod on earwigs, and they died. We even forked worms, but not people. We didn't know any people who had died.

We didn't cry, that was for later when the reality set in and we knew they would never come back.

My father's voice was very quiet when he told Pippa that it didn't hurt when they died, they just flew to heaven together and that God was now looking after them. The only words Pippa said to me before she left was . . .

"I hate Hitler, he messes up everything."

"I hate him too," I said.

SALZBURG

5

Few people were leaving for Salzburg on this crisp March morning: in fact, the plane was only a third full. Maybe the precipitous approach to the runway, one of the most dangerous in Europe kept the traffic minimal. I realized this was not a fictitious rumour, as the plane started to lose height and suddenly we were engulfed by the mighty Alps reducing us to the size of a fly, with only papery strength. We flew through the valley, between the snow-capped mountains soaring above us, as the overwhelming magnitude of nature became very close. Small glaciers held tightly between jagged rocks glittered in the sunlight. I felt the iciness of lingering winter and looked towards the pilot's cockpit, with the thought - I hope the hell you know where you're going and drew myself closer to the arms of the seat for comfort. When the bleep light went on for landing, my immediate reaction was, thank God.

Professor Frohmann's driver-handyman was waiting at the airport. I hadn't met him before but he approached me, with a note from the Professor and the important information that he didn't speak English!"

I read Frohmann's note, which gave me the name and address of my hotel: the Elephant, on Sigmund-Haffner Gasse. I wondered who Sigmund-Haffner was, that he warranted a street name: I would expect one for Mozart and I wasn't disappointed. The car passed through the Mönchberg mountain tunnel into the old Fortress City and stopped in a narrow street, just wide enough for one car.

Anton was right, I would go back in time and it started right here at the Elephant Hotel, unchanged by any technological advancement since the war - the great war of 1914. An old man sat behind a high fronted reception desk in a very small lobby, with a flagstone floor and a table with dried flowers.

'Passport bitte.' A crusty hand with fat fingers, like a farm workers' thrust towards me. I handed him my dark blue impressive English passport embossed with the Royal coat of arms, with the words, Honi soit qui mal y pense, on one side and Dieu et mon Droit on the other. The idiosyncrasy of the British is unending. We still write in French on our passports!'

'Ah, yes, Fraulein Edan, a reservation from the office of Professor Frohmann. Ein zimmer für ein wocke.' He looked up, 'mit frühstück?' I nodded. Breakfast, my favourite meal, certainly had to be included. 'Zimmer drei', he said, handing me a key the weight of a cannon ball. The lift swung precariously from side to side as it barely gathered speed to get to the third floor.

My room was like a prefect's in a boarding school: a bed, a bedside table, a rug, and a wash hand basin. I looked around for a phone. There wasn't one. I had a semi-panic attack. No phone! How could I work without a phone? I didn't unpack. I returned to the old man.

'Do you have a room with a telephone?' I requested.

His look was perplexed, as he stared at the antiquated switchboard with a wind up handle. 'The phone is there', he said pointing to a shelf opposite, 'that is for zie guests.'

'Oh - I see!' I said as if I had made a new discovery. 'What about messages? Do you take messages?'

'Yes, Fraulein, we will put them in your box.' His thumb lifted over his shoulder in the direction of little cubbyholes on the wall.

'And the bathroom?' I ventured.

'In the back of zie hotel.' I nodded, wondering if it was in the garden.

'Danke Schön' I said, and returned to the rickety lift.

Fortunately, I travel light, so my mix and match outfits, a Dior suit an "in case" Jean Muir clingy dress and a pair of trousers, fitted easily into the skimpy wardrobe. I sat on the bed, wiggled my bottom - no lethal springs attacked me. Good, at least I'll get a good night sleep. I re-read the Professor's note.

My driver Pieter will collect you at 5.30. from the Hotel Elephant. Regards Wilhelm Frohmann, Anif.

The bathroom towards the back of the hotel looked out onto the back courtyard. The bath must have been installed during the reign of the Hapsburgs: it was a throne in the centre of the room standing on ornate legs in the shape of great tiger claws, painted with gold leaf which had faded and were now turning brown. I turned on the swan taps and put my toe in the water, ah, ha, a miracle, it was hot. The mountain water was so soft and caressing, my breasts floated, the lavender soap lathered at a touch. I closed my eyes, relaxed, before hearing five deafening booms from the church bells.

At 5.30 Pieter arrived. We drove through the foothills to Anif, a small village some 20 minutes from Salzburg Stadt. Actually, it's not even a village, just a cluster of triangular shaped houses surrounded by vast fields with a backdrop of snow-capped mountains. Farms, scattered at random were dotted around the countryside, like dolls' houses on a vast green carpet.

Pieter veered the car over a cattle grid, past a water trough and parked the car in front of a gated garden. Two German shepherd dogs jumped and barked. I stood back as they looked predatory and I was averse to being on a dog's menu. The commotion brought Wilhelm Frohmann to the door.

'Don't be afraid Miss Edan, they won't hurt you,' he said as he pushed them into a pen. 'Come in, please.'

I had been looking forward to this moment since we first met. I was both curious and enchanted by this man. I wanted to know who he really was behind the rigmarole of conventional etiquette he projected. His suave persona intrigued me beyond curiosity. What goes on in his guts? What is he hiding? He directed me to the vestibule. 'Please' he said with outstretched hand. He saw by the expression on my face that I was surprised.

'Yes', he said, 'it's very different from our house in Vienna. This is where I like to be as often as possible.' I could understand why. The vestibule was minimally furnished: only a carved wooden rug chest and a wrought iron hat and coat stand: the flagstone floor was uneven, broken-down by time, square edges - now rounded, and pit holes added to the pattern. They shone like stones reflected in running water, and felt slippery underfoot. Off the vestibule was a pair of double doors, padded with traditional woven fabric in a diagonal pattern.

'This is the living room,' he said as he opened the doors. I stopped just inside a vast area, too big to be called a room, about eighty feet long and half as wide, with a white painted vaulted ceiling like the inside of a Gothic church. Again the furniture was minimal: a long church bench with cushions along one wall, a rocking chair, an odd assortment of carved wooden chairs upholstered in different coloured Salzburg weaves, navy, light blue, pink, bottle green. Against another wall was an ornately carved, long, narrow, light wood table, with a pewter jug holding dried flowers, two double candlesticks of wrought iron, and on a bookstand, an open bible displaying iridescent illuminated lettering.

I remembered my tutor going into raptures over the lettering on a manuscript, not really appreciating her enthusiasm at the time. Now, seeing the open pages of this ancient bible with the translucent colours and gold leaf in pristine condition, I can understand the devotion that made a book like this possible.

'I thought you would like it,' the Professor said.

'Oh - I do, it's remarkable, how old is it?'

'Fourteenth century, Bavarian.' he said as he stroked the leather binding. We walked across the stripped pine floor to the opposite wall where a cubist painting by Picasso in its original frame, was the central picture. On one side was a large Kokoschka landscape, a view of the Danube and on the other a dramatic painting by Eugène Delacroix. The Professor held my elbow.' We can look at the others later, Gerda has prepared dinner early.'

Wafting smells of cooking accompanied us as we went towards the dining room. At least that's where I thought we were going. Until, after passing numerous doors we arrived at the opposite end of the farmhouse - the kitchen.

'This used to be a cow-shed' the Professor told me, 'but now it's the most important room in the house, die küche.'

Gerda came to greet us wiping her hands down a colourful apron. 'How nice to see you again. Did you have a good journey?'

I wanted to say no, Salzburg airport should be banned, but my middle-class English upbringing controlled my tongue and I smiled politely and said 'yes it was very pleasant, thank you.'

'Wilhelm, maybe Miss Edan would like an aperitif.'

'Of course my dear, how about a little Secht?' Gerda smiled with approval.

Wilhelm Frohmann disappeared to the cellar, giving me a chance to survey the kitchen. A wooden table was in the centre of the room set with four pewter plates, rühmer glasses and an empty basket. I liked the cosiness of the room in spite of everything being exposed. Copper pots hanging on skewers, bunches of flowers hanging upside down to dry: massive wooden dressers with hanging cups and plates in neat rows, and crucifixes looking down from wooden niches. Its size belied the intimacy of the room, like a wood, where the trees are dominant, silent and enveloping. I felt very comfortable, soporific even.

Gerda was standing by a big black kitchen range built under a wooden Bessemer beam, stirring and seasoning. The surroundings didn't suit her: she had looked more comfortable in their sophisticated Viennese home, than the rustic surroundings of the farmhouse. 'I hope you are hungry. I have made a veal goulash mit apfel dumplings.'

I hadn't thought about food, but the spicy pungent paprika, bubbling in the goulash pot, provoked my taste buds. Wilhelm returned with two bottles of Secht.

'I took these from the coldest part of the cellar, so we can enjoy one now.' He unwrapped the gold foil, wrapped the bottle in a starched white napkin, and pulled the cork.

'Great sound,' I commented, as I watched the smokey fumes escape from the bottle and wondered if it tasted as good as Krug. It didn't, but does anything taste as good as vintage French Champagne? I remember as a child seeing my father open champagne and watching the genie escape from the bottle in a puff of smoke: then the magic bubbles appeared, and everyone was happy.

'I'll call Charlotte,' the Professor said to his wife. He turned to me. 'Our daughter, Charlotte, is joining us, I know she will enjoy meeting you.'

I didn't believe him. Why should I? He is a very social person. Visitors must have been part of his daughter's upbringing, which certainly didn't make me special.

When we were introduced, a rather limp hand casually took mine and Charlotte said "hello." She said something to her mother and then sat at the table.

I am, by most criteria, noticeable. Not because I am a tall redhead but because I convey security from within myself. Some might say confidence, others poise. At least, I know I have presence. Charlotte, for some reason, chose to ignore me. She was not rude, just indifferent. Although she spoke English throughout the meal, it was more a sulky rebuff than an attempt to know me at all. What she didn't know, was that I recognised her agitated disposition and deduced she had some serious problems, which her parents were superficially glossing over with champagne and hoping that I would not feel the atmospheric tension.

'Lotte, my dear,' said her father, will you stay the weekend, or will you go into the mountains?'

'Don't know yet,' came a rather sullen reply.

'Well' he said, 'we will be here all week while Miss Edan is in Salzburg.' Gerda was very quiet, sipping wine and smiling from time to time. I tackled the goulash, succulent soft veal in sticky red-hot paprika sauce with dumplings far better than any I had ever tasted. Charlotte didn't stay for the chocolate cake. When she left the table I noticed how small she was. Barely five feet, and very slight - she had her mother's creamy complexion but light brown hair, which fell straight to her shoulders.

'It was nice to meet you' she said, without a hint of conviction.

Professor Frohmann poured some more Secht, and asked if I was comfortable in the Hotel Elephant. I did not want to offend the Professor but this time I was more truthful. 'It's full of old world character, old world charm, old world plumbing, and old world hospitality. I am sure I shall be very comfortable, Herr Professor.'

'We have known the owners, the Reinhardt family,' he turned to Gerda for acknowledgment, 'for many years. Our son Kurt - you will meet him tomorrow at the Galerie - was at school with Dieter, their son. The family has owned the hotel since it was converted from a winery in the 1900's and believe me, apart from the Österreichischer Hof and the Goldener Hirsch, it's the best.'

Now that Charlotte had left, the Frohmann's were more at ease. The Professor had given only one concession to informality, a pair of red and gold embroidered slippers. He was still wearing a neatly placed cravat with a tiepin, and Gerda wore the traditional Salzburg dirndl. After chocolate cake and plum brandy, the Professor called Pieter his driver, to take me to my hotel, then insisting I take a bunch of dried flowers, to put in my room.

'You will wake to the smell of the pines and the ferns from the woods, far more elevating than anything man can concoct.'

One whiff, of the pungent aromatic herbal perfumes and I knew the Professor was right.

I decided to have an early breakfast and by 6.45. I was in the first floor dining room. The waiter nodded, and walked past me. I sat at a table under a musty yellowing parchment chandelier, the little shades crooked on their bases, and waited.

'The waiter reappeared with a tray and went to the only other guest in the room, then to me.

'Kaffe oder Tee', he said.

'Kaffe' I replied.

'Bitte Schön,' he said and disappeared.

Within minutes, a plate of assorted cheeses, wursts, sliced sausage, honey and jam, semmel rolls, schwarzbrot and a huge dish of butter were in front of me. The waiter asked 'Ein ei oder zwei?'

'Kein,' I replied.

'Kein' - he repeated as if I had committed a sin by not accepting an egg. The rolls were oven hot, crisp and crunchy, the cheeses, sliced, the ham lean, the sausage garlicky. Poppy seeds rolled about my plate, and fell from the long crunchy roll, which I had smothered in thick creamy butter. This was the best meal of the day, quite unique, breakfast at 6.45 a.m. - something my conscience normally wouldn't allow, nor my stomach either.

By 8.00 I was walking towards the great river Salzach: a commanding, torrenting river, carved through the mountains, and coming to its widest and most impressive when it reaches Salzburg. I stood on the Staatsbrücke and looked down. The river was clear and deep, running fast and furiously. Sea gulls swooped and cried, then a cold breeze suddenly made me shiver. I went to the end of the bridge, turned and saw the sun shining on the medieval city of Salzburg: its past unchanged, its present very foreboding. In spite of the magic of the view, tall narrow buildings, closely linked, painted in turquoise, pale yellow, watery green, shades of grey, a stunning mixture of pastels, like a theatre set, perfect in front, with a maelstrom behind.

I stopped on Giselakai by the side of the river. Large boulders trapped the mainstream of the waters, while little rivulets forced their way past, niggling at the land it would eventually invade.

The sun was high. Bright red reflections settled on top of the ripples like blood flowing through veins. A frightening thought raced across my mind as I pictured the heinous atrocities that had taken place on the banks of this river by feudal landowners bartering people for animals, then selling out to the Archbishops of the Catholic Church who ruled Salzburg with murderous intrigue. A lot of blood had flowed down this river, and that history, for my thinking, was too close.

Further along the Giselakai a sign over a very old wooden door, shaped like a Gothic portal, said Galerie Frohmann. Inside, it was quite dark. A pair of heavy velvet curtains separated the galerie from the hallway. I slid between them, not knowing quite what to expect. In spite of the antiquity of the building and the décor, the pictures displayed were very contemporary. A small desk in the centre contained catalogues and information on future exhibits. I looked around for a door, a telephone; any sign of life, no one was there. I looked at my watch: 8.30 exactly. I sat on a chair in a corner and waited. I looked at myself in the mirror and fiddled with my hair. Nice cut I thought but I was feeling anxious. Then the curtains flew back and Professor Frohmann apologized.

'I am sorry to keep you waiting Miss Edan. My assistant and Pieter are collecting a painting, and I have been talking with Kurt. Please,' he said.

The layout of the place was strange. I felt disorientated not knowing where exits and entrances were but I followed the Professor through the heavy curtains. Just inside the entrance was a door that opened into another galerie, which was long and narrow. I followed the Professor through a number of corridors to the back of the galerie. He turned and said to me.

'I'd like you to meet my son Kurt. He has his studio here.'

'How nice,' I responded. We continued along a small corridor into a large studio were Kurt was setting up a white screen.

'Kurt, come and meet Miss Edan.' He climbed down from a ladder and crossed the studio floor to meet us. He was not as tall as his father more inclined towards his mother's build, but looked agile and athletic. His hair was fair and he had a neatly trimmed small moustache, and looked about thirty.

'Miss Edan,' he said. 'My father has talked to me about you.'

The set-up of the studio and the equipment was typical for a photographer: a variety of cameras and tri-pods and backdrops of rainstorms, grasslands, cows and rivers were stacked around the walls. Most fascinating,' I commented' 'What type of photography do you specialize in?'

'Mostly advertising,' he said, 'but sometimes, travel commissions come along for magazines, if I'm lucky.'

As we were leaving the Professor casually turned to Kurt and in an abrupt manner said. 'Do you want lunch?' His reply was a frosty 'Nein.' I didn't know if he was anti-British or had some grievance like his sister Charlotte. Whatever the problem, it was for the family and no concern of mine.

I followed the Professor again. His office was off yet another corridor, and sitting at a desk was a young dark haired woman with hair glued to her head like a Spanish dancer without the rose.

'Miss Edan, this is Lisette Chenier. She is a research student here in Salzburg and is helping me with my book.' Another handshake.

'Please,' Professor Frohmann said, and indicated a chair.

I glanced at my watch. It was nearly 9.30 and I had achieved nothing.

I told the Professor that Anton Hempf had agreed to edit his book on Rembrandt, and that I would be the courier. I did not tell him that Hempf would not write a foreword. I waited to see if the Professor asked: he didn't.

'I am sure you are keen to know if there has been any progress for the exhibition?' Frohmann said. Keen, was certainly not the word I would have chosen. Desperate was more apt. He continued. 'Stephan Moser, my galerie assistant and Pieter, my driver, are collecting the final painting from the collection of Count von Sneider. His widow, at my suggestion, is offering some of the collection for the exhibition.'

I listened intently. 'That's a good start' I said 'but who is Count von Sneider?'

'Sneider,' said the Professor, 'inherited the salt mines at Dürnnberg and the coal mines at Hallein, and invested the revenue in De Beers, and Theissen steel, in the Ruhr.' Interesting economics, I thought but how did he build his art collection? At that moment, a man walked into the office.

'Ah, Miss Edan here is Stephen Moser, he will be helping you in Salzburg if I'm not available.'

He was thin, more bones than flesh, and his suit hung on his shoulders, requiring more padding in the shoulders to make it appear lived in. He spoke in a quiet staccato voice, his lips, surprisingly full in such an angular face.

'Herr Professor, I have the Nolde painting in the long galerie.'

The Professor rose from his chair, walked across to Lisette, looked at the lines she had written, then said. 'I'll be in the long galerie with Miss Edan and Stephan. If my wife calls, please, come and fetch me.'

Standing by the wall in the long galerie was the Emil Nolde painting, the corners of the frame wrapped in corrugated paper. It was a stunning portrait of a young girl. Her cheeks were green, her hair orange. Purple shadows sat at the corners of her eyes. Her head rested on a brightly painted yellow neck, then dissolved into multi-coloured rakish brushstrokes.

'It's one of the paintings from the Lucerne sale,' Stephan Moser told the Professor. I didn't know why Lucerne in Switzerland, should be of any importance.

'Reichtig,' he responded. He bent down, close to the picture; lifting his spectacles to see more clearly before he stood and turned to me.

'What do you think of the picture Miss Edan?'

I moved towards the painting, took off my shoes, knelt down, and sat back on my heels for a period of silent viewing before I turned to the Professor.

'It's a fake' I said.

Professor Frohmann looked first at Stephan Moser and with penetrating rage said.' How can you say it is a fake? That's preposterous!'

He turned to Stephan 'What number is this painting on the inventory?' Stephan mumbled . . . I don't know exactly, I would have to look.'

'Well, said Professor Frohmann; look - macht schnell.'

I saw the tension pulling around the Professor's neck muscles, and I realized, this man could get volcanically angry if provoked. I waited, quietly confident; Emil Nolde had not touched the painting.

Stephan returned and pointed to a number on a sheet. Nummer neunundzwanzig. The Professor scuffled through more papers and said something to Stephan, which I couldn't understand.

'Miss Edan, I can tell you, you are mistaken.' Frohmann said. 'That particular picture was bought by the Sneiders' in the sale at the Grand Hotel in Lucerne in June 1939, organized by the Berlin Art dealer, Karl Haberstock.' I was alerted by the name Haberstock.

'Correct me if I'm wrong, Herr Professor, but wasn't Haberstock the procurer for Adolf Hitler's private collection?' . . . I paused. 'Professor Frohmann, I think we must be honest with each other, or this exhibition cannot progress. I think it would be helpful if I could see the provenance of the painting before giving judgement; presuming there is one? I have spent the last ten years looking at works of art, and I know a fake when I see one. Professor, I am sorry to disagree with you, but that picture was not painted by Emil Nolde.'

Wilhelm Frohmann was disturbed by my reaction, but did not comment. The implications of exposure if forgeries were exhibited, would turn a graveyard of worms.

'Shall we continue this conversation in my office?'

The Professor asked Lisette to bring some coffee. When she returned, Wilhelm Frohmann sent her to the small library adjoining his office, leaving us alone and not overheard.

I took off my suit jacket and made myself comfortable. I felt like a dentist about to extract something rotten.

'I have some questions which I think are pertinent to our collaboration Herr Professor. I would like to know the significance of the Lucerne sale and why you're so sure the Nolde isn't a copy.' He drank some coffee before answering.

'I shall try to make it clear to you. The sale, in June 1939, was organized to raise foreign currency for the German Reich. The paintings included in the sale came from the 'Kitschi' trashcan exhibition of degenerate art, which was shown in Munich. Forty-one of Nolde's pictures were included from the one thousand confiscated.'

'I don't understand Professor. Emil Nolde was a member of the Nazi party, and had a huge following in Germany.'

'Quite correct Miss Edan, in fact Goebbels had some of Nolde's water colours in his home. But Hitler decreed him degenerate. At the close of the Munich 'Kitschi' exhibition the most valuable works were separated from the rest and designated for the Lucerne sale. It might interest you to know that the sale was reviewed by the London Daily Telegraph's art critic, who commented on the low prices the lots fetched: the highest price of £8,330 was paid for a Van Gogh self-portrait which was taken from the Munich State Gallery in 1938. A Picasso was bought by the Antwerp Museum. Paintings by Klee, Kandinsky, Nolde, Gauguin, Kokoschka, all went under the hammer. Count von Sneider bought the Nolde portrait.'

'Thank you Professor, it's clearer now, but the fact remains, it is a fake. Could we look at the painting again and I'll show you undeniable discrepancies.'

I was puzzled, I knew it was a fake but what was the motive for including it in the inventory for the exhibition of stolen art? Also I began to sense Professor Wilhelm Frohmann knew much more about looted art and its whereabouts.

Until now, I had been treated with polite acceptance because Dr.Hempf had introduced me. Now, I had to prove something about myself. As far as Professor Frohmann was concerned women were for charming, light relief, acceptable appendages, even prizes, but certainly never competition. I was tacitly on trial.

The painting was still on the floor and I suggested to the Professor we put it on an easel, to make it more visible. I could feel the Professor's challenging eyes on me.

'Please, come a little closer,' I asked the Professor. 'Now, look at the edge value of the face. It has a distinguishable line. Emil Nolde never painted a line as definable as that.' I pointed to a dark line delineating the chin.

'His handwriting rejects line: when he puts his brush on the canvas it spreads, each strand collects paint, diffusing the line, colours are integrated: the paint merges, no definition is left. Herr Professor, it's like squashing a lemon: the juice, the pith, the skin, become one. Nolde used vibrant paint with brutal force: the subject, landscape or portrait, was only a vehicle for his own expression. Whoever copied or forged this work, has made undeniable errors.'

Professor Frohmann's reaction was conciliatory.

'I can understand your apprehension,' he said 'but I suggest we see the rest of the inventory offered by Countess von Sneider before deciding if this piece should be included in the exhibition.'

When we met the following morning I asked the Professor if he could arrange a meeting with the Laufenbankgeschaft in Salzburg.

'I understand from Dr.Hempf that your father had been a director of the bank and you may be able to get sponsorship.'

I wasn't sure if the Professor had simmered down from our altercation the day before but it seemed pointless to continue looking for works of art when I didn't have financial backing.

'Dr.Hempf's right, I do know the bank: in fact I know it very well. My personal banker, Herr Steinhart, has an office in Salzburg. I will introduce you but I doubt if he will give you any money,' he said briskly.

The Professor called the bank, speaking in German, laughing and listening. 'Gut' I heard him say. He put the phone down. 'Steinhart will be free in half an hour.'

We crossed the bridge back into the old city. The bank was on the Getreidegasse, next door to Mozart's house, a narrow street crammed with small shops distinguished by their ornate signs protruding across a street originally built only to accommodate carriages. It was obvious from the moment we left the galerie that Frohmann was well known. People stared, nodded, smiled, said "Guten Morgen". Whether they recognised him from the press or television or his galerie, I had no idea. But it was obvious to me he was a media celebrity.

On entering the bank, the clerk at the desk greeted the Professor. 'Guten Morgen, Herr Professor, Herr Steinhart is expecting you, please.'

A wide marble staircase led to the first floor, then to a small-carpeted anteroom. Austrian architects, it appeared to me, specialized in double doors because this room had another pair of highly polished wooden doors, which swung open, and Herr Steinhart introduced himself.

He shook the Professor's hand, 'Good to see you, please come into the office.' I followed. Then he turned to me, hand outstretched, 'Jack Steinhart' he said, you're Miss Katrina Edan. Delighted to meet you.' The American accent was too identifiable. A cross between mid-west and New York. Oh, dear, I thought, this is going to be tough. The Americans aren't the best people to hand out money, especially for a European cause.

'Now' Steinhart said to the Professor, 'what can I do for you?'
Wilhelm Frohmann looked first at me, and then said.
'Jack, I don't want anything, unusual as it may seem, but Miss Edan has a situation which might interest the Laufenbankgeschaft.' The Professor was wrong. I didn't have a 'situation' I had a mission, and to achieve that, I needed greenbacks.
'Herr Steinhart' I said. 'I don't know if Professor Frohmann has told you, but I'm curating an exhibition of works of art, stolen during the Nazi regime.'
'That's unusual' he said to Frohmann. I was not distracted.
'To make this possible, I need financial backing. I shall talk in pounds sterling, if you don't mind. I need a contingency amount of £1,500.000. from four sponsors, each depositing £375,000 into a special account. That amount remains the bank's money, and I would have no call on it whatsoever. What I request is the interest.'
'Most interesting,' Steinhart said, 'but since the Laufenbankgeschaft and Imperial Chicago merged five years ago, our policy is no investment without return: so any money I put up front must work for the bank.'
'Mr.Steinhart, if your bank becomes a sponsor, you would make enormous impact on the American Jewish lobby just by association, and by default increase your investment income in the U.S. There isn't a bank in Austria that isn't tainted with blood money; yours would be the first to redress this anomaly. The advertising revenue alone, once I get into swing, will more than compensate for the £375,000 on ice. In fact, I only need to reveal one masterpiece before I have every museum in the United States, bidding against each other.'

I looked across the desk at Jack Steinhart. He was fair-haired, fair skinned, scrupulously clean-shaven and around thirty-six. He had a gazelle type physique, strong and wiry, square shoulders, square jaw, a face expressing an all American candour, which often belies an undercurrent of ruthlessness.
'Miss Edan, Professor Frohmann hasn't told me anything about your project. This is the first time I have heard of an exhibition of this nature taking form. It's difficult for me to even comment right now on the pros and cons, but as far as the bank is concerned, I can see there could be a problem.'

Before he had a chance to continue I interrupted. 'Of course there are problems. That's what this exhibition is about. The problem of theft, greed, fraud, cover-up, annihilation, every despicable action that was perpetrated outside the Geneva Convention, happened here: in this city - in this country - in this bank. Perhaps, Mr. Steinhart, it's time for the dice to be weighted in favour of the losers?'

'O.K' he said, 'give me five days, and I'll give you an answer.'

'I am sorry, Mr.Steinhart, but I leave in four days.'

He spoke in German with Professor Frohmann before saying, 'excuse me, you do speak German?'

'Only enough to avoid getting apples when I want chocolate.' Mr.Steinhart moved from his desk and said 'four days Miss Edan.'

Outside the bank the Professor suggested that I walk around the town to orientate myself. 'It will only take about one hour if you are not tempted to go inside shops.' He had a knowing smile on his face, as though all women were easy targets for shopkeepers.

'I'll meet you at the Weinstube on the corner of the Sigmund-Haffner-Gasse and the Frucht Markt for lunch.' He looked at his watch, which hung on a gold chain, before tucking it neatly back into his waistcoat pocket.

'Let's say, one thirty. That gives you a few extra minutes in case you get lost.' I thanked the Professor, and then wandered the length of the fascinating Getreidegasse.

***

Curiosity can become a serious addiction: consequently the proximity of Berchtesgaden to Salzburg, Adolf Hitler's mountain retreat and favourite home, tempted my inquisitiveness.

As I left the hotel, a cold wind nipped at my skin. Thankful for my cashmere coat, I pulled the collar high around my neck, and then walked towards the river. White steamy clouds had settled across the Salzach: a swirling mist, blotting out the landscape and the early morning light. They lapped the banks, then crept through the mediaeval town, giving the place a damp eerie feel, inviting evil spirits from the past, to disrupt and play with the present.

The journey to Berchtesgaden by bus took one hour. It passed through Anif, then towards the border with Germany. As I crossed this emotional barrier for the first time, my thoughts were disturbed and reflective. What was I doing here? The physical beauty of lake Königsee, the gem of the Bavarian Alps, tucked between soaring jagged rocks, was real enough, but evoked an irreverence in me, inbuilt by hurt and my first encounter with death. I looked up into the mountains, soaring vertically, unapproachable, dominating Berchtesgaden. I thought of Pippa, and Captain and Mrs Rawlings. I thought of the murderous tyrant who had lived there, who had curtailed their lives, along with millions more. The site of the Eagle's Nest, at the summit of Obersalzburg, was blown to smithereens by the allies, so no shrine would ever be revered: it did not obliterate my sadness, but it did gratify a morsel of revenge.

I walked away, back into Berchtesgaden, through streets selling leder hosen and embroidered blouses, and as quickly as I could, crossed the border. By the time I arrived back at my hotel, I felt drained. I looked into my cubbyhole for messages. Some papers were poking out of the wood, but there was nobody to hand them to me, and my arm wouldn't reach. So I went into the wine strüberl, next to the hotel lobby, sat at a bench and ordered a rühmer of red wine. It was unusually quiet for lunchtime, as many locals, shopkeepers, office workers, the Rotary club, the Innkeepers Association; all held their meetings noisily in the restaurant of the Elephant.

My glass was empty, except for a few drops of light red wine. The waiter hovered waiting for me to finish and order another glass. Instead, I decided to collect my messages from the lobby.

There were two calls. One from Sue in London: 'Phone me at the office, I think you'll need to change plans.' The other, from Jack Steinhart: 'Please phone me at the bank, before five if possible.' Hell, I thought, the quick brush off, Yankee style.'

The old man in reception wound the handle on his antiquated switchboard and I picked up the phone.

'Herr Steinhart, bitte.' I asked.

'Ja, Fräulein', Wie ist Ihr name bitte?

'Katrina Edan.' I heard the clicking of wires then the voice of Steinhart.

'Ah, Miss Edan, you received my message. Do you have plans for dinner this evening? I thought it might be a good idea if you filled in a few blanks before I put your proposal forward.'
'That would fine,' I replied.
'Good. I'll pick you up from the Elephant at seven.'

Dressing for dinner didn't present a problem. I could wear either the jacket with trousers, the same jacket with a skirt, or the snappy little number from Jean Muir, in dark green jersey silk, which was a bit clingy. As I had worn the trouser suit all day, I opted for the skirt. I luxuriated in a bath of bubbles, smelling of wild roses, then pulled a large warm towel off the radiator, wrapped it around me, walked to my room, rested on the bed and fell fast asleep. A knock on the door woke me. It was the chambermaid.
'Miss Edan, Herr Steinhart ist aufwarten.' I picked up my watch. It couldn't be: but it was, exactly seven.
Tights - where the hell were my tights? Ah, they were on the chair-back. And my white silk blouse: in the drawer, of course. Make-up, quick: foundation - oh no - it was smudgy - blusher, eyeliner, mascara, done. No - not quite. I grabbed the Givenchy L'Interdit, whizzed a few squirts over my hair, pulled on my jacket, looked in the mirror, and then at my watch. I tucked my coat over my arm and took the 1900's express to the ground floor.

Jack Steinhart was sitting at the lobby table, reading the local newspaper. He stood as he saw me leave the lift. 'Good evening.' he said. I didn't apologise for being late, just answered, 'Hello.'

He collected his coat from the arm of the chair, and said to me. 'You'll need to put your coat on; it's very cold outside. You don't mind walking? It's not far, a few blocks towards the end of the Getreidegasse.'

It was bitter cold and although it was only a five-minute walk I was pleased when we turned into the rounded portal entrance to the Goldener Hirsch, an old hunting lodge that is now an Hotel. Inside the hallway stags' heads commandeered the walls. There was a small bar, with an oriental carpet covering the flagstone floor. Jack Steinhart suggested we have a drink before dinner. I ordered white wine: he ordered rye on the rocks. 'It has just occurred to me,' I said as a plate of pretzels arrived with the drinks, 'I forgot to have lunch.'

'And what was so exciting that you forgot to eat?'
'Tragedy' I replied, 'Remembering tragedy.'
He looked at me, but made no comment, letting me pour out the recollections that Berchtesgaden brought to mind.
'Well, let's try and redress one part of the tragedy, and eat.'

The dining room was down a few steps from the bar. Built entirely of stone, a stone floor, a stone ribbed ceiling, stonewalls. A waiter showed us to a table by the side of a stained glass window, heavy with jagged uneven red and green glass, catching the light from the candles on the plain white tablecloth. I could not understand the menu but I didn't need to. Steinhart suggested Tafelspitz.
'What's in it?' I asked.
'Everything,' he replied 'Roast suckling pig, marinated chicken, a selection of smoked sausage, sauerkraut. Frankly, I'm not sure I can remember any more, except it's an experience on a wooden platter. And to start, take the wild mushrooms in brandy sauce. They're collected in the mountains above Salzburg. It's a great dish if you like mushrooms.'
'I do. And I'll have the "experience" to follow.'

While we were waiting for the first course, Steinhart wasted no time in grilling me with questions. But then, I thought that's why I'm here.
'Miss Edan, which other banks have you approached?'
'Samuel Hall in London, Rothschild Paris, and yourselves. I have one other in mind, the Ritzvah Memorial Bank, Tel Aviv but I haven't discussed the proposal yet.'
'Do you have any confirmations?'
'No. My proposal is being considered by Samuel Hall's board and Rothschilds will call me in London.' I presume they're testing their investors' reaction!'
'I'd go along with that. No investors, no money.' he said.
'I agree with you Mr.Steinhart, but, as I see it, the bank's hesitation has nothing to do with money. It's a no risk, one off payment, held in the bank's name. I know it's a sensitive and evocative proposal without precedence, but I think this makes sponsorship even more attractive.'
'O.K. you present a good case. What I'd like to know is, where are you going to get the exhibits? The dead won't rise and make claims from Austrians holding works of art. The Austrians won't

admit to grand larceny - that's for sure. Even if you get funding, I can't see how that will solve all the existing improbabilities.'

'Mr.Steinhart, you're right: except if families have kept works of art for over thirty years and they're getting old, what will become of the loot when they die? Will their children be answerable to theft? Do their children even know what their parents are concealing? It is an unresolved dilemma. Showing stolen works could be the only chance to legitimise paintings, with no questions asked. Guilt will not motivate the Austrians but greed will, Mr.Steinhart. The odds might be stacked against me but that doesn't mean I'll fail. In fact, once I have financing, failure is not an option.'

All the time I was speaking Jack Steinhart's gaze was penetrating. He could have accused me of misguided altruism, but he didn't. Instead he said.

'Tell me, Miss Edan, why did you choose such a difficult assignment? You will be messing with some pretty mean customers here.'

'I know it's going to be tough. But, to answer your question, the idea formulated some years ago, when I met Anna Frishman, a refugee from Vienna. Her story was festering in my mind. It became a bug, eating at me. At the first opportunity, I put a structure together for the exhibition. That was two months ago.'

Before he had a chance to ask any more questions, I said.

'And you, what brought you to Salzburg?'

'Nothing altruistic, I must confess. I was trading in commodities in Chicago. I felt like a Las Vegas pimp, only I was raping the market. Big bucks plus big burn-out.'

The waiter arrived with the Tafelspitz. I looked at the wooden platter with the sharp carving knife placed by its side. The little pig's head was sitting in the middle of the platter, looking up at me. I couldn't touch it.

'A problem' Steinhart said, as I sat back in my chair.

'Big problem' I replied 'would you ask the waiter to remove the inedible anatomy, from my plate? It's giving me a conscience.'

'Sure.' Within seconds my plate returned with a white turnip sculpted like a rose, in exchange for the pig's head, making the dish look more like normal food than a night out for a cannibal. Before sampling the delicacies in front of me, I said to Mr.Steinhart.

'You haven't told me what brought you to Salzburg.'
'I suppose, if I'm truthful, it was an accident of fate. I was ready for a change - so I put the word around that I wanted to move on, and then waited to see what came up. My timing coincided with the merger by Imperial Chicago and Laufenbankgeschaft. I was prepared to re-locate. It was a challenge, so I jumped on board.'
He deliberately turned his pig's head, so it wasn't looking at me.
'How long have you known Wilhelm Frohmann?'
'Five years, since I arrived here.'
'Did you know much about him before you met?'
'You mean the fact that he was a Nazi. Of course. The CIA briefs all bank staff before coming to Europe. This was the American zone after the war, I didn't want my hide kicked over the base line.'

My head was spinning, nobody - not even Dr.Hempf, had verbally accused Professor Frohmann.
'Are you sure?' I inquired.
He looked up from cutting a piece of sausage.
'Sure of what?'
'That Frohmann was a Nazi!'
'As sure as we're sitting here this evening, I have first class confirmation. He told me himself.' I sipped my wine in silent contemplation careful not to re-act impulsively.
'Miss Edan. As far as I'm concerned, they were all Nazi bastards. But that was twenty years ago. Now the dollar rules Europe and we hold the balance of power. It doesn't matter what happened in the past. It's history.'
'It matters to me,' I said.

It was getting late. I had a meeting with the Professor at 8.30. so I said to Steinhart. 'I hope I've filled in any gaps: is there anything else you'd like to know?'
'No, not right now, I think I have the picture.'

It was crisp outside as we walked along the Getreidegasse. Steinhart plunged his hands deep into his coat pockets and I pulled the collar of my coat over my ears. We paused a moment at the entrance to Mozart's house to read an ornate plaque with the words Wolfgang Amadeus Mozart. Geboren 1756. We turned into the Sigmund-Haffner Gasse and into my hotel. Mr.Steinhart extended his hand.
'Thank you for your company, I'll be in touch before you leave.'

I had a restless night. It wasn't the Tafelspitz that disturbed me. It was Jack Steinhart. I usually know if I've made a favourable impression but this man was like a well-bred racehorse, totally in control, every move preceded by thought. What's wrong with that? I asked myself. After all you are asking for over a million dollars.

***

Trusting Sue had opened the office early, I phoned at 8.45 a.m.
'At last' she said, 'where were you? Don't tell me. You were out with a punter?' I listened. 'Bernard Anderson's secretary called. Samuel Hall have agreed sponsorship, and they want you to sign the contract.'
'That's not a problem, I'm back on Wednesday.'
'Katrina, it is a problem. Corinne called from Paris. She leaves for New York on Thursday and wants to see you before she leaves.'
'Did she say why I had to go there? Couldn't we talk on the phone?'
'Tried that. She said no. I'll tell you what I've arranged.'
'You'd better,'
'On Wednesday take the Rosenkavalier to Vienna.'
'Hang on Sue, what's the Rosenkavalier?'
'It's the name of a train: it leaves Salzburg at 7.50 and arrives in Vienna at 10.45.' I could hear Sue chuckling down the phone.
'What's funny?' I asked
'The Mozart leaves half an hour later then Die Fledermaus. What the fuck gives with these Austrians?'
'Not sure,' I said, 'but I'm finding out - fast.'
'Take a taxi to the airport when you arrive in Vienna. You're booked on Austrian Airlines to Paris leaving at noon. Corinne will meet you at the Dauphine Restaurant at Le Bourget at 1.30 p.m, give or take a few minutes. You'll have to have your ticket re-routed. Just take it to the Austrian airlines office in Salzburg.'

By mid-morning Professor Frohmann and I had scrutinized more than twenty paintings when he suggested we stop for coffee. We went through the maze of corridors to his office.
'Professor Frohmann, how well do you know the Sneider collection?'
'Fairly well,' he admitted. 'Some I have seen on the walls at Schloss Lundwig. Others I haven't seen before.'

'May I ask you a personal question?'
'Yes, of course . . . well, it depends how personal.' he added.
'How long were you a member of the Nazi party?'

The Professor sat very erect, his head resting on the back of his chair. He lit a cigarette, which he fixed into his ivory holder.
'I joined in 1938, Miss Edan. Perhaps I should explain the circumstances of my involvement with the National Socialists.'

SALZBURG

6

Professor Frohmann pushed his glasses closer to his face as if the action could make him feel more comfortable with his past.

'I graduated from the Academy of Fine Arts in Vienna in 1938, the same year Austria became part of the German Reich. Hermann Goering, the founder of the Gestapo, the state police of Nazi Germany presented the scrolls to final year students. It was, I must admit an exceptional occasion. The old assembly hall was decorated with bunting and flags and, hanging as a backdrop on the platform, was a large portrait of Adolf Hitler bordered by two flags with the insignia of the Swastika: the emblem of the German Socialist Party. My parent's received an invitation to attend the ceremony as I was receiving my Master's degree. Lunch with the Rektor and the distinguished guest Reich Marshall Hermann Goering would follow the presentation.

My father, Ernst Frohmann, was a fastidious man, and started preparing for the ceremony soon after breakfast. I had joined him in his dressing room, at his request, for his approval. He was busy straightening his tie, making sure it was perfectly aligned with his starched white collar. Holding two mahogany-backed bristle brushes, one in each hand, looking into the long mirror, he smoothed his greying hair into impeccable shape. I remember every word he said.'

"Wilhelm. How's your new suit, is it a good fit? Are the sleeves long enough?"

I replied. 'Yes Father, the sleeves are long enough.'

"Are your shoes comfortable?"

'Yes, Father.' After 29 years with my mother Ilse, he must have known that she would have measured and taped and pinned, instructed the tailor, chosen the fabric and for such a special occasion, made absolutely sure the sleeves were the right length. He stood back, far enough to get me in perspective.

"A crease in your trousers, my lad, is a necessity for a gentleman. Knife edged shows precision of mind, attention to detail, self respect and creates a favourable impression. Don't ever forget that." The Professor gave a cryptic smile.

'I've puzzled over this didactic stance, and was, in my twenty forth year, a little bemused by it. Not that I didn't appreciate his role as my father, but his attitude was always biased in favour of conformity, without allowing me a hint of self-expression. Taking into consideration his thirty years in the international department of the Laufenbankgeschaft it would have seemed reasonable that his daily meetings with an eclectic clientele from Central and Eastern Europe - Russians, Poles, Hungarians, Czechs - would have tempered his attitude into a more moderate frame. This was not the case: his Teutonic affiliation was deep rooted. He spoke of the past glories of the Holy Roman Empire with pride and the defeat of the Teutonic race, in the Great War of 1914-1918, as an historical hiccup on the route to great expansionism.' Frohmann stubbed out his cigarette. "Now Hitler is in power," my father said, "we will have leadership, the renaissance will come, and when the momentum accelerates the whole world will revere our achievements."

'He never could understand my wish for self-expression. Maybe this was my reason for studying Art History: I was attracted to the melting pot of creativity. I admired individuals who reached within themselves for self-expression, oblivious of failure or success, recognizing both is only temporary. Art is always moving on: divorced from conventional mores it attracts minds wilful to change and experimentation and above all finding a certain truth. It's unimportant to artists that the trousers are knife-edged. They don't contribute to a fertile imagination. Father couldn't follow my reasoning. But on the day when my Masters degree was conferred I had to admit I felt comfortable with the sleeves and trousers the correct length! My final dissertation to the Academy caused me considerable anguish. Not that it was difficult, more a question of making the right choice. It was important that this last piece should clarify how astutely and clinically I could observe and how well I was able to convey that perception. My tutor, Alfred Kubin was not receptive to adventurous writing, nor was he, for that matter, prepared to look at my opinions on Modern Art.

"Frohmann" he said "I want your final and uncluttered opinion: an assessment based on historic fact, a rounded and well written précis containing the aspects of communication through art and the techniques used to promote that theory."

It was so important at the time to choose the artist who encapsulated every element that Kubin wanted. He had not stipulated the country: so - in my mind - I wandered around Europe, before settling at home. I selected the artist Franz von Stuck. It proved to be a fortuitous decision.

Rivalry between senior students was non-existent: respect for one another's ideas and open debate were always encouraged. Otto Prantl, Gerhard Hofer, Anton Hempf and myself, formed a society called "Revolt." Its aim was to disseminate past art movements, make way for new ideology and get as many students as possible to pay ten Austrian schillings to be members. We were respected seniors, about to be awarded the highest degree, so we had full houses for our debates and full pockets for our drinking sessions.

We particularly admired the stance taken by Gustav Klimt, in 1897, when the Secessionist movement rebelled against the constrictions of the Academy and built their own building known locally as the 'cabbage' to show their reactionary works. Their motto, ' to every art its time, to art its freedom,' was emblazoned in wrought iron over the main entrance. By breaking with convention in art and design, the Secessionists set free new ideas about what art should be. This group, especially the young Egon Schiele, disregarded convention, rejected the bourgeoisie and exhibited nudity, depravity, copulation, life and death, with such robust conviction and technical skill, the Viennese were outraged by his blatent effrontery. Thirty years after his death Schiele was our hero. Our magazine Revolt was the mouthpiece of the university's dissident students, in line with the innovative and radical newsletter 'Der Sacrum' printed by the Vienna Secession thirty years earlier.

Anton Hempf was academic dynamite, so, he was the editor. Gerhard Hofer managed distribution, as his father was a printer and gave us access to his press. Otto Prantl and myself solicited for articles. "Revolt" was a source of serious enjoyment to us, and sometimes Anton and I would sit in the Café Hawelka for hours discussing ideas.

My essay on Franz von Stuck elucidated the limits of naturalistic painting without going too far into the merits of contemporary art and steering well away from the avant-garde, just to satisfy the examining board. This would be the last time I would have to write to order. Anything, from that day forward I reminded myself, would be free from the constraints of tutorial prescription.

My mother looked very smart for the ceremony. She wore a new hat: brown velour with a tiny red feather in the hatband and a dark coat, which fitted closely at the waist and flared out at the hem, made by a tailor on the Kartnerstrasse. Her carriage was erect, and sometimes, I thought, a little immobile, as she moved slowly and with poise. But somehow, she effortlessly achieved the demands made on her by my father.

When my name was called I walked the long distance from the back of the hall along a central red carpet towards the stage. Goering was seated on the left side of the platform next to Professor Dreska. Alfred Kubin and other senior tutors sat behind; Dr.Ernst Kaltenbrunner, newly appointed chief of the Gestapo and Security Service for Austria, and Gauleiter Buerckel, head of the Austrian Nazi party sat on the other side. As I climbed the few steps onto the platform Hermann Goering stood. A surging power enveloped me as I took the rolled scroll with my left hand, and he vigorously shook my right. He said "Congratulations to you, Wilhelm Frohmann. I liked your opinions on Franz von Stuck, I am sure your career will be a credit to you and an asset to the German Reich." The flash bulbs clicked as I left the platform; surprised he had read my paper, and curious to hear what he had said to other students.

As the last student left the dais the Rektor went to the microphone and addressed the audience.

"This is a momentous occasion in the History of this University, and I am proud to be associated with it. We have just conferred degrees to this year's graduates and given Masters degrees to fifteen. I can now give you the results of our distinguished judging panel, for the two teaching posts available this year, together with research facilities for the title of Doktor. Those places are offered to Wilhelm Frohmann and Otto Prantl: both have shown exceptional insight and promise: the decision by the panel was unanimous." I heard the clapping, but it seemed distant, as if it was from some other place and had nothing to do me with me. The Rektor continued, "It is now, with pride that I can introduce our distinguished guest Reichs-marshall Hermann Goering."

After the applause had faded, Goering in the grey uniform of a German General, the insignia of the swastika on his armband, knee high jackboots, polished like silk, spoke.

"Members of the Nazi Party, ladies and gentlemen, graduates. I would like to thank all the Professors and tutors here to day for their success in steering you to your final goal. This achievement is of great value to us all. It is indicative of the way Vienna can now proudly move forward to a greater and lasting prosperity. But I must repeat what I said in March. Vienna will only become an important city when it is purged of the 300.000 Jews who live here. It is the duty of every citizen of the German Reich to help purify our future nation. You, the guardians of Vienna are given this power by our great leader, Adolf Hitler. A new Empire is being created and you are at the heart of our future."

Goering stood to his full height, raised his chin, took a step back, shot his right arm forward in salute and said "Heil Hitler."

The applause was rapturous; the entire Academy was on its feet. My father's hands were high above his head clapping continually.

I shall never forget his words to me. "Wilhelm," he shouted above the din, "This is a wonderful beginning for you, I am so happy and proud." My mother kissed me on the cheek. "Congratulations, my dear." She looked at me, with obvious love, and, I think, admiration. My father, then turned to me, put his two hands on my shoulders and said. "Son, for your own interest and advancement, now is the time to join the Nazi Party."

It was some time before Professor Frohmann spoke after his panegyric discourse. A far-away gaze and a smirk of satisfaction crossed his face. It was not without malice and indignation that he said to me: 'Now you know, Miss Edan, how I came to be a member of the National Socialist party.'

SALZBURG

7

Complex manoeuvres by Professor Frohmann appeared natural and instinctive. Whether he was preparing a barrier of duplicity for my benefit or destruction, I had yet to ascertain. This became apparent when he showed me the Emil Nolde painting, which I knew was a forgery. With this in mind I decided to go to Hallein, to look, albeit from the outside, at the home of the Sneider family.

I left the hotel early. Mist had crept down the river and into the city, taking away the light, menacing the buildings, and trapping the view. I waited at the bus stop by the river, as workers lined the pavement beside me in Loden coats and raincoats protecting them from the early morning chill before the sun had warmed the night air. A cold wind sliced down from the mountains and the fortress walls offered no reprieve.

Hallein is a small town, a collection of contrasts: solid merchants' homes and small shops selling everyday wares for the farming and local community. Bakers were selling the first bake of the day and the smell of yeast and dough clung to the walls in the quaint alleyways. I walked through a stone archway looking for any sign to Schloss Lundwig: then another arch, but still no directions. I went into a bakery, serving coffee, ordered a grand tasse mit sahne and asked for directions. 'Schloss Lundwig ist nicht hier. Das ist bei Dürrnberg,' the woman behind the counter said abruptly. A woman waiting to be served stared at me before collecting a large schwartz rye loaf, which she put in a wicker-shopping basket. As she was leaving she turned and looked at me with a hard-edged stare. As soon as I had scraped the last of the sahne sticking to the cup, I left.

The sun pierced the fog, the clouds were rising, the chill wind dropped. I decided to walk to Dürrnberg. The hill was steep but my eyes were fixed at the top and the air was fresh and crisp in my lungs. I stopped a few moments to look back down the valley. The Salzach River commandeered the landscape as it wove through the meadows towards Salzburg. As I approached the village I saw the castle and the spire of a church. Apart from these two buildings and a few farmhouses set in unfenced land this appeared to be Dürrnberg: until I turned a corner into an area with a sign 'Parkplatz fur die Salz-mine.'

On the far side of the Platz was a kiosk. Inside a man in a white overall asked in a very gritty voice if I wanted a ticket. He saw my vacant response.

'Zie mine opens Neun, und die erste tour ist neun und fünfzehn.'

I looked at my watch: it was 8.55.am.

'Yes please, one ticket. Does the guide speak English?' I asked.

'Ja, I do,' he replied.

His face had dark lines etched into leathery skin, sallow sunken cheeks below eyes which had long since lost their sparkle. His mouth was set rigid, tensed muscles distorted his thin immobile lips.

I took the ticket, which he tore off a roll and looked at the white piece of paper - nummer drei. By the time we had completed the transaction it was 9 am.

'Zie vomens change room is by der!' He pointed to a small wooden hut. Inside were two benches. A woman handed me a white overall with wide trousers and a hooded top. In sign language like a game of charades, she gesticulated I should put it over my clothes, and then remove my shoes. She gave me a pair of soft ankle boots with woollen tops and leather soles.

'Where do I leave my shoes?' I held them up.

She took them from me, then pointed to my shoulder bag, which she also took, then locked them in a free standing grey metal cupboard, which wobbled on the uneven floor as she struggled with the lock.

I was ushered into a waiting area at the top of the mineshaft where a young couple were sitting.

My limited knowledge of mines comes mainly from films except an incident televised in 1966. Those pictures were still clear in my head. Pictures of a massive slick of silt and coal dust, sliding downhill, quietly leaning towards a school of innocent children learning about the world's history, its geography, poetry and song, not knowing they would never experience any of its pleasures, as death rolled uncontrolled into their classrooms. This was the mining I remembered: a small mining village in Wales where grandfather, father, sons, nephews, automatically went into the pits. Destiny, previously prescribed and accepted, changed dramatically one day in

Aberfan when the earth moved and swallowed a generation of 114 children.

The young man sitting on the opposite bench with a young girl with short brown hair and no make-up spoke to me in English.

'I'm Heinrik and this is Delma - we're from Holland - and you?'

'English' - I said, not really wanting to get into inane conversation. Then the tour guide put his head around the door.

'We leave in vier minuten.' Then looking at me said 'four.'

At that moment, two German tourists waving their hands and shouting 'Bitte, bitte, eine Minuten, vier drei personnen,' as they dragged a fat boy of about ten into the waiting area. Anything that could upset the system by even half a minute is not in the Teutonic thinking.

'Zwei Minuten,' said the guide.

They rushed to get their white overalls, and panting and sweating were back just as a bell started ringing by the lift shaft. We all stood absolutely still as the lift plunged down. I wanted to shout - stop, I've just remembered an important appointment. My imagination was running amok as the lift went further into the blackness. Like the other passengers I was holding a rail on the side of the lift, but the open cage work only exposed rough rocks and grime. On the way down I'd wished I were going into a cave with stalagmites and stalactites and blue lagoons, and cave dwellings, with hieroglyphs inviting me to a pre-historic lifestyle. Instead, the lift suddenly jolted to a halt onto a rough wooden platform.

'All out' said the guide.

Small electric bulbs at about ten foot intervals cast shadows onto a chute. It was steep, with a fall of about one in six. 'I vant you to sit very close. I vant you to be sure your legs do not, do not, I say, go over the sides. I vant zie light vones in front and zie heavy at the back.'

We looked at each other, weighing and weighting our fat potential. The ten year old was first, then Delma, the Dutch girl, then myself, behind me was Heinrik, then the German Frau and lastly her very heavy husband. That's not quite correct, because the guide was last.

All my life I have avoided switchbacks, helter shelters, and fairgrounds. The big dipper was never a challenge: it was a worthless attraction for morons of diminished mentality. Cheap thrills, over in seconds: a penny's worth of excitement, with no recall. And here I was, about to shoot to the unknown with six strangers and no return ticket? I didn't hear the command, but suddenly we were off. I was tucked closely between the legs of Heinrik. I could feel his crotch against my lower back. We were travelling at God only knows what speed and the breath was sucked from my lungs and my sense of gravity was forever undermined. The incline flattened out and slowly we slid to a halt. Delma's back had been pressed between my legs and a sharp pain shot through my stretched thighs as I stepped onto creaky wooden planks.

'Wunderbar' shouted the German husband.

'Silence' said the guide. 'Dis mine is very old, not gut für vibration.'

We were standing in a large space with the flat roof held in place by crusty white pillars. It was airless and dry and I could taste the salt on my lips.

The guide gathered us towards the wall to explain the basic method of removing salt from underground mines.

'My name is Karl. I have vorked in dis mine für thirty years. I was Bergknappen, a miner. The method used here ist called room and pillar method. As you can see, pillars of salt hold up the rooms. First ve vould dig a deep shaft, then ve broke the rock salt with pick-axes, later with drills: the large chunks went to ground level through the shafts, leaving these huge empty rooms, separated by pillars of salt. Dis method required almost half the salt to be left behind, to support the upper side from collapsing. Ve are now at 300 metres below ground, for ze English 1000ft. Ve shall soon go to 550 metres - 1800ft, the deepest room in the mine.'

Fat boy shouted, 'down a chute?'

'Quiet' said his father 'we'll all be buried alive.'

We followed Karl through tunnels with electric light bulbs hanging like Christmas decorations on wires along the walls. Except the intervals of light were sparse, our shadows lost. We groped along the wall before arriving in a very large room, with pillars like columns on the facade of a Grecian temple. I could see ancillary tunnels had been excavated, forming spurs off the main room.

Karl explained, 'when ze salt seams became exhausted new tunnels ver excavated but ventilation was difficult and needed to be sealed once the lift had been lowered, to stop moisture seeping in and dampening the salt.' I licked my lips. They felt crusty, dry. All very interesting I thought, but I had a question: in fact I had many questions.

'Where do the spur lines go and where are we, at ground level?'

'Ah - you vish to know ver you are! - vell, I shall tell you. You are under Bad Reichenhall and that route,' he pointed to one of the spurs ' goes to Berchtesgaden, and that one to Königsee.'

Could this be one of the routes that Hitler used to move looted art when the Axis was in decline prior to its eventual destruction? It was rumoured the 'good burghers' of Munich and Salzburg had helped themselves to art and antiques stored in mines at Bad Auslee, Monshee, and here in Dürrnberg.

My attention was diverted from being underground and moved upwards to the Sneider collection. Could it have been supplemented from this underground source? Did Professor Frohmann know? It was inconceivable he didn't.

'Ve vill line up for the next chute' Karl said.

Activity had long ceased in the production of salt. What remained were a token fairground appeal, and a total rebuttal of the truth in relation to the very near past.

The descent, a long steady slope took forever. My crotch ached, bruised by the backbone of the Dutch girl: I wasn't in the least concerned whether I had ruined Heinrik for life. By the time we stopped I was completely disorientated until Karl revealed our geographic position.

'Now ve're on ze border with Austria and Germany.' He pointed to some deep recesses in the tunnels that were shelved and concreted: copper pipes lined the sides supplying a primitive heating system.

'That is ver der Fürhrer, Herr Adolf Hitler, stored his private treasures for protection from ze bombs of ze British and Americans.' I made a mental note of his reference to Hitler as the Fürhrer and his lack of reference to the British and Americans as allies. Surely this man knew much more than he intended to tell.

But then for ten Austrian shillings, what could I expect? An exposé of the criminals circulating in his village, the loot they had locked in their cupboards? I was relieved when we walked through another tunnel and saw by the electric bulb - a lift shaft. The fat boy ran to be first inside and we, and I speak especially for myself, gratefully followed.

As the cage edged its way upward, shards of light pierced the darkness and the bright morning sunshine made me squint. I thanked Karl for his 'interesting and informative' talk, and dropped a note in his palm. I went to the hut and hastily removed the overalls and the woollen boots, collected my bag, and left.

***

On returning to Salzburg, I went to the Café Bazaar, overlooking the river, frequented by the faculty from the Mozarteum and the nearby University and visitors to the music festivals. By most café standards it is impressive, with leather upholstered chairs and empire lights, glass top tables and starched collared waiters. I ordered frankfurters mit sempf, a semmel roll and tee. I looked at my watch, barely one hour before confronting the Professor. I rested my elbows on the table and cupped my hands to support my head. I desperately needed a plan of action to present to Professor Frohmann. The waiter arrived with a silver tray high over his shoulder, carrying my sausages. So much pomp for a pair of frankfurters: it was laughable. I held a frankfurter in my fingers and swiped it into the mustard. Bastard, I said, you bastard.

When I reached the Galerie Frohmann I had consolidated my thoughts, calmed down, and knew exactly what I should do.

The Professor, as always, looked immaculate in a grey pinstriped suit with matching waistcoat, a pink and grey cravat held in place by his pearl tiepin.

'Miss Edan, how are you? Are enjoying Salzburg? I hear Herr Steinhart took you to the Goldener Hirsch. Gut, Ja? It was unusual for Wilhelm Frohmann to comment in German, as his English was excellent.

'So,' he said, 'shall we start work?'

The array of assorted works, set out in the large galerie was, on first sight, impressive. The room was crammed with paintings resting against walls, even stacked one in front of another: too many to authenticate before the daylight faded.

'Firstly,' he said, 'shall we look at the largest piece.'

We stood by a ornate gold framed oil painting, with the title "Ansicht des Dogenpalasstes von Venedig" - View of the Doge's Palace - Venice. A small oval copper plaque had the inscription, Giovanni Antonio Canaletto 1697-1768. It was a perfect example of work by the great architectural landscape painter: smooth, translucent paint, no craquelure, no visible brushwork, with perfect symmetry and in immaculate condition. Regular, small white brushstrokes imitated ripples on the blue lagoon. Nothing to indicate it was anything but genuine.

'Very, very nice' I said to Wilhelm Frohmann. 'Do you have the provenance?' He consulted the list prepared by Stephan Moser.

'Yes... it is nummer drei in the inventory.' He shuffled the papers. 'It was bought by the grandfather of Sneider from Matrioni in Florence in 1923. He looked at me: 'Matrioni's galerie specialized in Veduta painting - and - this one - he pointed to a small Venetian Canal scene, 'is by Francesco Guardi 1712 - 1793. He didn't wait for me to ask about its history. He turned a few pages.

'Ah - here it is: purchased from an ancestor of Giambattista Tiepolo, Guardi's brother-in-law. No date is recorded.'

I looked down at the priceless gem resting on the floor: a setting sun over the Venetian lagoon radiates warmth from the canvas: light mystically refracts into the water, weightless gondolas glide slowly and gracefully, their passengers' mere dots of paint. A gondolier sinks a pole into the lagoon: no splash disturbs the tranquillity. I stood quietly, gratefully, admiring a masterpiece.

Next to the Guardi was a painting by Jan Vermeer 1632-1675. No title, no plaque, but the letters JV in a corner.

'Do you know anything about this one?'

'Nothing' Wilhelm replied: 'Stephan has written nummer dreiundzwanzig - no provenance, no date, no history!'

'Could be a fake,' I said 'like the Nolde.' There was a frozen silence.

'Miss Edan, we both know the war years produced fakes. It was inevitable. When Hitler's passion for Vermeer was known, it opened up avenues for crooks and fakers. Van Meegeren, the most prolific was also the most difficult to detect. He recreated many variants of great masters: pictures of undeniable accuracy. His intuitive talent and invincible confidence motivated him.

Everyone was duped, the Italians, the Germans, the Dutch. The problem Miss Edan is, they're still out there and I agree this could be one.'

We both looked very closely at the painting. The Professor removed his thick eyeglasses and was looking only inches from the canvas. I waited.

'It looks original to me,' he assessed rather too quickly.

'Looks O.K. to me too,' I said, 'from the front.' I took more time.

I turned the picture over, placed it on the floor with the back exposed, took a small penknife from my bag and scraped where the canvas met the frame. I showed the Professor the knife's edge.

'Not much dirt in two hundred years, don't you agree? The dust would have congealed much more - this is loose. I think Professor Frohmann, on analysis you'll find that it was reframed about thirty years ago. My question is why? Most Vermeer's are still in their original frames. I guarantee when the edge of the canvas is exposed it will look new. I suggest we remove this one and the Nolde.'

Proving my point was important and gaining the Professor's respect was equally important. Furthermore, I'm not someone who can be duped easily into accepting forgeries or fabrication.

'Would you like me to remove it from the canvas?' I asked.

The Professor said, 'It's getting late Miss Edan, I'll have my assistant remove it in the morning.'

'It's no trouble for me, I work very quickly,' I said as I lifted the nails with my penknife before he had time to object. As I removed the canvas from the frame, the unpainted edges, which wrapped around the stretcher, were white. I held the painting up for the Professor to see more clearly. I pointed to the edge.

'You can see, Herr Professor it is white. Proof this painting has not been in this frame since Vermeer created it or the canvas would be discoloured, yellowing, frayed, and the nails rusted with time. Proof enough that this is a forgery.' Swiftly I asked 'Would you like me to remove the Nolde?' Professor Frohmann conceded. 'That won't be necessary, I'm sure it came from the same source.' A fact, which I think, he knew beforehand.

It was late, so I asked the Professor if I could take Stephan Moser's list to London for the preliminary work.

'I can also show it to Dr.Hempf.' I said.

'Certainly. I'll have a copy made for you.' He tucked the inventory under his arm, adding.
'A great deal happened in Austria since Anton Hempf left that he wouldn't know about.'
'I'm sure you're right, Herr Professor. I'm relying on you for an accurate update.'
On the way back to his office, I casually asked if he thought Jack Steinhart would become a sponsor.
'It is difficult to anticipate Jack's moves. He is a shrewd negotiator. If he thinks the exhibition will profit the bank's image and not cost any money, I can't see why he shouldn't agree.'
We waited in the Professor's office for Lisette to bring the copy of the Sneider inventory.
'If there's anything confusing or improbable, call me.' said the Professor, 'I'm sure I'll be able to find a solution.'
'Professor. I have enjoyed Salzburg: it's a delightful town: I would really like to see it in the spring - it must be beautiful!'
'It is, and spring's not far away either: melting snow from the mountains cascades into the valleys: wild flowers go absolutely crazy, reaching for the light.'
We shook hands. 'Please give my regards to your wife and Charlotte.'
As I was leaving, Kurt Frohmann came into the office.
'Ah, Kurt, just in time to say auf Wiedersehen to Miss Edan.'
We shook hands. 'I hope to spend more time with you on your next visit,' he said formally.

***

During breakfast at the Hotel Elephant scoffing crunchy rolls and jam, the waiter told me there was a telephone call waiting. I walked downstairs from the salon to the front desk, where the phone sat on its shelf like an obsolete antiquity.
'For you, Miss Edan,' the receptionist pointed.
'Miss Edan, this is Jack Steinhart. Can you possibly manage lunch to day? I have a meeting this morning and another after lunch?' He didn't wait for me to answer. 'Could you find your way to the Hotel Österreichischer Hof - it's over the bridge, next to the Café Bazaar?' I remembered it clearly.

'I've seen the Hotel, I know where it is.' I said.
'Good, I'll see you there at one.'
The phone clicked. So, at least he was good for his word - four days exactly. I returned to my coffee, stuffed another roll with plum jam, and then decided to call London.

The line was busy. I waited in the hotel lobby as a French couple were checking in. They had flamboyant clothes - he with a camel coat draped over his shoulders, she clutching a voluminous beaver coat around herself. A jaunty, Jackie Kennedy pillbox perched on top of her head. The distinctive smell of Worth's Je Reviens accompanied them both. The receptionist was pulling wires out of the mini-exchange and plugging them in different holes.
'Your call,' she said, as she pointed to the only phone in the hotel.
'Sue, it's Katrina. Is the office ticking over?'
'Of course it is. No firecrackers here - apart from a few phone calls and the odd request for you to lunch with the Queen! It's normal.'
'Any changes on the plans for Paris, Sue? Good. I'll be in London on the last flight on Wednesday.'
'Katrina, did you get any money from the Laufenbankgeschaft?'
'I'll know by this afternoon - could go either way. By Thursday, I'll have everything or practically nothing.'
'If this guy Steinhart doesn't bite, let's shop him to the Chicago Jewish community. They won't have an account left!'
'Goodbye, Sue.' I put the instrument back on its hanger.

I crossed the river by the pedestrian Mozartsteg Bridge, a narrow walkway that I shared with swooping seagulls tilting their wings and zooming low over my head. After changing my airline ticket, I still had some time before lunch. I wandered along the Rudolfskai looking in shop windows. I stopped in front of a hat shop with an entire display of hideous, old-fashioned models, something my grandmother might have worn, certainly nothing I would wear, except for one, which caught my eye. I was propelled inside either by jealousy, envy, or both, since seeing the chic little number that had checked into my hotel. 'Guten Tag, madam.' I pointed to the small black pillbox in the window. 'Ja' said the assistant, 'das ist eine Paris model.'

She removed the hat from its wooden stand, showed me the label inside, and with a big smile, said 'Paris.'

Not quite what I had seen earlier but I plonked it on the back of my head. My long red hair waved loosely to my shoulders, and the assistant moved the hat forward across my brow, and then tilted it slightly to one side. I looked in the mirror. Saucy - I thought. It looked good with my cashmere coat. I've always liked black and tan, they complement each other, like Guinness and lager, or a breed of horse, and now, part of my wardrobe. I paid the assistant, walked out wearing my pillbox, feeling smug and self satisfied. Although the hat was on my head, it gave my feet a jaunty gait as I crossed the street to the hotel.

Jack Steinhart was waiting in the lobby. The cloakroom attendant took my coat: I kept my pillbox on. With a black skirt, a black high-necked sweater and now a black hat, the only relief breaking the monotony, was my scarlet lipstick.

We were shown to a table overlooking the river and the old town. I looked at the panoramic view through the floor to ceiling glass that looked like a cut-out from a children's book of medieval fairy tales. Crystal chandeliers hung from a high ceiling, silver cutlery and slim long-stemmed glasses stood on crisp white tablecloths; a stark contrast from the strüberl at the Elephant.

'Would you like a drink Miss Edan?'

'A glass of champagne would be nice.' I said reasoning the bank was paying the bill.

'Pink or white?' he asked.

'Pink, please.'

'And I'll have a vodka - straight up - with a twist,' he told the waiter.

When the drinks arrived Jack Steinhart settled back in his armchair.

'I guess you want to know what the bank thinks of your proposal.'

'Absolutely' I replied.

The waiter handed me a heavy leather bound menu, which I briefly scanned. My stomach was tight, I wasn't even sure I could put any food inside. 'I'll have blue trout.'

'Good choice,' said Steinhart 'let's make that two.'

The waiter held my chair back: we went to a large fish tank near the entrance. The trout were busy, darting between fronds of green leaves, looking at us, looking at them. The waiter was in attendance with a small net. I didn't point at the fattest one as its tail whipped through the water, but a small sized, very blue skinned fish.

'That one, please.'

'And you sir.' said the waiter.

Steinhart peered at the tank. 'They all look the same to me. Just give me a medium size.' he said to the waiter, 'and no heads.' The net plunged in and they were en route to the kitchen.

Dishes of pretzels, olives, Liptauer and croutons were waiting on our table. I looked across the river at the sunlight highlighting the painted buildings. Grey next to green next to pink; yellow, blue, sand; tall, narrow, touching. An arch in the fortress of this sugar facade is the entrance into the old city.

I spread some Liptauer onto a crouton and waited for Jack Steinhart to tell me whether my proposal had been accepted. He had his arms on the table and the tumbler between both hands.

'Imperial Chicago called me this morning. The bank will give you the £375,000 on deposit, which is what you requested. They'll pay interest into a feeder account at the fixed rate of 12%, also what you asked for but it will be in dollars.'

As he was speaking, the wine waiter placed a bottle of wine in a wrought iron cooler stand by the side of the table.

'With the exchange rate around $3.50 to the pound,' he said, 'I calculate the investment at $1.312.500 and the annual interest $157,500 and no cents.'

I smiled. 'For how many years, Mr.Steinhart?'

'Well, I reckon three - at a stretch four - that should see it to the close - or should I say opening!'

'Where will the checking account be?'

'Here, in Salzburg, transferred from Imperial Chicago.'

'Mr.Steinhart' I said, 'how long before the money is available?'

'Just as long as it takes to make the transfer from Chicago.'

'That's excellent. I must thank you. I can assure you any publicity for the exhibition will mention your bank as a sponsor. Now I have £750.000 at 12%. Oh, I didn't tell you, my secretary confirmed on the phone, Samuel Hall, have agreed to sponsor -

giving me £90,000 to date. Tomorrow, I'll know if Rothschilds will join the consortium.'
'You have enough finance to get started but the tough part will be finding the paintings. And when you do, take my advice, keep quiet.' I didn't follow the drift of this remark.
'I'm not being threatened Mr.Steinhart and I doubt if I will be. The exhibition will be high profile - anyone making menacing overtures to me, or anyone working with me, will have their nose put out of joint.'
'And how are you going to do that? Personally start a punch-up? The guys around here have track records that leave Al Capone looking like a saint.'
'I know,' I replied, 'but I can't rewrite their histories, I'll just have to match up to what's thrown at me,' I said with conviction.
I asked 'Did the Professor mention the Sneider collection to you?'
'Sure, but not in detail. I'm not his confidant, but we do have a good working rapport and I like the guy.'

The blue trout arrived, beautifully dressed with translucent glazed cucumbers on its back and resting on a bed of red paprika rice. I started to relax and enjoy the ambiance, the food and the company.
'Where's your next port of call?'
'Paris, tomorrow for lunch, then London.'
He popped a large piece of trout into his mouth.
'What did you think of the Sneider paintings Miss Edan?'
'I didn't see many but what I did see leaves me very suspicious. One painting in particular I know is a fake.'
'And the Professor, what was his verdict?'

I was cautious with my reply. 'We agreed. It's a Vermeer which we scrutinized very thoroughly.' Steinhart nodded, not revealing whether he'd ever heard of Vermeer, or for that matter cared. I looked directly at Jack Steinhart. His blue eyes floated into the distance, calling to mind something or someone - whatever - that was not available to me. After a few minutes silence he said.
'That must have been an early wake-up call?'
'It was Mr.Steinhart, but only sooner rather than later.'
'Interesting. Interesting,' he repeated.
'Coffee?' he asked as he looked at his watch.

We walked over the Staatsbrücke into the old city. His handshake was reassuring and firm and lasted a fraction longer than needed.

'Good luck in Paris - I'll call you in London when the contract is ready for you to sign.' He gave an American style salute, and turned into the Getreidegasse.

I felt good. Pleased I had the support of two banks, pleased to have one collection, pleased with myself and even pleased with Salzburg. I paid my bill at the Hotel and went to my room. I studied the inventory for some time, and then fell fast asleep in my clothes. Fortunately, I'd removed my pillbox hat!

PARIS

8

Austrian airlines flight 071 arrived on time at Le Bourget. I threaded my way through the mass of people zig zagging across the concourse, towards the Dauphine restaurant. It was very full. I looked around for Corinne, but couldn't see her. A waiter asked if I had a reservation. I hadn't, but Madame Rothschild had booked for 1.30.

Corinne and I had been friends, albeit through business, for a long time. Strategy was no longer a prerequisite for negotiations. Every aspect of our dealings was substratum: this gave us a freeway to circumvent rigmarole and get on with what we needed to do. My current project however, had different demands, requiring her to delve into painful experiences, ones she wanted to forget.

We had at various times discussed the assimilation of the Jews in Germany, the cosmopolitan eclectic mix of cultures in Paris: all this advanced civilization, had not helped Corinne during the war: a branded, hunted and haunted Jewess, hiding in haystacks, in horse dung, in foxholes. Always afraid someone would expose her. It is hard to let go of grave fear and I am not sure that Corinne ever will.

Having a surfeit of wealth, affords no real protection: the gates guarding ones soul are vulnerable. There are no locks.

It was 1.45.when Corinne arrived.

'Katrina, excusez-moi, I'm late.' She kissed me on the cheek. 'It's good to see you, ma Cherie.'

I left the ordering to Corinne, as I was busy talking, explaining all that had happened in Salzburg. I told her both Imperial Chicago and Samuel Hall in London had agreed to sponsor on the original terms.

'That is really good news Katrina, I'm pleased for you.'

'Corinne, it's not enough. I need your support and the support of the Mitzvah Bank in Israel.' Corinne replied with disappointment.

'I want to help you, because my sentiments are 100% for your cause, and believe me it has been a difficult decision, but the Baron, is reluctant.'

'What does that mean, Corinne?'
'It means, he will not have the Rothschild name involved as sponsors. He fears for me, and would rather let the past alone.'
'And you?' I asked.
'I am equally apprehensive; especially as the neo-Nazi movement is getting a stronghold in Southern Germany. There could be repercussions in Paris. We would be the first to be targeted.'
'I can't argue on that level Corinne, and I don't want you to feel insecure. But if everyone backed down for fear of reprisals, crime would be triumphant - and I'm talking about 6,000,000 crimes.'

She looked at me with moist eyes.
'I know, ma Cherie, that's why I persuaded the Baron to take a different stance. We are prepared to open a fund in Switzerland for the equivalent of £375,000 in a secret numbered account. The interest will be paid to you in Swiss francs and will only be available through a coded number. But there is one condition.'

The waiter put a bowl of salad nicoise on the table and filled our glasses from a bottle of Beaujolais.
'No-one must know who opened the fund. The Swiss banking laws will protect the account and I need your word, Katrina, that under no circumstances, whatever those might be, would you reveal the source.'
'But, I've already told Professor Frohmann, and Jack Steinhart that I'm meeting you Corinne and I've told them you're a prospective sponsor.'
'Firstly, Cherie, who is Jack Steinhart?'
'He's the investment director of the Laufenbankgeschaft which merged with Imperial Chicago five years ago. He works from Salzburg, but he's an American. According to Professor Frohmann, he's dynamite.'
'Well, my dear, I am afraid I will be your first failure. When you talk to either the Professor or Steinhart, just tell them we said no, and tell them why.'
'You mean that Baron Rothschild is scared for your safety?'
'No, Katrina, we are wine producers and everyone in Europe knows it has been a disastrous year. We have millions tied up in rotting vines. We have no money to give away or to loan.

Totally plausible, my dear.'
'If that's what I have to do Corinne, consider it done.'

While I appreciated the money, I had hoped Corinne would co-operate on a more involved level, but to put any guilt on her for not being involved was tantamount to theft of her liberty and totally unfair.

'Corinne, I am truly grateful for the loan. The exhibition is now secure and I'll keep you up to date. All I have to do now is find the exhibits.' I said this with raised eyebrows.

Corinne nodded … 'Even with your intrepid attitude, it could be a rough ride.'

'You're right, but it will not deter me. Corinne, how will I know when the account is in situ?'

'I'll call you from New York. I will give you a telephone number. Discard the first three digits and use the alternate numbers following: that will be the code for access to the account.'

'Corinne, you sound like Baroness Bond, and I thought I knew you?'

At last she smiled, 'Good luck to you, and go carefully.'

LONDON

9

The idea for an exhibition had been festering in my mind for a long time, its realization undefined, until a meeting in 1968 with a refugee from Vienna. I was curating an expressionist exhibition in London at that time when I received a telephone call from Anna Frishman, asking if I could include an Emil Nolde painting which she owned. Unfortunately, the exhibition space was already allocated, but during a subsequent meeting with her the seed of exposing stolen art really took root. Her story was so poignant, I knew that at some time, I would have to use my energy to expurgate the tyranny of the losses caused to her and others, by bringing back onto public display those works of art, supposedly lost to posterity.

Anna Frishman was raised in Vienna, the youngest of three daughters. Her parents were the owners of a galerie on the Kartnerstrasse showing works by the Expressionists, Impressionists Jugendstil, Die Brucke, and other contemporary movements. Anna was sent to a boarding school in Switzerland, where she studied art, languages, and history.

In 1938 she returned to Austria at the end of her final year. At the frontier police boarded the train and her passport was confiscated. Unknown to Anna, Kristallnacht (the night of the broken glass November 9-10) had erupted in German and Austrian cities, culminating in the burning of Synagogues and wholesale looting and destruction of Jewish owned property.

As the train pulled into Vienna station, thousands of people were on the platform, pushing to get into the train, even before it had stopped. Long queues waited at the ticket booths. Trains were leaving, packed beyond capacity. Crying, children, wandered the platforms, separated from their families in the maelstrom of humanity desperate to leave. Police were everywhere: checking tickets, documents, and passports. Anna arrived at her home tired, hungry and bewildered but no one was there. She tried to phone the galerie. There was no reply. It was not until she walked in the Jewish quarter that the real horror of the night of terror confronted her. Jagged glass clung precariously in shop windows, and empty spaces were all that remained of the merchandise that had been its energy. Windows in houses were broken, doors torn from their hinges. Everywhere she looked there was devastation. More horrific was the silence. Where were the people? Where were her friends? She hurried to Judenplatz. She looked down a narrow street, and then walked to number 10. The door was ajar. She pushed it open. The shock of what she saw that night, she told me, would never be erased. The inside of the room was unrecognisable, reduced to a heap of rubble. The Star of David was daubed on the walls. The crunch under her feet frightened her, so she stood still. Then a sound came from the yard, a whimpering soft cry. Slowly she moved towards the door and looked around the yard. All it contained was broken crates, cardboard boxes and rubbish. Suddenly, the lid of one of the crates moved, and through a small slit, two very frightened eyes appeared. A voice rasped. She stood back against the wall, too scared to move. Then again, a barely audible sigh. A small hand grasped the side of the crate and Josef her cousin eased himself onto the ground, shaking and too weak to stand. Blood was leaking from deep scratches. Anna wrapped her coat around him and carried him into the house. She washed his face with some rags and then slowly cleaned his arms and legs. He didn't speak. Vacant, staring eyes watched every movement Anna made. 'It will be all right soon,' she said to Josef, not knowing what she really meant. Josef was eight and Anna ten years older: their times together during her holidays from school had always been precious. She loved Josef. Taking his hand, they walked out of the house into the Judengasse, through the small streets into Am Hof. Anna told Josef not to speak, although, she realized later, he couldn't. Anna kept a tight grip on Josef's hand and walked quickly. When they arrived at St. Stephen's Platz, she left Josef on a seat and told him not to move. She continued to her father's Galerie. The front was unrecognisable. Wooden boards covered the windows and the Star of David was painted in yellow on the front door. Anna went to the back, where a small alleyway led to the delivery area. She rattled the door handle and waited. She banged on the door. After a few minutes, it opened. Standing in the doorway was Johannes, the Frishman family handy-man who had worked for her father for over twenty years. 'Fraulein Anna,' he gasped, pulling her by the hand into the back of the building. 'What are you doing here?'

'I am looking for Mama and Papa.' They are not at the house and terrible things have happened in Judenplatz. Please, Johannes, where are my parents?' Johannes looked sheepish. Casting his eyes away, he said.
'I do not know where they are.'
'But they can't just disappear. You must know where they have gone?'
'Fraulein Anna, you must leave here immediately. I cannot help you. It is very dangerous. You must leave now.'
Ignoring Johannes' warning, she went into the galerie. At first glance, everything appeared normal. Like most European galeries in the thirties, it was divided into a series of rooms, each able to show individual artist's works. The galeries at the rear had works of young emerging painters on the walls. Slowly she went to the front room and saw that a number of works had been removed and placed on the floor. In the second room, the floor was stacked with crates, and as she walked through other rooms, the reality of what was happening became apparent. 'Johannes, Johannes,' she called.

He was standing in the doorway, looking at the young girl he had known since she was born. The baby he had pushed in his garden wheelbarrow, the hand that had held his so tightly when he took her to school, and the eyes that looked into his with innocent trust. A tear rolled down his cheek as he moved towards her.
'Please, please, Johannes, what is happening?'
'Fräulein Anna, I can only tell you that I have my orders.'
'Yes, Johannes, yes, but who gave you the orders?'
'The new owners of the galerie.'
'Are you saying that Papa has sold the Galerie?' Johannes was silent. Anna walked to her favourite room, the Expressionists, stood for several minutes in front of a painting by Emil Nolde, then turned to Johannes.
'Please take that canvas off the stretcher.'

With Anna watching, he removed the wooden stays from the corners and pushed the painting out of the frame. One by one he removed the nails from the edges of the canvas and placed the limp painting on the floor. As Anna carefully rolled the picture, she turned to Johannes and said.
'Thank you'.

In the alleyway behind the galerie she carefully wrapped the canvas around the top of her skirt and walked assertively back to St. Stephen's Platz to collect Josef. The square in front of the church had always been a favourite place for children. They watched the beautifully groomed horses with head plumes in different colours and polished brass head plates tethered to closed fiacre. Waiting to set the whole picture into motion, horsemen in top hats and gold lapelled tailcoats were swishing their whips. Josef was unobtrusive among the other urchins, his ragged state making him part of the scenery. They walked towards the Frishman home on the Singerstrasse, not knowing who or what they would find. Anna pushed the large carved door open and heard the commotion inside. Before she had time to investigate, her mother rushed towards her and enveloped Anna in her arms. Her eldest sister Bertha lifted Josef, wrapped her arms around him and cried.

The ensuing events are a catalogue of the traumas that faced the disenfranchised population of Jews, and others who were against the dictates of Nazism. Harassment of Jewish school children had started in 1933, culminating in 1935 with the Nuremberg Decrees, when Adolf Hitler, as Reichschancellor in Germany, denied Jews the right to own land or property, or to enter any profession or State service. Anti-Semitism was spreading rapidly and irrevocably through Germany. By 1938 it was established and thriving in Vienna, culminating in total racial incitement and the eventual annihilation of 400.000 Jews.

Anna Frishman recalled the date of March 11 1938 when the capitulation of the Austrian Government led to the annexing of Austria by Germany. Within three days, 100,000 enthusiastic Viennese greeted Adolf Hitler as he rode triumphantly through the streets. Red flags, with the insignia of the swastika were fervently waved from every hand, Josef watched sitting on Anna's shoulders, as the high booted Wehrmacht army thundered through the streets of the old city on their conquering route from Germany. Not a single shot had been fired in resistance.

Anna had been spared the indignities suffered by her parents as she was away at school. Anna's mother explained what led to the horrific episode known as Kristallnacht. Herschel Grynszpan, a seventeen-year-old Jewish student in Paris had received a letter from his father in Hanover, telling him all Jews of Polish origin would be deported back to Poland. Grynzspan's family had escaped the pogroms by the Poles years before. Grynszpan refused to accept, that like his parents, he had become a homeless refugee. He bought a gun, walked into the German Embassy in Paris and made his protest. He shot an official, Ernst Vom Rath, who died three days later. This act was the catalyst for revenge. This act was the trigger the Nazis needed and led to the edict, already existing in Germany, whereby all Jewish businesses and property would be confiscated and Austrian cities cleansed of "Untermensch" (sub humans).

Anna and Josef were reassured by her father that they would all leave Vienna at the first opportunity. Josef's dark brown eyes were blank as an empty page, unable to believe anything. They sat silently in the ruins of what had been 'a life'.

Emanuel Frishman, the respected and trusted art dealer, was a broken man, humiliated and unable to protect his family. With humility he said to Anna "that her first priority in life must always be honesty. Nothing can replace it, except lies."

LONDON

10

Sue Hepple had documents on her desk, waiting for my signature. I looked down at the green coloured tape holding them in place. She handed me the file.

'On the move,' she said. 'They're the papers from Samuel Hall, for your signature.'

'Do I need to read them?'

'Not really, I've vetted them pretty well, they're in line with the original proposal.'

Her office was very tidy and the tiny kitchen spotless. With surprise, I asked, 'did you move in while I was abroad?'

'Katrina, what a thought!'

'Well, did you move anybody else in?'

'Certainly not. If I'm going to have it off, it won't be in this backwater.'

'So tell me, why am I walking into a clinic? You know I only activate in yuck. What's happened to your dirty mind?'

'Wait till you see your office Katrina, it's been blitzed.'

I looked at her in disbelief before going into my adjoining office. There was a file on the light antique oak desk and pencils sharpened in a tray. Books in the bookcase were in alphabetical order; a rug with angular patterns was on the carpet, wine glasses on a shelf with a decanter. A map of Austria was pinned to one wall: a map of Europe on the other. Thank God she hadn't moved the Henry Moore from my desk, I would have throttled her. I sat in my high backed tartan upholstered chair and looked through the file. I signed the Samuel Hall papers noting their request for the name and address of my accountants. I called Sue on our connecting line.

'I think we need to put our heads together. Are you in the middle of anything?'

'Give me five minutes to finish the proposal for Israel - then I'll make some coffee.'

I fondled the Henry Moore sculpture on the desk, so small yet so monumental. The eight-inch Marquette lost none of its majestic quality by size. In fact, this small, reclining female nude, clarified for me that I was in possession of a tiny portion of genius.

Sue came into the office carrying a tray with a silver coffee thermos jug, two china cups and saucers, a matching milk jug and sugar basin.

'Don't tell me' I said, 'Royal Doulton.'

'Quite right,' came the response.

'I have a question, Sue. Who's paying for this fancy crockery?'

'You are, of course.'

'Where's my mug? . . . I liked my mug.'

'Katrina, it's in the bottom drawer of your desk.'

'Why?'

'Because, boss, if a sponsor comes to this office, the writing on your mug says - "of all my relations I like sex the best." It could impede your credibility.'

'Hasn't so far. Anyway, I only use it when the bloke's good looking. I use the other mug, the one with "Be nice, I'm rich," on the other punters.' A lovely aromatic smell came from the pot as Sue poured the coffee.

I was debating whether to go to Israel and complete the sponsorship or return to Vienna and start the search. I asked Sue.

'Well, you have pounds and dollars coming in,' she said, 'wouldn't it be more productive to uncover some of the stolen paintings before approaching the Israelis?'

'Maybe you're right.' I held my cup up for more coffee. 'This is much better than the washing up water you usually serve. Sue smiled and turned a page in her notebook.

'You'll have to needle those bollixed-up Nazis,' she said, 'shove some guilt up their backsides. Make them know you'll be around for three years.'

'That's just what I intend to do and I'll start with Gerhard Hofer, because he's avaricious. If I can get an offer for his Gustav Klimt painting, this might tempt him to reveal what else he has stored in his vaults.'

'He's thoroughly ruthless, Katrina. He'll ask for every penny in advance and double-cross at the first opportunity.'

'Only if he has a choice,' I said. 'I'll remove choice then he'll have no alternative.'

'And how do you intend to do that?'

'This is my plan Sue. I want you to set up a meeting with

Elizabeth Cuthbertson at the National Gallery. I will offer them the Klimt painting of Hermine Gallia.'
'Then what?'
'If they agree to buy, and there's every reason why they should, because there isn't an original Klimt in any Museum in this country, I might gain Herr Hofer's confidence.'
'I don't follow, Katrina.'
'You will - it's a sprat albeit a very large one to catch a mackerel.' The expression on Sue's face was whimsical.
'Do you want me to set up a meeting with Dr.Hempf before or after the National?'
'Sounds like a horse race, Sue. I suppose, in a way, it is.'

The phone rang. Sue answered. Looking at me she indicated, with silent lip movements, that Otto Prantl was on the line from Vienna.
I nodded and picked up the phone. 'Katrina Edan speaking.'
'Otto Prantl said, 'I have located some paintings at a Museum in Hanover. The curator has no knowledge of their history. They do not appear in the files of any purchases prior to 1938. He has agreed that your exhibition might indicate the source of some of these paintings.'
'Could you send me a list with titles and dates, if possible?'
'Certainly' came the reply. 'Do you have a date for visiting Vienna, Miss Edan?'
'I'm working on that right now. I'll tell Professor Frohmann as soon as I know.'
'Gut' came the reply. 'I'll have ectochromes here when you arrive.'
'Coo,' said Sue, 'talk of the devil and he'll breathe down the phone.' She poured more coffee: it was steaming hot.
'Good purchase,' I said, looking at the silver thermos.

While Sue was making calls in her office I looked at the Israeli proposal. It differed somewhat from those I had confirmed with London and Salzburg: in as much as any immigrant who could prove, through documentation, old photographs, or corroborated evidence, that an exhibited painting had been looted from them or their families, then the cost of coming to London to substantiate their claim would be paid from the exhibition fund. In other words, as sponsors, the Israelis would be sponsoring reparation for their own nationals.

I had no idea what their response would be. It was only 20 years since they became an independent state. During that time they'd fought two costly wars, and they were by European standards, poor. But, Dr.Levine the curator of the Tel Aviv Museum had gained the respect of curators worldwide for his endeavours in collecting donations to the museum, in cash and works of art. The new Helena Rubenstein wing, named after the American cosmetician, was the result of his tireless efforts.

Sue came back into the office holding another green file, announcing efficiently.

'Elizabeth Cuthbertson returns to London on Monday. Your appointment is at 2 pm. Monday afternoon. A seat, on the outward flight to Vienna is reserved for Tuesday morning. How long do you intend to stay?'

'Leave the return open - I'll book that from Vienna when I know I've made enough headway.'

I took my spring route home through Regent's Park, which I always do in April. It's a precarious month, never sure which way it will turn. This year, in spite of a cold winter, the sun had warmed the buds, and now the first flowering trees were showing their glory. Spiky yellow forsythia, soft pink almond blossom, tulips in full flood, and daffodils, proudly waving their heads in the wind saying, I'm here - it's spring - look at me.

I visually absorbed the colours, wishing they were permanent but knowing they are always transient. Every hour, every minute, the toll bells rings for nature, a time barrier on beauty falls, everything fades. Human intervention has no power in this everlasting scenario.

When I arrived home I could still smell the perfume from the flowering trees. My fingers smelt where I had touched a blossom. It was a soft white flower and I had intended to pluck it from its stem, possess it, and steal it from its thriving branch. Then I stopped and thought, what would a lone flower look like severed from its grand flora?. . . Nothing. . . Just a wilting relic of my greed to possess, a confirmation of my vandalism.

Home is not a lonely place, just a place to be alone; I chose the house for its simplicity. Its eclectic heritage appealed to my minimalist taste. Sparsely furnished, each piece with enough air around so it could be visually appreciated. A red Chinese lacquered desk, an Arne Jacobsen chair upholstered in black and white striped silk: a scarlet sofa, and hidden in a smoked glass cabinet, a music centre. The most extravagant indulgence in the house was the hand cut slate floor, which sometimes looked green, others blue, depending where the light caught the irregular cutting. Upstairs, from the balcony outside the bedroom window, I could watch the sunrise: sometimes a sliding line of fire, obscured by wisps of grey clouds across the horizon, before turning turquoise, gold and yellow, like a Raphael painting, and sometimes it was angry like Delacroix, or abstract and unrelated to anything man has ever envisaged.

***

This is the first time in my adult life, that I had felt really nervous. Of course, there had been times when plans had not gone smoothly, when I had been let down, mislead, but somehow, they hadn't presented the tension which I felt from the enormity of the programme I had set myself this time.

My meeting at the National Gallery needed some preparation. Their spending budget was tightly controlled and extremely frugal. I had to devise a way for money to be advanced for them to make a purchase.

I asked Sue to compose a letter for Directors of National Institutions: Lord Sieff of Marks & Spencer's, Sir Sidney Weinberg of General Electric and Lord Delfont of Granada. If I could get payment or part payment from the private sector, a format could be worked out for the National Gallery to pay on an instalment basis over a period of time. It was a long shot, but might tempt them to consider the purchase of the Gustav Klimt painting.

I had not met Elizabeth Cuthbertson before and found her rather formal. A stout lady, wearing a loose grey gathered skirt, topped with a darker grey top, very subdued and unflattering. Her background was academic rather than high profile and she came to the National Gallery following an exceptional research programme she introduced at the Courtauld Institute, and followed that, with three years as Keeper of Fine Art at the Ashmoleon in Oxford. I knew her track record was impressive. I was directed to her office over-looking St. Martins-in-the-Fields. I outlined the offer for the Klimt painting and I had correctly anticipated the response.

'The National would really like to add a Klimt to our collection but we would never get permission to spend that amount of money, even if we had it.'

I continued with my proposal.

'If we could supplement the purchase from public and private donations, would that make a difference?'

'The difficulty is, Miss Edan, we are committed to an expensive restoration programme and £500,000 is absolutely prohibitive.'

'Miss Cuthbertson, if I could find funding, would the National Gallery consider an instalment plan?' She lifted her chin high and looked down her nose.

'That would depend on too many issues for me to answer. Have you researched the painting's provenance Miss Edan?'

'Oh, yes, very thoroughly I have a full provenance from the time it left the studio of Gustav Klimt, to the present owner.'

I gave her the file Sue had prepared. She said.

'Just give me a rough outline for the moment.'

Moritz Gallia commissioned Gustav Klimt to paint his wife, Hermine, in 1903. She was born Hermine Hamburger in Silesia, the daughter of a brewer, and married Moritz, her uncle. They moved to Vienna. The portrait hung in the green drawing room of their home on Wohllebengasse 4 where Gustav Klimt and Emile Flöge were regular visitors.'

'Is that information from photographs or have you seen the painting, Miss Edan?'

'I saw the painting in Vienna a month ago. It's in excellent condition except it needs a light cleaning.'

'And what are the conditions of sale?'

I explained my exhibition project. She listened without comment, her hands wrapped across her chest, and her eyes firmly on me.

'Miss Cuthbertson, I'm curating this exhibition because many atrocities happened during the second world war culminating in the disappearance of unknown quantities of irreplaceable

masterpieces. I'm trying in some small way to redress the balance, by bringing into the open works of dubious background, so anyone from any country will have the chance to make a claim. One of the conditions of sale is that the National Gallery would agree to exhibit Hermine Gallia.'
'Is the Klimt painting suspect?'
'No, that has a recorded and authenticated provenance.'
'By whom, Miss Edan?'
'Dr. Anton Hempf.'

Mentioning Anton's name to anyone involved in the arts always produced a respectful response. His contribution to art literature was unrivalled. In the past twenty years his books and essays had been translated and published worldwide. His association with any project demanded acknowledgment, especially in the hierarchy of the art cognoscente.

Miss Cuthbertson stood holding the file. I was not sure if she would hand it back to me. But she said.
'I really can't comment at the moment. I will give the offer some thought and if I think the board of trustees will consider the purchase, I shall be in touch with you.'

Abruptly the meeting was over leaving me convinced her response would be negative.

***

It was a lovely sunny Saturday afternoon, so Dr.Hempf suggested we walk in Regent's Park. We entered through the Jubilee Gate, a massive ornate twisting of black wrought iron, embellished with gold, and fronting the broad walk: a wide paved promenade lined with wooden benches. Families with prams and dogs and grandma in tow, strolled in the bright April sunshine. Children on roller skates weaved between them, laughing, struggling on wobbly knees, before landing on their bottoms. We found an empty seat near the fountain and listened to the rippling sound of the water: watched the spray turn to mist as it cascaded into the air, then fall back, to start over again. We sat silently gazing at the fountain.
'Isn't water soothing?' I said,
'Maybe,' Anton replied 'it's the comfort of repetition, like rain. We know where it's coming from and where it's going . . .we're

in a state of uncomplicated acceptance.'
'Until we get wet,' I said.
'But - here we know we won't, so we're comfortable.'
'You mean, Anton, we always anticipate predicament?'
'I suppose we do - if we think about it.'
'Surely, that's just preservation. We're not always on a knife's edge.'
'Consciously - no - but subconsciously - we are. We live with fear. There's nothing tangible to preserve us.'
'That's morbid, Anton!'
'I disagree. Goethe said, "man cannot stay long in a conscious state; he has to plunge back into the subconscious, for that is where his living roots are." That confirms we're seeking harmony within ourselves.'
'And mostly, not finding it?' I asked.
'Unfortunately, you're right. We're always, continually and irreversibly, dying. Nature regenerates. We the human race - do not.'

This pessimistic view of life was understandable within Anton's vision. I hadn't suffered deprivation, starvation and man's inhumanity to man. My generation was reckless with life. I didn't fear death - I felt immortal. Yet, hidden in my subconscious, were the nights and years spent in an air-raid shelter, not knowing if I would wake up to see a tomorrow.

Anton appeared relaxed and was casually dressed in a tweed jacket, with a polo-neck light woollen sweater and a hat that might have come from the Scotch House.
' Does your hat have a title?' I asked.
'What do you mean, a title?'
'A style, then, a special type of style. I'm sure it does.'
'I think it's called a peaked cap - but there's not much of a peak.'
'It's smart' I said, 'it suits you.'
He smiled, his pink lips curled, the sun caught a sparkle in his eyes. I knew he liked the cap too.
'I bought a hat in Salzburg,' I said. 'Well - it's not really a hat - it's a piece of nonsense - I bought it on impulse.'
'So Katrina, what was behind the impulse?'
'Jack Steinhart' I replied. 'He's the American I told you about, who's running the investment office of the Laufenbankgeschaft

in Salzburg.'
'Strange connection' Anton said, with a questioning look.
'Well, we were lunching and I needed something to contain my brains, and the little pillbox - did just that!'
'Ah-ha, so, you've met your match, young lady.'
'I don't know about that - but he did confirm the contract for sponsorship.'
'Good, so you're operational. What about the Rothschilds?'
'They had to turn the proposal down.'
'But why?' questioned Anton.
'Their reasons are complicated but basically the wine growers are having a terrible year - too much rain. So they have to conserve all their assets, to balance the books.'
'That's a pity. Will you manage with only two sponsors?'
'It could be three, I haven't seen the Israelis yet.'
'So, tell me Katrina, what else did you achieve?'

Those words reverberated in my ears, a reminder of the repetitious questioning from my parents when I was a child. "What did you achieve to day, Katrina?" my mother would ask. "Now - what have you achieved?" my father wanted to know.

Why, I would ask myself - did I always have to achieve? Couldn't I just "do". One day - I'd tell them. "I've just been happening. I walked, ran, sang, laughed, and achieved nothing." But - I never did.

Anton Hempf was thirsting for information. I told him my strategy and also that Otto Prantl had located pictures of indiscernible background in Germany. Anton thought for a few moments before saying.
'It might be to your advantage to keep Otto Prantl at arm's length. He's a suave operator from an over privileged background.'
'What do you mean "over privileged?"
'Spoilt is another word that comes to mind' Anton said. 'Otto's father, a diplomat, moved around the world taking his family with him. To compensate for the disruption to Otto, his only son, he lavished him with new toys, then later new inventions, at every posting. By the time he arrived at Vienna University, Otto spoke five languages including Russian. Otto boasted he had three cars. He was seventeen and very devious.'

'So why did you take him into your group?'
'Because he was clever and attracted a lot of attention, which is what "revolt" wanted. My advice to you is concentrate on Gerhard Hofer: I think you'll find more leads, even in his murky background. His father Werner Hofer was the printer for German propaganda as far back as 1933. He had a coterie of boys distributing hate leaflets, gathering a retinue of followers for Nazis ideology. With the annexing of Austria by Germany in 1938 Werner Hofer was already a prominent Nazi, waiting in the wings to activate the "final solution." His son, Gerhard, was his chief lieutenant.'

The slats on the wooden seat were hard. I could feel marks being imprinted onto my flesh and suggested we walk across the grass, towards the open-air theatre. The gardens next to the auditorium were spectacular, with plants packed closely in banks of colour. I carefully digested what Anton had told me before saying.
'Anton, I know Gerhard Hofer is arrogant and devious and likes money - big money, but - if I can sell the Klimt to the National Gallery I'll have power of persuasion which could lead to further offers. But, I doubt if he'll give permission for any paintings to be shown in the exhibition.'
'Do you need permission Katrina? Surely, you can make it quite clear, that your prime motivation is "the exhibition". Any interim sales are incidental. You can make it a question of alternatives. The art market will become very suspect when your exhibition becomes public, and Gerhard Hofer won't risk a penny with unscrupulous dealers: he knows how money can get side-tracked, especially when dealing in stolen property.'
'Absolutely true, Anton.' I said. 'Crooks never sue for stolen goods: they shoot each other.'

Anton smiled. We had arrived at the entrance to the outdoor cafe on the inner circle and spoke in unison . . . tea. We stood in line with our little trays. 'What will you have Anton, a big piece of chocolate cake or a fat sticky bun?'
'Just tea, my dear, with some lemon.'

Our table overhung a choisya bush, sweetly smelling of citrus. I squeezed some lemon into my tea.
'One thing is worrying me Anton. What will stop you from

making a claim on the Klimt portrait? After all it is yours.' Anton seemed surprised by my remark. He said firmly.
'No, that's not correct. It is only morally mine; legally the Klimt is Hofer's. Additionally, I give you my word.'

Having survived the despicable, he would not, for any reason, jeopardise his personal integrity.

VIENNA
11

Sue had reserved a room at the Hotel Graben on the Dorotheergasse, in the centre of the city near to the Galerie Frohmann. It was built at the turn of the century and in keeping with the rest of the narrow thoroughfare was built of slabs of stone. The hotel frontage was drab and uninviting. I peered at the long windows covered by very heavy cream lace curtains. The entrance door had no distinguishing features, until I looked up to the plaque above: Franz Kafka and Max Brod lived here. The inside reception hall was depressing and excessively outdated; but then, all Vienna was outdated. Since the end of the war in 1945, the Viennese had striven to recapture their past: now, 25 years later they were introspective and provincial. This reflected in their architecture, theatre, arts, crafts, clothes, activities, like a time warp. Even the younger generation were still mimicking their parents. More importantly, there was no hint of remorse, no guilt, no regrets even, just an arrogant justification for being hi-jacked by the Germans. The city still smells of collaborators posing as the victims of Nazi domination.

My room was carpeted, which surprised me, as the corridors were covered in faded green linoleum. But there was a radio, a private bathroom and a telephone. Certainly not designed by David Hicks but the essentials were there, which was what I needed. And the lift hadn't creaked on the way up, its heavy wrought iron frame and sliding gates, indestructible. I threw my case on the bed, checked my telephone number and dialled Professor Frohmann.

'Welcome back Miss Edan, I hope you had a good journey.'

'Can we meet to-day Professor?' I asked. I could hear him talking with Frau Stolz.

'Yes, but not until 5.30?'

'I look forward to seeing you Professor.'

My photographic memory had recorded every street I had walked during my first visit in February. Now, a hint of spring tweaked the air, retarded by comparison with London, but to day I was fortunate. The sun was splintering the clouds; streaks of bright light came through my window. By the time I left the hotel for the Galerie, the skies were blue and hopefully I was wearing my cashmere coat for the last time this season.

Wilhelm Frohmann, for some reason unknown to me, looked grey. His face hadn't the usual mischievous sparkle. His eyes were distant, his shoulders rounded over his desk. He was smoking a cigarette.

' Professor, I'm pleased to see you, Are you well?'

His reply was not curt, but excluded any explanation as to why he was looking in a state of dejection. He hastened to get on with the business we needed to discuss.

'Miss Edan, I've made an appointment for you to meet Dr.Gutman Holbeck, the Director of the Albertina. He has some drawings and watercolours, which he feels should be included in your exhibition. We have discussed them but he will give you all the details when you meet.'

'Thank you, what time is the meeting?'

'Eight tomorrow, breakfast eight, not dinner eight.' he said. He smiled although it appeared to be an effort.

'I'd like you to look through this catalogue' he said, as he handed me a slim green covered book.

'It's for the forthcoming auction sales on Monday and Tuesday at the Dorotheum.' I looked at the frontispiece, then at Frohmann.

'Is there something of interest in the sale for the project, Herr Professor?'

'Two stolen paintings are being offered for sale.'

'How do you know they are stolen?'

'I've seen the works before. They were shown at an exhibition in Vienna in 1942: then they went to Linz for storage.'

'Why Linz?' I asked.

'Because Adolf Hitler was building a new museum at Linz.'

'To fill with loot?' I replied.Professor Frohmann did not respond.

'I suggest you read the catalogue and see what you make of it. We can discuss the individual pieces later.'

I could see the Professor was tired. He lit another cigarette and inhaled deeply.

'Frau Stolz will give you directions to the Albertina. It's very near here.'

'That won't be necessary,' I said. 'I saw the building when I met Gerhard Hofer at the Café Mozart. By the way, how is Herr

Hofer?' The Professor didn't answer, confirming my assessment that Hofer's well being was immaterial.
'Gerhard wants to see you' he said. 'I gave him your hotel number, I'm sure he will call.'

***

Tourism had not invaded Vienna in the same way it had London, Paris and Rome. It was still a city for the Austrians and the dubious flotsam that stalked the iron curtain illegally. Blackmarketeers, illicit traders in forged passports, diamonds, art and people. Any saleable commodity that could be turned into money was traded in Vienna. It was the first drop off point from the East: the city where the iron curtain metaphorically went up, and the first act of any deal was struck.

Spies were commonplace. Russians, Hungarians Czechs, Cubans, Germans and of course the British and Americans. Everything was for sale . . . at a price. Uranium, the central component for the atom bomb, armaments - from tanks to small weapons was being traded. And operatives of the super powers exchanged technological information, the currency of spies.

These surreptitious activities were known and condoned by the Viennese administration. They suppressed information - gave false reports on suicides and accidents when they were actually murders. In this whirlpool of subterfuge people like Gerhard Hofer flourished: they were the "risk merchants" , small bait in the highly sophisticated espionage rings operating for the benefit of the super powers. The professional agents destabilized governments, weaved between bribed officials at the highest level, at the same time mixing with cheap opportunists who could be bought without risk to their own valuable operators.

When the OPEC chief Sheik Yamani was being driven to a meeting in Vienna in 1970, he was abducted and held hostage. At the time, with the amount of protection surrounding him, it was tantamount to abducting the Queen of England or the President of the United States. Except for one point – collusion - a word indelibly stuck in the mouths of the Austrians: after all - they had thirty-five years experience.

Dr. Gutman Holbeck custodian of the Albertina's collection of drawings (second only to the British Museum in London) was, like most museum directors involved in research and revelation, balancing education with administration and passing historical facts to the next generation. He recoiled from sensationalism: what appealed to him most was the preservation of art works relevant to the History of Art and maintaining an ethical front for his own preservation and that of his museum. This must have been a contributing factor for agreeing to assist me.

He was a dark haired stocky figure with small round shaped glasses, and chubby hands, which he covered with white flannel gloves for handling the drawings laid out on a long wooden cabinet.

'Miss Edan' he said, 'Professor Frohmann has told me what you are trying to accomplish.' I nodded and waited.

'These drawings are not recorded in any inventory at the Albertina. According to a receipt, a Fraulein Ester Isazsohn handed them to the museum for safekeeping in 1937, but no purchase order or record of payment can be traced. Because of their value, I thought your exhibition might throw some light onto their provenance.'

I looked at the drawings, slowly walking along the line to take them in one by one. A Chagall sketch in pastel and ink, a Paul Klee pencil and charcoal drawing, a Rembrandt etching, then a sepia wash of a head, heightened with white, by Ingres, an Egon Schiele pencil drawing of a young nude girl and lastly a devastating drawing of the art dealer Alfred Flechtheim by Otto Dix. These were of remarkable quality. Whoever selected these drawings either had a good adviser, or knew something of their artistic worth. I counted the number of works - six. Not many, considering the size of the museums collection. Maybe these were just a token quietener for my benefit.

'Do you have photographs?' I asked.

'Everything here is recorded, some photographs could be available for you in a few days.'

The conversation was polite and stilted, until I asked.

'Do you think the owners were murdered in the holocaust?'

'Miss Edan, it is not within my power to speculate on the fate of the unknown. When, and if, I have historical facts, I shall share them with you.'

'Dr.Holbeck, do you think you might find further unrecorded

pieces?'
'That Miss Edan, remains to be established, we have only investigated to 1937, but I doubt we have more.'

I didn't believe him, but with that remark the meeting concluded. No one and I emphasise - no one - ever had any knowledge of the exhaustive pattern of annihilation that happened on his or her doorstep. The participants of genocide of the Jews and the wholesale looting of art and antiques were shrouded like a cataract under a veil of silence. Many still believed Hitler's "final solution" was justified. Hate was a consoling companion for the defeated Austrians.

***

There was a message at the hotel from Gerhard Hofer with a telephone number, one from Jack Steinhart in Salzburg and one from a Tatiana Orlanofsky, but no number. I called Steinhart first. He was in a meeting but I was told he would call in half an hour. Then I arranged to meet Gerhard Hofer in his Galerie at noon.

I shuffled through the auction catalogue Professor Frohmann had given me till I came to a page marked with an asterisk. The written reference stated: oil painting on canvas: 'The Bible-reader', Rembrandt Harmensz van Rijn 1606-1669, signed and dated 1659. Provenance: Bought by the family of the present owners in Amsterdam, 1914. Exhibited in Vienna, 1942. The second asterisk by an illustration of a painting by Ernst Ludwig Kirchner stated: slight marking at right hand corner of the canvas, in original frame. Privately owned.

A piercing ring came from the telephone. It had an old fashioned bell, similar to those mounted on kitchen clocks, by the side of the mouthpiece, and designed to wake the devil in Hades. It was Jack Steinhart.
'You'll be pleased to know, Miss Edan, the contract papers have arrived from Chicago. They're here waiting for your signature.'
'Thank you. Is it possible to send them to me in Vienna?'
'I'm afraid not. I think the papers should be signed in my office. Then I can get an account processed immediately.'
'You mean I should come to Salzburg?'
'If you want the money to start working for you, yes.'

I had not intended to go to Salzburg as I wanted to progress with my search. But securing financial aid from Mr.Steinhart's bank was more important. So I said.
'In that case I'll complete as much as I can here, then come to Salzburg - is Friday convenient?'
'Friday's fine. Just call and give me your arrival time. Have a good stay in Vienna.'

***

Gerhard Hofer's galerie had changed dramatically since my first visit. The walls were hung with a selection of canvases from the Bauhaus period of German Art and the long modern galerie with its white walls and polished wood floor, was an appropriate setting for the exhibit.
'For sale - or for show?' I asked
'Both' replied Hofer.

His office was chaos: masses of papers strewn over a lightwood desk, copies of magazines - stacks of papers tied in bundles on the floor and sitting on his desk a bronze twelve inch pen holder, in the shape of an erect penis. I looked at the crippled figure of Hofer and his dishevelled clothing accumulated around his fleshy structure then at the phallus. He was looking at some papers as though I didn't exist. Then without looking up he said. 'Have you sold the Klimt painting?': his impatient attitude an indication of his own anxiety.
'All I can tell you at the present' I replied 'is I have offered the painting to the National Gallery in London for half a million pounds. The curator will discuss a possible purchase with the trustees at their next meeting.'
Quickly he barked. 'Ven's dat?'

I lowered my voice to accentuate the contrast.
'I think they meet every three months - so I should have a response by June. And I made it clear, that if they buy the painting, it must be shown at my proposed exhibition.'

Hofer stood up, rested on his walking stick and limped to the window, his back to me. Then he turned. His face was red with anger, his mouth twitching. Words tried to escape but the constricting muscles around his jaw line held them in. Then he exploded . . .
'You must tink me an idiot - Fräulein Edan. You're telling me

that any corrupt Jew can make a claim on MY painting!'
'Herr Hofer - my aim is an exhibition; I am not concerned with the politics of evil. If you prefer I'll withdraw the offer to the National Gallery immediately.'

He returned to his chair and sat with his head resting slightly to one side. He leaned forward: the outburst had caused a digestive eruption as the smell of stale garlic hit my face. He farted with no apology. It was not difficult to estimate his potential for murder, he had killed before and I reckon the act was not mandatory. A man so internally driven by bitterness was a dangerous adversary: Francis Bacon said, "revenge is a kind of wild justice", and right now, I was the target of his hostility. He leaned further forward. 'Don't blackmail me Fräulein Edan.'

I could see the acid fall-out on his tongue, as foam formed at the corners of his mouth like a hungry bloodhound: if this miserable specimen of humanity left his body to science I hoped the will would be contested.

I had anticipated a volatile reaction and mentally prepared myself but being intimidated and threatened had implications I'd never dealt with before. I could not predict what he would say next except I knew he was calculating the risk factor: after all, risk was his business!
'Do you have another buyer?' I asked. He'd modulated his tone somewhat and answered indirectly. He was searching in his desk drawer, rummaging through papers.
'Vot guarantee vud you and zie Galerie give zat zie painting vud not go to any false claim?'
'I'll explain.' I said. 'The National Gallery would not purchase any work of art without a full documented provenance. This work fulfils all the criteria for acceptance: it can be traced from the time it left Klimt's studio to the present day.'
'Go on,' he said curtly.
'But, the Gallery will need a record of purchase from the present owner, yourself.'

Gerhard Hofer was listening, his hands resting on the desk twisting a fountain pen. Sweat trickled down his temples. He unbuttoned the collar of his checked shirt exposing light brown wiry hair around his throat that looked as if it had travelled upwards from his groin. His floppy knitted cotton tie drooped

down his front.
'You mean a letter of sale?'
'We call it a receipt. You have one I presume?'
'In zie files - ya. It vas bought by mine Vater.'
'From the Hempf family?' I said in a questioning voice.
'Correct' he replied.
'That is all they would require, and to make it absolutely clear that no claim can be made, certain items will be catalogued as "loan" exhibits, and not for sale, including the painting of Hermine Gallia.' I pushed a little further into his mean transparent mind.
'Think about the sale, Herr Hofer, you have plenty of time.'
He settled back, picked up the phone and asked for some tea.
'Have you any more works here?' I asked.
'Nein, but I have vorks coming from Dresden.'
'Isn't that behind the iron curtain?' I inquired.
'Right, it is. But zie Soviets are returning zie paintings they took when they occupied the city including the Raphael Madonna.'
'Why?' I asked.
'Because zie Russian trophy brigade found them in zie Gross Cotta mine in 1945, stored for Der Fürher's museum in Linz, and zey took them to the Pushkin in Moscow - now we get zem back.'
'I assume,' I looked at Hofer with haughty indifference 'they were looted in the first place.'
'I tink you should remember you are in my country: we set zie rules here. You English know about playing zie game, so play it Fräulein or you vil be very unfortunate.' He paused. Then a young girl put a tray on the desk.
'Tee,' said Hofer. 'Milk? You English always have milk.'
'No milk. Just tea. Thank you.'

I knew I was worrying him. He wasn't sure how much of a pushover I was: my youthful appearance, my red hair and clear porcelain complexion, belied my lack of timidity. I held the strings and did the pulling. But I knew he needed a legitimate link for laundering art, while he posed as an altruistic benefactor for restitution of works stolen by the Nazis. I suspected it was his first chance since the end of the war, to get even for his personal loss of liberty and the fall of the Third Reich. I believe he expected me to exhibit paintings, knowing they could never be claimed. He knew who had been exterminated - I knew his father had printed Nazi propaganda in Austria: so forged receipts were an undeniable fact. I put my teacup down, collected my briefcase and handbag.

'If you decide to proceed with the offer to the National Gallery in London, I'll need photos and ectochromes of the painting. I'll call you on Monday morning.' I looked down on Hofer.

'I can find my own way out.'

The receptionist at my hotel gave me the room key and a note listing telephone calls. I dialled Professor Frohmann first.

'Guten Tag, heir ist Frau Edan,' I said in pigeon German, 'Herr Professor bitte.' The phone clicked as they wound the handle to transfer the call, then he was on the line.

'How was your meeting with Gerhard?' he asked.

'As expected, he is considering my proposal for the Klimt painting and told me works are arriving from Dresden. I will need to discuss these with you before Monday.'

'I have a suggestion. Come for dinner to-night. Could you be at the Galerie at 5.30, then Pieter will drive us home?'

'Thank you Professor. I'll be there on time.'

I phoned Sue. 'Everything's going to plan, I've given Hofer time to sweat and to-night I'm dining with Frohmann - at his home.'

There was the usual pause I expected from Sue before she blasts a one-off crack.

'Don't stay too late, Katrina, you know what happened to the bears in the woods!'

'Any developments in London?'

'Nothing really, except some joker from New York phoned and asked if you wanted to ski over the Easter holiday. I told him to fuck off and put the phone down.'

***

My meeting with Otto Prantl on Thursday would complete the Vienna triangle - Frohmann - Hofer - Prantl, leaving me free to go to Salzburg on Friday. I asked reception for the train times to Salzburg on Friday morning. Within seconds the phone shook

and clanged and a young girl's voice said.
'The best train to Salzburg is the Orient Express leaving at 7.30am, arriving 10.50am. It is not possible to reserve.' I dialled Jack Steinhart.
'Steinhart,' came the sharp response as he picked up the phone.
'Edan, I replied, 'Katrina Edan.'
'Sorry, I was expecting a return call from the Ministry of Finance but I'm pleased it's you. One of the papers needs your passport number and confirmation signature. Could you bring it with you when you come to Salzburg?'
'I'm leaving Vienna on the Orient Express, arriving Salzburg 10.50 on Friday.' After a pause, he said.
'That will be an experience you'll never forget. Could you be at my office by 11.30? We'll complete the paperwork, before lunch.'

I dialled the Hotel Östereichisherhof - it was full. I tried the Elephant - that was full. My idea of spending the weekend in Salzburg rather than Vienna seemed doomed. Then I remembered the Goldener Hirsch. They had a double room available for Friday and Saturday. With my weekend settled, I changed into a simple black wool dress, slung a Dior scarf of yellow red and black silk around my neck and walked to Frohmann's office.

Wilhelm Frohmann was in the galerie talking to a group of visitors admiring the Picasso exhibit.
'Ah, Miss Edan, come and meet Herr Feininger and his family. Miss Edan is from England,' he said, as we were introduced.
He opened a gold cigarette case, which he offered around before pushing his own cigarette into his ivory holder.
'You must excuse us,' he said to the Feiningers 'my wife is expecting us for dinner but Herr Breiter, my assistant, knows this collection better than I do.' He beckoned to the young man, 'He'll show you the rest of the collection,' he said with a smile.

The drive through the Vienna woods was quite different in the company of the Professor. Although I sensed his agitation he attempted to make the journey along the winding road interesting, giving the names of houses owned for generations by the same family, as each one appeared between the fir trees. The Haflinger house, the Börsdofer house, the Radl. But Professor

Frohmann was looking and not seeing, speaking without hearing, the words automated, tense. If I had known him longer I would have asked what ailed him. No doubt there was a problem that was eating into his personality and stifling his exuberance. Hopefully, it would either become apparent or better still he would tell me. More likely, he would be nonchalant and pretend, for the sake of appearance, that everything was in order. As we rounded the last bend in the woods I could see the lights of his house, darting in and out of sight as the car moved between towering tree trunks, so close at times, our speed was reduced to a crawl.

The massive wooden studded door to Frohmann's house was not locked. He turned the wrought iron handle and called to his wife: 'I'm home.' The house was very silent; no response came from his wife.

'If you don't mind Miss Edan I'll take a short rest, then, we'll have time to talk before dinner.' The Professor took me to the salon and offered me a glass of wine and a magazine in German.

Magazines in general I find boring, their main purpose being the exposure of extremes, whether it's the antics of a jaded aristocracy, money legally or illegally gained, stick thin models wearing clothes no one else can, or politicians making promises they never keep. All this, printed on glossy coloured paper creating tortuous envy among the young and unsuspecting. So - this is how life is supposed to be lived? I turned another page. I looked at the headline. I looked again.

Professor Wilhelm Frohmann, the eminent art Historian will escort Her Majesty Queen Elizabeth II on her tour of Salzburg. The distinguished Professor is pictured below, in conversation with the President of Austria, His Excellency Dr. Bruno Kreisky at the premiere of the Cantata by Gottfried von Einhem at the Musiksverein in Vienna.

I glued my eyes to the picture trying to identify the attractive dark haired woman in red velvet . . . no name was accredited to her. Oh how nice and discreet. Typical. Just as I was turning the page for more revelations, Gerda came into the Salon. Her hair slightly dishevelled and her skin pallid. As she moved towards me I could see her eyes were bloodshot with dark grey shadows puffed underneath. I stood when she came into the room, usually something only men do for ladies, but at my school we always had to stand for an older woman, and somehow it still made sense. She took my arm.

'Miss Edan, shall we go into the dining room?' she said formally.

We walked together along a hallway decorated with drawings and watercolours in the direction of the kitchen, as wisps of smoke from something cooking on wood floated in the air.

'We shall have dinner in the small dining room tonight as we're just three. I'll call Wilhelm.' A few minutes later Frohmann joined us.

'Miss Edan, excuse me, I fell fast asleep - we'll have to discuss our business after dinner.' He'd changed into his velvet embossed slippers and a navy blue woven linen jacket.

Hardly any conversations except polite comments were exchanged between Gerda and her husband during dinner. I suspected some marital conflict was being suppressed. Maybe the lady in red was the cause of the animosity, but that seemed unlikely, as the Professor was notoriously fond of women, and I'm sure after more than thirty years of marriage Gerda had come to some inner arrangement, nullifying her husband's infidelities. Whatever was happening was having an obvious effect on them both. While I enjoyed the meal and the setting I felt uneasy in the tinderbox atmosphere.

We had coffee in the grand salon - the room that impressed me on my first visit. Gerda stayed only a few minutes before leaving.

Professor Frohmann took two glasses from the cabinet and filled them with apricot liqueur. 'This is gut medicine. Try.' He offered me a long - stemmed glass with a blue fluted edge, filled to the brim with orange liquid. He watched me as I sipped.

'Gut?' he questioned.

'Excellent' I replied. It was smooth, silky and clingy, with the aromatic sweetness of aged and ripened fruit, pungent with alcohol. The Professor smiled, 'It's fifty years old, and I often wonder how it's lasted that long without going sour. Actually, Miss Edan, I hide it, in case someone like Helmut Wingler is here. He'd drink anything, even if it was made from acorns.' We laughed. Then I asked the question that was troubling me.. 'Professor, Gerhard Hofer has paintings coming from Dresden. How does he get them through the iron curtain?'

'A difficult question, Miss Edan: I have some idea but that's all.'
'Any information you give me is helpful.'
'Well, he uses runners, stateless refugees using false passports who need money. They cross at points along the border where guards have been bribed, changing the position frequently.'
'I understand - but how do they hide paintings, especially if they are large?'
'Mostly they are rolled, maybe in sixes or more but if they are too big, they go into a metal compartment like a thin narrow drawer built under the cars' base.'
'Isn't that risky?'
'To the paintings or the runners?'
'Both,' I replied.
'Certainly, but there's nothing to lose. Hofer pays on delivery, the runners get paid on delivery, the border guards get paid on return trips - so where's the risk?'
'Not getting paid, Herr Professor. Hasn't Hofer ever reneged on an agreement?'
'I can't answer that, but sometimes a body gets washed up along the Danube beyond identity. So I leave it to your own conclusion.' I responded with a touch of sarcasm.
'I'm surprised Herr Professor, you still keep such desirable company!' The Professor tipped his head down and looked at me over his glasses. I continued.
'So whatever Hofer offers I must presume will be without provenance.'
'Not necessarily: many works were held in care in museums.'
'Please Professor: "in care" means they kept the works knowing they were confiscated?'
'If you like, Miss Edan, but surely that's an advantage for the exhibition.' He filled my glass with more apricot liqueur.
'I'm seeing Otto Prantl tomorrow.' I said. 'Is there anything I should know in advance?' The Professor took a cigarette from a silver box, placed it in the holder, but didn't light it.
'You already know about the works coming from Hanover, I am sure he will have everything documented and ready for you,' he said.

The wooden grandfather clock resting in a corner of the room was ornately carved in a leaf pattern picked out in gold and blue.

It was so voluminous the time seemed incidental, except when I really looked at the face, blue on blue with big gold hands dominating the dial and pointing to eleven, I realised it was time to leave.

'Professor, thank you for a nice evening, but it's really getting late.'

'Of course, I will call Pieter to take you to your hotel, it's safer than a taxi at night. Sometimes the drivers are night owls, prowling for illicit business. So be careful when you are alone.'

'I'm always careful, Herr Professor. It's built into my character.'

***

My meeting with Otto Prantl completed the trilogy. Like my previous visit, I found the Kartnerstrasse busy with traffic and people. It's the fashionable street for the Viennese, if fashion can be equated with the past, because everything about the street has a revivalist approach, quintessentially déja vu.

As I approached the galerie I remembered my first meeting with Prantl, the absolute opposite of Hofer inasmuch as he exuded suave refinement complemented by a matching appearance: hair drawn back, greased smooth, dark gipsy eyes, thin frame responding erratically to movements. His eyes darted constantly from one thing to another, to the paintings, to the visitors in the galerie, to the door, unable to hide his nervous anxiety.

Anticipating Hofer's motivation wasn't difficult: in one word, greed. Prantl was different. I knew his background: I knew he had traded in stolen property. As assistant to Hans Posse, Hitler's acquirer of paintings, he was more than qualified. But that was past. What now? The receptionist told him I was waiting in the front galerie. Unlike my meeting with Hofer, I was unprepared. Not for lack of time, just the inability to anticipate what to prepare for. If, for supposition, I had to assess Prantl, I would liken him to a snake, a malevolent graduate of high intellect who had misused his learning and now in his late fifties found it too late to change. Like many Austrians, defeat was never foreseen, and Prantl's visible attitude to the present, as far as I could see, conjugated a guilt ridden past.

He took long slow strides towards me.

'Miss Edan,' he dropped his head in a nod, 'would you come to the lower galerie? All the pictures are assembled for you to see.'

At the front of the building, some steps led down into a series of small rooms. The light was poor with just a centre light in each room holding a low wattage bulb. The basement rooms were stacked with crates.

'Are these the pictures from Hanover, Herr Prantl?'

'They are in the upstairs galerie, we can see them after.'

'After what?' I asked.

'These' he pointed to the crates 'have been stored here for some time. I can't tell exactly how long. My father bought the galerie and this is the remains of the inventory: the rest have gone.'

'Gone where?' I asked

'My father is dead, Miss Edan so I cannot ask.' He shrugged his shoulders. 'Sometimes we take out works and show them, some we have sold, but as we are short of space, they stay here.'

Short of space! I looked around the series of rooms and then thought of the galerie upstairs. No shortage as far as I could see. It was obvious by the connecting layout of the basement rooms that at some time they had been galeries. Now, twenty four years after the end of the war they were filled with crates. This did not add up. The allied art brigade would have scrutinized every galerie space for hidden artefacts in 1945. Why were these crates not found? Then something occurred to me.

'Do you have a garden Herr Prantl?'

'Ein garten,' he said, in a surprised tone looking down at me from his full height. 'This is a galerie not a café, we do not have ein garten.' His words were brisk.

'Maybe a courtyard?'

'Courtyard?' he questioned. 'A delivery area at the back, yes.'

'Maybe we could go back that way?

Otto Prantl was mystified. He had no idea I had recognized the galerie from Anna Frishman's description to me in London, when as a young girl she had returned from the seminar in Switzerland the day after Kristallnacht on the 11 November 1938. I remained outwardly cool but I was trembling inside. Not with fear, but reality. The past was now the present, and everything Anna told me became graphically visual. We walked silently to the courtyard. As we approached the rear door Otto

Prantl stood back to let me through. I turned the brass handle, and hesitated just long enough to see letters on the polished surface, their edges worn flat but clear enough to see GF, the initials for Galerie Frishman. This contact went much further than the back door, the transference of terror, which consumed Anna, passed through that handle to me. The flashback was so strong I had to constrain myself, as I feared my thoughts would become transparent. I hardly noticed the paintings, as I looked at the structure and layout of the rooms. Nothing had changed - the rooms led one to the other just as Anna had described them to me. I felt claustrophobic, desperately wanting to escape from myself, as breaking point became imminent. My head was talking: it's Anna's galerie; everything here belongs to Anna. Each stick of furniture each light fitting, the mirrors, the crated paintings. Everything.

I looked at Otto Prantl with disbelief. So this was the son of a bitch who had crippled the life of an innocent eighteen year old, leaving wounds so immeasurable, only death would be the cure.

My appetite for any paintings from Hanover ceased from that moment. I made delaying excuses to Prantl, and arranged to return after the weekend.

SALZBURG

12

I arrived in good time at Vienna's Westbahnhof to wait for the Orient Express to arrive from Istanbul, a scene unchanged in decades. Anna Frishman's description of her arrival at this station from Switzerland the day after Kristallnacht, became crystal clear to me as I envisaged the chaotic exodus of desperate thousands fleeing Nazi pogroms. People en route to anywhere, anywhere that would give them a life. The smoky atmosphere of the platform with its massive engines and tracks gauged to support tons of steel, were the same tracks that transported millions to the gas chambers. I could not avoid the old wooden cattle wagons resting in sidings opposite the platform. They were the coffins of thousands of incarcerated Jews and dissidents who suffocated or starved to death. I visualized the crates of paintings, stolen from museums across Europe, rolling into Germany and Austria, trophies for the hierarchy of the Third Reich.

My head ached when the great engine of the Orient Express nosed its way towards the buffers, a filthy mass of metal, smoking and smelling of oil, black smoke steaming from its funnel. It slowly came to a halt and the surge of people on the platform pushed forward, I was carried forward with them. Inside passengers were hustling between compartments looking for seats. Fortunately I found a seat next to a window, which was so dirty I couldn't see outside anyway. I put my Samsonite bag on a rack above the worn brown leatherette seating. I looked at the other occupants: a family of Turks. They must have started their journey in Istanbul. Father, mother and three children. One child of about three sat on her father's knee; head slumped against his chest, eyes watching me curiously, then quickly looking away, nervous and insecure. The father's trousers were stained and greasy, tied at the waist with thick cord. He was chewing the end of a brown dead cigarette, which he turned and sucked before chewing again. His nails were encrusted with grime, hands of the soil, softly holding his kin. Their luggage: four threadbare carpetbags smelt of stale sweat and rested under their feet. The mother silently gazed out to the corridor, a shawl tied across her head and shoulders. Passengers peered into the compartment looking for seats.

Three young boys pushed their way into the carriage. One scrambled to the window seat opposite me, the others squeezed into spaces either side. The moment the train started to move the boys opened packages and started eating. Pungent garlic sausage and bread, was pulled from their rucksacks. The boy opposite ate at Olympic speed pulling a fat egg sandwich from his bag that he stuffed into his mouth without looking up. As the train gathered speed I tried to sleep but there was nowhere to rest my head, except against the smoke stained window. I had no alternative other than watching this greedy boy. The young Turks also looked, their parched lips licked with their own saliva, resigned observers, silently communicating between each other as they slumped backwards against the brown unforgiving seating. The boy opposite was drinking fizzy Fanta orange, eating Mannen biscuits, and chocolate. He was too busy eating compulsively to even offer his friends a taste. As the train slowed into Linz and pulled up abruptly the boy started to go white. He will be sick, I thought. I was right. No sooner had the thought left my head, he dashed to the corridor. I have no idea if he made it to the toilet before his stomach emptied, but in the crush of luggage and people standing in the corridor, I doubt it.

When the train slowed into Salzburg station I felt a wreck, albeit a grateful one, and as the Orient Express chugged out of the station it took with it distressed families of the Turkish nation in decline since the fall of the great Ottoman Empire and now unable to support its population. The train also carried the voracious offspring of the defunct Austro-German alliance and my vision of a legendry romantic journey.

The taxi to the hotel Goldener Hirsh took less than ten minutes. The decor was of no interest to me. I ran the bathwater almost to the rim, and climbed in. All I wanted was to soak away the dust and smells accumulated on the train. But the comfort of the warm water could not alleviate the plight of the hungry Turks, desperate for work, and the Jews escaping along the same route from annihilation.

A junior bank clerk from the ground floor escorted me to Jack Steinhart's office. I must have looked like a ghost, I certainly felt

transparent. He offered me a scotch, then poured a large amount of whiskey onto an even larger quantity of ice.
'I'm sorry, I should have warned you Miss Edan about the Orient Express, but trains criss-cross all over Europe crammed to the gills with manual labourers from Turkey and the Balkans.'
'Does that include children of fat over-fed parents inducting their offspring into ritual eating, then throwing up in front of starving peasants?'
'Oh dear, you did have a rough ride. If you prefer we'll complete the papers later.'
'No, I'd prefer to sign all the documents now.'
As usual with bankers every paper was quadrupled. Copies for the acting branch, for head office, for the client, and one for the archives. I had to sign sixteen copies.
'Aren't you going to read them?' Steinhart asked.
'What is there to read?' I replied. 'You're giving me money according to my proposal. I read that line!'
'One point you may have missed Miss Edan, every dollar you spend is accountable to this office, not Chicago.'
'Don't worry Mr.Steinhart; I shall report every item up to a million dollars. After that, I'll cheat.'
He ignored my remark, which was I admit, snide - but I was blaming him, unjustifiably, for not warning me that my romantic image of the Orient Express which I'd held for years would be scuppered in one miserable train journey.
We completed the mechanics for the account. I now had currencies that could talk; dollars in Europe, sterling in England and Swiss francs anywhere. He offered me another whiskey which I refused.
'Dare I ask what train you're taking back to Vienna?'
'I'm not. I'm staying here in Salzburg.'
'Oh, I didn't realize you were staying. That's a pity, I'm having dinner with a colleague from the States.'
'Please, don't be concerned. A little aloneness right now is the right prescription.' I put the papers in my briefcase.
'Would you join me for lunch tomorrow? I finish at noon.'
'Thank you.'
'Good, I'll call you around eleven thirty. Where are you staying?'
When I told him, he smiled. The Goldener Hirsch was the first

place we had dined and the first time I had really looked at him as a man and not "the banker." Good looking - yes. But I suspected his looks - long lashes over sea blue eyes and blond wavy hair, belie a ruthless streak, which no doubt I would eventually encounter.

I returned to my hotel and read the papers I had signed. Not that I suspected anything might be wrong, just prudence, and if, with a big IF anything was amiss, now was the time for correction.

The comfort of the hotel revived my senses. I went to the bar and ordered a scotch and a sandwich. I sat by the log fire, watching the flames darting around the wood, creating patterns like crepe paper, edged with glinting lights before turning to ash. Blue flames, tinged with yellow licked at the pine logs adding a sweet scented aroma.

I was more than ready for sleep and the comfort of my own room. I passed the stag heads garrotted to the walls in the hallway, antique paintings of hunting scenes, before getting to the blue door, hand painted with wild mountain flowers. A canopy of printed blue flowered cotton hung over a small four-poster bed.

To tackle this project single-mindedly I needed to clear my head. Useless emotions crowding my thinking would inhibit rational judgement and impair my professional consistency. As my eyelids flickered open and closed, sleep was difficult to arrive. I was still thinking of Anna Frishman, questioning myself if I should conceal what I suspected or reveal what I had seen, knowing the inconceivable hurt I would inflict upon her.

Saturday morning in Salzburg is market day. As the sun was warm, it felt good to meander along, not going anywhere in particular. The Collegiate Church dominated the square where colourful awnings covered stalls selling produce from the farms and mountains. One stall required a dictionary of fungi to identify the varieties of mushroom. Curly orange ceps, ugly mutilated field mushrooms, tiny white pinhead marsh mushrooms, flat toadstools, special angel whites perfectly shaped, displayed in a white wicker basket. Another stall was selling dried flowers, carefully made into posies in warm winter shades and cool blues, wrapped neatly in little gold doilies with a message dangling on gold thread "handmade in Salzburg".

I wandered from stall to stall, looking at spinach, and radish, and potatoes. It is surprising how different a potato can look in a foreign country. Even the earthy ones in Wendover I remembered, had a different look from ones in Camden market. Untravelled, and not cosmetically treated, I supposed. The clean crisp air and bright sunshine combined with the smell of fresh vegetables had revived my energy. I strolled around the square, through Schmuck alley, the arcade for jewellery; every window powered by thousands of watts of electricity so even the smallest diamond shone like the Kohinoor.

Steinhart was waiting at the bank's entrance casually dressed in grey flannels and a dark grey corduroy jacket, what I would call smart weekend. By contrast I was wrapped in a big hand-knit sweater in cream wool over a pair of sand coloured check trousers. A comb and lipstick in my pocket, I had left all semblance of my working life in the hotel bedroom.

'Did you have a good morning, Mr.Steinhart?' I asked, out of politeness.

'Jack, he replied, my name's Jack, O.K. And what did you do, Katrina?'

'I wandered in the market with my hands in my pockets, looking.' We went towards the Mönchberg tunnel.

'Where are we going?'

'To get my car, then we're driving to Parsch, a village on the outskirts of Salzburg. I know a small Inn, we can sit outside and eat whatever we fancy.'

'Sounds good to me,' I said.

When we reached the car park he directed me to a white convertible Alfa Romeo, I looked at Jack, then at the car.'

'Don't bankers usually drive navy blue or black sedans?'

'You mean, show the right image and drive some heavy heap of metal across these mountain passes. Not me. Even if I were working in Kansas, where the road bends slightly every five hundred miles, I'd still drive a racer. He pulled a lever below the dashboard. I'll drop the hood: it's O.K. with you? There's a scarf in the glove compartment, if you want to preserve your hairdo!'

I looked in the offside mirror at my hairdo, and said.

'Frankly, the more wind going through my hair the better, it might even blow away some of the predatory thoughts.'

We crossed the Salzach River and followed its bank for a few miles before it turned into a tributary flowing into a tiny village with wooden houses and an old farmhouse, converted into an Inn.

'This is it,' Jack said, pulling into the car park, 'my secret rendezvous.'

Tables were set in the garden between willow trees. The farmhouse walls were painted with turquoise waves and mermaids and sea horses of unusual proportions. I smelt herbs roasting on a wood burning stove and wondered what succulent concoction was being prepared.

We sat at a green iron table with matching green seats on green grass. It was good the tablemats were red or it might have ruined what nature was offering free. We looked at the menu.

'I don't know if you like beer, but it's really good here. It's stored in caskets in the cellar, so it's really cold.'

'Don't tell me,' I said, 'Englishmen drink warm beer?'

'Absolutely. But wait a few years, it's one piece of history they'll dump, I'll put money on it. Seriously, Katrina, don't let my taste for beer interfere with your choice. Wine's good, too.'

As we were looking through the menu, a robust woman with a patterned apron and hair tied in a bun, came to our table.

'How nice to see you, Herr Steinhart. Are you comfortable outside? It's not too cold to-day.' She smiled. After a little banter Jack watched as she walked across the grass.

'Nice woman, and a great cook, I can recommend everything.'

'The beer sounds good, with a ham sandwich mit zenf und chen.'

'Is that all? Did you manage breakfast?'

'No, I lost my appetite on the Orient Express. Also I walked into a hornets' nest of intrigue in a galerie in Vienna.'

'Which one?'

'The Prantl Galerie on the Kartnerstrasse.'

A young plump waitress, the daughter of the owner, took our order. I could visualize her, ten – twenty - years on, fat, big breasted and still waiting on tables.

Jack then asked. 'What disturbed you so much in Prantl's Galerie?'

'Everything. Firstly he had crates of stolen works in the cellar.'
'Isn't that what you're looking for?'
'Of course, but I suspect every item is property owned by a refugee I know in London.'
'What makes you suspicious?'
'Hedging, unconfirmed dates, dead relatives, and his disposition - enough?'
'Strange,' Jack said, 'what do you intend to do?'
'I'm not sure. I stalled till Monday. I'll discuss the implications with Frohmann, I'm sure there's not too much he doesn't know.'
'You had dinner with him and Gerda, I hear.' Jack said, changing the subject.
'Umm, that's right, so you spoke to him?'
'Of course, I do regularly.'

Our food arrived, my sandwich and his order of duck salad. The beer was ice cold in big pottery mugs, froth swilling on top.

Close by, the river rippled over stones, licking the grass. Little birds hopped around, sometimes dipping into the waters edge then shaking their tiny heads. It was idyllically peaceful. But I was concerned about the Professor, and made a point of asking.

'Do you know what's troubling the Professor? The tension was like stretched elastic, one further pull and it rips into shreds. Do you know what's going on?'
Jack finished eating some salad and took a swig of beer.
'You haven't read the newspapers?'
'No, well not the Austrian ones, if that's what you mean.'
'His daughter Charlotte is suing him.'
'Suing her father? For what?'
'Her inheritance. In Austria, when a daughter marries she is entitled to a sum commensurate with her father's estimated wealth. That's the law.'
'I don't believe it, it's feudal.' I said in disgust. 'But why are they going to court?'
'Because the Professor doesn't approve of the future bridegroom.'
'What's wrong with him?'
'The papers say he's been married twice before, has two children and Charlotte is just twenty-one.'
'Sounds very murky to me, No wonder there was an atmosphere during dinner. How much is the Professor worth?'

'You know I can't answer that - I'm his banker, that's absolutely confidential.'
'Will you have to go to court if she sues?'
'I haven't the foggiest idea - I've never seen this ancient right in motion. Maybe it won't get that far, I hope not for the Professor's sake at least.'
'Sounds like the press is having a party.'

He called the waitress and asked for the bill.
'I have to be in the city by five for a drink with a guy who's going back to the States. Do you plan to eat dinner or are you staying on sandwiches?'
'Why?' I asked.
'I'd like to take you to the Winkler, a restaurant on top of the Mönchberg mountain. Fantastic view. Anyway, there's music - so you could just listen. What do you say to 8.30? At your hotel?'

There really was nothing to say. He was totally in command, knew the best places, and knew the language, friendly with the Professor, successful in banking, absolutely made to measure. But, he was an American, and in spite of our common language, they play by different rules. So far, I hadn't crossed them, but I was warned they play rough when the chips are down. Now they ruled Europe with their mighty dollar, and this guy was not around for peanuts, he must be turning over quite a lot of financial muscle, and could be, apart from a sponsor, a good ally.

***

I looked in the mirror at my blown apart hairdo. I realized every inch of me had to be revitalized. Hopefully my nerve endings, which were tense, would soon feel soothed. Small packets of soap, bubble bath, body lotion, hand cream, his and her perfume, shampoo, all neatly wrapped, waited in the bathroom in a blue lined basket. I had packed frugally as usual: one casual outfit, which I was wearing, one suit for travel, and two dresses. I shook the dress, which I had hung in the wardrobe. A simple purple crepe with a high neck and long sleeves, it fitted where it touched and curved where my body curved. Understated English chic and not competition for the French or the Italians.

Jack was on time and reception called to say he was waiting.

He looked stunning in a dark chocolate brown velvet jacket, accentuating the blond hair resting neatly on the edge of his collar, a white silk polo necked shirt and dark brown serge trousers. Everything about his casual elegance was tasteful.

We walked to the end of the Getreidegasse, crossed to the mountain's rock face, which reached directly to the pavement and waited for the funicular. It was an antiquated affair with vertical tracks on the side of the mountain with the body of the lift slotted into the rails.

'Is it safe?' I queried.

'Don't know, it's been running for years, guess it'll last this evening.'

An Austrian party of four joined us in the lift, the men in dinner jackets and the women in everything they could find a space for. One woman had a second pair of earrings pinned either side of a décolleté neckline. I wanted to laugh.

The Maitre D who greeted Herr Steinhart with the proverbial 'nice to see you again Sir', received us. He took my coat then escorted us to a table by the window.

'Isn't it stunning,' Jack said. Millions of lights twinkled far below and into the distance and the more we looked the more appeared.

'Breathtaking.' I said. 'I'm not sure which is more spectacular, this or the top of the Empire State building.'

'They're different,' he replied. 'This one God made, the other one, man made. You know, even the electricity from one dam, from one lake, into one river, powers the whole valley. They can't do that in New York.'

The wine sommelier arrived with a bottle of champagne, which he put in an ice cooler by our table. The restaurant was built into the mountain, oblong shaped, curving slightly as it hugged the rock face. In the centre was a dance floor surrounded by tables and a band was playing Strauss. The musicians were really serious: two violins, an accordion, a bass, and drums. The average age was "deceased", but they were tuneful, looked like they were enjoying themselves and changed the mood of the music often. A number of couples were on the floor waltzing to the strings of the Blue Danube. Even teenagers, dressed in their best parentally approved frocks were whizzing round as the music became faster.

Jack saw me pondering over the menu. 'Still no appetite?'

'It's coming back,' I held my fluted glass up. 'I think the champagne helps. Do you know it's the only alcohol allowed in hospitals at home.'

'Seriously, I'd have thought it was stout!'

'No, it's recommended as a digestive: that's if you drink it slowly and don't have a second bottle.'

'I can just imagine, a whole crowd of geriatrics doing the polka up and down a ward, waving the Union Jack and champagne corks.' Jack said.

'Only on Lavender Hill,' I replied.

'That's such a beautiful name. Does it really have lavender or was it a scriptwriter's dream?'

'Well, it doesn't have any lavender and hardly any hill but it's there all right. It's on the south side of the Thames across Wandsworth Bridge, where you can be very unwelcome, even to day. It's wide-boy territory: petty criminals, dodgy measures in pubs, stolen goods in lock-up garages. It's a shame, it has such an inviting name.'

'So, Swiss Cottage must be a chocolate factory? Or is that too obvious' he asked.

We'd drunk half the champagne and still hadn't ordered any food. At the flick of Jack's finger the waiter was at my side.

'Would you care to order madam?'

'Yes, linguine with ceps,' a nice light dish, which I felt I could manage. Jack asked for scallops of veal in white wine. The band was playing a slow foxtrot. Jack held out his hand, 'dance?' As we reached the dance floor his hand wrapped around my waist and he held me very close. My left hand rested on his arm, but he took my right hand and held it between us, in the American nightclub style. He didn't speak and moved slowly and assuredly not going very far around the floor. He could dance. He could feel the rhythm of the music. He didn't tread on my toes, except once, and then he whispered in my ear, 'sorry, that big guy shoved me.' The music stopped and he held my arm as we left the dance floor. The meal was ready and the waiter asked Jack if he could serve.

'Sure, and please bring another bottle,' he said, pointing to the champagne.'

'Feel more relaxed now, or are the Viennese bugs still biting?'
'They're not biting but they're still here. I can't run from depression, I take it along like a snail leaving a silver trail behind. Going forward only produces more activity and the trail gets longer. That's how I feel right now.'

To include Jack in the mechanics of my exhibition negated his role as a sponsor. His money - well - the bank's money was invested in me for return: value for money is the passport to American thinking: if for any reason one's off track - get a shrink - but never forget your commitment to 'deliver'.

He was sitting opposite me looking very intent. Not worried, but his eyes narrowed, as if he were holding something back. Then he put his hand on mine across the table.
'Katrina - I should like you to feel free to speak to me on any matter that's worrying you. I know it's not for me to give you advice, and I'm pretty confident you wouldn't take it, but I know the Austrians. I know how they think and how they operate. There might come a time when a thumb up or down might save you a lot of heartache.'

I was watching every move he made, listening to every inflection trying to sum up his motivation. I didn't know about his personal life, I only knew how I reacted to what he chose to tell me, and I felt at ease with him - comfortable. BUT, pour my heart out, that would overtake my natural reticence, but maybe - just maybe, it's what I craved.

The band was playing "dancing in the dark" 'one of my favourites.' I said. He pushed his chair back and offered his hand.
'Mustn't waste a good song.' The champagne was having the desired effect. I felt relaxed and malleable, my body overtaken by the rhythm of the music. Jack's hand was low down on my back and I could feel his erection close to me. He didn't move back, just held me as if it was the right place to be. When the music stopped we stayed on the dance floor, waiting for the next tune. The musicians knew how to pace their music but when they played "I like New York in June, how about you" we walked off the floor, and lingered over the last of the champagne.

On the way to the funicular I suggested we hike down.

'No way. Jack retorted imitating a gruff voice. 'It's a vertical drop of 800ft. Anyway, you're wearing the wrong shoes.'

The Goldener Hirsch was minutes from the mountain face and once again we were passing the bodiless stags and the hunting scenes on the walls, to my blue door. Jack held it open.

'Thank you, I enjoyed the evening, I will call you.'

And he was gone.

I was pleased he'd made the decision for me that sex wasn't mandatory. Even with the attraction between us, he was able to walk away. I was curious though. What criteria had he for sex with a client? Was I out of bounds? Could I be a moral issue? Certainly not! I never became an issue. It would have been easier to sleep together and talk later I told myself, instead of being frustrated by imponderables.

***

The telephone rang in my room. I slithered from under the silky sheets and managed to engage myself with the offensive machine. 'Yes' I said. There was a pause 'Yes' I repeated. The voice at the other end said.

'You must be very careful who you say yes to. This is a foreign country, remember.'

'Oh, good morning Jack What time is it?'

'It's ten o'clock. Did you miss breakfast?'

'Breakfast, that's for the working classes. It's the weekend, remember?'

'Do you have any plans for to-day?'

I rubbed my eyes and squinted, looking for the bedside clock.

'Did you say ten. Oh, hell. I'm due at the Frohmann Galerie at ten. Kurt's opening the galerie so I can look at the Sneider collection.'

'I'll call you at the Galerie later - I'll see what's happening around town.' I dialled room service for a large glass of fresh sweezed orange juice and a pot of coffee.

The sign on the door of the Galerie said Geschlossen: I rang the bell beside the brass plaque and Kurt opened the door.

'Gutentag' Miss Edan, please.' He held the door open for me. 'There's an envelope for you from mein Vater's assistant. One moment bitte.' I waited in the lobby of the main galerie before

following Kurt along the maze of corridors to reach the room where the collection was being stored. The galerie was crammed with paintings. The inventory that I had studied meticulously in London listed forty-two items. The new list Stephan Moser had put together listed one hundred and twenty six.
Kurt said 'If you need any help, please call me; I will be in the studio. Just walk along the corridor and turn left.'

I thanked him and started looking at the works, trying to match descriptions with their inventory numbers, and then checking the provenance. After some time I thought, did it really matter? After all, whatever I exhibited, the provenance might have been falsified. It would be for prospective claimants to prove that their deceased families owned them. All I needed to do was identify fakes, and make absolutely sure they were catalogued, as copies. If the provenance had been doctored a search could then be instigated for the original documents. This made the scrutiny easier and set a trend I would follow. It was more important to have possession than proof: once the paintings were in England, what I printed in the catalogue would be out of the jurisdiction of the Austrians, Germans, Russians, or any other country including the Swiss. Kurt came into the Galerie. 'Would you like some coffee Miss Edan?'
'That would be most welcome,' I replied.

He seemed by his demeanour an affable young man, a little repressed maybe, but then with such a forceful father, that is often the case. Or maybe he disapproved of his fathers past? Kurt represented the new generation of Austrians, who were force fed denial of wartime atrocities by their parents, even when they knew of their involvement because they had served a jail sentence. But their children were too conformist and inhibited to rebel.

Kurt brought two mugs of coffee on a tray and was apologetic that he couldn't find cups and saucers - as if it mattered anyway.
'Do you enjoy your work here, Herr Frohmann?
'Sometimes, especially landscape photography. I am a good climber, so I can get some rare shots. I am not keen on fashion, but it is not possible for me to choose in this line of work.'
'Have you ever wanted to be involved in the art world - I say that because in some ways it's global. Do you understand what I

mean?'
'Oh yes, mein Vater has tried to get me to work in the galerie, but I prefer to work outside his comprehension. Is that the right word Miss Edan?'
'I think you mean jurisdiction. Your father has great knowledge and a deep feeling for the substance of art . . . it's impossible to emulate: dedication can't be inherited - it's simple - it's either there - or it's not.'

Kurt was listening, translating word for word into German but somehow there was a distance, coolness, and a lack almost of belonging to the environment in which he existed. Then the phone rang, breaking any train of thought that might have revealed more about him. 'It's for you Miss Edan, Herr Steinhart.'
'Katrina, there's a good concert at the Mirabell Palace at four, could you make it? Or are you doing proletarian hours?'
'I have to be careful. It's your money I'm spending, and for the record I'm absolutely dedicated to thrift.'
'I'm pleased to hear that.' he remarked
'I'll finish by three, then I'll grab a sandwich.' I said.
'You're not back on those things?'
'No choice Jack, the chef's off duty here.'
'I'll meet you at your hotel at three forty-five.'

In Salzburg every historical venue is within walking distance and by four o'clock we were in the small salon of the Mirabell Palace, sitting on gold painted chairs with red velvet seats, waiting for the Mozart Quartet to appear. The room was full. I looked up at the pink and blue painted ceiling with nude cherubs floating around attending seductive women with fat breasts and classical features, servicing the whims and fancies of men in some Arcadian heaven where the sexes could never be equal. Thy will be done on earth as it is in heaven. Oh, dear. I smiled at Jack, then looked up again at the voluptuous nubile figures who ravished a man's strength and forced his satiated body into involuntary recline, while Pan played the flute and the women, complacently, waited.

The quartet entered, dressed in black tuxedos with white shirts and bow ties, two violins, one viola, and a cello. Applause greeted them. They played a Telemann suite that was exquisitely lyrical, each musician producing clear defined sounds, which reverberated throughout the room. But I was only on the fringe of listening. Jack's presence next to me disturbed my concentration. I was conscious of his breathing, of his hands resting in his lap. Every movement he made, I felt. I fidgeted, crossed and uncrossed my legs, looked at the wall panels, with their vertical gold, pink and blue pilasters. I was impatient for the end: I knew I shouldn't be, but when the last note sounded, I clapped with relief rather than appreciation.

We left the splendour of the Palace and walked through the Mirabell Gardens. Early spring flowers, all placed in neat rows, were bursting with colour.

We stopped to admire the comparative expressions of pansies.

'Those are arrogant,' Jack said, pointing to a mauve cluster,'

'And they're sulky,' I replied, as I looked at acid yellow flowers.

'Look closely' I said, 'at their painted faces - see how piqued they are?'

'No they're not, they're proud.' He held his jaw high in a pansy parody.

'But look at the black ones with white eyes and orange Picasso eyelashes. I would call those domineering pansies.'

He looked at me with a huge grin. 'Maybe you're right, but frankly, Katrina, I like the blue ones.'

I knew why. They were the same colour as his eyes: pools of watery blue - concealed under long blonde eyelashes, neither proud nor resigned nor aware of their devastating effect on me.

'You didn't enjoy the concert, very much?'

'Oh, I did, but I found it hard to concentrate.'

He didn't press for an explanation as we walked along the quayside listening to the gulls making their own music. We strolled towards my hotel, in no hurry, just shop gazing, when Jack spotted a pair of walking shoes with soles like door-steps and uppers that would have given me misshapen ankles. I shook my head. My blue hotel door was becoming very familiar. This time Jack didn't walk away. As the door closed he was in front of me and very close, one hand on my shoulder holding me back, his other hand, slowly undoing the buttons on my blouse.

VIENNA

13

Success is a word I would not use often nor for that matter is failure. But, after three months the formation of the exhibition was taking shape. Legitimate and illegal sources were aware of my activities and paintings were materializing at a steady rate. With this in mind, I arrived at Gerhard Hofer's galerie, to see the works he expected from the Soviet Union.

'Ve vill take a taxi to Grinzing,' he said as soon as I arrived. 'All zie works are there.' He took his black beret from an old-fashioned hat stand, manoeuvred it into place, negating any influence of French sang-froid and limped to the door. I suspected this beret represented the last remnants of possessions from his time in the Hitler youth movement. The swastika, the badge of allegiance had gone, but the power vested in it still operated silently within him.

Grinzing is known for its wine Kellers and Inns during Heuringer when the new vintages are tasted in more than abundant quantities. I had only read about this ritual, but it sounded equal to the bier fest in Munich, except in Austria, they get drunk on wine.

The taxi driver stopped outside a private home with a low white picket fence, on the outskirts of the village. Gerhard Hofer pulled a long black iron handle at the front door that activated a bell high above it. A tinny sound brought a tall thin man, wearing metal-framed glasses to the door.

'Guten Tag Herr Hofer' he said, and looked over his glasses at me as he beckoned us through the front door. The first room had bare boards, two worn armchairs and stacks of paintings resting against the walls. We passed through another room where an elderly woman was sewing. We left through the back door to the yard. Hofer flicked a stone with his walking stick and it rattled against a rusting rod of metal lying on the ground with other pieces of assorted debris. Beyond the yard was an orchard, long and narrow, overgrown with trees so old they couldn't possibly bear fruit. At one time it must have been a pretty garden, now it was neglected and sad.

I followed like a dog on a leash, trudging through the grass till we reached a large corrugated shed the width of the orchard. We crossed a concrete forecourt and Hofer unlocked a large new padlock, slipped open the bolt and slid the door back.

Electric light bulbs hung at ten-foot intervals along a central rail and continued as far as I could see. I watched my footing carefully as we stepped round canvases stacked one on top of the other like milk crates in a dairy. Others, their frames chipped and dirty, rested against the sides. It was impossible to estimate the number of paintings. One still life lying on the floor, its stretcher removed, looked like a Chardin but it was caked in black dust, so at first glance it was impossible to know. Hofer pointed his walking stick at a Eugène Bourdin. 'In good condition, ya?' I had my doubts.

My baptism by Hofer had been hard won, and I didn't want to exacerbate controversy, which would be counter-productive. What I wanted was "possession": any investigations could follow, once the works were in Salzburg.

'How long have you had this warehouse, Herr Hofer?'

'Vy do you ask, Fraulein?'

'Because Professor Frohmann has a depot in Salzburg to store works for the exhibition and all the paintings will be dispatched to London from there.'

I watched his brooding face as he lit a cigar, first licking the end and spitting the tip on the floor. He twirled it in his hand before lighting it with a cheap plastic lighter. Then he puffed and sucked. I casually turned a canvas over to the painted side but dust caught my breath and penetrated my nostrils. I breathed in and felt the irritating burn of coal dust. Then I knew. This was part of the Dresden collection from the Gross Cotta mine. But, who owned them? Had the Museum kept stolen works? Had they paid for them? Could the Museum make a legitimate claim? Questions I asked myself, not Hofer. But he did ask me for money. 'I need to pay zie shippers.'

'Shippers,' I queried

'Ze couriers zen.'

'Of course - Herr Hofer, but I must check the items first - I'm sure you understand.'

Whether he did or didn't was immaterial, but handing out money before seeing a listing wasn't on my agenda. To keep him sweet and prevent any more obnoxious outbursts, I told him. I had money available in any currency he wanted.

He chewed on his cigar, taking the soggy end from his mouth, turning it round, looking at its shape: the rich pungent smell of smoke lost in the cavernous warehouse. Then he spurted out.

'You can look right now. Everytink is here. And zie cost is five thousand dollars before anytink leaves.'

I heard the revving of an engine and the noise of tyres moving over the crusty stone forecourt, then the slamming of a car door.

Hofer went to the entrance - slid the door back and spoke to a thick set man wearing a workman's check shirt and grey trousers, with a stomach poured precariously over his belt. Hofer shouted. 'Ve vill leave you and come back in two hours. You can list for two hours.'

'One moment,' I said as I hurried to the entrance. 'I have no idea which pictures to look at?'

'Oh, ya, the two pallets on the front and the ones on the right side.' He pointed with his stick.

'You'll be back at one o'clock?'

'Nein, Zoffman will collect you.'

They left and I heard the bolt rattle across steel and the padlock click shut. The shunting outside sounded loud and final. I looked up at the cobwebs around the light fittings, at the metal walls searching for windows or ventilation and I walked the length of the warehouse looking for another exit. The walls were sealed. Nothing existed but stagnant art on rotting pallets, each with a history, but no one so far had liberated their stories. I started to sweat but felt cold: I was shaking uncontrollably and doubted whether trusting Hofer wasn't positively irresponsible. In this claustrophobic, filthy metal shed, smelling of mould and coal dust, I needed something to sweeten my imagination. Without any enthusiasm, I took a canvas from the stack and looked at the grubby signature. I held the picture to the light and looked again: I remembered what Francis Bacon said in the 16th century: "all colours will agree in the dark". Not these colours. They belonged exclusively to Gustave Courbet - the first painter to paint outside en plein air, in the open. I felt momentarily liberated, transported outside to where he had been, where he had stood, where he had looked. This landscape of incalculable historical importance made any discomfort I was feeling, recede into insignificance. Universally acknowledged as a stepping-stone to impressionism, Courbet went where no artist had dared - into the freedom of the outside - into the sunlight and warmth. I shivered at the thought of the millions who had prematurely been denied this everlasting spectacle, and my resolve to get on with the job at hand, hardened.

Then I heard the lock click . . . I looked at my watch - only forty minutes had passed. I watched the entrance from behind one of the pallets. As it opened the old woman from the house, stood silhouetted against the light. She put a mug on a shelf near the door. "Heiss chocolade Fräulein" and closed the door.

I started the listing. Paul Cézanne (landscape)
Gustave Courbet (landscape)
Frans Hals (Torso of a man)
Claude Monet (Park scene)
Joshua Reynolds (Portrait)

It was becoming increasingly evident that this cache was NOT from the Soviets. More likely the Germans hid it, when the Russians advanced in 1945. This was genuine loot, maybe from a Museum, or from the private collections of wealthy Jews, who had paid for their lives with fluchtsteuer (escape tax). If this was the case, they might still be alive to substantiate a claim. At one o'clock the padlock clicked open and Zoffman pulled back the iron door. He had an old black Citroen car parked on the concrete outside. He turned off all the lights in the warehouse and drove me to the Hotel Graben without uttering a word.

***

That evening I decided to eat at a restaurant on the Seitzgasse, a cobble stoned alleyway near the Amhof, recommended by Professor Frohmann. The Gösser Bier Klinik, owned by the brewers and had a reputation for lake fish: carp, zander and trout, prepared in a variety of ways: fried, baked in exotic sauces, flaked, marinated, smoked.

A waiter took me to a marble topped table with a wrought iron base, which reminded me of my grandmother's sewing machine stand. 'Bier?' he asked. No question here of which variety, only a question of size. While I was reading the menu he placed a cork mat on the table and a tankard full to the rim. Mirrors lined the walls stencilled with the Gösser emblem, a yellow circle with red inset. I ordered zander, fried in breadcrumbs with tartar sauce and chips. Just ordering fish and chips made me think of home - until, I must add - it arrived. It was an oblong of fish about one inch thick, an extraordinary shape that must have been formed by a kitchen knife. It was accompanied by a sauceboat filled with creamy tartare and a silver platter of dry fried golden chips. Dare I ask for tomato sauce? I dared. The first bite into the crusty coated fish and I had reached the succulent white inside. I fingered a chip. There's something special about eating chips with fingers - they taste different. A hangover maybe from the days when they came wrapped in yesterday's newspaper!

The tomato sauce arrived, freshly squashed. The chef had peeled cored and de-seeded them, before beating them into a pulp. Heinz could take a lesson. I ordered another bier.

During my private culinary celebration I had finished every morsel put in front of me and hadn't realized it was past eleven.

By the time I reached my hotel I decided to walk a little longer, or would never sleep. Dorotheergasse is narrow with high buildings on either side concealing courtyards of hidden activity. I had to decide whether to continue towards the Opera House or turn left into a smaller dark street, as the route back was not so long. I turned. There weren't any people around at this time of night and I could hear the tread of my heels on the stone pavement. I glanced back - someone else was in the street behind me. I just walked on. Then I walked a little faster and heard the footsteps behind move faster. I looked back again and saw the silhouette of a man about a hundred feet away. The permutations of why I was being followed rushed to my head. He's a rapist, I thought whose been stalking Vienna for months - uncaught? I started to panic, then my feet worked in a bicycle motion propelling me along - then I ran. My heel caught in the ridge of a paving stone, I stumbled and saw the figure getting closer. I ran as fast as I could, catching my breath in gasps, looking for somewhere to turn. The lights were dim and far apart; I thought I was tripping over shadows, desperate for somewhere to turn. I reached the Singerstrasse and thankfully saw the lights of the Graben in the distance. I was exhausted and tempted to hide in a doorway to regain my breath - but panic propelled me onwards towards the lights of the main street. Couples were walking home hand-in-hand, unaware of my distress; street vendors had removed awnings. The sweet aroma of roasting chestnuts on a brazier wafted in the night air. I dodged between people trying to become invisible until I reached the Dorotheergasse. I looked back before approaching my hotel entrance, expecting the figure to be there. He had gone. With relief I took my key from reception and double locked my door. Then fear took hold. I couldn't sleep and my imagination was in overdrive.

Vienna is a sham city. Like the Gothic buildings of its past glory it masks offstage depravity perpetuated by its geographic border with the eastern block, and has become a playground for criminal deviationists, escapees, rapists and murderers, making the oldest profession, by comparison, virtuous. This is contemporary Vienna, where the computations are extended to a rampant spy network, where east meets west in the twilight hours, where hush money is agents' everyday currency and the individual in this climate is dispensable. The cold war is a misnomer: it's hot, dangerous and without laws. The terms of the Geneva Convention play no part or reference for the controller of any foreign desk. They are licensed manipulators, sanctioned by governments, killers for good or evil, surreptitiously working without ever showing their country's flag.

***

Feeling fear was not alien to me although it had been twenty-three years, to be precise, when I was eight, that fear became part of my life. I believed that bones of dead people were lying on the surface of the waste ground opposite my school in Aylesbury. I believed it because I was told by my superiors', prefects with badges of office: green for Cavell, red for Nightingale, blue for Darling. At first they were my heroes. Fiona was my favourite: her team always won the school prize. Priscilla was pretty, with long blonde hair and blue eyes and had a boyfriend who collected her from school. I didn't like Tessa, the head girl and captain of Cavell. She sent notes to juniors, telling them to clean her hockey boots, or her tennis shoes.

Juniors like myself thought this was the privilege of her position and did as we were told.

At four o'clock when I left school, I always hurried past the waste ground in abject fear, not daring to look at the bones in case they moved. But fear followed me. Juniors were regularly targeted by the three girls and notes placed in blazer pockets, which hung in the cloakroom. "We're coming to get you! It's your turn." It never said when. I was on permanent alert.

I knew, when I saw the girls on the bus to Wendover, it was my turn, and it was me they were after because they lived in different directions: Priscilla and Tessa in Stoke Mandeville and Fiona in Weston Turville. It was a twenty minute walk from the bus to my house and often I would stop at my favourite sweetshop, where I bought a slab of homemade toffee or an aniseed ball, which I would suck until it became a pinhead. It lasted exactly the time it took me to get to my gate.

I pretended I hadn't seen them on the bus and put my head in a book: but I was the first one on the platform ready to jump off the moment the bus stopped. Fortunately I could run fast, very fast, and although they were older than me I was tall for my age, and my long slim legs could out-run them. This did not minimise fear, it only perpetuated it, because I was told, that soon, very soon, they'd "get me". What they would do with me was a matter of conjecture, but all sorts of horrors came into my head. Maybe, they had put the bones in the field, and were looking for more victims. I wished Pippa had been with me, but she'd been sent to Wickham Abbey, as a boarder after her parents died. I missed her.

If I had told my Mother she would only have told me not to be silly. "You're imagining things, my dear. Just do your homework, and stop being babyish". My only consolation was my secret hiding place, which I made bigger as I grew. In there, I talked to the animals, a lonely worm sliding along, or a butterfly that wandered in by mistake. Mostly, I cried.

I was tempted to phone Jack for consolation but what would I say. "I was followed?" So what? Par for the course he would tell me, and he would be right. I called Sue in London instead.

'At last Katrina, where have you been?' came her response.

'Working' I said, 'what else would I do in this outsize Baroque

Mausoleum?'
'Yoo-hoo, something's gone wrong?'
'Not really,' I said, not wanting to whinge. 'Have you completed the Tel Aviv file? Good. I'm seeing Prantl this morning and Frohmann this afternoon, I will return to the office on Friday. Anything I need to know?'
'Just one thing, Imperial Bank Chicago wrote to Samuel Hall for suggestions on profile etc. They phoned here too.'
'Stall them Sue till I get back, but run a short progress report. I'll check Steinhart to see what they're up to. I want you to prepare a draft letter for circulation to all European Museums asking for declarations on works taken in under any conditions, between 1938-1945.'
'Is that all?' came the sarcastic reply.
'Isn't that enough.' I retorted. 'See you by the end of the week.' I hung up, knowing that Sue would prepare a draft of consummate dimensions, with the envelopes stamped, waiting for my approval.

***

Prantl, unlike Hofer was meticulously organized. When I arrived at his galerie he had listed all the paintings. He handed me a folder. I opened the dark blue cover noting the number of items listed. Prantl was nervously fingering his navy and red tie. I hesitated at page three.
'Something wrong?' he asked.
' No - but I'm surprised by the number of works - two hundred and eighty. Are they all from Hanover?'
'Oh - no, I have included some from my own inventory.' He shifted his gaze.
'Are they indicated in the listing?'
'No' he replied. I wondered why.
'It would be helpful Herr Prantl, if you would mark your galerie pieces with a star.' I gave him the list. I hastily said. 'I intend to exhibit museum pieces separately so I need to identify them.' He looked at me again with a degree of suspicion but proceeded with my request.

Otto Prantl could not have known Anna Frishman had survived. The Frishman family were deported to Bergen-Belsen and this would have been recorded. The list I held was testimony in itself, that Anna Frishman had been robbed of her inheritance.

LONDON

14

My friendship with Anna Frishman grew from our first meeting, in spite of the dichotomy of personalities and backgrounds, age and interests, the common denominator that perpetuated our empathy was, justice. Justice for any cause that created an under-dog, countries that rejected human rights, and cultures that denied their bloody history.

It was a fine early spring day as Anna and I watched the gardeners planting spring flowers in Regents Park their wheel-barrows filled with young seedlings. Anna said.

'I'm always fascinated how they get the colour schemes right. Never a pink flower where a blue one should be, and so tightly packed, not one rogue flower anywhere ... Amazing.'

'I agree Anna; the head gardener must have ex-ray eyes or come from a family of geneticists. We'll come back in six weeks for confirmation. How about a bet Anna, I'll lay ten to one he gets it right.'

'Ten to one,' exclaimed Anna 'pounds or pence?'

'Pence of course, we're gambling on mistakes, so the odds should be loaded!'

We arrived at my home as the sun was going down and settled in the living room for a glass of wine.

It was not easy for Anna to recall the circumstances of her flight to England but now, in relaxed mood, she revealed to me what had happened. She started her story in a disjunctive way, events out of context and time, searching for rejected memories.

The historical background, Anna told me, was both important and exceptional as it pinpointed both gratitude and disbelief engendered by the British reaction to Kristallnacht in 1938. In the summer of that year President Roosevelt instigated a conference at Evian on the French side of Lake Geneva to discuss the mounting numbers of refugees fleeing Nazi Germany. Delegates attended from Belgium, Canada, France, Holland, U.S.A. and Great Britain. The conference proved futile when Great Britain refused entry of Jewish refugees into Palestine, which was under British mandate, justifying their stance as "being fair" to both Jews and Arabs. To appease this stance, the British delegate, Norman Bentwich, agreed to instigate an agreement offering entry to ten thousand Jewish children at risk from pogroms, which were escalating in Germany and Austria. First priority would be given to orphans, then to children of parents in work camps, then by selection by the Gemeinde and the Quakers.

'Who were the Gemeinde?' I asked Anna.

Her hands were wrapped around her glass. She put it down on the coffee table. 'Katrina, they were officers of the Jewish communities who selected the children.'

'Was there any corruption?' I asked. I knew the moment I had used the word that I had made a horrible error.

'Corruption, for what? For sending children away alone to unknown destinations. No Katrina, there was no corruption, only begging.' She continued. 'Children were taken to main stations across Europe. The export of infant untermensch (sub-humans) from the Fatherland helped Germany solve the problem of disposal, as yet unresolved. Between November 1938 and September 1939 when war was declared, one thousand children arrived a month, a total of over nine thousand. The last train to England was stopped at the Dutch border in September 1939 when war was declared, and returned to Germany. Anton Hempf was on that train. Anna Frishman's hand was trembling as she held her glass. Don't worry Katrina, I'll be alright, it's just my nerves.'

But I did worry. As a silent bystander of tragedy, I was grateful for the twenty-one miles of sea that protected the British Isles from the horrors of Hitler's mania and his crippling of creativity regardless of race or religion.

In spite of the traumas and horrendous fate of her family in the gas chambers of Bergen-Belsen, Anna was a handsome woman, neat and well groomed: grey hair tinted light brown. But it was her carriage which gave her presence: silent pride radiated from her, never looking for sympathy, eternally grateful for living, for a place in the world, and the country which gave her help and hope as a young woman. She had never come to terms with her guilt at being the only family survivor - the loss was too great. I poured some more wine for Anna and myself.

'Excuse me, Katrina, I'm wandering. I'll explain. My passport had been confiscated on my return from Switzerland. Father wanted me to travel on a Kindertransport train coming to England.' Anna stopped speaking and looked out of the window, her eyes far away searching for some meaning to the words she spoke. 'Father applied for Josef, as his parents were still in detention. I travelled with him as his older sister. Father's accounts in Austria and Switzerland were frozen and my sisters were not allowed to work.' In a whisper Anna recalled.

'Vienna station was jammed with parents putting their children on the train, waving shouting, "see you soon in England, repeating "soon". Anna's voice was cracking: "soon" never came. Children with identity tags dangling from their necks were crying, holding their only possessions, a toy and a small suitcase. From that moment we all became orphans.'

I saw the blood rushing to her cheeks, the tension building, her voice becoming distant, a speaking shadow.

'Please Anna, ' I asked . . . 'perhaps another day?'

'No, Katrina'. She shook her head, took a white embroidered handkerchief from her handbag, blew her nose, and cleared her throat. 'That's better. Ah - where was I - I remember.' Her eyes were darting from memory to me, pulling at the past, expurgating ghosts, and repressing melancholy. Holding her screwed up handkerchief in her lap, she continued.

'When the train reached the Dutch border, women brought cakes and cookies and chocolate. On the boat to Harwich, Josef spoke for the first time since Kristallnacht. He said. "Wohin vir gehen?"

'To London, I said, to see the Queen: reality being I didn't know where we were going and all I could recall was the nursery rhyme. I tried not to cry, but hearing Josef speak was overwhelming: looking back they must have been tears of joy, but all I felt then, was despair.'

I left my chair and crossed to Anna on the scarlet sofa.

'I'm going to the kitchen to rustle up a little supper, Anna.' As I passed I stroked her cheek: little consolation but genuinely felt.

Anna was standing by the window watching blue tits darting from tree to tree: one perched on the windowsill, quickly to be joined by another.

I put a plate of smoked salami, ham and a plate of assorted

cheeses and a yard of French bread on the dining table, joined Anna by the window and watched the fading light fall behind the trees and night descend. It became increasingly obvious that Anna had to unburden everything to me, as if she had passed into another life and desperately wanted to come back.

'I was an 'illegal' she said, 'and put into a camp in Kingston-on-Thames. After two months I was sent to work in a factory and billeted with a family in Reigate. An incident happened after I accidentally answered the factory foreman in French.
"You," he said. "Yes, you," he said, pointing at me. "Come 'ere. What you fink you're up to, I don't need no Nazis 'ere talking foreign. Report to the office, PRONTO." Ironic, that pronto for him, was English. I was ordered to return to my billet and told that under no circumstances must I leave the house. What they didn't know was I never left the house, as the owners Mr.& Mrs.Butler, made me do the housework and the washing at night. The following morning two interrogators, Lieutenant Warren and Corporal Sheppard, arrived from the foreign office with copies of my papers. I was scared they would intern me as an illegal again. Mrs.Butler offered them tea, smiled and said I was no trouble. She was paid 7/6d a week for my keep but did not tell them she also kept my pocket money. Mrs.Butler stood by the living room door waiting to hear what I said, her arms folded, her hair wrapped in a scarf with a knot on the top.'
'Was she unkind to you Anna?'
'Not really, just indifferent, but her husband tried to abuse me. He'd put his hand up my skirt at the table - I'd nowhere to move. I locked my door at night. I wanted to console her, apologise for my countrymen, but she went on quickly.
'The officer thanked Mrs Butler and asked to speak to me alone. He was very formal. "I have your papers Miss Frishman and I can't see any declaration that you speak the French language? Could you tell me why?" He looked about twenty-four years old with an air of haughty importance. He stood very erect and had two pips on his shoulder. As we spoke the corporal was taking notes. Herr Captain, I said, I speak five languages. My English was good Katrina, but I didn't know a Captain from a General.'
"Then why aren't they listed?" he asked.

'Because no one asked me. So I listed German and English.'

Lieutenant Warren reviewed the file. "Where did you learn French?"

'At school in Switzerland.'

"And what other languages do you speak that aren't listed, Miss Frishman?"

'Italian and Spanish, I replied.'

He turned to Corporal Sheppard. "Make a note that this report must go to market tomorrow."

Anna looked blankly at me 'I had no idea what he was talking about. A market? Anyway, I soon found out. The next day a car came to collect me, and I went to Whitehall for an interview. From then on I worked in the translation department at the War Office on codes and classified documents. The war became close and sometimes what I translated was beyond belief.'

Anna tore a piece of bread from the French stick, but left it on her plate.

'I never returned to Mr and Mrs. Butler in Reigate. Nor did I ever tell what happened until after the war, then only to our mutual friend, Dr.Anton Hempf.'

LONDON

15

Sue was huddled over files of papers, her light brown hair falling over her forehead. 'Thank God you're back' she said. She always thanked God for my return. Why I deserved this miracle I have yet to find out.

The mug on her desk was inscribed overworked and underpaid and the capital letter "Y" formed the handle. She wore a white shirt with the buttons open to bra level and a large bubble bead necklace in different shades of brown.

'It's been like a telephone exchange here.' she said. 'The Americans have been nudging and neighing. What's going on? The Chicago bank wants a résumé of costs you expect to incur on the exhibition: your advertising schedule, which journals, newspapers, television channels, and radio you're targeting?'

'Sounds reasonable,' I said.

'That's not all. It goes on. Who's covering the U.S? Have you contacted the Jewish Agency? How many items do you have to date? Katrina, these yanks want to know how often you change your knickers. Typical!' She put her pen down with a bang. 'If I were you, I'd tell them you're advertising in the Zulu News and the Maori Gazette.'

'Good idea Sue, but come into my office, and I'll give you an update.' Sue put our newly acquired silver thermos jug on my desk and I took my "be nice I'm rich" mug out of my drawer.

'After I spoke to you from Vienna, Jack Steinhart came to my hotel and I asked him why his head office was pounding the daylight out of you in London and writing to Samuel Hall.'

'And?' Sue said.

'I made it clear to Steinhart that unequivocal control on all levels must stay with the curator, myself. That, I told him was normal procedure, in order to keep continuity and avoid memos or correspondence passing unseen which could impede the exhibitions progress.'

'Good', responded Sue, 'did he get the message?'

'He listened and then told me, in his controlled American way, "Interference can often be productive."

'Ooh,' said Sue, 'right out of the book, how to be successful

without really trying.'
'Anyway, I wasn't in the mood for Steinhart's wit, I wanted answers, and made it patently clear. Then he gave me $500 for Prantl. I recorded it in the expenditure column in my notebook, right under his nose.'
'I have a request for Mr.Steinhart,' Sue said. 'Ask him to tell his London office gigolo to keep out of my knickers. The arse-hole wanted to know if I had blue eyes? I told him, black, and so would his be, if he didn't lay off.'

After she had poured the coffee, she handed me her draft letter for circulation to the museums.
'I don't understand the strategy behind this letter, it doesn't make sense to me.'
'Well Sue, I reckon if the museums do not reveal their inventory records to us and hold back information on works that could have been looted, they'll be looking for a scapegoat to justify themselves. And who better than the curator currently in charge?'
'What's he got to do with activities twenty five years ago?'
'Exactly. If the current curator can't get access to records it's tantamount to concealment.'
'And who's going to put a gun to their heads for an answer?' Sue asked.
'No one, because if they don't reply they'll be open to suspicion and every investigative agency will be on their doorstep. I think you'll need another paragraph.' Sue poised her pen at the ready.
'Just add - a copy of this letter is being sent for distribution to the National Press, Reuters, the International News Service and all the main information agencies. To my thinking, the museums will react.'
I sipped my coffee. 'Any toast? I'm starving.'

Sue went to the kitchen and shouted. 'Marmalade or honey?'
'Why?' I answered 'Is the bread stale?'
'You're so suspicious lately.' came the reply. 'What's happening to you, Katrina?'
'Come on, Sue. It's always stale this or stale that. What's happening to you?' She sat by my desk with a wedge of toast.
'Actually I was constipated and went off my food. When my taste buds came back, everything here tasted foul, so I've been

going to the Olympic bakery every morning. What's left at the end of the day is for the ducks.' I bit into a slice of sesame toast as I read the Tel Aviv file. The phone rang on my desk. Sue answered. 'For you, says it's personal.'

A man's voice asked, 'Is that Katrina Edan?' The voice hesitated. Then in a thick European accent said, 'I hear you are dealing with the Nazis. I am phoning to warn you. God invented man, the devil, and the German.'

'Who's speaking?' I asked . . . 'Who's speaking?' I asked again.

'That's not important, you are collaborating with an Austrian criminal. Just stop, Miss Edan, stop.' The line went dead.

I sat back in my chair and looked blankly at Sue She had a pen in her mouth and was holding the draft she was working on. 'You caught me in the middle of a great para!'

'Sue. I've just been accused of collaborating with the Nazis.'

'You're kidding?'

'No. The personal call was an anonymous diatribe.'

'Did he name anyone?'

'No, but if he rings again, put him through.' Sue gave the thumbs up sign. 'That all?' she said, as if being accused of being a traitor had no significance.

Sorting through the accumulated letters on my desk, an intriguing envelope, written by hand, caught my eye. It was post-marked Swiss Cottage London NW3. I remember the name well, as my mother told my father, during the latter part of the war "one needs a passport to cross Swiss Cottage."

I didn't really understand why, nor did I ask. I thought - what a quaint name. One day I'll see that cottage. The passport I later discovered was a derogatory expression alluding to the number of Jewish refugees resident in Swiss Cottage and the Cottage itself was a run down pub on an island between two main roads. I opened the envelope. This was the transcript.

Dear Miss Edan,

My name is Ester Rosenbaum. I was born in Vienna in 1928 and I came to England in 1939. Unknown to me, my Mother had lined my attaché case with linen to protect my clothes from getting damp. On arrival in England, I was sent to a family in Bristol named Ann and Derek Granger. When they unpacked my clothes they removed the linen lining and found a painting on the reverse side. I remembered the picture. It hung in our living room. In fact Miss Edan, it always made me laugh, and my brother and I giggled at the man with a starched moustache and prissy lace collar. He also looked drunk, red in the face. People always look silly when they are drunk. I am writing my recollections, as they might be useful to you.

The handwriting was neat and carefully set on the page. The letter continued.

Mrs. Granger said she would iron the linen but I never saw it again until 1947, when I queued for three hours to see the first exhibition after the war at the National Gallery. In the room showing Dutch paintings was the picture from our living room wall. It was framed in dark wood with a plaque under the picture: Franz Hals 1580-1666. Portrait of a Gentleman.

A long time has elapsed. I have no records and I lost contact with the Grangers. I still go to the National Gallery to see my picture. I call it mine, although it belonged to my parents. They both died in Auschwitz. Ester Rosenbaum.

I looked at the wall clock Sue had installed in my office. A huge white knell stared down at me, unforgiving, ticking forward relentlessly.

***

Exactly as I had expected, the mystery caller rang again a week later. This time I was prepared. Before he had time to speak I said. 'Whatever you tell me on the phone I'll reject as personal recrimination. If you want me to take anything you have to say seriously, then tell me to my face.' I could hear papers being shuffled in the background before he spoke.
'There's nothing I can tell you personally that is different from what I can tell you now.'
'Then show me something,' I replied. 'Anything. I won't be party to wild anonymous accusations.' Before ending the call, I said, 'my work will continue regardless of any malicious interference. As far as I'm concerned, this conversation never took place.'

I was about to hang up when he said.
'The Cosmo Restaurant in Swiss Cottage. I'll be there at four fifteen. I know what you look like.'
I didn't question him but hastened on.
'Your name please, I must know who I'm meeting.'
'Daniel Lerhmann' he said.

***

When a café, becomes an institution it's unusual, especially in conservative Britain where tea is taken 'at home.' But the Cosmo was different. Its popularity grew because it was close to the office for rehabilitating refugees. It became a hub: men sipping lemon tea, drinking coffee, and trying to salvage memories and create a semblance of café society.

From outside it resembled a double fronted workman's caff. Yellowing net curtains covered windows misted by condensation. Inside the image changed. It was crowded with people in small groups speaking German, Hungarian, Czech, Polish: raising their voices and gesticulating to make their point-of-view heard. Cigar smoke clouded the vaporous atmosphere. Through the haze I saw a man sitting on a green banquette against the wall, waving a newspaper.
'I am Daniel Lerhmann' he said as I stood by the table. He wore a crumpled suit with leather patches on the sleeves that seemed to weigh him down. A bald avenue parted dark bushy patches of hair, involuntarily moving in all directions. Steel rimmed glasses perched at an angle on the end of his nose.

I said. 'Thank you for coming to meet me, Mr.Lerhmann.' We ordered coffee, which came accompanied by a small glass of water, another relic of nostalgia from Vienna, where water is considered the city's nectar.

Before Lerhmann spoke, in good English with a strong European accent, he put a newspaper cutting in front of me. It was a copy of Die Presse, dated 1945. Beneath the headline was a large photograph of Professor Wilhelm Frohmann. I looked at Lerhmann. 'Would you translate for me?'
The paper was flat on the table as he moved his fingers nervously across the lines. 'I'll read the headline,' he said.

Professor Wilhelm Frohmann indicted for war crimes.

He looked at me over his glasses.

He is charged with grand larceny, denial of human rights and collusion.'

I was looking at the newspaper waiting for him to continue, when Lerhmann put it down. 'Would you like me to read on?'

'Of course,' I replied,

He has also been charged with exporting stolen paintings to South America, looting, colluding in barter, and theft from the collections owned by the Barons Louis and Alphonse Rothschild.'

Daniel Lerhmann stopped reading. 'I have more evidence Miss Edan,' He pointed to the newspapers on the table 'This, and this, and this,' his forefinger stabbing at the photographs of Frohmann. 'He's a convicted war criminal - living on stolen money from stolen lives.' I didn't interrupt. 'He should be hanged like his running mates Ernst Kaltenbrunner and Alfred Rosenberg. Yes, Miss, he ran with the vermin and survived. Don't be taken in by him. He can charm the hind legs off a donkey.' This, I already knew.

'Mr.Lerhmann, I would just like to say that I am trying to redress the balance. If I have to lie down with the devil to achieve this exhibition, that's what I'll do.'

Lerhmann said, 'and Wilhelm Frohmann will look like a saint for helping you find stolen works of art?'

I sat silently for a moment, searching my thoughts for clarification of my actions.

'Mr.Lerhmann,' I said, 'I am not my brother's keeper. If there is any retribution to come it won't come from me. But I believe it will come.'

His face was white and strained. He put another newspaper in front of me. 'And this, how will you justify this?' I looked at the headline from an American newspaper.

"The bell tolls for Wilhelm Frohmann - Austrian Art Thief. Hundreds of looted paintings have been removed from his home in the Vienna Woods. As the confidant and private adviser to Hermann Goering he has acquired a cache estimated to be worth millions."

I looked at the date of the newspaper: November 4 1946.

'What do you really want to tell me, Mr.Lerhmann? I know Frohmann was a Nazi. They were all Nazis. That's why I'm working with them. As far as they were concerned they'd committed no crimes: they were always "doing their duty" following their leader, Adolf Hitler. This was not a crime. Outside of Austria, Frohmann has no celebrity. But his countrymen need idols and who better than Goering's art supremo. It's painful, I'll admit. But my aim is for restitution of looted art, and Professor Wilhelm Frohmann is a specialist.'

Lerhmann was rolling the edge of a newspaper, winding it round and round, trapping the words.

'If you recognise any works in the forthcoming exhibition, belonging to you or members of your family, I shall do everything I can to help you reclaim your property.'

His head was bowed when he said, 'Family, I have no family, they were murdered by men like Frohmann, members of the SS, after being forced with many other Jews to scrub the streets of Vienna with tooth brushes.'

There was anger in his voice. He said. 'Miss Edan, they laughed. The Viennese watched and laughed until the drunken soldiers were given the instruction to shoot. My parents were on their knees. I watched. I was five.'

I was not yet acclimatized to horror and every story I heard I stored, making me more determined to accelerate my attempts for restitution, when justice had clearly failed.

It was five thirty. I phoned Sue from a call box at Swiss Cottage and asked her to ring Anton Hempf.

'I want to see him to-night. Try Sue. It's important.'

Sue had waited for my return. 'I spoke to Dr. Hempf but he's lecturing tonight at Senate House. He can see you to-morrow.'

'What time?' 'Two' she replied, 'I've checked the diary it's OK. You look bushed. Did Lerhmann work you over?'

'Not exactly. Let's go to the pub, I'll tell you the whole story.'

The following morning I was at the office by eight. The telephone was ringing. By the time I had unlocked the door and picked up the receiver it went dead. Within minutes it rang again. It was Jack Steinhart.

'Katrina, I'm in London for a meeting. How are you? Keeping the pack at bay I hope?'

I was surprised to hear Jack's voice. He could have called and told me he would be in London, that he'd like to see me, even missed me. But he hadn't. In fact his voice sounded brusque.

'I need an update on your expenditure including who's received money in Austria: I'd like to collect it later. Are you free?'
'Hold on. Why do you want an estimate so soon? I've hardly started.'
'Right, but Chicago picks up the tabs. They want to know what for.'
I was meeting Anton at two, so I arranged to meet Jack at five.
'Could you come to my office? It's off Camden High Street. The cab driver will know. One end of the street is the fruit market, the other end, a row of houses. Mine is the Georgian house on the left, with the large bay window. I'm on the first floor.'

When Sue arrived around nine I told her what I thought of the Americans. 'Harassment' I said 'bloody nitpickers. I've only spent a couple of thousand dollars. What'll happen when I spend fifty thousand? They'll arm the statue of liberty - ho, ho ho, the Brits are on the rampage!'
'Lovely morning,' Sue informed me. 'I'll just take my coat off and I'll come and soothe your ego.'

Together we opened the post. Sue was sitting opposite me and slowly my desk became covered in correspondence. She shifted the letters into piles titled: Now, Later, Not-At-All. Then I opened a letter from the National Gallery in London. I turned to Sue. 'Listen to this.'

> **Dear Miss Edan,**
> **The Governors at their quarterly meeting have agreed in principle to pursue the purchase of the Gustav Klimt painting of Hermine Gallia for the National collection. Would you please phone for an appointment so we can discuss the details?**
> **Yours sincerely,**
> **Elizabeth Cuthbertson.**

'Great,' I said, banging my clenched fist on the desk 'I've got him - got him.'

Sue leant back in her chair and rested her hand on her chin. 'I've come to barmy park this morning. First you scupper the Yanks, now some mystery man's been "got". Could you explain or shall I call for a man in a white coat?'

'Sorry, Sue. Just thinking aloud. It's nothing really, just swinging from despair to elation. I'm a little off balance this morning.'

She took the letters from my desk and said as she was leaving. 'I'll call the National Gallery. Anytime you can't make?'

'Yes, 'I replied. 'Five this evening, Jack Steinhart's coming here. Don't leave early.'

LONDON

16

The weather is a constant guessing game in Britain, played by everyone. We greet each other with the news, A Nice Day, Good to see the Sun, or Terrible Weather, isn't it? Optimism is rare after years of irregular patterns, and inaccurate forecasts have turned us into a country of weather whiners. The most reliable source is a piece of seaweed nailed to an outside post and stroked daily for moisture. The meteorological office totally dismisses this analysis as folklore, but the British, being addicted to quaint superstitions unrelated to reason or evidence, believe in historical hearsay.

With this in mind I crossed the park to Anton Hempf's house. On route I tipped a bag of stale bread into the lake and disappointed hungry squawking ducks as they tussled with the hard crusts. I felt cruel. An elderly lady in a beige velvet beret, her face evenly powdered, said, "Isn't it a nice day to-day?"

'Lovely,' I replied,

"Let's hope it lasts," she said.

June is the precarious month of hope when I rush out and buy some ridiculously scant dress, and freeze every time I wear it. But sometimes it is essential to pretend it is summer, otherwise it will never happen. I was apprehensive about meeting Anton because I wanted answers. I wanted to know how he had escaped to England. I wanted to know why Wilhelm Frohmann had become the advisor to Goering and more importantly the details of Frohmann's trial. While I didn't doubt what I had heard was true, I needed clarification.

Anton as always was welcoming. He suggested we sit on the terrace in the warm sun overlooking the lawn. I slipped my suit jacket onto the back of the chair, and put a note pad and pen on the table.

'Is this an interview?' Anton asked.

'I'm afraid so, Anton, because some facts are unclear to me.'

'All right, young lady, fire away.' I told him about my meeting with Daniel Lerhmann and the newspapers I had seen.

'What I want to know is how did Frohmann become involved with the hierarchy in the Nazi party?'

'Katrina, he told you that his final dissertation at the University was on Franz von Stuck.'
'That's right - but what happened after he left the University?'
'Well, he taught for about eighteen months, then he was called to the office of Dr Ernst Kaltenbrunner, the head of the Gestapo and Security Services in Austria.'

Anton removed his jacket and placed it on a spare chair by the table. 'I'll ask Eva, my housekeeper, to make some fresh lemonade.' Anton left the table and I made a few hurried notes. He returned, moved his chair out of the sun and sat silently as if to re-access his thinking.

'There's not much more I can tell you, except that in 1938, the year Wilhelm graduated, the dissertation he presented was on the favourite painter of Adolf Hitler.'
'You mean Frohmann had the same taste in art as Hitler?'
'Certainly not. He wrote on von Stuck just to keep Kubin, his tutor, happy. Anyway, Goering made it clear to Kaltenbrunner at the graduation that he should keep an eye on this young art graduate and find something more in keeping with his talent.'
'So he became Goering's procurer?' I added.
'That's right.'
'So why was he accused of war crimes, Anton?'
'Because he was guilty. Guilty of theft and selling looted art at high prices to fill the coffers of the Third Reich.'

Eva put a jug of lemonade and chocolate biscuits on the table.
'Anton,' I said, pointing to the biscuits 'they'll melt in the sun.'
'Not if we eat them, my dear.'

The aggression I felt when I arrived at Anton's home lessened, and I felt calm enough to press for more intimate details of his past. Also, he liked me. Not that he had said so, I just felt it: he respected my forthright approach and had once said "there's an imaginary fire around red-heads, a little too hot to handle!"

I picked up my notebook and turned the pages back. They were clammy from the heat so I dipped my finger in the lemonade to separate them. 'Terrible waste of juice,' I said, as I licked my finger, but I found the page I wanted.

Anton spoke slowly. 'Frohmann was tried by an International War Crimes Commission and sentenced to three years in prison. His private art collection was confiscated and bank accounts

closed. He was stripped of the title Professor which he was given gratuitously by Goering.'
'That doesn't make sense to me. Both his homes are awash with treasures and he is still Professor.'
'There's a simple answer,' Anton said, 'because when the British and American investigators left, the hidden loot emerged.'
'And the titles, Anton, what about those?'
'They emerged too. So I suggest you look suspiciously at privately owned paintings, they could be works sequestered by the Nazis.' . . . You,' he said - pointing a finger - 'may have one last question.'
'I'll be brief. I know from Anna you were on the last Kindertransport train coming to England, and I know it was stopped at the Dutch border when war was declared in 1939 and children on that train, returned to Vienna. My question is, how did you escape?' Anton undid his tie and pulled his chair close to the table. He spoke quietly, levelling his eyes at me.
'The train journey back was gruelling: we had no food, it was cold and the children couldn't understand what was happening to them. When we arrived at the Westbahnhof in Vienna, volunteers collected the children, as almost all were orphans. I had no money, my home had been ransacked, and I had to survive somehow . . . Just a moment Katrina.'

He left the table and walked to a rose bush, studied the blooms before taking a small penknife from his waistcoat pocket to cut a stem. He put the yellow pink-rimmed bud on the table.
'Such a comforting flower,' he said. 'This one's named Peace.'

A light breeze blew floral scent towards us from the garden and the single rose became resplendent in its isolation. Anton said. 'You were asking how I came here. Well - I had two choices in Vienna, escape or die. I had no money and nothing to barter and nowhere to go. I waited outside the University until I saw Wilhelm. I told him what had happened at the Dutch border. He didn't know how he could protect me, as it was a criminal offence to harbour a Jew. We tramped the streets until he decided the only solution was to hide me in the cellar of the university library.'
'How long were you there?'

'Three months, but it seemed like three years. I saw Wilhelm every day when he brought my daily rations.' Anton picked up a biscuit; an involuntary movement triggered no doubt by a lingering reminder of hunger.

'Sometimes,' Anton continued 'Wilhelm would stay and talk about what was happening in the city and how Jews had been taken to work camps to help the war effort. Wilhelm told me he did not trust Otto Prantl and he was suspicious Prantl might inform the Gestapo if he knew where I was hiding. One day Wilhelm didn't come to the cellar. I was cold and hungry. There was a small grill, which let daylight in, but the nights were long, and I had to talk to myself to remain sane. My memory of pictures sustained me. I wandered into a Millet painting with corn shivering in the breeze. I sat with Titian while he painted the eighty-year-old Pope Paul lll. I felt the soft velvet resting on the Pope's shoulders: watched Titian's brush, soaked in paint, become a long grey woolly beard, while the sly, penetrating eyes of Alexander Farnese looked out of the canvas at me. But, it was Titian whom I remembered. He subjugated the power vested in the Pope by the power of his own genius. That power also sustained me.

I picnicked with Giorgione at the Concert Champêtre, joining his erotic juxtaposition of naked women and clothed men; I compared Manet's pastiche, "Déjeuner sur l'herbe."

I grew old with Rembrandt.

Anton was tiring, his shoulders rounding as he put his arms on the table for support.

'Three months ' he sighed, 'that's how long it took Wilhelm to save enough money to buy me a forged passport. I was scared he had abandoned me but after four days he came to the cellar: gave me a bratwurst and some bread and told me I would have to leave that night or it would be too late. He handed me a wallet. Inside were a passport, false work papers from IG Farben and 50 marks. I couldn't see him clearly but his voice was breaking as he put his arms around me and said, 'God be with you, my friend.'

When I arrived in my office, Jack was waiting. Sue had kept the door open so she could observe him and make sure his fingers stayed in his pockets.

'Mr. Moneybags is in your office complete with the Wall Street journal, and Desmond Hegarty wants you to have dinner tonight.'
'What did you tell Desmond?' I asked.
'Nothing. Just said I didn't know your plans.' She'd obviously scrutinized Jack's appearance and concluded he'd qualify for dinner - at least.

Jack rose as I entered my office. I slammed the door behind me, took off my jacket and sat at my desk opposite him.
'I believe you want some figures Jack, for Chicago's accounts department?'
'Hang on a minute. Give me time to say hello.'

He was about to move across to my side of the desk when I picked up a file and threw it across the desk.
'So Chicago wants an update. Well, there it is. It's the contract we agreed in Austria.' Jack picked up the file.
'Read it, and then you can remind Chicago that I made no agreement to produce petty accounting at the whim of your office. It clearly states that a full expense account will be produced and sent to all sponsors half-yearly. I shall not default on that agreement.'

Jack was sweeping his eyes all over me, calmly digesting the attack. I waited for a response inaugurating me into the principles of banking - American style. It would have fallen on deaf ears. He sensed it - and said nothing. Instead he asked 'How is the search coming along?'
'O.K. I replied, I expect a consignment in the next few weeks.'
'Do you know where from?'
'Yes, Russia.'
'Any chance of a drink, Katrina, I've been on the move since six this morning, I could do with a pick-up.'

I opened the wall cabinet Sue had installed during her rampant transformation of my office. Whiskey, Red or Black label, Smirnoff and Gordon's. Not a fruit juice in sight. Trust Sue.
'What would you like?' I asked.
'Scotch on the rocks, please. I hope you're joining me?'

I put two glasses on the desk, called Sue on the intercom and asked for a bowl of ice. Jack tipped his glass from side to side,

watching the ice cubes melt the amber liquor before taking a hefty swig.
'Who's your Russian contact. Can you trust him?'
'No. Absolutely not. It's Gerhard Hofer.'
'Have you seen any of the paintings?'
'Yes, the horde in Grinzing: definitely from a mine because I could smell the coal dust.'
'How's he getting them through the Iron Curtain?'
'I can only tell you what Frohmann told me. It could be lies, but he has a series of couriers who bribe the border guards. The whole operation seems well organized.'
Jack looked concerned. 'Be careful, Katrina. He's a user. He's motivated by money and revenge, in that order.'
'I know, I've already worked that out. But how do you know?'
'I've had dealings with him through Frohmann. He'll use you for cover to get the paintings to the West hoping to sell them.'
'He could lose the lot if they're claimed.'
'Not from the dead, Katrina, and the Russians won't claim them because they stole them from the Germans and the Germans won't claim because they stole them from the Jews. That leaves a free run for Hofer. Has he asked you for money?'
'Only 5000 dollars for transportation and a 10,000 dollar deposit for the Klimt painting the National Gallery is purchasing.'
'Congratulations, who's paying your commission?'
'Gerhard Hofer,' I said. Jack's face relapsed with a look of quizzical disbelief.
'Oh, I'll get my 1%.' I said. 'I'll deduct it from the half million the National are paying.'
Sue called on the inter-com. 'Desmond Hegarty's on the line. Can I put him through?'
'Yes, Desmond', I said, holding my pen in my hand while listening. I wrote The White Elephant eight thirty.

There was a silent space between Jack and me. Pride would not allow my emotions to be tampered with in an off-hand desultory way. If there was to be any mutual respect, now was a good time to set the parameter.

***

The entrance to the White Elephant was lit by one dramatic chandelier: shadows sprayed the dark green velvet walls and double engraved glass doors led into the bar and restaurant.

Desmond was perched on a stool, holding a cut crystal glass of champagne.

'You look stunning, love,' he said, and planted a warm kiss on my cheek. 'You should always wear red silk, it makes you look divinely mysteriously innocent and devilishly seductive.' He held his glass up, 'Champagne?'

The White Elephant is an exclusive club for celebrities and successful businessmen. Desmond is an exception: never suited and tied in the stereotyped uniform of an architect. He flaunts a nonchalant disrespect for convention that makes his presence both noticeable and questionable. Maybe he's an actor - resting, a titled Lord of some unknown patch of English countryside, a sophisticated crook!

'Do you like my purple waistcoat, Katrina?'

I hadn't really noticed it in particular, more the overall pattern of his appearance. I looked more closely. The waistcoat was partly obscured by a black silk Raj jacket and a white silk collarless shirt. His light brown hair dropped across his brow as he looked down at his attire for my approval. An almighty scream escaped from me and I laughed too loudly. Heads turned in our direction. Earrings swung from the lobes of sedately dressed women and their starched husbands pretended not to hear. I calmed to a giggle.

'I expected you to pluck the ace of spades from your inside pocket and turn it into a frog. Please, Desmond, make a frog.'

'You're mocking me, Katrina. All I want to know is if you like my waistcoat?'

'Sorry Desmond, I had to laugh. You're so serious. It's a beautiful waistcoat.' I whispered in his ear, 'it makes everyone here look absolutely dull!'

We sipped our drinks as the bar started to fill. The headwaiter handed us two menus. Mine was the one without the prices. It's that sort of club. Never creates a gold digger from a woman with a healthy appetite.

'You can order anything' Desmond said, 'Just got a fat cheque from the Arts Council AND a new commission. Guess what?' There was a supercilious grin across his face.
'Can't,' I replied, 'I'm hungry. You'll have to tell me later.'

We were shown to a table for two. The waiter held a deep red velvet chair back and I sank into the space like a nesting swan, comfortably enveloped for the evening. Lord Denning, master of the Rolls, sat with three admonishers of his trade, Laurence Olivier was there and so was Kenneth Tynan.

After I had eaten some king prawns in garlic mayonnaise and Desmond had devoured a half-a-dozen oysters, I was ready to talk.
'So tell me?' I said, licking my lips and looking approvingly at Desmond, 'what's your new commission?'

He swished his fingers in the finger bowl, wiped them on the starched napkin, took my hand and said. 'You won't believe this. I'm going to build a new grand stand for Brands Hatch and I know fuck all about motor racing, and less than fuck all about bikes.'
'I can guess why they commissioned you. It's because of all those people you funnelled up and down at the Festival Hall. You're a mass transit architect.' Realizing what I had said, a cold shiver ran down my spine, when an involuntary thought crept uncontrolled into my thinking, of train wagons rolling into the concentration camps and the cargo they trapped for servicing the gas chambers. The blood had drained from my face. Desmond raised an eyebrow, concerned by my lapse of attention.
'Are you alright, Katrina, you're very pale?'
'Sorry, my mind wandered. Tell me more about your new commission?'
'Have you ever seen motor racing, Katrina? It's a laugh. Thousands of heads darting from side to side like puppets, as the cars flash past. Seconds later, they're gone.'
'Can't wait to see the model,' I said, 'Are you going to have revolving seats? It would save a lot of neck strain. You should fit every seat with a periscope and angled mirrors so no one moves.'
'Katrina, you've just got me sacked. How's the Art business?'

'Art is not business, Desmond, at least my branch isn't. Anyway most businessmen don't know or care about it. '

I gave him an up-date on my activities without mentioning the name of Jack Steinhart.

'Did I ever tell you Desmond about the meeting I attended, when twenty captains of industry sat around a lunch table boasting about their financial triumphs? One chap said complacently that his company had laid a two thousand mile pipeline across the Saudi desert, costing a million pounds. That's £10 a foot. Guess what I said?'

'Tell me?' Desmond asked

'Well, I told them that a Van Gogh painting of sun flowers had just fetched forty nine million pounds, and that worked out at £56.000 a square inch.'

'You kidding?'

'No. God's honour. Sad thing is I don't know if they knew who Van Gogh was?'

Desmond and I became steadily drunk. We chatted inarticulately on the progress of world power, when the Iron Curtain would fall, the antics of Nikita Khrushchev, and the danger of Brezhnev and Kosygin's policy on China. We planned to assassinate the prime minister, Edward Heath, concluding he was less than useless, responsible for inflation, imposing direct rule of Northern Ireland from London, and the most heinous of all - strikes. And anyway why should the Americans have a monopoly on bumping off Presidents? Mostly, we forgot about anything outside the walls that confined us, and revelled in each other's wild and fanciful dreams.

***

Elizabeth Cuthbertson didn't waste time. She made it clear at our meeting at the National Gallery that the purchase of Gustav Klimt's painting of Hermine Gallia would be over a period of three years.

'You see, Miss Edan, we can't raise half a million pounds at once, we must wait for donations.' She took a buff folder from her desk and handed it to me. 'That is the list of patrons. The trustees have notified them of the importance of the painting for the nation, we are waiting for a response.'

She left very little room for comment but there wasn't much for me to add anyway, except to agree that the painting would be included in my exhibition with a green NFS - not for sale sticker on its label.

'I see absolutely no reason why that can't be agreed. One other point' she said. 'Payment will only be authorized when the picture arrives here.'

I was a little puzzled by this. 'Is there any doubt about its authenticity?'

'None whatsoever. Normally I would look at any prospective purchase myself, but one of our directors knows Dr.Hempf and discussed the painting with him.' We shook hands. The rest was paperwork.

ISRAEL

17

Perched on a sand dune, wild flowers sprouted yellow heads, nodding in the sea breeze as a warm wind blew. This thriving plant called 'chicken fingers' spreads in masses along the dunes between the Mediterranean Sea and the coastline. Through the glass window of the shanty café, with its tin roof rusted by wind and salt water, I watched as a lone diver emerged from the sea, a black rubberised figure lifting his fins slowly, an amphibian predator, edging towards the beach where a dark line of seaweed fringed the shoreline. Dappled lights reflected in the calm water as I paused, sipped my coffee and cast my mind back. Four thousand years have passed since the bible records that it was here, in Jaffa that Jonah emerged after his encounter with the whale. Here, according to Greek mythology, Andromeda was chained to a rock, then rescued by Perseus. Here Richard the Lion Heart and Napoleon passed with their legions, and here St.Peter was born. I felt the history burning under my feet, in this place set apart from all others.

I looked towards the Citadel, the monument in the Holy Land for pilgrims who came over the centuries from east and west, seeking shelter on their way to Jerusalem: a sanctuary en route to the promised land, now a derelict shamble of ruins, raided and pillaged by invading armies, a monument of culpable neglect for its historic past.

Behind the seashore, hugging the sides of narrow sand and cobblestone alleyways was a tangle of crumbling concrete hovels covered by corrugated tin roofs. The smell of herbs and oriental spices clung to the air, and the muezzin called the Muslims to prayer. Open bread ovens were being dowsed and Arabs moved swiftly along the streets, their white robes billowing in the evening breeze as the light started to fade. A lone rider, a ragged boy on a saddle-less horse moved past, a static toothy grin, proud in a dirty dark brown skin. He was a King, elevated. He was the past, the present and the future. I watched as the King rode slowly away, and the horse's hoofs shifted the desert sand, as the blood red sun melted slowly over the horizon, sinking into the sea bringing blackness over the old port of Jaffa.

***

My hotel, the Sheraton Tel Aviv was a tall building elevated on a high dune, an isolated mass of grey concrete and stone, an incongruous invasion on a skyline unchanged in thousands of years. With a small map in my hand I decided to walk to the museum for my meeting with the director, Dr. Chaim Levine.

The main street - Dizengoff Street was near my hotel and named after the first mayor of Tel Aviv. The shops were dismal, stocking cheap unfashionable clothing, mass produced jewellery, stalls with a variety of local nuts, seeds and dried fruits and pavement cafés totally devoid of any aesthetic appeal. A young man was frying falafel on an open stove; the sizzling fat fumes swirled around in the hot air. He deftly filled pitta bread pockets with the nutty chickpea balls he had fried, then dolloped chopped onions, tomatoes, peppers and cucumbers on top. Within seconds it was in paper, into a waiting hand, and he started again.

In 1932 Tel Aviv was a village. It was a strange place, a point where the desert meets the sea, yet: even then, it had two theatres, an opera, a library and eventually a museum on Rothschild Boulevard in the home of Meir Dizengoff. Slowly, donations of art were elicited to start a collection. One of the first paintings came from Marc Chagall. With time, many more followed, including complete collections from families in Israel and abroad. Dizengoff's "lesser temple" became a focus of awareness for the muses to explore all aspects of creative expression.

Eventually I found King Saul Boulevard, a wide street fringed by palm trees, an oasis of calm. The museum was perched on stilts, a very modern concept in white concrete and stone.

As I entered, a security guard watched me carefully as I took an introduction card from my bag. I was shown to a small first floor office. It was a modest working room with an architectural model of the museum displayed on a table. Art books and catalogues lined the walls and one painting by Chaim Soutine hung behind the director's chair. I moved close to look at the thick impasto paint piled on in layers so thick, I had to step back to get the paint into perspective, and then, what had been indistinct in close-up became realistic at a distance. A blob of red paint became a deep cut in a chicken's neck: cobalt blue revealed the gut and white over cadmium evoked a rotting smelling skin.

Why, I have been asked, do artists paint such horrendous images when there is so much beauty in the world? For me this is innovation, another kind of beauty, and deserved attention: I was compelled to compare a dead rabbit hanging by its neck, or a speared falling horse, romanticized in the eighteeth century, with the same subject painted in the twentieth. Both had the guts gouged from the animal, but one is painted meticulously with a sable brush, every hair separate, so the animal is so ennobled, death was incidental. Not so with Soutine's chicken. His carcass smelt. Its bloody crusty paint scraped on with a palette knife was fused together with violent action. It spoke to me. It told me about the artist: his torment, his hunger, his abandon, and his dedication to the medium, not the subject. This is tomorrow's history. I was still looking at the painting when a small man wearing beige cotton trousers, a white short-sleeved shirt came into the office. 'Miss Edan' he said offering me his hand, 'Chaim Levine. I am sorry I kept you waiting: I had to over-see a large piece of sculpture safely into the building. We had some difficulty with the pulleys. Now, it's in place, I can relax.'

I had tried to imagine what he would look like from his telephone voice, but he was different in every way. Firstly, he was only about 5'5", smaller than I had thought, slim and lithe, his actions quick and jerky, as if they were trying to keep pace with his mind. He was informal, had a cherubic smile that made me feel at ease immediately. Unlike most high achievers he looked unaffected by success. In creating a world-class museum he had earned the respect of curators worldwide, and far from being arrogant, which I had been told was a national characteristic, he was quietly spoken but very direct.

'I have read your proposal' he said, 'and I think the concept is admirable: it's also pertinent to many Israeli citizens and as much as I would like to endorse the exhibition with sponsorship,

it is impossible.' He spoke with authority without being dismissive. A frown furrowed his brow as he thought silently.
'I am sorry, I could not persuade the Mitzvah bank to loan any money, but perhaps I could help you indirectly,' he volunteered. 'You know we have many survivors from the holocaust living here: I suggest I write an open letter to our two leading newspapers, Yediot and Ma'ariv about your planned exhibition.'

I was disappointed that he was offering nothing more than advertising, something I could easily handle. He was writing notes on his desk pad, lifting his pen slowly between words. 'How about something like this?' He handed me the paper.

"ENGLISH CURATOR SCANS EUROPE FOR STOLEN ART TREASURES"

'That could be the headline.' he said, 'Followed by a request for survivors to write with any information of paintings looted during the Nazi regime. Then details of how to make a claim.'
'Who will pay for the advertisement, Dr.Levine?'
'I would expect the papers to donate the space and collate all correspondence or enquiries. I could arrange for translations to be made for you, so everything will be forwarded in English.'
'That would be an excellent start' I said.
'Miss Edan, I should like to make a suggestion. If a painting remains unclaimed after your exhibition and the sponsors do not purchase the work, could I make a sealed bid?' It was obvious to me that I was talking to a shrewd negotiator. The Tel Aviv Museum is proof of his power of persuasion and the network he had created. He could and no doubt would target every Jewish director on the boards of the sponsoring banks, letting them know of his interest in orphan works. After all, the paintings were stolen property from Diaspora Jews. So, to hang them in the Holy Land, where pilgrims of all denominations could view them, would be a fitting testimony to justice.

'This museum' he added 'is visited by thousands of people who experienced the horrors of death camps. What they endured and survived is indelible, but it is diminished in front of great works of art.' I could not argue with his reasoning.

Like everyone else, I was impressed, not by his audacity more by his feelings for his country, and for art. 'Would you like to see the museum?' he asked. He called on his inter-com. 'I have asked my assistant Miriam to take you round. She knows the collection well, and I am sure you'll recognize some of the pieces because you have had them on loan.' There was a kindly smile on his face and a hint of pride, well deserved and hard earned.

'When you've finished the tour, maybe you'd like a little lunch. It will be little' he said, 'because, unlike the rest of the Middle East, we don't have a four hour siesta. We work right through.'

'Now I know how the falafel became a national dish' I said. 'It's quick.'

'Miss Edan, I am afraid we Israelis are in a hurry. We have a lot of catching up to do.'

The collection was an eclectic mix of paintings and sculptures by famous Israelis and Europeans: Lipchitz, Leonid Pasternak, Mane-Katz, Reuven Rubin, Menashe Kadishman, Marcel Janco and Chagall, Henry Moore and Mark Rothco. It takes a long time before I get visual indigestion and no way had I reached my capacity for looking when Miriam said it was time to meet the Director for lunch.

Dr.Levine suggested a small local restaurant in Leonardo da Vinci Street where I could sample a local Yemeni speciality. We left King Saul Boulevard and walked to the narrow street where restaurants spilled onto the pavement and sat at an outside table in the shade of a Jacaranda tree: the temperature must have been over 90F and the bustle that I'd seen in Jaffa at dusk was a sharp contrast to the stillness here at this time of day. 'I suggest we order the Mlawah. It is a fried dough covered in Zhoug.'

'By what?' It sounded like crusting cement.

'It's chilli paste with parsley and coriander,' he translated. 'What would you like to drink?'

'What do you usually have?'

'Water', he said 'but the beer's good, especially Maccabi.' I chose the beer. While we were waiting for our order he asked after Dr.Hempf.

'Is he well? Has he finished his book on Van Gogh?' Before I could answer he said. 'You may know I was at the Academy in Vienna with him in 1936?' This was a totally unexpected revelation.

'No, I didn't know, he never told me. How long were you there?'
'Two years. Then I went to Paris.' Levine said.
'So you must know Wilhelm Frohmann?'
'And Otto Prantl and Gerhard Hofer' he added. 'They wrote the magazine "revolt".'

It had not occurred to me that Chaim Levine had been educated in Central Europe. He ate quickly and said little while he was busy doing so. When he rested his knife and fork, he wiped his brow with his paper napkin, 'It's very hot to-day, I think we will get a khamsin later. That's a hot wind that comes from the desert and covers everything with sand.'
'Dr.Levine, how much has Anton Hempf told you about my progress so far? I assume you know he's giving me contacts in Austria?'
'Yes. Anton keeps me fully informed on anything which might be of interest here and fortunately much more.'
'What exactly do you mean?'
'Miss Edan, I've known about your activities since you first approached Samuel Hall and Rothschild for money. I was actually asked about your suitability to carry such a challenging project as I had loaned paintings for exhibitions you had curated.'

Dr.Levine looked at his watch. 'My goodness, nearly an hour has gone.' On the way back to the museum he explained the changes in architecture from ramshackle to modern box only as "a means to an end."
'One day we'll afford more elegant and challenging designs. It will come' he said, 'it's only a question of time?'

As we entered his office Miriam said there had been a telephone call for me. I had not expected London to call within one day. Dr.Levine smiled and handed me a note with a telephone number. 'That's in Tel Aviv' he said.
'But I don't know anyone here except you,' I replied.

Miriam took me to her office and I phoned the number. A switchboard operator answered it. 'American Embassy, can I help you?'
'Extension 402 please.' I asked
'Brooks,' a voice answered.
'This is Katrina Edan, you left this number at the Museum.'

'That's right, Elgin Brooks, I'm a friend of Jack Steinhart, he asked me to call you.'

'Why?' I asked suspiciously. 'Oh, he just thought you might need a little company as you'd not been here before. We wondered if you'd like to join us for dinner tonight?'

'And who are us?' I asked. He caught my frosty apprehension.

'My wife and I. And we don't eat raw sheep's eyes. We'll collect you from your hotel at eight, if that seems reasonable to you?'

Elgin Brooks wore thick lenses, had a Southern American drawl and wore a white tea shirt with a leaf emblem embroidered on the pocket. Maybe it was a cloverleaf, maybe he was Irish, I didn't ask. I know he was too young to have brown stained teeth but he chain-smoked. He introduced me to his wife, Bunny. I suppose it was short for Barbara or Beatrice - no - she didn't look like a Beatrice. The Americans have a knack with the unusual, like calling a boy Flint, after his great great-grand Daddy, who lit campfires with flintstones.

I envied her bronzed body punctuated by a skimpy sleeveless shift dress, brown arms draped down her sides and long thin legs finished in backless strappy sandals. She was the archetypal cute American blonde, who lived and thrived on men, unlike the founders of American feminism, she had to be kept - well kept - and indulged. HER man was a vehicle for HER success. Match up he must, or she would move on to another fall guy with a bulging chequebook and promises of eternal love.

I felt white and exposed, a naked office dweller dredged from the northern hemisphere. The only resemblance between us was my skimpy mini dress. I felt like a doll on white stilts. I shook my mane of red hair hoping to bring some sense back to my head. Who needs to look half-baked anyway, I concluded. I'm thirty-one years old and pink or white I can still rustle the whistle and the wow, especially in a bikini.

We drove along the coast on a wide stretch of unmade road, it was bumpy, dark and eerie until twinkling electric light bulbs strung on wires waving in the sea breeze, appeared in the distance. The lights were decorating the restaurant, a ramshackle shed in need of urgent repair. Tables with flickering candles were scattered on the bleached white sand. Close by the sea foamed gently. Teasingly near, it lapped its lacy edge forward, and then was sucked back into the parched beach.

We ordered St.Peter's fish, a fresh water fish from Lake Tiberius. It arrived with salad.

'It's not like fish and chips in England' Bunny said.

I smiled, thinking, there's no comparison with that rare delicacy which, wrapped in newspaper or served on Royal Worcester china, lingered in the memory buds of the English traveller and eternally with the expatriate.

Elgin asked 'How are you managing at the museum? Dr. Levine's a pretty forceful guy.'

That remark surprised me and I said so.

'I didn't find him forceful, forthright maybe, but very straightforward. Do you know anything about his background?'

'What do you mean?'

'Where he came from, how long he's been here? Bunny answered. 'I read an article about him in the Jerusalem Post.

Great I thought she actually reads!

'He came from Latvia when he was nine with his parents. His father was a musician and his mother taught in an infants' school.'

'Why did they send him to Austria to study?' She put her knife and fork down, drained her glass and pulled a bone from the fish.

'Many Israelis sent their children to Germany, Austria and of course, England, for higher education. It was considered the best option, if you could afford it. The Jews did the same in the United States: Alfred Steiglitz, who married Georgia O'Keeffe, was sent to Germany to be educated. His parents considered it culturally superior.'

At that point Elgin called the young waitress and asked for another bottle of wine. He was edgy, unable to relax, running his fingers through his mousy hair, and then twisting the packet of Camel cigarettes lying on the table, tweaking at the cellophane wrapping, before lighting another cigarette from the stub of the last. He ate very little before saying.

'You asked if we know more about Chaim Levine. I can only tell you what we've read and what's whispered. He has good connections in the German speaking countries but treats all transactions with lethal scrutiny.' He filled Bunny's glass. 'He's achieved a lot here, and I'm sure he'll be a good ally for your exhibition.'

How much more had Jack told him about my activities, I wondered. Bunny said. 'It must be quite scary working with all those ex-nazis?'

'Cut out the 'ex' honey, there's no such human being as an ex-nazi. I'd say it's more dangerous being near the Iron Curtain. Does it worry you, Miss Edan?'

'So far, no, but I have met a few unsavoury characters.'

'I'm surprised, I thought art was for art's sake, if you know what I mean.' Actually I didn't.

'Where's your next port of call?' he asked.

'Mr.Brooks.' I said.

'Elgin' he replied.

'What is your job at the Embassy?'

'I'm pretty low down the ladder Assistant trade attaché. You see, we're not big here in Israel compared to the U.K. or Paris, but big enough to matter!' I drank some wine, watching the candlelight playing shadows on our table.

'How do you know Jack?' I asked

'We met at Harvard – I liked him, so we kept in contact. He's threatened to visit me - but banking's such a time taker, he's permanently wrapped in dollar bills. No time for friends or fun.'

'I'll report exactly what you've said when I see him.'

Elgin laughed and for once during the evening seemed more relaxed.

'Tell me Katrina, it's O.K. if I call you Katrina?' he said, not waiting for my reply - 'how'd you do with Levine? Get any money?' So Jack had discussed my visit in some detail.

'No, but he'll support me in a different, more active way.'

'What sort of support will he give you?'

'Are you asking on your own behalf or Jack's?'

'Both,' he replied.

'I can tell you off the record Jack won't see you go under for a few extra green backs. He knows a good investment when he sees one.'

Bunny's voice was raised and she spoke with a slight alcoholic slur. 'Come on, Elg, you can't make insinuations like that.'

'Like what? Honey.'
'Like Katrina's an investment. She's arranging an art exhibition not a take over bid.'

I was about to change the subject, but Elgin called for the bill, preventing an on-going argument.

I decided I liked him - her too - and any feeling of jealousy diminished when she took my hand as we walked to the car in the darkness.
'Don't want you to trip on a reed and damage your gorgeous English complexion,' she drawled.

LONDON

18

Typical English weather played havoc with the summer. It was now late August and the central heating was already on. I tucked myself between pink cotton sheets and sneezed my way to September. Crisp sunlight made a brief trellis pattern on the white wall of my bedroom, and then rain clouds swooped and battered against the windows. Autumn was making an early start. I dozed in and out of sleep: my head pounded like a gavel on an auctioneer's lectern.

Bang - bang "five hundred, one thousand, two thousand, two thousand five hundred. Do I see three?" The auctioneer was staring at me, "thank-you madam, I have three thousand, any advance on three thousand?" A voice in the rear of the room said four, another said five then six. Then it was silent. I hesitated, so did the auctioneer. Then he stared at me again. "All finished at six thousand?" His eyes became fireballs, his head like a wolf's. His pointed nose had prickly hairs, his finger a knife's blade, menacing, threatening. In desperation, my voice almost a squeak, I said "seven". His gavel crashed down. "Sold to the lady on the right." He pointed at me, "Yes, you madam." Gloating bastard had forced me to bid thousands more than I had intended. I had bought Lot 132. I looked at the illustration in the catalogue resting on my lap: a full frontal fox leaping out of the canvas, open jawed with blood dripping from its long fanged teeth, and in the background the body of a ravaged maiden, prone in the woods. I bought - THAT!

I woke up screaming; not knowing where I was and heard chimes in the distance. I covered my head with the sheets and slowly moved them back as the chimes grew louder. Hell - it was my front door. I held onto the central pole of the spiral staircase and felt I was in a vortex spinning round. My feet stuck to the mahogany treads as sweat dripped from my exhausted body.

'Good Lord,' Sue said 'shall I call an ambulance?'

'Don't joke please, I feel lousy.'

'I guessed that, so I've brought you some oranges, lots of vitamin C, some throat sweets, a packet of Disprin, a box of paper

tissues and in case you're hungry some porridge oats and milk.'
'Yuk' I said.

I clawed myself back upstairs while Sue made some tea. I was wearing satin pyjamas, which stuck to my body. I showered and put on a long sleeved voile granny nightie. I sipped some lemon tea, which made me hot, then I felt freezing, all the signs of a temperature. My voice was fading, trapped in its box and my throat felt as if razor blades had been dragged across my enlarged tonsils. Sue did the talking and I nodded and grunted.

Answers from museums in response to our letter arrived daily: France, Germany, Switzerland, the United States, and Poland, responded, mostly saying they would look at their inventories, purchase dates and receipts. Some admitted items had been left for "safe keeping" and would agree to participate. Nothing came from Austria.

'Something's worrying me,' Sue admitted. 'What will prevent any museum from concealing important works and releasing the lesser valued pieces?'

'Nothing,' I managed to say.

'So they could release works onto the market anytime in the future - when all the survivors of the holocaust are presumed dead.'

'Right.' I nodded my approval and put up a thumb. Sue said thoughtfully, 'O.K. so they cheat, but unless we can have access to museums' inventories, we are impotent.'

I nodded again, and put a thumb down. She handed me the draft of a letter replying to the museums.

'Do you want me to read it to you?' I nodded. Sue made herself comfortable on the white sheepskin chair by my bed. White sheepskin slippers sat under the chair but for some bizarre reason I had never put them on and now they had become sculpture, like Oldenburg's soft typewriter.

'Thank you for your response to our letter.' Sue read. 'We should appreciate photographs of the items referred to and information on the date and place they were received, the subject or title, if known, and the artist. We shall need an enlargement of the signature. Further information will be forwarded at a later date. Thank you for your co-operation etc.'

She picked up another file from the floor.

'Are you ready? Telephone calls. Elizabeth Cuthbertson wants to discuss money with you. I offered to take the details. She said she would wait till you returned from Israel.' Sue continued as my eyelids became heavy. 'Frohmann's received calls from Austrian museums, that's why we haven't had any replies. Anyway, he seems to have the coals burning and the sooner you're out there the better. Frohmann wants to know if Hempf has looked at the chapter on Rembrandt. I called Dr.Hempf. He said it would be ready in a couple of days. Shall I tell Miss Cuthbertson you're laid flat?'

'No other choice, Sue, I'll be here for ever the way I feel.'

I had not heard the last part of what Sue said next, except a brief, "Sod it she's going." When I woke, there was a note on the chair.

"Back at the office if you need me. I'll call again this evening. Taken the spare keys. Desmond rang, he's bringing you some soup later and a dirty story to cheer you up."

It was almost two weeks before I became mobile. Still in low gear but ready for the fray, I went to the National Gallery to meet Elizabeth Cuthbertson.

Her precise manner cut quickly through any chitchat, and straightaway she said.

'I have the £10,000 deposit for the Klimt painting, but the board have made it quite clear no other payment will be made until the painting is here. Then we will pay the first instalment and the rest over the next two years. I think that's what we agreed?'

'Yes,' I replied, 'that's correct, except you'll need the bank details.'

'Quite' she said.

I started to cough, my throat dry and tense, a hangover from lack of use. 'I'm so sorry, Miss Edan, I should have asked if you'd like some tea. You've been unwell, your secretary told me.'

She left the office and came back carrying a tin tray with two cups, some tea bags, sugar and milk. 'Won't be long' she said 'I've put the kettle on. Now, where were we? Ah.Yes, I need to have the bank account number.'

For a large rounded lady she moved swiftly. While superfluity surrounded her body, her mind was lean and tidy. I gave her the

exhibition fund account number at Samuel Hall, and the sort code. 'Is there anything else you'll need?'
'Only your written assurance that no claim can be made on the painting and a corroborated authentication of the provenance from the vendor and one from a Klimt scholar.'
'I'm sure, Miss Cuthbertson, the history will prove one hundred per cent authentic and the purchase a great addition to the National collection.'

While we were drinking our tea, Miss Cuthbertson, whom I considered to be overtly formal, surprised me by saying, 'I think in future you should call me Elizabeth, as it looks like we may be working together for quite some time.' From that moment our working relationship became recklessly friendly.

***

I decided, mostly for reasons of diplomacy, that Elizabeth should meet Bernard Anderson, the director of Samuel Hall bank. On a crisp November morning we left the National Gallery, crossed Trafalgar Square, threading our bodies in snake lines through masses of pigeons competing for seeds thrown by exuberant tourists. One pigeon alighted on Elizabeth's head. 'Shove off, you beast.' She whooshed her hand across her new coiffure and turned to me, 'I hate them, dirty destructive birds. They're pests. We have to fumigate the eaves. If I had a gun licence I'd abolish the lot of them.' She held her hands up in mock shooting stance. 'Bang! That'll fix 'em.'

Elizabeth was looking smart. I had recommended the salon of Vidal Sassoon in Bond Street after she had told me her local hairdresser in Hammersmith was on holiday and she really felt in need of a little "tidying up". Now she had a casual, neat fluffy bob, an easy style that she could shake into place instead of a mass of hair piled into a bundle on top of her head.

We were sitting in a small conference room, overlooking King Street around an oval glass topped table. I had not seen Mr.Anderson since we first agreed the contract whereby Samuel Hall would sponsor the exhibition of stolen works of art. We had numerous conversations and our rapport was easy and I wanted him to feel more involved and up to date on the progress of the exhibition.

On meeting Miss Cuthbertson she told him the National Gallery was purchasing an important painting from Austria.
He looked at Elizabeth. 'It must be very important to interest the National Gallery.'
'Eventually it will attract a lot of visitors; it will take some time but it will happen.' Elizabeth said.
'You already have one of my favourite collections, and it's so accessible for me: I just nip across Trafalgar Square.'
'In spite of the pigeons?' Elizabeth said.
'Oh, yes. I would negotiate the M1 on foot to see your renaissance collection, it's remarkable.'

The vision of Giovanni Bellini's Doge Leonardo Loredan, painted in the fourteenth century, swept into my sight. When I was a student, the portrait had captivated me. In a small panel, only twenty-four inches by seventeen, everything there is to tell about a man was encapsulated in this small, intensely perceived painting. Bellini depicts the evil behind the fragile sly face of the old man: a man empowered with status and majesty, a tyrannical doge who ruled the Venetian Republic with a bloodied rod. In the renaissance this riveting portrait extolled the power and the glory of the Doge; in the twenty-first century, it is only the artist Giovanni Bellini who is revered.

For bankers, every commodity has a value and sentimental attachment, especially to a picture, would provoke disapproval. But Bernard Anderson was shrewd. He had convinced his board to invest in the art market, and then watched the investment treble on the walls. Elizabeth remarked to Mr.Anderson how attractive the picture was in his boardroom.
'It's a Pissarro,' he told us, which of course we both recognized. 'I specifically asked for it to be hung here as he is a painter I particularly admire. His style appeals to my mathematical mind.'

My eyes clashed with Elizabeth's.
'But Mr. Anderson' I said, 'mathematics have no expression, only conclusion.'
'Yes,' he said, 'but all those little dots add up.'
Elizabeth added, 'I understand what Mr.Anderson is saying. If yellow is put next to blue, you see green. It's a simple illusionary fact and the pointillists knew it.'
'It's the precision which fascinates me,' he said to Elizabeth. 'The

overall coercion of two colours sitting side by side, making another entirely different.'

We discussed how the transfer of money would be made for the purchase of the Klimt painting of Hermine Gallia. Elizabeth explained that the deposit of ten thousand pounds would be transferred within the next few days into his bank, then added 'but before we make the transaction, Miss Edan has a request.'

'And what is that Miss Edan?'

'The National Gallery will be paying into the exhibition fund in sterling. Could you transfer that amount to the exhibition account at the Laufenbankgeschaft in Salzburg?'

'To Mr.Jack Steinhart's department?' he asked.

'Yes' I replied. I had no intention of concealing anything from Bernard Anderson so I told him the money would be transferred from Austria to Liechtenstein, where the owner of the Gustav Klimt painting had an account. Bernard Anderson gave a knowing smile without saying "to a tax haven."

SALZBURG

19

The year was running fast like a ladder on a silk stocking, slipping into the second phase of my programme. I was always apprehensive after the first year, not having learned to hold on to what had been achieved, without racing ahead looking at what had not. The jungle of ideas never thinned and activating them with caution and forethought was paramount to planning a successful exhibition.

I had come to Austria after a shopping spree at Harvey Nichols with Elizabeth. She accused me of extravagance. I retaliated by taking her to the outsize department, convincing her she looked ten years younger than her forty five years in a gorgeous plum coloured suit costing two hundred pounds, with a matching pure silk shirt for another fifty pounds. "I never spend that sort of money," she complained. But I knew she was pleased as she floated into the coat department with me clutching her carrier bags to her chest like a defiant child. I bought a natural sheepskin coat reaching almost to the ground with a matching hat trimmed with white sheepskin around the brim: a pair of beige suede trousers and a white polo neck cashmere sweater. It was an outrageous extravagance. I also bought some new satin underwear. I wanted something sexy and fetching, nothing my grandmother would have worn.

"It's so skimpy," Elizabeth had said. "I don't know how they have the audacity to charge thirty pounds for a pair of knickers with less than five inches of fabric." But I didn't buy them to keep me warm, only to take off.

The focus of my visit to Salzburg was to ensure delivery of the paintings promised by the museums in answer to my circular letter. An Austrian journalist had written an article in Die Presse accusing the exhibition organisers of interfering in Austrian cultural affairs. "They are trying to revert "heirless" Jewish art, the property of the state, into the hands of unscrupulous art prospectors abroad." The article concluded that, "A court injunction could be served on any curator exporting works of art without government approval. Curators and directors could be held personally responsible for any infringement of the law relating to export of works of national interest."

I had been forewarned of this on the telephone by Jack when he had called during my bout of 'flu. I really didn't care at that time what was going on in Austria, but now I had to be realistic and deal with the problem before it festered. I called him at the bank.

Half an hour later I was sitting in his office on the first floor of the old building with its unusually modern interior: soft carpet, glass top table with flowers, a tidy desk with a leather notebook, a telephone and a tell-tale American Mickey Mouse ink stand, the only concession to anything personal. 'Glad you made it Katrina. You have a real problem on hand!'

'Right', I admitted, 'but problems are meant to be solved and this one must have a loophole somewhere. Do you know if Wilhelm Frohmann has a solution?'

'No, I haven't discussed it with him. I called you for two reasons, the most important being this article.'

'And the other?' I asked.

'Just to check on my investment.' That was a lie and I knew it. He handed me the copy of Die Presse. The headline was in dense black Gothic lettering, emphasizing the severity of the charges.

'Is this an injunction or just press bravura?' I asked.

'That's unimportant. I suspect the wording is a thinly veiled threat to you. The text reads "a court order *could* be served", not *would* be served, so the law might be up for interpretation.'

'Does Frohmann know the law?'

'If he does, he hasn't told me. I do know he's due in court himself in three days - his daughter is suing for her dowry.'

'What a mess,' I said, 'how is he reacting?'

'He's playing a part in a scenario totally out of his control.'

'And his wife, how is she managing?'

'She's not - she's putting pressure on her husband to give the money to Charlotte and he's saying he won't support a gold digging gigolo. So it's up to the court to decide.'

'Has he discussed it with you?'

'As his banker, yes, but not on a personal level. Everything I've told you has already been reported in the press. Every day some journalist leaks a little more gossip. It was said that Frohmann's wife hasn't been seen at any of the preliminary hearings, which

is true. But the reason, that she is dying of a broken heart, is untrue.'
'Is she dying of anything?'
'She wasn't last week, but then, who knows in this cockeyed world.'

***

Professor Frohmann was surprisingly calm when we met, and apologetic about the article in Die Presse. 'There was no way I could stop them printing, that's the way they work here. Print and argue later if you have to - if not, unglücklich.'

Without co-operation I could not proceed. It was not enough to rely on illegal traders and individuals dumping 'hot property' when the institutions were clandestinely holding the bulk of the loot.

Wilhelm Frohmann was holding a magnifying glass and a set of photographs. 'What do you think of this, Miss Edan?' He handed me a picture of a Raphael Madonna. I studied the image for a few minutes. 'It's magnificent' I said, as I put it back on his desk. 'Who's the owner?'
'I don't know, It was handed in at the Collecting Point which I set up in Badgastein.'
'In Badgastein! Why Badgastein? That's eight thousand feet up a mountain and half way to Italy!'
'Well, I discussed the idea with Otto Prantl and we agreed to keep the collecting point very discreet.'
'Just a moment Professor, are you telling me there's a hush-hush point, where anyone can clear their conscience by handing in the odd work of art?'
'No, Miss Edan, I'm expecting the contents of a bank vault and a collection from a castle at Neuschwanstein to arrive any moment.'

I could not understand what was going on. Firstly, I was told the Austrian government would sue anyone who exported works to the exhibition, and then I was told more looted art was arriving at a ski resort in the mountains.
'Excuse me, Professor, but I think I need some explanation. How can works be collected if your government intends to sue anyone who exposes them? It doesn't make sense.'

'Confusing to you Miss Edan but not to me. I will explain. In 1945 the three occupying powers, the British, French and Americans, set up Collecting Points in the major cities of Europe to enable works of art confiscated for protective custody during the war, to be handed in.'
'You mean stolen during the war.'
'If you prefer,' he said without argument. 'This plan resulted in thousands of works returning to museums and many more thousands to private collections. During 1946, the first year the Monuments, Fine Arts and Archives commission were active, over 23,000 items had been returned to the Munich Collecting Point and 340,000 items to Wiesbaden. It was a cultural amnesty with no questions asked.'
'Then why are so many paintings still on the missing list?'
'Because they weren't returned.' He quickly clarified this. 'They most probably were blown up in the bombing, or hidden and the owners are dead.'

This conversation was going nowhere, so I said. 'Professor Frohmann, that was twenty-five years ago. What has it to do with now?'
'A lot,' he replied. 'This is why. Between 1945 and 1947, when the Collecting Points were set up, works were coming out of hiding like rabbits, including the Rothschild horde. But a law was later passed that any works not claimed by December 1949 would become national property.'
'What a loophole' I said. 'I wonder who passed that one?'
'It was a universal decision by the three powers. The Russians didn't participate and it was ratified in a court of law.'

Professor Frohmann sounded like a record player, speaking in copybook style unconvincingly. I felt uneasy, He knew exactly what had happened: after all he was there. The big lie at the defence trials at Nuremberg rested on quotes like, "pillaged by the Russians", "burnt" "bombed", "records lost", subterfuge for records doctored, sequestered, hidden underground, anything other than the truth, to enable the sale of art worth billions, to flourish. The aftermath left millions of displaced objets d'art, paintings, sculptures, tapestries, books, religious artefacts: the wealth of Europe taken by the fleeing Nazis and the Russians, undetected in institutions and collections worldwide and still missing to-day.

Now I was being told, the exercise, which had been so successful in 1946, would be repeated! I had every reason to doubt its success.

Frohmann removed his glasses, hunched over his desk, rubbing his eyes with a white handkerchief. He concluded. 'All I can do with Herr Prantl is gather works together, but I can't guarantee our government will allow anything to leave this country. Maybe, and I repeat maybe, they will allow an exhibition here, but by law, they don't have to. All unclaimed works of art after the 1949 deadline were declared "heirless" and became the property of the state.'

'Professor, if it's a point of law I need proper advice. Without it, I am completely in the dark.'

That evening in Jack's office I asked if he knew of a lawyer conversant with the 1945 laws?

'Katrina, I think you should visit the Jewish Agency in Vienna.' He handed me a piece of paper. 'Ask for Daniel Clipstein, he'll point you in the right direction.'

'A client?' I asked.

'No - a research historian into souls.'

My mind was very centred and I needed to concentrate on the work without any emotional complications. Jack read my mood and made no attempt to allude to anything personal.

'I'll tell you for free Katrina, you'll get by-passed in Vienna. The museums here are getting together and forming a block to offset anything you might try to do here.'

'What is going on Jack? Firstly I get the Sneider collection, and then I don't. Then I get pictures via Prantl from Hanover, and then I don't. Russian works are in transit. I'm being given the run around. These scare tactics, won't work, I'll only become more determined. I'm organizing an art exhibit not a trial.'

Jack Steinhart had no chance to speak. I raised my voice.

'These bastards are all guilty of war crimes, still lying and cheating, still anti-Semitic, still justifying their horrendous pasts as "doing our duty", "only what we were told to do". No one, I repeat no one, ever admits to having a single self-inflicted thought. God, they make me sick.'

I was running my hands through my hair, holding my head in my hands with my arms on the desk. Jack took hold of my wrists and put my arms on the desk, holding them there.

'Listen, Katrina Edan, no one will ever accuse you of not trying, should this exhibition fail. The forces of evil have unprecedented roots here and your allies are in short supply, but they're there, and my advice is to take a deep breath, move slowly and keep your head down.'

'What the Hell do you think I'm trying to do?'

'Move too quickly. Try thinking you're a tortoise. Hibernate, keep them guessing. Come out when you're ready and have the right ammunition. Remember they're only helping you for gain.'

'Even Professor Frohmann?'

'Yes,' Jack said, 'and personal absolution. Maybe he's preparing to meet his maker and he's scared - who knows - conjecture is only animated thinking, neither positive nor negative.'

I looked blankly at him. 'Whatever their motives, especially the Professor's is not an issue for me to even think about.'

He let it rest, but not before he warned, 'Take my advice and move only when you have positive evidence of the law, otherwise you'll be liable for prosecution.'

VIENNA

20

Winter comes early in Vienna. Winds sweep in from the east and ominous black clouds swirl towards the city heavy with snow. A relentless biting cold gave no concession to my delicate English complexion unused to the stinging harsh invasion.

At eight in the morning the city was bared of charm. People walked briskly to work, children huddled like Michelin tyres walked hand in hand to school, their backs weighted down with satchels.

A wild draught gusted into the doorway as I waited by the bell to Gerhard Hofer's galerie. He answered himself, smoking a cigar and wearing a brown knitted scarf wound around his neck. 'Guten Tag, Fräulein' he said. I noticed his limp was more prominent than I had remembered. His eyes were watery and he sneezed into a grey handkerchief. As we entered his office, he picked up the phone and asked for tea mit rhum.

'Tea?' he said to me, 'Make zwei tea.'

Papers in a chaotic mess covered his desk. He scrambled through them before getting the one he wanted.

'Ve must talk about zie Klimt first.' he said. 'Did you get zie money?'

'Herr Hofer, I said, 'I have arranged everything as you requested - the deposit will be paid in pounds sterling.'

'Um . . .' he was chewing the end of his pencil. 'Pounds sterling' he repeated. 'You vill send them to Liechtenstein?'

'If that is your request, the money will be sent.'

He was calculating on a small adding machine.

'Pounds sterling' he repeated.

'Is there a problem?'

'Nein, ven vill zie money arrive?'

'As soon as the painting is crated and delivered to Professor Frohmann in Salzburg.' He was twisting his pencil and stabbing onto the paper, making a line of dots, which he crossed out with a dash. 'Right' he said.

'When will it be packed and sealed?' I asked.

'Vy do you ask that question?'

'Because, Herr Hofer, I cannot allow a valuable work of art to be crated without being present.'
'Fräulein' he said in a low slow tone, 'you vill have to vork mit trust or you vill get nothing. I can have every picture confiscated before it gets to Salzburg. I suggest Fräulein, you make your plans according to the vay I vork, not the vay you vant.' He was sitting back with a supercilious grin on his face when the assistant arrived with the tea. He poured a large measure of rhum into his cup.
'Herr Hofer, trust has nothing to do with seeing the Klimt crated and sealed. It's normal professional practice.' Fortunately not a win or lose argument, so his reaction was conciliatory.
'Right, I shall have ze workmen here at five this evening. You can see vot you vant'.

***

Daniel Clipstein's office was part of the Simon Wiesenthal organization, the hub for hunting Nazi war criminals and bringing them to trial. I didn't know if they could or would help me, but to continue without knowing the legal implications, would be irresponsible.

Clipstein was about fifty-five, a rounded man with dark piercing eyes and a busy moustache, which lay on his upper lip like a moveable broom. His office was in the back room of a very old building, in need of much repair. The hallway plaster was peeling and his office smelt of damp wood. But he was pleasant and extended a warm hand.
'Come Miss Edan' he said in broken English with a strong Eastern European accent, which could have been Polish or Russian. 'How can I help you?'

I hardly knew where to start - there were so many gaps in my programme.
'Mr.Clipstein, do you know of the work I'm doing here?'
'Yes' he replied, 'It has been exposed in all the newspapers and there is not too much this office does not know anyway. So, to answer your question, we have known about your exhibition since your first visit to Vienna.'
'In that case, Mr Clipstein you know the problems I'm faced with?'

'I do, but how can I help you?'
'I understand there is a law prohibiting the movement of "heirless" art outside of Austria? I need to know the details of that law and if it can be by-passed?'

He walked to the wall stacked high with books on rickety shelves, put on a pair of half-framed gold glasses and fingered his way along the line. 'Yes, this is a start - I'll look at a few past clauses and see what turns up.'

He put a dark green book with a torn spine on to his desk and ran his forefinger down the index page, speaking aloud '1945-46-47.' He stopped, turned a page in the book and started reading.

I looked at the photographs on Clipstein's oak desk. A portrait of a woman with dark tightly curled hair, sitting between a boy of about eleven wearing a prayer shawl, and a girl about eight. The only other object on the desk was a carved wooden pen and inkstand. He turned a page, still not uttering a sound. Then he looked up and beckoned with his forefinger.

'Look at this paragraph, Miss Edan', he handed me the book. Under a heading Post-war Germany 1945, I read: - "In April 1947 following Collection Points being set up by the Allied Monuments, Archives, and Fine Arts Commission, Law 59 was passed in 1947 by the occupying powers, Britain, America and France".

'I can tell you,' Clipstein said, 'this law failed because hordes of loot stayed at the checkpoints, unclaimed.'

I looked at Clipstein not really understanding the implications.

'Read on' he said.

"The Germans wanted a deadline of December 1948 to be added to Law 59 whereby they would be free to pass their own regulations for placing "heirless" Jewish property. The allies rejected this cut-off date especially as it could not be applied to the Russian Zone, where restitution was an unheard of word. Law 59 was eventually passed in the German Courts in 1948 with no codicils." I stopped reading and asked Clipstein.

'Does that include Austria?'

'Yes', he told me.

'Mr.Clipstein, I understand what I have read, but it doesn't answer my question.'

I looked at the shelves hoping their dusty covers would reveal something more comprehensible to me.

'Please, Miss Edan, be patient. We will just have to read a little further.' He turned some more pages, scanning the words, then in a quiet unshakeable voice read aloud.

"Law 59 does not address the problem of "heirless" Jewish property, only unclaimed cultural property which will revert to its state of origin for distribution to museums within that state."

Mr.Clipstein was deep in thought, as if his memory was activating faster than he could read. "Following the ratification of Law 59, a clause was added in the American zone, giving an organization founded in New York in 1947 named the Jewish Restitution Organization, the right to claim Jewish Property instead of it reverting to the state or country in which it was found. This Organization was set up to represent Jews in Europe and Palestine. A second organization, the Jewish Cultural Reconstruction committee was instigated to collect and distrib-bute cultural and religious objects. This clause was finalized in 1949." He put the book down looking directly at me.

'Would you like a further explanation?'

He adjusted his glasses. They now perched on the end of his nose. His voice was clear and decisive.

'After the war the three occupying powers, Britain, France, the United States, and USSR, split Europe into zones. The demarcation lines were drawn up with Russia holding most of the land it took, including Czechoslovakia, Poland, and almost half of Germany, including Berlin and Dresden. The rape of museums by the Russians was unprecedented. The "Collecting Points" were set up in the zones occupied by the allies, so nationals could return items with no questions asked and it is recorded that art and artefacts arrived by the truckload from designated storage sites instigated by the Third Reich. Masterpieces were being moved from one zone to another as museums were in chaos and ruins.'

I was hanging on to every word, then Clipstein said, 'Miss Edan, the clause to Law 59, added in 1949, giving the restitution organization powers over Jewish owned property, is still operational.'

'But what power does it have after 25 years?'

'If an item is detected on the auction market or surfaces at an exhibition or is recognized by a survivor, the restitution organizations can make a claim. You see, Miss Edan, many items were withheld by the Germans, Austrians, French, Americans, and more especially by the Russians, to allow enough time to elapse, so the ill-gotten gains from the dead could not be identified.'

He removed his glasses from the end of his nose and looked at me directly, his chin down like a prowling animal before making a pounce.

'You must understand the situation here in 1945. There was no food - people were hungry and they traded anything they could for sustenance. Soldiers had been sending home loot throughout the war, their attitude being "we have only taken what we have earned." Stolen watches, gold cigarette cases, pictures, silver, porcelain, manuscripts, religious objects, all lost their value in defeat. Because of the magnitude of theft and the enormity of the operation,' Clipstein said; 'a lot passed the inspection points undetected. At the Munich collecting point a Yugoslav falsely claimed and removed, 165 paintings - which are still unaccounted for to-day. And - believe me Miss Edan - this was a mere skirmish compared to what is still to be found.'

'So what you're telling me is they all lied and schemed, the Germans the Austrians, the French and any other nationals holding looted treasure?'

'Indirectly, yes. Sometimes a Picasso was traded for a loaf of bread, an icon for a packet of cigarettes. The aftermath of war in Europe left a desolate, corrupted population, who had collaborated in wholesale genocide in the name of "cleansing". They had lost all moral values, and in defeat they remained defiant losers.'

I shifted my chair to the desk and placed a red spiral notebook in front of me. 'I'll just make a few notes, if you don't mind?'

'Of course. If there is anything that is not clear, please ask.'

I thought very carefully about my questions, as too many would cloud the real issue.

'Mr.Clipstein, I need to know why Professor Frohmann and Otto Prantl have set up a Collecting Point in Badgastein, when the

Austrian Government has decreed that works of national heritage would be forcefully withheld from my exhibition?'
'That is two questions, Miss Edan. I will answer the first part. What they are doing by setting up a Collecting Point is re-enacting the process of the Monuments Enforcement Officers after the war, in the hope that anyone holding stolen works of art will declare them and send them in. Second question. Law 59 only applies if proven bills of sale can be shown with dates and provenance.'
'That sounds like catch twenty-two to me. Who can prove a document is legitimate anyway?' He responded with a knowing nod.
'That is true but it is no longer important - what is important is what is returned. I suspect Professor Frohmann and Otto Prantl will use the Collecting Point in Badgastein to filter works undetected during intensive interrogation. Both worked closely either with Herman Goering or Adolf Hitler, and many paintings - like war criminals - have still not surfaced. In twenty three years I've followed trails of evidence, some false, others genuine, and I think my sifting mechanism is still intact.'

Like Professor Frohmann, he knew much more than he would reveal to me, but he did offer some advice.
'What I suggest is you put an advert in the newspaper quoting Law 59 and its successor clause, making quite clear that any works handed in at the Collecting Point in Badgastein, will be included in the exhibition. And you, "the exhibiting organization will not have to sue in the Austrian Courts for withholding property known to be of dubious ownership.'

I felt the blood draining from my face. Mr.Clipstein asked. 'Are you feeling all right, Miss Edan?'
'No - I mean - yes, I'm all right. But I have never in my career had to deal with international law. It is very intimidating.' I pushed my chair back from the desk. 'From my point of view, it would be unwise to even consider a legal tangle even if I could afford it – which I can't, and it could frighten off museums prepared to co-operate.'
'On the contrary,' Clipstein said. 'It will force them to reconsider. Your article must give a loud signal to the Austrian government

that you are within the legal parameters of Law 59. They will have to respect its existence.'

Until now I had been out of my depth with the intricacies of political manoeuvring which formed the basis of allied settlement at the end of the war in Europe in 1945.

'Thank you. I'll do what you suggest but could I request your support if I get into difficulties?'

'I think Miss Edan, that is part of my job here.'

He spoke with conviction and sincerity not trying in any way to influence me, but giving strong signals that this would be the only way to go forward.

***

My first call after leaving Daniel Clipstein's office was to Jack Steinhart in Salzburg. But he was with a client. I gave the number of the Hotel Graben. I sat at a small desk in the hotel lobby and wrote notes pertinent to Daniel Clipstein's advise for an article.

It was quiet until a busload of peasant farmers and their soaped up wives smelling of cheap perfume arrived to check in. A poster on the wall advertised the annual Gasthaus event for Inn Keepers. The receptionist was calling them by village, Westendorf, Saalbach, St.Anton; they put up their hands and collected a room key. They were a hideous bunch of rough and weathered mountain men, out of place in the city, speaking dialects of their region, which sounded like a cross between German and Slavonic. But it was the women who looked more incongruous, vulgar even. One round faced blonde, a long plait down her back, a toothy smile protruding from ruddy cheeks, wore a dirndl shirt too tight for her ample proportions, her bust and hips bursting to escape. She made herself the centre of attention, her penetrating voice pitched high above everyone else, gesticulating and pointing, then doubling over with laughter before elbowing the thin man next to her. These annual jaunts from the mountains must have been the highlight of their year (I told myself) as most of their time was spent underneath a cow or looking to the sky for snow. They were rough and inbred, hardened by weather and poverty, tasting for the first time, an industry unheard of before the war, mass tourism. And I had discovered since starting this exhibition that whether they were lowlanders, city dwellers or simple mountain folk, all participated in murder, and justified their past by affirming they were foot soldiers obeying orders.

It no longer washed with me. Guilt is guilt, even in war. There were rules, and in spite of them, the rate at which hatred was so easily spread by propaganda, made any excuses null and void.

I always believed what I was told. It wasn't in my thinking or comprehension to even consider that people deliberately lied. Even the bones in the field opposite my school were real and belonged to dead people, because I had been told by my prefects. Naiveté maybe, yet in retrospect, trusting one's fellow human beings is not too bad a trait - in fact - it is an advantage. Being comfortable with honesty can be a barrier from intrusive abuse.

The telephone rang. It was Jack. I told him what Clipstein suggested. He said, 'Hold everything. I'll be in Vienna tomorrow and we'll work something out.'

'You mean sit still, and do nothing?'

'For one day, yes.'

'That's difficult Jack, because I'm seeing Hofer at five this evening to oversee the Klimt being packed.'

Jack interrupted. 'Say nothing, just look pretty and dumb - even if it's an effort. It will pay off, I promise.' Though he spoke softly, the urgency of doing what he asked was clear.

***

The Gustav Klimt painting of Hermine Gallia fitted perfectly into its wooden crate. The two men handling the piece were wearing grey pinafores and obviously knew the value of the work they were handling. Gerhard Hofer asked them to be careful not to let the crate touch the walls of the galerie. My school German was enough to understand the answer. "Nothing gets damaged, not even a light bulb mister, when I'm on the job". Hofer didn't reply, and as instructed I stayed absolutely mute. The younger man took some red sealing tape, wrapped it around the crate in diagonals so it looked like a tartan pattern all over. Then he took some hot wax and sealed the end with a stamp.

'What is the imprint on the seal?' I asked.

The young man was about to answer when Hofer said 'AR'. It meant nothing to me. 'Austrian Republik,' he added.

The crate was loaded into a shelf, made to size, in the lorry waiting in the courtyard outside. I took a deep breath as I watched it disappear into the Am Hof en route to Salzburg and eventually London. I looked back at Hofer's Galerie; I was laughing inside and out.

***

Promptly at eight I walked the few hundred yards to Professor Frohmann's office. We collated the information he had received from Badgastein without discussing the feasibility of the plan.

'You will see, Miss Edan, that some of the important works appear on the official list of "missing" works of art. The Modigliani and the de Chirico will probably be claimed by the Italians, but the Cimabue altar piece is a mystery.'

I looked carefully at the listing. A total of one hundred and fifty had already been sent to the Collecting Point.

'Very good Professor, it looks like your plan will work.'

I was following Jack's advice to the word: no opinion, no questions, and no reaction.

'One hundred and ten pictures came from Castle Doeniz where they were stored for protection.' Frohmann said.

'Yes Professor, I noticed.' He folded the list before putting it in his desk drawer. Then he said.

'Herr Steinhart will be in Vienna tonight, he is joining us for dinner, Please, I would like you to come too.'

***

It was dusk when Pieter collected me in Frohmann's car. Jack was in the back of the black sedan. We had not spoken since he'd arrived in Vienna and I was anxious to know why I had to act dumb. I was poised to ask the question when he took my hand and gripped it tightly, his piercing blue eyes moistened by the cold, looked straight at me.

'Isn't it a great view from here?'

I looked out of the car window then back at Jack. His forefinger brushed his lips. He glanced at the driver, then back to me. The message was clear. We sat silently, admiring the beauty of the woods, the density of the dark green pines, broken sometimes by a clearing revealing the panorama of Vienna. As the car swung around the last bend, Jack released my hand.

As we walked towards the front door, Jack whispered. 'Don't be surprised by what you see Katrina, I'll explain later.'

Professor Frohmann was waiting, looking immaculate as always in a dark blue smoking jacket and cravat, the pearl pin perfectly placed. Frohmann greeted us cordially. 'You're looking smart, Miss Edan.'

'Thank you Professor,' I said, rather surprised he had commented. To Jack, he said. 'Steinhart, I need to have a talk with you.'

We went to the salon where iced schnapps was set on a tray.

'Would you prefer something else?' Frohmann asked.

'Schnapps for me - nothing better!' Jack took two glasses and handed one to me.

The salon had a quiet unlived in feel, as if the covers had been removed from the furniture for the evening and tomorrow they would be back in the shadows.

'I apologise for Gerda. She'll join us for dinner. I'm expecting the Weisskoffs', you met them on your first visit here, when Helmut Wingler was well under the table!' He laughed, but it was an effort.

The Weisskoffs arrived minutes later. He is a balding man in his mid-fifties, not a great conservationist I recalled, but a good client of Frohmann's. When introduced to Jack he said. 'Nice to put a face to a telephone voice.'

'Good to meet you too,' Jack said.

Mrs Weisskoff is very short and compact, had blonde tightly curled hair with a Mamie style fringe and wore a black suit with embroidery on the lapels. She looked around and in a New York twang said.

'Where's Gerda?'

'Upstairs, she won't be a minute,' Frohmann appeared agitated.

'The Professor asked. 'Schnapps?'

'Sure,' said Weisskoff. 'You'd like one too,' he said, and handed a glass to his wife. Jack initiated the conversation by asking the Weisskoffs how long they were visiting Austria. 'Well, it depends if I can buy what I'm looking for here in Vienna or if I'll have to go to Italy.'

Professor Frohmann picked up on this remark quickly. 'Italy! You can't buy anything there - only spaghetti and glass jars to put it in!'
'Professor,' said Mrs.Weisskoff, 'that's not fair. We might find a Leonardo or a Botticelli. Who knows?'

We were admiring a painting Frohmann had recently bought by Hundertwasser, a contemporary Austrian artist, when Gerda came into the room. She greeted Mrs.Weisskoff first, shaking her hand formally and smiling, then me, and when she came close I could see the red rims round her eyes, the sunken cheeks where she had cleverly applied rouge. She was extremely thin; a mere shadow of the woman I first met almost a year ago. Her delicate beauty remained, but the light in her eyes had dimmed.

Dinner was informal served at the table in the salon with general chatter about artistic events in the capital, and the proposed visit of Sergie Ozawa, to conduct at the Salzburg festival.

I was sitting between the Professor and Mr.Weisskoff. Jack kept the conversation lively without introducing anything sensitive like my exhibition or the election of Bruno Kreisky as the new Chancellor of Austria.

Kreisky was a controversial choice: a Social Democrat who initiated neutrality for Austria in Europe, and was accused of sympathizing with terrorism in the Middle East, at the same time, purging his own Jewish background, His election should have been an emolument for Austria, but resulted in a backlash of disloyalty to the remaining Jews in Europe. and to those who had escaped to Israel.

As we left Professor Frohmann's home, I turned and looked out of the taxi window. The Professor was standing with his wife. It was the last time I saw Gerda Frohmann.

I went with Jack to the lounge of the Palais Schwarzenberg. We ordered coffee, which came accompanied by a dish of whipped cream and a bowl of lady fingers. The waiter wore the livery of the Schwarzenberg's with gold embroidered epaulettes. Only one other couple were in the room. Jack looked at me, waiting for a barrage of questions. I didn't deliver - I was still on hold, my conversation limited only to what was strictly necessary.

'O.K. Katrina, you can drop your guard. I'm not giving sentence this evening.' I was in no mood for smart quips.
'Christ, Jack, what's going on?'
'O.K - O.K - cool it, I'll tell you.'
'I'd appreciate that,' I said sarcastically. 'Why the hell do I have to play games because you say so? What's it to do with you anyway. You're just a sponsor - remember?'
'Listen Katrina, there's three ways of playing here - upfront - underground - and cheat, and there's not much difference.'

I looked away, avoiding his gaze. 'God, this is getting like a B movie.'

Jack poured the coffee, offered me the ladyfingers and smiled, his eyes heavy with nuances. If I was supposed to melt it had the opposite effect, I exploded.
'Fuck you and fuck the Professor and all the bloody liars I'm dealing with.' I shouted, 'it's enough to have the fucking Austrians pushing me into no-mans-land: you're an interfering bastard! Just keep your opinion to yourself and stick to folding dollar bills, that's all you're good for.'

Jack picked up my coat from the back of the chair and called the waiter.
'Take this tray to room 110 please, with two double whiskeys. "Bell's" Jack added. He took my hand and led me like a wimp to room 110. Once inside I covered my face with my hands, burst into tears and sobbed uncontrollably. I sat down in an armchair and mopped my stinging eyes. Jack pushed an armchair in front of mine.
'Double scotch?' He said, as he put a glass in my hand. I took an adult sized gulp, then another.
'Sorry' I said. It was not an apology, more a rebuke for my weak behaviour: I was letting circumstances upset my emotional balance. I felt I was losing control. Jack didn't take advantage, although I knew he could. He said,
'I know there's some explaining to do and I won't waste time: you're in the dark because certain events have been kept from you.'
'How do YOU know? You're in banking.' I snapped.
He pulled his chair closer and removed his jacket. 'Yes, you're right to wonder, but as a banker I have to investigate deposits

which are placed for laundering before I can invest on the open market. Mostly it's legal but sometimes, when I get a flush from any one source, I have to validate authenticity.'
'That means?'
'Looking into the background history of the investor.'
'And Daniel Clipstein? Where does he fit in your filing system?'
Jack caught the cynicism in my voice
'Katrina, it won't help you if you're antagonistic, I'm trying to keep you informed.'

Another slap on the wrist! This time he was right.
'Clipstein is an account of mine. That's why I wanted you to keep quiet about your meeting with him. I didn't want you to repeat anything he had told you until certain recommendations were in place. Some of the investment for your exhibition came from the fund I manage for Clipstein's organization. They receive money for research from Jewish charities and individuals worldwide; I invest on their behalf. Imperial Chicago knows about the investment, but Professor Frohmann does not.'

Jack poured more coffee while I silently mulled over this revelation.
'So Clipstein's advice was in collaboration with you?'
'No - his recommendation is based on the laws here, with one exception, and this is why I wanted you to stay stumm.' He took a newspaper cutting from his pocket and showed it to me. It was an article written in Die Neuepresse by Anton Kodech on proposals for Austria to join EFTA, the European Free Trade Association, which allowed member countries freedom of movement across borders.
'Good idea. Anything that limits bureaucracy is fine with me. Who is Anton Kodech?'
'He's the guy who will write an editorial on Clause 59, so you won't be exposed as the advertiser.'
'Who fixed that? You or Daniel Clipstein?'
'That's not an important question and it's aggressive. What you need right now is a clean image, and some allies.'

I threw the rest of the scotch down my throat in an act of defiance, and wished I hadn't.
'Another?' Jack asked.
'Why not?' I waved nonchalantly.

He walked across the thickly carpeted room to a walnut cabinet and held up a bottle. 'It's Teachers. That O.K?'

By the time I had finished the third double scotch I could barely keep my eyes open.

Jack said 'You'll fall asleep in the taxi Katrina, I think you should stay here to-night.'

I kicked off my shoes and found my way to the bathroom, pulled the dress over my head, hung it on a hook, peeled off my tights, looked in the mirror at the mascara smudged over my cheekbones, as my eyelids drooped involuntarily. I wet my hands and ran them through my hair, vainly trying to reinstate myself. I floated into the bedroom, sat on the edge of the king-sized bed with my toes curling into the thick piled carpet and slowly rested my head on the pillow.

When I woke Jack was lying next to me in his shirt and trousers. He'd removed his shoes, socks and tie. Sunlight was breaking through a slit where the beige velvet curtains met. I turned to face him.

'Why aren't you wearing pyjamas?' It was all I could think of at that moment.

'Because, my dear Katrina, I was too tired to put them on.'

I looked at his toes poking out from the turnups under his trousers. 'They cold?' I asked, pointing to all ten.

'Nope, they're used to it.'

'Used to what? Sleeping uncovered?'

'Sure, in the open too. In my cowboy days.'

'You a cowboy?'

'Well sort of, I was raised on a ranch in Northern New Mexico. My dad bred horses.'

I was looking up at the ornate tracery on the ceiling, the patterns picked out in beige and blue. I wanted to know more about his childhood but the warmth of his body overpowered my thinking.

'I put a "do not disturb" notice on the door.' he said.

His hand gripped mine and the message was electric.

Jack ordered breakfast in the room, we sat at the table by the long French window overlooking the gardens, crunching Kaiser

rolls, and thinking private thoughts. I thought about the Professor.
'What's happening to the Frohmann's?' I asked.
'Hell, I thought you knew - they lost the case, or at least the Professor did. The judge awarded Charlotte her dowry - a quarter of the Professor's assets.'
'No wonder Gerda looked ill.'
'That's only part of the scenario. Charlotte wrote an open letter to the newspapers, disowning her parents and stating she will never visit them nor have any contact with them, in her lifetime.'
'What a bitch! She really spelt it out.'
'What's more unbelievable, Katrina, is they printed it.'

Who paid for that privilege, I wondered.

We were munching through our breakfast when Jack made a surprising suggestion. 'How do you feel about dumping all this shit and going to the mountains for a few days? I know a delightful village, Filzmoos, high in the mountains.'
'The best suggestion I've heard in years, but I can't.'
'Why not?'
'It's really critical I get back to London to set up a venue for the exhibition. I haven't even applied for Government Indemnity yet, and that's due a year in advance.'
'Can't Sue handle it?'
'She will, but it needs my signature. Believe me there's nothing more I'd like than rid myself of this charade for a few days.'

I looked up over my coffee cup, my eyes firmly fixed on his.
'Please - ask me again.'
He smiled, but the disappointment showed.

LONDON

21

One week later a newspaper cutting arrived in my office from Vienna. It was the translated article by Anton Kodech, challenging the Austrian Government's stance on Law 59 by elaborating on the second clause passed in 1949. It was a tightly written piece, no frills, only facts. Kodech did, however, speak out on the chances for Austria joining EFTA the European Free Trade Association, while withholding dubious National treasure. "This" he wrote, "would be a contradiction. Austria seeks acceptance to market freely with the West while denying free access to show works of art in case their origins prove suspect. This dichotomy will lead Austria into isolation and relegation from the rest of Europe."

I put the article down, picked up the phone and read the gist of the article to Anton Hempf. His reaction confirmed what I had thought: accurate but would it change the status quo?

'It will certainly give them something to think about,' he said, 'but they won't react immediately. It's not politically advantageous.'

As I put the phone down it rang immediately. It was Elizabeth Cuthbertson. 'Did you have a good trip, Katrina? I have just returned from Manchester.'

'Yes, if going from anguish to ecstasy is a good trip, yes I did.'

'Can't wait to hear. Come to dinner to-night, or are you too tired?'

'Love to. All I have in the house is a tin of sardines.'

Elizabeth's apartment in South Kensington is a riotous collection of objects acquired during her many years of travel. Small mementoes from exhibitions like the bronze Mannekin Pis from Brussels and a scarab from Egypt.

'The only practical things I've ever bought,' she told me, 'are beds and rugs.' I looked at the deep carmine and navy Kashan carpet covering the floor of the drawing room and knew she had spent a considerable amount.

The apartment was on the first floor of a four storey white stucco house. It was large by most standards, with French doors leading from the drawing room onto a balcony. A massive horse

chestnut tree, its last remaining leaves grounded, dominated the view. Elizabeth opened the doors.
'I love that tree,' she said. I put my head over the balustrade and looked up to see how far it actually grew.
'That tree - has almost nine lives,' Elizabeth said. 'In winter it starts with fat dark brown sticky buds which slowly turn ash coloured at the tips, then in spring they turn lime green, before breaking into huge flat leaves with wonderful tracery until the tree is transformed by huge pink candle flowers in May. When I think it's all over, it showers horse chestnuts onto the ground wrapped in spiky green shells, which hang on the tree until they're too heavy. And that's not the last,' she said with excitement. 'The shells crack and rich dark chocolate chestnuts fall out.'
'It's a pity they're not the roasting kind', I said. 'We could become chestnut ladies, with a brazier and some bags, we'd be in business!' Elizabeth closed the French doors, frowned at me, as though 'business' was a dirty word.

She had set the polished mahogany table with mats, linen napkins and an empty wine coaster. 'I'm not a great cook Katrina, so I only use simple recipes which don't take too much time.'
'That's more than I can say. I've just broken my third tin opener!'
I felt relaxed with Elizabeth: she is wise, and experienced enough not to ask questions, knowing you will volunteer information anyway, like a psychotherapist prizing out your most private secrets till you reach silence, then saying, "and?".

I did not recount all that had happened in Vienna, except to tell her about the Austrian Laws, adding 'I'm waiting for clarification. I hope it will be resolved in a few days'.
'How's my Klimt?' she asked.
'In bed in Salzburg. Wrapped crated and sealed. Waiting with all the other items for shipment.'
'Good! I haven't prepared a press release; I decided to wait till it's in our vaults. By the way, have you set a date for the exhibition?'
'Elizabeth, I haven't even found a venue. I was hoping you might come up with a suggestion.' Her answer was decisive.

'I'm sure the National Gallery won't give it space, even if it's available. Too controversial, politically risky.'

Elizabeth put a piece of grilled halibut with a white parsley sauce in front of me. 'Please help yourself to vegetables. Sorry, no potatoes. I'm slimming.' I took some broccoli and carrots.

'Have you tried the Tate?' Elizabeth asked.

'I haven't tried anywhere, but my nose points towards the Royal Academy.'

'Do you know Sir Hugh Casson?'

'I've met him. He's adorable, like popcorn. He's ready to jump into anything controversial if he thinks the idea is right. He's flush with space too, if it's not all booked.'

'I'll call him if it will help and give you a little boost.'

I looked up from my plate at Elizabeth with raised eyebrows.

'I know you can manage without insider preference' she said, 'but it's not Sir Hugh I'm thinking about, it's that bunch of old R.A. buggers who live life backwards that concern me.' As she was speaking she was collecting our dinner plates.

In the years I have been curating I have learned never to refuse an offer of help. If that offer fails, you are only left where you were in the first place - on your own. It is the difference between interference and mediation; one takes away initiative, the other pushes it into place.

'I really appreciate your offer Elizabeth. I'm keen to push the project forward. Anyway it would be a coup for the Royal Academy to have the first showing of a new National acquisition, wouldn't you agree?'

Elizabeth understood exactly the psychology of my salesmanship, giving a firm nod of approval. We really do speak the same language, I concluded.

LONDON
22

Sir Hugh Casson is a man of many parts. In his capacity as President of the Royal Academy council he set the programme of exhibitions for all the galleries in Burlington House. By profession an architect, an artist by talent, a travel writer, an illustrator, an historian, but mostly a humanitarian. I am a consummate admirer and was excited to be meeting him. As I climbed the wide staircase from the foyer, white lilies and exotic foliage in giant urns cascaded either side in honour of the Queen Mother who was attending a special dinner that evening. At the top of the stairs I turned right. A door marked private, led to a corridor with paintings on the walls by past academicians.

I knocked on a door on the left. A muffled voice said 'Come in.' Sir Hugh was up a ladder retrieving a book.

'Hello m'dear, won't be a sec, just get this dusty old thing down.'

The ladder wobbled and I was about to grab it when he shouted. 'Don't worry it's been like this for the last hundred years.' He held onto the sides of the ancient antique and came down.

'We've met before,' he said as he shook my hand. 'Never forget a redhead. Now, what are you up to?'

'Do you know about the exhibition I'm arranging?'

'To be honest m'dear, Elizabeth told me how far you'd progressed. I already knew about the exhibition.' We were sitting side by side at an oval table on rickety wooden chairs with worn silk upholstery seats. I undid my scarf and unbuttoned my jacket. 'Too warm?' he asked.

'It's fine Sir Hugh. May I ask how you heard about my research?'

'From Anton Hempf. You know he's a frequent visitor here - like him - nice chap - bloody good Rembrandt scholar.'

Barely five foot five tall, of slight build, Sir Hugh wore a comfortable Cambridge blue buttoned cardigan over a pink shirt. Sir Hugh Casson defied his seventy odd years with alertness and athleticism and gave no concession to his age. He is a firecracker in this austere outpost of British art, and apart from Sir Gerald Kelly, who swore on television when describing a painting as "bloody marvellous," no word and certainly no foot had ever been misplaced again by an active Academician - until Sir Hugh: not so much by breaking rules, just by creating new ones.

'Don't tell me,' he said. 'I know m'dear, you're looking for exhibition space!'

'Yes sir.' I said rather feebly.

'How many exhibits do you have?'

'They're still coming in, but at the moment I have about six hundred.'

'That's a lot.'

'Yes Sir, but many, like the Vermeer's are small. The largest piece is the Gustav Klimt painting, which the National Gallery is buying. Have you seen Klimt's Hermine Gallia?' I asked.

'Only in book illustrations.'

'Do you know, Sir, it hasn't been exhibited since 1938? It would be exciting if the Academy could show the piece.' Sir Hugh was listening but his thinking was elsewhere.

'Six hundred' he said. 'I doubt I'll have a room large enough. Six hundred,' he repeated. 'Tight. Very tight. I'll look in the events diary and see what's booked. Won't be a tick.'

I waited apprehensively in his room, looking at the walls stacked with bound books, static and unmoved, their message outdated, their pictures uninspiring. The dust had gathered on the Edwardians and Victorians, the interceding wars erupting to force painting into new directions, which would shock and revile the followers of the old established schools of naturalistic reproduction, which for decades had set the criteria for acceptance as an academician.

Sir Hugh returned holding a black leather diary. 'Doesn't look good, m'dear. We have three retrospectives listed, an exhibition of Ingres drawings, then we're painting the walls.' He stopped speaking for a moment, 'I'd really like to help you but I just can't find a date.' He was running his finger down the page, then he stopped, turned the page, then back again. I watched every move.

'There might, I say might be a possibility in 1973.'

He was turning the page back and forth. He dialled an extension on the phone. 'Lucy, will you come to my room?' A tall thin girl came into the room wearing a black skirt to her

ankles and a black and white shirt from Marks & Spencer. I knew because I had the same one.
'What's happening in the Private Rooms in late 73?'
Lucy looked at the diary. 'That period's allocated for the electrians to put in the new lighting tracks.'
Sir Hugh scratched his head.
'Ah - yes, new lights.' His finger ran up the page. 'Couldn't the lighting be changed when the walls are painted?'
'It's risky Sir, they could get splashed,' she said.
'Still looking at the diary he said, 'It's a tricky business trying to fit everything in, Miss Edan. The only possibility I can see is October 1973.'
'That would be ideal. How long is the space available?'
'Four weeks, absolute maximum. Sorry, m'dear, it's the best I can do.' He closed the diary. Lucy reminded Sir Hugh that the table settings for the evening were being placed. Before I left, I made one more suggestion.
'I could extend my expenses to include the repainting of the private rooms. I have also set aside a contingency for security. So we would not incur any expenses for the Academy.'
Sir Hugh Casson did not react to my bargaining; in an authoritative tone he said, 'if the exhibition is approved by the other nine members of the executive committee, I'll get Lucy to call you. We meet next week, so you will have an answer very soon.'
On leaving the Academy's arched portals in Piccadilly I heard the tinny chimes of the clock on the facade of Fortnum and Mason and watched the medieval figures moving round. A guide holding a yellow, red and blue golf umbrella shepherded a group of tourists. He told them in an exaggerated unfashionable upper class voice, that the store dated from 1707 and that Mr.William Fortnum lodged with a small shop owner named Mr. Hugh Mason in St James' market. Fortnum persuaded his landlord to become his partner. They started a grocery shop, for the purveyance of exotic spices and fruits. Their establishment became so successful they were awarded the royal coat of arms. A voice shouted 'What's that?'
'That madam,' said the guide, 'is awarded when an establishment supplies a member of the Royal family.'

'You mean she buys her groceries there?'
'If you mean the Queen madam - yes.'

***

I worked at home till late into the night, presuming the Austrians would eventually co-operate or Professor Frohmann and Otto Prantl would pull some strings. After all they had more to gain by legitimising paintings they could sell on the open market than withholding them under some controversial law. I started putting together the rough plan for transit, delivery, and security. It seemed useless co-ordinating dates for a one-month exhibit but there was no alternative.

In the morning I walked briskly through Regents Park concentrating on the mechanics of the project with no thought of Law 59. A few runners passed swiftly in singlets and shorts, puffing and sweating in the damp cold air.

Sue was at her desk, completing the drafts for a press release.
'How's it going?' I asked.
'Getting there. Anything you want me to add?'
I picked up the typewritten page. 'Seems O.K. The usual advance press gabble, approximate date, year, venue to follow.' I waved the paper about in the air. 'Sue, something's missing.'
'What's that boss? Hitler's death certificate?'
'Shut-up and listen.'
'I want a heading - how's this? Capital letters: -

"THE EXHIBITION DIFFERENT"

Sue wrinkled her nose and made sniffing sounds like there was a bad smell. I gave her an icy look. 'I haven't finished. By-line.' I made writing signs with my forefinger.

NO ONE OWNS IT - NO ONE'S SELLING IT, NO ONE'S ACCOUNTABLE FOR IT, AND NO ONE CARES.

Sue pushed her typewriter forward on the desk.
'You sound one sandwich short of a picnic. You really want me to write that apeshit?'
'Yep, we gotta get the press out of the pubs with something!'

The phone gave a piercing ring cutting short our deliberations.
'Katrina Edan's office.' Sue held the phone with her hand over the mouthpiece. 'It's Jack Steinhart from Salzburg.'
'Put him through to my office.' I threw my coat on the chair and sat on the corner of the desk. 'Hello Jack, how are you?'
'Katrina, are you sitting down?'
'Sort of' I said.
'There's been a hitch here in Salzburg.'
'What do you mean, a hitch?'
'There has been a robbery in Frohmann's Galerie. The Professor called this morning. He's coming from Vienna later to-day.'
'Do you know what's been taken?'
'No. He just told me the thieves spent the week-end on the job.'
'Oh my God, what a cock-up.' I held the phone looking at the mouthpiece in anguished disgust.
'Katrina, are you O.K?.'
'No, I'm not sodding O.K. I'm shocked.'
'My advice is, you get a ticket and get yourself here on the first available flight.'
'Jack, why can't Stephan Moser handle it? He has the inventory, he knows what the galerie owns.'
'Katrina, it's more complicated: the theft wasn't from the galerie inventory: it was works for your proposed exhibition. Frohmann can't handle it, he's depressed and on God knows how many pills. Anyway you'll have to identify as much as possible for the assessors.'

He was absolutely right. 'Jack would you call the Elephant for a room? I'll get Sue to call the airline.'
'Hang on a minute.' I could hear indistinct voices, then Jack said. 'I'll call you later - take it easy - don't worry. The Professor's insured for a hundred and fifty million schillings.'

As I replaced the phone in its cradle, I thought, that's not the point. What good is insurance? It's only money. It can't compensate the ultimate losers, the disenfranchised refugees who might have received some consolation from their lost past. I called Sue into my office. She sat opposite me while I picked at the edge of a notebook.
'Trouble?' she asked
'Frohmann's galerie has been burgled.'

'Has the Klimt gone?'
'Shit, I didn't even ask.'

Sue realised the serious complications this might cause and waited for me to tell her what to do.

'I'll leave for Salzburg as soon as possible. Try and get a ticket for tomorrow. Any route, any airline. I'll fly to Munich if necessary and take the train to Salzburg. While I'm away make an application for Government Indemnity for the exhibition, but check with Lucy at the Royal Academy beforehand to confirm we have the space. You have a specification on file on humidity, ventilation, fire and lighting - just copy those. Set a temporary value of three million with a cover note explaining the circumstances. Post it as soon as written confirmation comes from the Royal Academy.' Sue stopped writing.

'Didn't you say the Royal Academy was changing the lighting?'

'You're right, you'd better find out if it's tungsten or fluorescent, total wattage and the cooling system. You'll need to add that on the application. And Sue, ring Desmond Hegarty, give him the dates before he gets overbooked.'

'What about the press release with the No One Cares headline?'

'Hold on to it Sue, till I give you the go-ahead.'

SALZBURG

23

An early morning fog draped over London airport like the curtains in a theatre waiting to open and the action to start. All flights before 8 a.m. had been delayed and anxious business travellers craned their necks, scanning the clicking flight indicators, hoping they would change from delayed to boarding. This had the effect of slowing my adrenalin, which was running at such a pace, if it had a boiling point, I had reached it.

One irate passenger, a man wearing a Burberry raincoat and carrying a Gucci briefcase, stormed to the Lufthansa desk with a German accent that was a parody of itself, shouting "Hasn't dis airport ever 'eard of radar?" An Englishman in cords and a leather jacket, who was standing by the ticket desk took offence and replied.

'Yes cock, we invented it!'

At that moment the tannoy announced, "Flight 226 to Munich was boarding at gate No.5." Less than forty passengers boarded the plane. The pilot apologised for the delay.

"The weather en route and in Munich is clear and the temperature 35F - 3C" he said. My sheepskin coat became a comforter.

***

Sue had reserved a seat in a first class compartment on the Munich-Salzburg express. Only one other passenger, a well-dressed man, maybe fifty-five, joined the compartment. He closed the sliding doors to the corridor and sat in the window seat opposite me. As the train pulled out of the station I made notes on the questions I needed answered, listing the Klimt's fate as my first and most important.

The man opposite was reading the Süddeutsche Zeitung. He didn't look up but must have been as aware of my presence as I was of his. At the first stop, a few people joined the train. No one came into our compartment.

As the train started to move, the stranger said to me in English, 'that's good, no noisy kids munching and clacking: I knew exactly what he meant after my experience on the Orient Express.

'How did you know I was English?'
'I read the label on your luggage.'
I tried to identify the accent and concluded it was German/American. Since working on this particular exhibition I have become cynical and distrusting, an alien feeling, as I had always looked at my fellow human beings as civilized. But now I've met the dog-ends of my species, rat-assed individuals whose sales tag on life is zero, I'm more than guarded.
'Are you from Munich?' I asked.
'No, I'm American.'
'I couldn't place the accent,' I said.
'That figures. I was born in Germany at Rosenheim. It's the next stop.'
'Do you have family there?'
'I had. They all died in the gas chambers.'
'I'm sorry' I said, the only cliché, I could find.
'I'm Sam Rosenheim.'
'Katrina Edan.'
He pulled a watch chain from his top breast pocket with well-manicured fingernails.
'Only an hour to Rosenheim. Where are you going?'
'Salzburg.'
'On business or pleasure?'
I hesitated. If I said business he would want to know what business, so I said, 'pleasure.'
'Interesting city. You'll like it,' he said.
'I hope so. What's Rosenheim like?'
'Small German town: Herman Goering was born there. But that doesn't make it special. It's a typical Bavarian mix of rustic and concrete. I'm going to sign documents of reparation.
'And in twenty five years you haven't been recompensed?'
'Oh, yes, I was given ten marks an acre for our land and nothing for our factory or my home.'
'But why did you wait so long?
'I didn't. The Germans waited. They have been prevaricating for years with excuses to delay or refute reparation.'
'So you're hoping to set the calculations right?'

'Not hoping. The Germans want papers. They always want papers regardless of the content. Every detail must be in writing.'
'That must be difficult after so long.' I said.
'It's very time consuming. Anyway it will cost them a lot more now, with 25 years interest added.'

When he left the carriage he handed me his card. 'Just in case you're ever in New York perhaps I could show you around.'
'Good luck,' I said.

I looked at the address on the card. Sam Rosenheim, Attorney at Law, 55 Park Avenue New York.

The line of taxis at Salzburg station depleted quickly. I stood on the pavement waiting, looking into a shop window selling Mozart souvenirs. Mozart's face looked at me from a variety of mugs, chocolates, miniature china pianos, with white wigged look-a-like dolls tinkling ivories, and music boxes enticing us to hear the highlights of the Marriage of Figaro, Don Giovanni, and The Magic Flute. I doubt that Mozart would have approved, but the City of Salzburg certainly did. Mozart's head is now the symbol of carnival kitsch, and the source of insatiable revenue.

A police car was parked outside the Galerie Frohmann, its flashing lights dimmed. Inside it was surprisingly normal. I had expected the chaos associated with burglary, but there was no evidence of damage or vandalism. Paintings were in place on the walls and a glass cabinet containing filigree sculptures was untouched. Books and postcards still stood in neat rows on the shelves. Strange that a burglary had taken place yet everything seemed normal.

Stephan Moser came into the galerie as I arrived.
'Guten Tag Miss Edan, Herr Professor is with the police.'
'Herr Moser, do you know what has been stolen?'
'No,' he said abruptly. 'I do not have the complete list.'
'When was the robbery?'
'Saturday night and Sunday morning.'
'Do you know what's missing from your incomplete list?'

He took a sheaf of papers, held together with a paper clip from the drawer of a table covered with catalogues of past exhibitions, and gave it to me. Moser said, 'I have marked some that are missing but most of the crates have not been checked.'

'Would you ask the Professor if I could see him now?' He looked startled, as if I had asked to take a moonwalk with him. 'I can ask Miss Edan,' he said with emphasis on the word ask.

A few minutes later he returned and beckoned me to follow him. We walked through the winding corridors. On the way we met Kurt Frohmann who squeezed back against a wall so we could pass. He held a large photographic plate above his head. He smiled.

When we reached the long galerie, two uniformed policemen were talking with the Professor; one taking notes the other asking questions. Frohmann had his head bowed looking down at the floor strewn with empty cartons, corrugated paper, packing filler and loose nails and screws. I looked around for the large crate from Vienna containing the Gustav Klimt for the National Gallery. Many unopened crates were stacked but not the one I wanted desperately to see.

Professor Frohmann turned and saw Stephan and myself waiting at the entrance and with the two officers came to join us.

'Gott im Himmel,' Frohmann said after the police left. 'We cannot touch a thing until forensic have dusted for fingerprints. Then we will have to give them a full report on what has been taken.'

I showed him the list Moser had given me. Frohmann ignored it.

'Miss Edan, a large consignment arrived from Badgastein too late on Friday evening for us to record them.'

'Do you know if the Klimt has been stolen? I can't see the crate in the galerie.'

'Because it's in the other galerie. Probably too big to move.'

His gold watch dangled on its chain outside his waistcoat pocket. He looked at the time, then held it closer to his glasses, then slid it into his pocket. 'It's nearly two o'clock. I think we should have some lunch and then we can make some plans. The Chief Inspector is coming here later this afternoon,' he said, 'for an official statement.'

Stephan Moser drove the Professor's car to the farmhouse. Marta had set the pine kitchen table with red chequered napkins, wine glasses, a basket of black bread, butter, and a soup tureen.

'I think we should eat and talk at the same time, if you don't mind, Miss Edan?'

Marta filled the tureen with hot noodle soup. The Professor explained exactly what had happened.

'I will try and get everything in order Miss Edan. Firstly, the police suspect the thieves knew what they wanted, because the robbery did not follow a pattern. Usually they would take the items nearest the door first, to make a clear way, then as much as they could safely load. In this case, because the burglars had plenty of time, they selected items of high value and left the others.'

'How do the police know if you haven't checked the inventory?'

'Because some of the crates were opened and the contents left inside.'

'What happened to the alarm system, Professor?'

'It was cut off at the main switch, so it would not ring.'

The neck of my sweater felt tight. I took a deep breath and filled my lungs with fresh air, trying to relieve my tension. Marta brought a dish of steaming hot gnocchi and a bowl of minced meat, which she set in front of us.

'These,' the Professor said as he pointed to blue pills, 'are before meals, the pink and white for after.' He threw them into his mouth and swallowed, drinking some water, then some wine.

'I have been thinking about this mess, Miss Edan. We could turn it around to our advantage.'

'That's interesting. What do you propose?'

'We could use it as propaganda for the exhibition. The press will be reporting from the police files. Maybe we should make a statement in advance.'

I remembered what Jack had said: stay out of the limelight.

'I agree it could produce some results but I would prefer that my name or the exhibition were not mentioned.'

The Professor looked surprised, put his knife and fork down, took his glasses off, wiped the thick lenses with his napkin: a move to see more clearly into my reasoning? Then he tried persuasion instead of suggestion. 'It will bring the exhibition onto the front page, might even rattle a few memories. The police will be out looking for stolen property with search warrants, people holding loot will be wary.'

'After twenty-five years Professor? I doubt it. We are already on the front page and threatened with court action if we remove national treasures. Or has that story died?' A leading question that made the Professor react immediately.

'Miss Edan, nothing has changed. The Government threat still exists, but it does not mean we change our plans. We just carry on till it's resolved.'

Frohmann smoked incessantly while we had coffee, his hand trembling each time he set another cigarette in the ivory holder.

We returned to the galerie at four for Frohmann's meeting with the police chief. While he was being interviewed I studied the list of stolen items. Sixty paintings were missing, mostly works by important modern masters: Cézanne, Vlaminck, Braque, Picasso, Matisse and a Titian. I concluded the thieves were stealing to order and the works were already out of Austria.

When Professor Frohmann left his office after the interview, he was visibly distraught. If a butterfly had landed on his back he looked as though he would collapse.

'Please, Miss Edan come into my office.' He picked up a bunch of papers angrily. 'I have to answer question after question. Some I cannot. This is not a routine robbery.'

Is there such a thing, as a format for art theft? I asked myself. Frohmann continued. 'I don't know when, where, why, or how the paintings came into Austria. Nor, who owns them. The police don't know what line of inquiry to follow.'

'Professor Frohmann, the robbery only happened two days ago. They haven't had much time.' He calmed a little and settled heavily into his chair.

'Maybe a cup of tea will help?' I suggested.

Lisette brought a tray with tea and placed it on the desk, speaking in German she told Frohmann something about Herr Steinhart. The Professor translated. 'Steinhart's coming here soon to tell me what to say to the assessor from the insurance company. Dummkopf. I know what to say. There was a break-in and sixty paintings were taken. Got, I'm not an imbecile!'

I sat in a small leather armchair sipping lemon tea, while Frohmann puffed continuously on his cigarette.

'How is your wife, Herr Professor?' I was genuinely concerned.

'Not well. She's very upset by Charlotte's behaviour. She can't understand why her daughter's so ungrateful. Charlotte has broken her ties with our family. It's difficult for me to see Gerda so distressed and I can't console her - believe me I'm trying.' He removed the lid of an enamel pillbox and put two pills on the desk, one blue, and one yellow.
'My doctor insists I take these tablets.' He swallowed them with his tea. 'They don't do any good, I just take them to keep him quiet.' The phone rang to tell Frohmann that Jack Steinhart was in the Galerie. The moment he entered the office I knew something was wrong as he hurriedly said.
'Has Wilhelm given you all the lurid details?'
'Not really. He's waiting for the police to do that.' I looked at the Professor for reassurance.
'It's right, Jack,' the Professor said. 'The chief inspector suspects the burglary was carried out to order.'
Jack turned to ask me, 'Why?'
'Because it's too neat. The police even suspect they had a copy of the inventory, it's been so well picked over.'
'That will complicate the insurance claim,' Jack said. 'The company will ask for proof that it hasn't been set up as a ruse.'
'Are you suggesting, Jack, the Frohmann Galerie would create an insurance fraud?'
'No, Wilhelm, I'm not but the insurance company might. They'll dig around the paper work looking for anything to lessen their responsibility - that's the assessor's job.'

Jack moved across the room, looked at a picture on the wall, not thinking about it, just talking all the time. He was irritable, acting out a scene, rushing to get it finished without knowing the next part of the plot. 'The only proof you have is an inventory list,' he said. 'You haven't seen the paintings, you can't even prove they exist.'

This seemed unreasonable to me, so I asked Jack. 'Could Professor Frohmann be held responsible?'
'You mean personally? No, because the Galerie is the custodian and it's the Galerie that's been robbed.'
'That's clear enough, Jack, but the Galerie doesn't own the stolen works. We don't know yet who does.' I said.

'That, Katrina is irrelevant. The galerie policy covers everything under its roof.'
'O.K, but what if the insurance company say they're fakes with no value, stolen goods without provenance? What proof would we have? None?'

Wilhelm Frohmann joined in the argument.
'Miss Edan both you and I have seen the paintings stored here and authenticated most of them.'
I interrupted. 'But Herr Professor, if we don't know what was in the consignment from Badgastein, how can we know what's been stolen?' Jack was getting more agitated.
'There's nothing more I can tell you, Wilhelm. The assessor will be here tomorrow morning. His name is Helmut Rotenberg.'

It was five thirty. I was tired, I had been on the move for eleven hours and my concentration was ebbing. Jack offered to take me to the hotel and carried my small case across the Staatsbrücke to the Hotel Elephant. The snow was deep and crunched under my sheepskin boots. The receptionist recognised me immediately: 'Grussgott, Frau Edan, welkommen,' and gave me my room key. We took the boneshaker lift to the third floor.
'Thank goodness my room's at the back, I said, 'no noise from night hawks.'

Nothing ever changes at the Elephant. Every room is the same: a bed, a wardrobe, a bedside table, a table and chair, all recognisable as simple utility furniture.
I told Jack, 'I feel a wreck - I need a bath, a change of clothes and some food.'

I took the copy of the Royal Academy's offer from my briefcase.
'Something for you to read,' I said.
'Great, I'll pick you up at seven thirty, O.K?' He planted a light kiss on my cheek.

Monday night isn't a great dining out night. Jack suggested the Hotel Österreichischer Hof. I remember having lunch in the restaurant when we first met but tonight he suggested the Zirbelstube, the converted wine cellars which had a special local charm. We entered through rounded stone arches painted with mythical stories of Salzburg folklore. Locals liked the good food and authentic atmosphere and were regular habitués. An Austrian man with his family nodded to Jack as we passed.

It didn't take us long to order. Speck mit dumplings for me, Hungarian Goulash for Jack. He was more relaxed than he'd been at Frohmann's office. He ordered a pitcher of red wine. I had forgotten till it arrived in the glazed flower decorated stone jar, that a pitcher contained a litre of wine. Jack filled our glasses.

'I know what you're thinking' he said.

'God forbid' I replied. He smiled but I could see there was something serious he wanted to say.

'You're wondering what that charade was all about in Wilhelm's office?'

'How right you are.'

'I'll tell you Katrina. It's serious. I've talked to Rotenberg, the assessor. He thinks there's been a tip-off. A rat's been nibbling somewhere but not strong enough to bite through the alarm cable. That means someone gave the position of the mains.'

'Do you suspect anyone?'

'Sure, I suspect them all. These guys have been double dealing all their adult lives. It's the language they understand: lies covering more lies, tricksters camouflaged by respectability. They're whores Katrina.'

'Jack, slow down.' It was my turn to put some sense into what was happening.

'I'm getting ready to sling this job.' He poured some more wine.

'Not because sixty paintings have gone missing?'

'No. It's the pressure of banking I suppose, especially now the Austrians want into EFTA.'

'So what? It's more likely to keep them in line. Once they're in they'll have to stick to the rules.'

The waiter put our order on the table accompanied by dishes of thinly sliced cucumber salad, and assorted mustards.

'I guess you're right Katrina. Maybe I'm in line for a vacation, a nice cruise in the Caribbean, a safari in Africa, anything to kick all this shit out of my life for a few weeks.'

'Come to England,' I suggested.

'Great idea if I could swim the channel so no one would find me.'

'Why are you trying to hide Jack? Just tell your head office you're going on leave or better still say on holiday.'
'I've a better idea. Come to New York and meet my Mom. She's a great lady. You'd like her.'

Sounded like wishful thinking to me! I put my knife and fork down, drank some wine, moved the napkin on my lap and sat very erect, my chin high, my eyes cast down my nose. I pushed the sleeves of my black sweater slightly over my wrists.
'Meet your Mom?' I said. 'The last time I met a friend's mother she accused me of cradle snatching. Christ, he was thirty-two and I was twenty. Thank God he still lives with her, not me.'

Before he had a chance to exaggerate the qualities of his Mom, I said. 'Don't tell me, Jack - she's different.'
'Dead right she is. Vivacious Steinhart's been married four times. After every divorce she reverts to my Dad's name. I pop up occasionally to take a look at my latest step-father!'

It was a flippant statement of fact without sentiment or sadness.
'Another statistic of the American dream,' he said as he scooped a dollop of mustard onto his plate.
'Come to England,' I repeated. My mother's Cynthia and my father's Richard. They've been together for thirty four years and as far as I know, have no intention of swapping.'
'In that case Katrina, I'll think about it.'
'Did you read the acceptance letter from the Royal Academy?'
'Yes, but how prestigious is this Academy?'
'Jack, it's not West Point. It's been an Academy of Art since 1840 and owns a building slap in the middle of Piccadilly. How much more prestige would you like?'
'Couldn't you get the Bank of England?'
'Could you get the White House?'

SALZBURG

24

At Salzburg station I watched the big steam engine of the Rosenkavalier crawl towards the platform, turning everything into miniature before grinding to a halt. I walked along the corridor and found an empty carriage and settled into my seat for the journey to Vienna. The massive iron wheels started to roll. Their rhythm became words in my head - here we go - here we go - the same sound heard by the captive human cargo, on the same tracks three decades earlier. Steel girders stirred the wheels of the giant engine, black smoke ejected from its funnel, sending an odorous smell into the carriages and a leaden shroud across the daylight.

***

My meeting with Gerhard Hofer in Vienna was at noon. A hazy sun pushed splinters of light, like glinting swords through the taxi window, as it drove along Mariahilferstrasse to Am Hof.

Every meeting with Gerhard Hofer is different. His mood swings from minimal tolerance to outrageous effrontery and are impossible to anticipate. His smouldering disillusion with life is only compensated by power, and power for him is money. It is difficult to imagine him having a friend: for him, everyone has a use, a price. People are bought like cattle or rented like things.

We left for Grinzing, where Hofer had his latest consignment. He sat in the front of the car with the driver speaking occasionally in German. I was non-existent, which suited me as I was in no mood for confrontation. I recognised the surroundings immediately, but this time I was taken directly to the storage huts to the rear of Grinzingasse: corrugated metal huts similar to those erected by troops in the war for offices, sleeping quarters, and canteens.

Hofer unlocked a thick steel padlock and let it hang on the holding bar. The inside of the hut was pitch dark until he switched on the meagre electric bulbs swinging silently from cheap wiring. I sneezed from the dust and the smell of wood mould. My eyes watered until they acclimatized to the dim

lighting. Hofer was not affected and made no apologies to me. He unlocked a partition door that led into another hut.
'Here,' he said, 'is the Russian consignment.'

Wooden boxes stretched the length of the hut in rows of about ten. At a quick guess there must have been at least two hundred. They were grimy and some were dented: all were the same construction just varying in size.
'From one collection? I asked Hofer.
He looked at me as if I hadn't spoken. It was a curt message.
'You have ze money for ze transport?'
'Depends how much, Herr Hofer?'
'Five thousand Swiss francs?'
Of course I should have remembered he only works in multiples of five and ten.
'Is there a list of contents?'
'No, Fräulein. That vill go to Wilhelm Frohmann after I receive ze money.'

The whole operation was over in half an hour, and whatever the contents, I was convinced Hofer knew they would never be claimed.

I arrived at Westbahnhof station for the four o'clock train to Salzburg and had coffee in the grand Empire style buffet; far to ornate to be on a railway station.

The train was slow, stopping at St.Pölten, Linz, and Wels. I started to compile a list of prestigious names to approach for patronage, names that carried either weight in the business field or credibility in the arts. I short-listed names for the catalogue introduction, including Anton Hempf, Sir Hugh Casson, Lord Delfont, Sir Simon Marks.

It was dark when I arrived at the Hotel Elephant. The night concierge took a note from my pigeonhole on the wall and gave it to me: a message from Jack, asking me to phone him at his apartment.

The grime from the journey felt clammy on my skin. After fifteen minutes soaking in bubble bath, I changed into a black trouser suit and went downstairs to phone Jack.
'You survived?' was his first comment.

'Yes, but if arseholes were an Olympic event Gerhard Hofer would win gold.'
'And who'd get silver?'
'Jack, I'm tired and jokes won't find an audience with me tonight.'
'O.K. We'll go for a light snack. I'll be outside the hotel with the car in fifteen minutes.'

We drove to the foot of the Kapuzinerberg mountain through meadows lit by a cold fading moon to a wooden chalet with log seats outside and paintings of saints on the door. Inside, a few local farmers were playing cards, drinking from steins or chewing on pipes held in dirt ingrained unwashed hands.

A massive fire burned in a cauldron hanging in a blackened brick recess. Benches and tables were on either side. We ordered frankfurters mit zenf and beer. I told Jack what I'd seen, or rather not seen, in Vienna.
'Hofer didn't mention Law 59.' I said. 'Maybe the cunning bastard is bribing someone in Government, just waiting for it to look as if "reason" is taking its course?'
'Doubt it, Katrina. The Government is sitting tight on the article by Anton Kodech: not a word about it has appeared to date.'
'Strange. I'd have thought they'd have capitulated by now.'
'No, they'll have to acknowledge the amendment exists without losing face, so they'll allow a cooling period, get it off the front page before backing down.'
'Do you think Hofer knows this?'
'Certainly.'
'And the Professor?'
'Him too, although he's holding a big crying baby of his own. He told me he's seeing the Minister of Arts tomorrow. Regular stuff Katrina, but it's worth a dollar bet that the meeting's not about humidity in the museums, more likely the climate outside.'
'What's Otto Prantl up to, Jack, besides siphoning paintings through check-point Badgastein?'
'He's a wily fox I'm told. I haven't had any commercial dealings with him, so there's not much I can tell you.'

We finished our beer and drove back into the glow of the city lights. A haze diffused them, turning the white snow into shades of warm yellow. I was in bed and fast asleep by ten thirty.

At eight thirty the following morning, while I was having breakfast, the waiter told me there was a phone call. It was Sue from London.
'Katrina, the Arts council want a firm value on the exhibition before they'll consider Government Indemnity.
'Sue that's impossible. It's changing daily. Will they accept an estimate with a rider for alteration?'
'Only if it's completed within a month.'
'Right, this is what I'd like you to do. Give them a ballpark figure: the Klimt's worth half a million, so quote that as an indication. Who's your contact?'
'Peter Quilliar.'
'He's O.K. He knows us. Tell him the problem, person to person. Try to get some leeway.'
'Shall I mail the first press release?' Sue asked.
'Yes, let's do it our way. Send out what you have with a "more to follow" footnoted. Get it out as soon as you can. And don't give the exhibition a title.'

I knew Sue would pacify the Arts Council and get the press interested. It is news we are selling not just an art exhibition.

While the Professor was in Vienna meeting the Minister for the Arts, I studied the inventory from Badgastein. It was a motley collection of Italian, German and French paintings, some appearing on the official list of lost works of art, under the heading "whereabouts unknown". Kurt Frohmann was most helpful, moving heavy pictures and just being around if I needed a hand. He was always a little aloof and involved in his own artistic work, avoiding contact with visitors to the galerie and the colleagues of his father.

Promptly at five, Professor Frohmann called from Vienna.
'Miss Edan, the meeting went well at the ministry. I think the government will announce an amnesty for works of art held without bills of sale that are handed in at Badgastein.'

It was obvious that the remnants of the Third Reich were alive, well, and active. Even at ministerial level, there were activists holding dust-encrusted secrets, which would not survive scrutiny unless protected by a political arm. Protection money for politicians in exchange for the "occasional favour" was not in short supply, a useful tool to have in place.

Many times during the last year I'd felt frustrated and apprehensive. To-day, completing the list of paintings we had received to date and knowing that the Austrians would rescind their threat of court action, revived my enthusiasm.

***

For the first time Jack suggested we had dinner at his apartment. He lived on the Makartplatz; five minutes walk from his office and five minutes from my hotel. I arrived at the imposing baroque building and looked up at the long windows set between undulating stone pillars. Inside it had all the features of a classical baroque interior: high ceilings, pediments over the double mahogany doors, ornate cornices, with a crystal chandelier hanging from a central ceiling rose, heavily embellished with stucco.

A table was set for dinner in the salon and Jack took a bottle of wine from the refrigerator in the enormous kitchen. It had been refurbished to include modern amenities, but had not lost its charm in the makeover.

'Hungry?' he asked.

'Always. Did you cook dinner?'

'No, but I selected it from the best *to go* service in Salzburg.'

'Oh, I've never eaten a *to go*.'

'Snob' he said, 'you're a semantic left over of Empire.'

'Anything else nice to say about me?'

'Katrina, it's an English take-away with class.' I looked anxiously to see what would arrive on the table.

I sat waiting to be served, fiddling with the buttons at the neck of my red knitted dress, while Jack collected a steaming hot dish of veal in wine sauce decorated with paprika.

'No potatoes?' I called.

'They're coming. The waiter service is crummy to-night.'

We talked about the problems involved by the theft and I said to Jack. 'It will not alter my programme. In fact, sixty missing paintings could give us publicity in media journals we would not normally target. The tabloids aren't interested in art exhibitions but they thrive on theft and intrigue, especially if a few war criminals are involved.'

After dinner I followed Jack into the kitchen.

'Do you wash dishes too?'
'Like hell. They're for the maid in the morning.'

Shame, I thought. I really appreciate a man who can scour a dirty great saucepan. While Jack made coffee I wandered around the apartment looking at my image in eight-foot high gold-framed mirrors, running my hand along satin-topped marquetry furniture, holding china figurines of women in crinolines and bewigged men of the Mozart variety. I went into the bedroom, stood by the door and calculated the yardage in the floor to ceiling pale green and gold damask curtains. The four-poster bed was draped in green silk and white netting. Jack was standing behind me. I turned towards him. 'Oh dear, you have mosquitoes?

'Ignoramus. I thought you came from the enlightened classes.'

Jack sat in a Biedermeier chair with a cup of coffee, watching me as I stroked the shot silk cover on the bed. Then, for no reason, I started to remove my clothes, flinging them in stripper fashion across the room. First my dress, then my bra, which landed cup size up, like two halves of abandoned orange skins. My briefs slowly dropped around my ankles and I stepped onto the thick pile of a green and beige Chinese rug, naked as the day I was born except for my pearl necklace. Jack was watching every move, while I pretended he didn't exist and the whole show was in reverence for my own body. From the corner of my eye I could see him unbuttoning his collar, removing his tie, then folding his trousers over the back of the chair. We fell into bed laughing like teenagers. He said 'tramp.'

I said 'gigolo.' He was still wearing his pants and singlet.

'You're overdressed,' I said as I removed his briefs.

'You're tickling me,' he said.

'Intentional. Part of the Edan service,' I said.

But the laughter stopped as our breathing quickened and our bodies warmed against each other and his lips caressed my body and the tide of sensuality took us into that unrivalled state of oblivion.

LONDON
25

As anticipated, a statement appeared in the Austrian press. Jack telephoned and read a rough gist of what it said:

> **'The Austrian government will honour the ratified clause added to Law 59, which has now come to their notice, the article continued 'it is a gesture for dispersed Austrians to reclaim items of personal sentiment.'**

'That's about it,' he said. 'Frohmann's sending you a transcript.' I put the phone down and shouted: 'Hypocrites, bloody hypocrites,' angered by the one shaming word "dispersed". .

Sue charged into the office almost tripping over some books on the floor.

'What's up with you? Seen a ghost?'

'Almost,' and I told her what I'd heard.

'Calm down Katrina, you're getting too emotional about this project. The Austrians have to justify their mistakes, it's called diplomacy.'

'Too emotional!' I repeated, 'what sort of response is that? I have responsibilities, Sue. It's the way I work. When I cease to be involved, it's time to get out.' I went on venting my anger in a loud voice.

'What am I supposed to do, stand on the sidelines and wave the Union Jack?' I said.

Sue sat opposite me nibbling the end of her pencil, chin down staring at me, waiting, with no intention of trying to appease me. Only someone with her tenacity can calmly reject what she doesn't want to hear: like a British bulldog, her fat paws firmly placed in her four corners, steady as a rock, the face of typical British resolve.

I asked her to check back copies of auction house sales for any items that were on our list. 'Then get Professor Frohmann on the phone.'

Sue picked up her notebook and went to her office, kicking the books on the floor on her way out, leaving behind a waft of Guerlain perfume and a room filled with tension.

Curating always has its disappointments, especially when a museum refuses to loan an important painting because it has exceeded the time allowed for it to be away. Rules can be bent but only for a grand retrospective when the museum would lose prestige if its masterpieces were not included.

My current exhibition had no rules, no precedents and certainly no limits. Knowing this, I had to make ad hoc ones en route, create a framework, set guidelines and, most importantly, shout.

Then, through my anger, I had an idea. If I could borrow Edvard Munch's "The Scream", it would be a metaphor for every aspect of what I was trying to achieve. The image of a lonely skeletal figure standing on a bridge, hands clasped across the ears, desolate, wrecked with fear and creeping death: every brushstroke pregnant with torture: this pictorial statement says more in twenty four inches than any literary lineage could ever say for the victims of Hitler's tyranny. It could be the theme, even the title of the exhibition. I felt excited. I called Sue on the inter-com.

'Take a break, let's have some coffee.' This time she walked round the books put the tray on the desk and sat down.

'Boss are you going to scream or be moderately normal?'

'Scream,' I said. 'That's exactly what we need.'

Sue looked puzzled.

'If we use Munch's "The Scream" as our focal point, its ramifications pictorially and verbally are limitless. It sums up every aspect of what I'm trying to do.' Sue was pouring two mugs of coffee. 'What do you think?' I asked.

'It may be a good idea but what makes you think you'll get the loan?'

'I haven't thought - it's just an idea to work on. This is what I would like you to do. Get in touch with the National Gallery in Oslo and see how the loan position stands. I think we have a good chance of getting it for four weeks: even if it's out on loan, we could borrow it for a month. Also find out if any of their museums have sent "orphan" works to Salzburg. The Germans occupied Norway during the war, so it's possible works were taken. Sue was making hieroglyphic markings on her pad, and then she picked up her mug.

'Good coffee-eh? It's Costa Rican. Thought I'd try the best.'

I hadn't even thought about the coffee, but I sniffed the nutty brew steaming from the top of my mug.

'Umm, you're right, it is good.' Sue was more serious.

'I've been thinking. I can't visualize a formal document for refugees to fill in for a claim. What can we ask? When was the last time you saw the painting you claim is yours? Where was it displayed? What was the subject? Who was the artist? How long had it been with your family? Katrina, we're talking about surviving children who were deported when some were under five years old. They can't be expected to give details. And the older survivors could be too embittered by bureaucracy to even bother.'

I knew what she meant and told her about a refugee, Esther Kalkowitz, who now lived in Israel and returned on a nostalgic visit to see her home in Vienna, where she'd spent her childhood. It was exactly as she'd remembered: the street was the same, and the facade of the house unchanged. Only one thing was different: the occupants. She had arranged to visit the house, but on arrival the door was slammed in her face. She was told to go away and get burnt with the rest of her tribe.

Sue was right, formal documentation was expecting too much.

Putting together a format that wasn't aggressive yet gave enough credibility for a claim, forced me to decide that a form would be implausible. Not only would it intimidate, it would most likely deter anyone from coming forward, fearing they had insufficient evidence.

Instead, I decided on a loosely written invitation asking for any information that would help restore a painting to its rightful owner. This initial request would be helpful in identifying works of art that had been held in "safe keeping", awaiting a claim.

I was looking at my desk: full of clutter, pieces of paper with ideas, exhibition reviews, assorted photographs, invitations to previews, and bills which I had to pay, when a telephone call came from Professor Frohmann. Only ten days had past since the burglary and I was surprised to hear that some of the paintings had been found.

'The police located them in a galerie in Munich,' Professor Frohmann told me.

'So close to Salzburg?' I said in amazement
'The police checked the borders and a van similar to the one owned by my Galerie, crossed the border on Sunday night with papers for an exhibition in Hamburg. The paperwork was in order and it was waved through.'
'How did the police know which galerie to search, there are hundreds in Munich?'
'I don't know Miss Edan, that's the only information I have.'
'Well, Professor it's lucky they were found before reaching Hamburg - obviously the shipping port. I still can't understand why they stopped in Munich?'

Professor Frohmann didn't answer immediately and when he did he changed the subject. I could hear the click of his lighter and the draw on a cigarette holder.
'I believe one of the missing Rothschild paintings has been handed in at Badgastein, when I get an ectochrome I'll send it to you.'
'Thank you Professor. How's your research?'
'I'm managing but my eyes get very tired with all the close up work, and I'm behind with the Rembrandt, but I'll manage.'

There was a sigh of resignation. I guessed the repercussions of his daughter's lawsuit and his wife's withdrawal, were draining his energy and saddening his heart. I hoped it wasn't affecting his judgement.
'Jack Steinhart on the phone.' Sue called.
'Katrina I'll be in London in four days, I'll bring the transcript from Frohmann with me.'
'Why didn't you tell me last week you were coming here?'
'Because I didn't know last week. I'm going to Cambridge first. I'll call you from there. I'm booked into Blake's Hotel in Knightsbridge. Save some time Katrina.'

***

I phoned Desmond and invited him for dinner. When he asked where, I told him 'Alfie's on Waterloo station. It's the second caff on the left.' He refused, but settled to meet me at Langan's brasserie, one of my favourite eateries.

The restaurant was buzzing when we arrived. We sat on high stools at the long bar, ordered champagne and looked at ourselves in the mirrored wall.
'I've got a pimple,' Desmond said, holding his head high and slightly to the left. 'I hate pimples - they appear without invitation, burst their innards and leave you to clear up the mess.'

I watched Desmond surveying the contours of his face, turning left then right. The barman was unmoved, having seen vastly more bizarre antics performed in his arena. The owner, for example, regularly greeted guests wearing a chef's apron wrapped around his wide girth, with an empty champagne bottle tucked under his arm, swaying indiscriminately. When diners entered through the heavy velvet curtain at the door, he'd be waiting.
"Go home, we've no fucking food left," he'd say. Or, "Sod off, we're full." Everyone stayed, as though being insulted was an intimate privilege. In fact, tables were at a premium. One French guest I took to the restaurant remarked, "Peculiar race the British. You accept eccentrics as part of your culture. In France they'd be burned at the stake, comme un filet bien cuit: how can you tolerate such arrogance?"

Certainly Britain has a monopoly on this breed, inherited no doubt from mad King George lll. Now most British families can lay claim to at least one eccentric in their midst, and in some cases a relative in the exclusive Eccentrics Club.

My Aunt Ellie comes closest in our family, a rude frustrated spinster who could cripple any conversation with her rigid hangover from Victorian virtues. She condemns the disgraceful behaviour of young people to-day, never giving leash to youthful experiment nor high-octane energy.

Once I arrived at my parents' home for dinner in purple woollen trousers, and high-heeled shoes and a black jacket. Aunt Ellie was staying for the weekend. When she saw me, her chin dropped, the sides of her mouth dropped, her glasses dropped to the end of her thin nose, but her voice didn't drop. It boomed. "Cynthia, come quickly." My mother came into the room, pecked me on the cheek, and turned to Aunt Ellie in surprise, "what is the matter?"

"Cynthia, your daughter looks like a tart and smells like one too. Just look at her - in trousers for dinner and purple ones to boot." I ignored her comments on taste and kissed her on the forehead.

Desmond and I were seated at a table by the window.
'I know what I want' Desmond said, 'Bangers and mash with onion sauce and a bottle of Brouilly 62.' I didn't read the menu either. 'Mushroom soufflé and fish cakes.'

The waiter collected the long green leather folders holding the hand-written menu inside, leaving space for Desmond's pad and pencil. Sue had kept him informed about progress in Austria and given him dates for the exhibition.

Firstly, he told me the exhibition wouldn't be easy to hang.
'You have two choices: either show them grouped according to their period or country, or the country where the painting was found. Then you can start at the earliest icon and finish with the 20th century.'

He was scribbling on his pad, short and long lines, dark and light, like hatching on an etching.
'What are you doing Desmond?'
'Thinking,' he said.
'I know that, but what are you thinking?'
'About colour.' He was still shading on the paper till the pencil marks became the faintest grey. My soufflé arrived. Desmond continued scribbling. Usually, one touch on top of a soufflé, and they collapse. Not these. They're high, proud and independent. The chef is equally high-minded, refusing to serve soufflés on the first floor, in case they collapse en route to the table.

Desmond, between eating and doodling was deep in thought, speaking aloud to himself.
'Black and white is too depressive, too concentration camp. Green, too Victorian, and primaries, too hard. So what' s left?' He rubbed the pencil lines with his thumb till they merged like clouds. He pushed the hair back from his eyes.
'That's it,' he said, still looking at the smudged lines. 'Pastels. This is the way I see it, Katrina. We have four or five rooms, depending on the number of exhibits and dividers.' I was listening attentively. 'We use five different hues, pink, yellow

turquoise blue and salmon, each wall outlined with a white four inch border.'

I started to visualize the rooms and the quiet calm background effect of soft colours.

'The other reason I think pastels will work,' Desmond said, 'is for identification. If a work of art is recognized and needs someone to corroborate the claim, reference is easy. A single claim in room three, colour yellow, exhibit number x, couldn't be simpler,' he said.

Desmond's idea would not only identify a position, in the exhibition, it bridged any language barrier. I lifted my glass.

'To you, Desmond. Good to have you on board.'

Desmond started tucking into his sausages and mash. I attacked my fish cakes.

I do love Desmond. He's the quintessential good friend. We're non-competitive, non-manipulative, never trying to upstage one another, tuned to each other's thinking and beyond being offended by trivialities. If attractiveness can be measured on a scale of one to five, Desmond's a four, but Jack, on the other hand, rates a five.

What sets this devastating life-changing programme of sex appeal into action is totally arbitrary. Even before I knew Jack as a person, his proximity aroused my senses and created without my intervention, need. Then the search for compatibility followed. With Desmond, regrettably, everything's in place except the elusive sexual magnet.

'Do I get another bottle of wine?' He'd already called the waiter.

'How's the Austrian connection? Any more leads in Munich?'

'None, Desmond. I'm baffled. The robbery wasn't recreational: too professional. On the other hand, it's amateur to unload in a galerie so near to Salzburg.'

'You know what I think, Katrina, there was a tip off. The Munich galerie was just a sleeper till they'd filtered the rest over the border.' This concurred with my own opinion.

Over the years we had worked together, his advice had always proved substantial. His gut reaction was balanced by experience and artistic gift. His Festival Hall project was due to open in December, and it would revolutionize crowd control and give Desmond another well-deserved feather.

'Something has occurred to me Desmond.'
'When something occurs to you, sweetheart, I know you want something.' He took a packet of cigarettes from his pocket.
'Don't smoke, Desmond. Have a dessert.' I pointed to the menu.
'How about Death by Chocolate or Raspberries on a Rocking Horse?'
'Darling, I know you're paying, but I'd rather have a ciggy. So, tell me, what occurred to you?' He pursed his lips and blew smoke rings in my direction. Then he poked his finger through the hole, like a child with a bubble kit.
'Concentrate, Desmond. I don't want you to miss a word.' The restaurant was very full and noisy, so I lent halfway across the table and beckoned with my forefinger so his face was near to mine.
'When the Festival Hall opens, you'll be bombarded by the media. Television, radio, and chat shows, you'll be hot. Every architectural journal, newspaper, magazine will want a piece of you!'
'So, Katrina, I'll give them want they want.'
'Then you can tell them about your next project: my exhibition.'
'Cunning! But pastel colours won't get the press shouting.'
'But it won't do any harm to mention it,' I told him.
'Katrina, it will be positively detrimental to my career. Here am I' . . . he sat back and adjusted his tie, swept the hair from his eyes . . . 'telling some chat show smoothie about a technological innovation for people to hold tagged tickets that channel them to escalators, and into their seats, and bleep if they take the wrong direction, and you want me to tell them I'm painting the walls of the Royal Academy?'
'But you'll do it, won't you?' I pleaded.
'Bloody hell I won't.'

CHAPTER 26
London

I had taken the short route through the park and walked briskly, anxious to get to my desk and complete the application for insurance and the new press release. Sue had her hands tucked into the sleeves of her sweater as I walked into the office. 'I think the heating's on the blink, it's freezing in here.'

I gave Sue a card from my desk drawer. "Ken Bates Everwarm Service".

I phoned Professor Frohmann. The German police were collaborating with the Austrians, and had found the rest of the stolen paintings in a warehouse in Munich. Forensic were dusting for finger prints, which they would compare with those found in Frohmann's Salzburg galerie. 'I'm very pleased,' I told him, 'I hope this whole episode can close quickly.'

Jack Steinhart called from Cambridge. I invited him for dinner, and then phoned Elizabeth. And invited her too. 'I'd like you to meet another sponsor?' I told her.

She accepted and asked me 'who's the other sponsor?'

'Jack Steinhart from the Laufenbankgeschaft, he's an American.'

I telephoned Anton Hempf.

'Anton, will you come for dinner to-night?'

'I'm so sorry, I can't. I'm too tired - it's Friday, remember?'

'Anton - I can't take no for an answer, and dinner's not till 8.30. I'll send a cab to collect you at 8.15. And I promise you'll be home by 10.30.' I waited. Anton sighed.

'I want you to meet my other guests, Elizabeth Cuthbertson and Jack Steinhart. You have such irregular schedules, it's almost impossible to get you all in London at the same time.'

'Alright, Katrina, send the taxi, but I'll leave early.'

It is fortunate having an office in a street with one of the best outdoor markets in central London. As usual I had next to nothing in my refrigerator so I hastily put a menu together in my head. Avocados stuffed with feta cheese and black olives from the Greek delicatessen, owned and run for over thirty years by a Greek man and his wife, and later, joined by their daughter. The shop sold superb olive oils, goat's cheese, olives, artichokes and sweet baklava dripping in black honey.

'I have a problem' I told Sue.
'Not another one Katrina. I'm not in the queue for problems.'
'I've invited Elizabeth, Anton and Steinhart for dinner. What can I give them?'
'Tripe and onions. That'll give the Yank something to talk about!'
'Any other bright ideas?' She buttoned the top of her red cardigan. Something with chilli, it's good and hot.' She rubbed her hands together.
'Seriously Sue, what can you suggest?'
'Get a salmon. It's Friday, Elizabeth and Steinhart might be Catholics, so you'll be on to a good start.'
'How shall I cook it? Sue went into the office kitchen and collected a large roll of tin foil and stood in front of her desk as she spread it flat.
'This is a Fish on Friday menu by Faye Tipper in Women's Own.' She smoothed the wrinkles from the silver paper till it looked like a mirror, then she said, 'First you butter the paper, then cover it with thyme, parsley and thinly sliced onion, salt and pepper the fish, stuff the gut with more herbs, put a dab of butter on top and wrap it up.' She sat down with relief.
'You eat the first course and in half an hour the fish is ready - couldn't be easier.'

Table setting is an art, but for me the activity is cursory. I have one set of black Chinese place mats, decorated with tiny red clad kimono-clad figures, languishing on bridges over water gardens with weeping trees touching the water's edge. Often the mats become a topic for conversation and lead to China, Nepal, Hong Kong, any exotic place in the Far East a guest had visited and a good story usually follows. I set white dinner plates on the mats, and an avocado shaped white china dish on top.

As a child, I had collected china edelweiss or cuckoo clocks, toby jugs and teapots and though I've graduated from this commercial trap, I am now attracted to the esoteric. Once I bought a set of drawings by Adolf Frohner of grotesque fat women, nude except for suspender belts holding up stockings that barely covered the folds of fat above their knees. Other Frohner drawings captured the frustration of trying to secure a brassiere while fighting scrolls of flesh: breasts like cows' udders merge onto swelled inflated bellies. My mother and father thought they were horrendous, a mockery of female beauty, refusing to accept that this was art. But only a few brave draughtsmen elect obese women as a model. That's why I like Frohner. His art becomes a metaphor. These fat ladies with scrolls of tissue and extra creases, their weight heavier than muscles can hold, become icons of stature, at the behest of the artist. For me, this is drawing at its best - limited line and visually convincing. I put the thermostat up on the heating and took a navy pleated skirt and a white shirt off their hangers.

I dislike aprons; they're the quintessential class divide. The Dutch artist, Jan Stein in the genre scenes of bawdy life in Holland paints drunks, interfering with servants. And the British gentry play with the aproned classes, in pictures by Hogarth.

Elizabeth was the first to arrive, promptly at 8.30. An icy wind gusted into the hall like a Siberian warning.

'Ooh, it's cold ' she said. 'I think it's going to snow.' She was wearing a heavy brown overcoat over wide brown trousers and a chunky sweater. Anton followed a few minutes later wrapped in a big woollen scarf and woollen gloves and a long navy blue overcoat. I introduced them. They'd met before but only in the company of many people at a function in the Banqueting House in Whitehall. Both were aware of the other's position in the arcane hierarchy of the art scene.

Anton extended two hands to Elizabeth.

'It's a pleasure to meet you. Katrina has told me about you.'

'Oh dear,' she said, looking at me, 'I hope she was truthful?'

I asked them to help themselves to drinks from the cabinet. Jack was apologetically late.

'The iron horse had to slow to a creep: there was frost on the points. Anyway, I made it. Good to see you Katrina,' he said as I took his lined raincoat.

I introduced him to Elizabeth and Anton as a major sponsor of my exhibition. Anton was quietly surveying this good-looking blond American in a light blue shirt and light blue tie. 'Cambridge?' asked Anton.

'No, Sir,' Jack replied. 'Harvard, but I wasn't a rowing blue.'

The conversation continued at the dinner table.

'I majored in politics and economics' Jack told Anton, 'which tracks one either to the White House or banking.'

'And you chose banking,' said Anton.
'Yes, Sir.'

Jack turned to Elizabeth. 'I believe we have something in common?' he said. Elizabeth looked at me then at Jack, with a perplexed expression. I intervened.

'Elizabeth is the curator who's buying the Gustav Klimt for the National Gallery. She's not a sponsor.'

'Excuse me,' Jack said, 'now I remember. Recently I had some money from Samuel Hall bank and concluded you were a sponsor.'

Elizabeth is far too generous to get offended and quickly replied. 'In a way I am, but only indirectly.'

From then on the conversation flowed easily, except when Elizabeth, Anton and I became animated and excited discussing an uninhibited painting by Francis Bacon, as sheer genius. Jack was relieved when the subject changed to banking, his territory, and where he felt more comfortable. Anton asked 'Is there still enough money in the fund for Katrina?'

'To be truthful, Sir,' he said seriously, 'Katrina is mean with money. She keeps a very tight budget, so I guess she'll make it even with some left over.'

'Doubt that,' I said. 'The catalogue has to be printed and mailed. There's transportation, advertising, port fees, clearance charges, hanging, and security.'

'Katrina, you'll frighten the sponsors away.'

While I was collecting the salmon from the oven I could hear them chattering and laughing. I put the fish on a long lalique dish my grandmother had given me, threw parsley on top, put vegetables in tureens, put them on the table and proclaimed 'Self Service.' Jack poured the wine.

'It's Sue's recipe,' I admitted, 'via Woman's Own. I've never prepared it before. You're my guinea pigs.'

'I object,' Anton said. Jack followed suit. Elizabeth, keeping the female morale intact said 'it's delicious.' Heads nodded. While I was preparing the dessert I could hear the verbal animation coming from the dining room. I filled the glass coupes with fresh fruit salad and vanilla ice cream topped with an amoretto. As I took them to the table, the smell of percolating coffee drifted in behind me.

Elizabeth had taken a photograph from the top of the Chinese cabinet of my parents in the garden in Wendover, against a backdrop of a flaming orange sun setting over the fringe of the Chiltern Hills, and was studying my parents intently.
'You're more like your father, Katrina,' she said tentatively. 'No, maybe not. You have the same chiselled face as your mother. They're a good looking couple.'

Anton and Jack were sitting on the sofa talking. As we drank coffee Anton brought the conversation back to the exhibition. He said to Elizabeth. 'I'm so delighted you're buying Klimt's Hermine Gallia. I remember when my father bought it and I asked my mother if she minded sharing her drawing room with another woman.' Anton put his coffee cup on a side table and sat forward. 'I will never forget what she told me.'
She said, "Anton I am sharing a room with a great painter not a person: she is only the vehicle for the skill of the artist, a muse, an object for interpretation. The painting will survive and have a place in history, but she, my son, will die." I was fifteen.'

He had remembered every word but his eyes were searching for the memory of his mother. We sat silently, not wanting to arouse memories painful to him. Within seconds he said to Jack.
'I believe you know Austria well. What are Katrina's chances of finding enough work for the exhibition?'
'Difficult to answer Sir. She's achieved a lot in one year. Katrina's determined and resourceful: good ingredients by any standards.' Anton looked at his watch. 'Oh dear, how time flies.'
'May I get your coat Sir?' Jack said.
'You certainly can, Katrina told me I'd be home by ten thirty and it's already eleven.' Anton turned to Elizabeth. 'I look forward to meeting you again.'
Elizabeth asked Jack if he would like a lift to his hotel.
'Thanks,' he said as he slipped into his raincoat, 'but my hotel's in South Kensington. Not this side of town.'
'That's where I live Mr.Steinhart.' 'Jack,' he corrected.

Anton said as he was leaving, 'Thank you, Katrina I enjoyed the evening very much. Would you call me on Monday morning?' Elizabeth and Jack left together, both saying how much they had enjoyed the evening. 'We'll talk soon.' Jack said.

In the morning I called Blades Hotel and asked for Mr. Steinhart. 'Just one moment' came the reply. Then 'I'm sorry Mr.Steinhart isn't answering his telephone.'
'Would you try the breakfast room please?' The line went dead. After a few minutes the voice came back 'I'm sorry Mr.Steinhart is not in the hotel.' I looked at the time: 7.50 am. He made an early start! Maybe he didn't stay in the hotel last night.

Sometimes my imagination plays havoc without any justification: self torment on issues that are irrelevant, controlling and mostly unfounded, except when my intuition intervenes with warning signals that all is not as it appears. This was happening now. I'd never really been in Jack's confidence, in fact, I knew very little about him except what he had selected to tell me. Strange really. I sat up in bed and dialled Elizabeth with the feeble excuse she'd left her scarf on the back of a chair.
'I hope I didn't wake you.' I said.
'No - I was sweeping the garden, I was going to call you anyway to thank you for dinner.'
'Did you find Jack's hotel?'
'Easily - I've been there before.'
'I hope Steinhart didn't keep you chattering, you know what Americans are like.'
'Katrina, we did chatter. In fact I had coffee with him.' She didn't elaborate and it would have been impudent to ask. But she added, 'Anton Hempf invited me to his home. Wasn't that kind. He's calling me next week.'

I was suspicious of everything and everybody, drawing conclusions from nowhere, craving reassurance on all the levels in my life, a sure recipe for disappointment.
At noon the phone rang - it was Jack. 'Thank you Katrina for last night. Great to meet Hempf, and Elizabeth's a very interesting woman - I really enjoyed the change.'
I felt grumpy and neglected. 'Change from what, Jack?'
'Banking of course. I even had it for breakfast this morning at Grosvenor House. Elgin Brooks was in transit from Israel.' What a coincidence. Sounded more like an excuse to me.
'Oh, so you have his account too?'
'No Katrina, I don't, and I don't want to talk work anymore. How about lunch?'

'The Rotunda in Hyde Park, is nearby. Is one thirty O.K.'
'How do I get there?'
'Go into the park at the Albert gate by the Memorial and the Rotunda is on the right.'

Jack had arrived late for dinner, now he was late for lunch, and at one forty five I decided I would wait another fifteen minutes, and not a second longer. I had made no particular effort to look alluring; in fact I wore a knitted black cloche hat, pulled down over my forehead leaving my red hair falling around my shoulders. Through the spaces in the bare branches of trees, the icy water of the Serpentine looked grey and uninviting. Why do people swim in its murky water every day of the year? The thought left me shuddering. Eccentricity at its extreme - my father would call it bulldog stamina. A group of children riding ponies held on lead reins passed the window. A rider on a polished brown thoroughbred walked past them, its ears haughtily high, turning its head from its superior height, then galloping off into the distance, leaving the ponies plodding on.

Jack arrived by taxi: 'I'm sorry I'm late, I have been at the Embassy to collect some information and the guy I was supposed to meet didn't show, so I've been hassling around the department looking for the papers I need. Would you like a drink Katrina, or are you passing out with hunger?'

As I'd already had a glass of wine I said 'I think we should order,' although I had passed being hungry and his off hand manner, and being late, didn't encourage conviviality on my part. There wasn't anything on the menu I fancied. 'Maybe a dish of assorted sandwiches with mixed salads?' the waiter said.
'Sounds O.K. to me. And you, Katrina?' I nodded.
'And to drink Sir?' 'A bottle of Muscadet de Sevres - make sure it's well iced.'

My curiosity forced me to ask his opinion on Anton and Elizabeth, but I made light of my question by saying.
'I enjoyed dinner last night. Everyone seemed to gel. What do you think?'
'I liked Anton, a convivial gentleman for someone so eminent.'
'And Elizabeth?' I asked, my voice rising.
'I suspect there's a lot going on around her that isn't obvious.'

What an obscure reaction. I had always found Elizabeth to be outspoken and predictable. Could I be foolishly naive?

Jack's sandy polo neck sweater matched his hair, which reached just below his chin line, accentuating his firm contoured jaw line. He pushed the sleeve of his sweater up from his wrist and looked at his watch.

'There's been a change of plan,' he said, 'I have to return to Salzburg to-night.' He looked out of the window towards the still water of the Serpentine, 'I have a six-thirty flight.'

'Aren't you staying the week-end,' I said in disgruntled surprise.

'I was, but the Chicago office has other ideas.'

'Can't you deal with it from here - you are connected to the telephone,' I remarked sarcastically.

'It's not that simple. I wish it were.'

'So - tell me Jack - what's not so simple?'

The waiter placed a tray of sandwiches on the table on a fancy white doily that fluttered around the edge of the dish like the collar on an old fashioned nightdress. Jack tasted the wine.

'What's going on in Salzburg Jack, I want to know? If it's nothing to do with me, say so. If it is, tell me!'

Jack put his glass down, wiped his mouth on his napkin, then threw it on the table.

'Indirectly,' he said, 'it's a lot to do with you, and directly, absolutely zilch.'

'I don't understand. Is this a personal issue?' I responded, as though he'd thrown a gauntlet - not a napkin. 'Don't tell me you're lost for words, you never are.'

'No Katrina, I'm not and until I know exactly what I'm talking about I'm opting for the 5th amendment.'

Smart arse American! 'If you haven't an answer, I have.' I took my handbag from the back of my chair, threw it defiantly over my shoulder, and said, 'Don't bother to get up' and I walked out.

Curled up on the couch at home, I contemplated my actions. I had no remorse, nor an inkling of regret, although my reaction was emotional, it was also prudent. Isn't it reasonable, I argued with myself, that a relationship should engender a few mutual secrets excluding everyone except the personalities involved?

Isn't it reasonable that I know something of the pattern of his life, or is that being unreasonable?

I kicked a cushion off the couch. It fell on the floor in a floppy heap. Then I picked it up and put it back in place.

I phoned my mother. 'Are you and Daddy home to-night? Good. I'll be home about six. Hope there's plenty of ice in the freezer.'

WENDOVER
27

The A41 is a winding road with undulating hills that get steeper on the approach to the Icknield Way, the old Roman Road to Wendover that looks out to the vast expanse of Aylesbury basin, where gliders gracefully topple on air currents and thermals, like swooping sea gulls, before rising again. There's a section of the A41 at Hunton Bridge with a "SLOW Hump Bridge" sign, which became a symbol of my childish excitement, when I would shout to my father, 'faster, faster'. We would fly off the top of the hump nearly hitting our heads on the car's roof. My mother always, but always repeated, "One day you'll do that once too often Richard, and then what?" I giggled and my father, with his foot firmly down on the accelerator said, "Yes dear."

Wendover village is a collection of thatched cottages, a thatched general store and the Wendover Arms where my father bought wine. Sometimes he took me with him and Mr.Atkins, the owner, gave me a packet of crisps which I dived into immediately, looking for the little dark blue paper that was filled with salt. I would sprinkle it over the crisps and eat them till the bag was empty. My father said to Mr.Atkins once.

"It's the only time she's quiet, when she's eating." I didn't think that funny, but they laughed.

The white wooden bar gate to my home was open. I parked the car on the pebble drive outside the garage. Smoke coming from the chimney curled into the air spreading a potent scent of burning pinewood and my heels sunk into the grass, making pockmarks on the lawn. The front door latch was open. Mother came into the hall, her hands green and smelling of fresh herbs.

'Darling, what a lovely surprise, she said with her arms outstretched like a duck in flight. Daddy's upstairs changing. He put his shoe in a cow pat and he stinks!'

I had bought fresh bread from our regular stopping place on the Finchley Road: one tin loaf, one cottage loaf and eight scones. Father was waiting by the door as I returned from the car.

'How are you my dear. What a lovely smell,'
'My perfume or the bread Daddy?'

My bedroom hadn't changed since I left for university. I still felt it was exclusively mine. I had chosen the decor as I grew from teddy bear wallpaper to flashy silver stripes, and later, as an art history student, to plain academic white.

"It doesn't distract me," I had justified. "I have to imagine colours and anything glaring from the walls will spoil my picture." Mother always consented, though she did baulk once when I wanted to put Alphonse the tiger skin rug on my wall. She absolutely refused to remove it from the floor in the drawing room.

"You can go to Selfridges and buy three yards of mock leopard and put that up," I remember her saying.

"But it's not got any shape," I had protested.

"What are you saying, not got", you mean it hasn't.'

"If you say so," I said.

I like my room. The big double bed with its white wrought iron head and tail, covered by a white lace bedcover, with white lace cushions scattered over the pillows. The curtains are made of white muslin lined with Egyptian cotton and tied back with white cord. I have a small white television set and a white painted desk, although it was originally green before my parents reluctantly gave it a lick of paint. Above the bed is a Mondrian painting with abstract squares in shades of white from pure titanium, the whitest, zinc white, then flake white, to cremnitz the most opaque. My room faces West over the Aylesbury basin and our house is high on a ridge commanding dramatic views of golden sunsets more often seen in the Mediterranean or a Rembrandt painting. I watched from my window as the spherical ball of fire hovered on the horizon, before slowly sinking into another sunrise.

I heard the familiar call from the stairwell, 'Drinks time.' I took a comfortable red cotton kimono from the wardrobe, and went downstairs.

Daddy was pouring. 'Whiskey?' he said. 'Double' I replied.

We sat quietly enjoying our drinks by the fire. My father never asked intrusive questions, especially when he knew I had something to tell and that I would tell him in my own time. It is his army training, I presume: a lifetime of listening to subordinates, where yes or no only confirm guilt or denial, success or failure. The grey areas of why or when or how are not for consideration. In a way father had lived in a black and white world, with very little room on the sidelines for opinion. He is both tolerant and intransigent in turn, according to situation, but whatever the circumstances they must fit into his channelled mind. He is not demonstrative but I know he loves me. I wondered why he had married my mother, until I was told by a psychotherapist that most children face that question, especially girls during puberty, when they become competitive, seeking unrivalled attention, testing their sex appeal on the first man in their lives, their father, who is totally unprepared for this type of disruption. Not the case with Richard Edan, he was programmed to repress sentimentality. In the army focus is paramount, often vital for survival and any diversions were negative.

But since retiring he had let slip the constraints of army life, and appeared more relaxed and comfortable. He discussed the Cold War, our troops in Germany, sent letters to The Times and rigorously hiked the countryside between forays to London to the theatre with my mother and occasional holidays abroad. They went on a cycling holiday in France one year. Well, that was what they told me! Actually, they biked along flat country roads in the Auvergne between relais chateaux, while their luggage was transported ahead, in time to wine and dine in dedicated French style. They rode from eleven till one, lunched and ended the day at four. I admired their fortitude and sense of adventure, and was secretly thankful they weren't overtaxing their energy.

The embers of the fire crackled like sparklers on Guy Fawkes night, and the scent of wood penetrating the house was a perpetual source of comfort to me: timeless and natural - no intervention by science, just a flick of a match, and a world of imagination is released.

I used to see hidden caves in between the logs, as blue flames danced with red ones, running into little holes seeking fresh wood to keep them prancing, then slowly vanishing when the wood turned ashen and cold.

'Lovely fire Daddy,' I said.

'Isn't it, but I can tell you it's a beast to get going, something to do with the wind direction in the flue, but once it's started . . . whoosh, and it's all guns firing.' He took a brass poker and turned a log, igniting new flames that leapt up the chimney.
'Cynthia's putting something in the oven: you know what that means?' I smiled and looked knowingly at my father. Mother's "something's" being untried recipes she couldn't resist. She came into the drawing room holding a glass, 'I'm ready for a top up,' she said. 'I hope you're both starving?'
'Do I look starved Mother?'
'Yes you do. You're too thin. Are you overworking and living on sandwiches?' I thought of Jack and the Rotunda and the abandoned lunch, admitting only to myself that I hadn't eaten all day.
'What's on the menu Mummy?' guessing she was dying to tell me.
'Well,' she said, putting her whiskey down next to her armchair.
'We're having duck pâté which I had already made for the week-end, then I've experimented.' Daddy and I grinned at each other.
'Stop teasing. It's from Flo Meredith's new book, "Country Treats", mother said.
'Oooh - can't wait, can we Daddy', still trying to illicit ridicule like an immature child. He sipped his scotch without responding. He reckoned the game had finished.

Dinner was set in the kitchen. It's a big friendly country style room with dried flowers and a long narrow wooden scrubbed table which once served as the counter at an Aylesbury drapery store. Scissor marks made from cutting yards of fabric left odd shaped dents and the edges curved where heavy sheaves of material were pulled onto it for measuring. It seated ten comfortably and was continually used for every meal, except Christmas, birthdays, and when my parents gave dinner parties. The pâté, was a treat, lots of duck pieces nestling in aspic with fresh herbs from the garden. My father poured some red wine. While we waited for the "something" Daddy asked.
'How's the exhibition, darling. You must be getting towards the end?'
'No, Daddy. Only the end of the first year but I've managed to get the R.A. for October 73.'

'Clever girl,' he said.
'Not really. It's only for one month.'
'That's a short time for so much work!'
'I know. The whole venture's a lottery anyway. With so much undercurrent, I sometimes wonder if it's worth the hassle.'

Mother called across the kitchen, 'won't be long,' My father looked at the engraving on his silver napkin ring with thoughts of his own, not intruding on mine. My parents have a dedicated interest in my work, my welfare and personal involvements, but without criticism. When I brought boy friends home for a day in the country, they didn't ask about his history or his intentions or if it might be permanent. Just commented 'nice chap' or 'good sense of humour' and left me to my own conclusions.

Mother had her hands in leaf green printed oven gloves and set a casserole shaped like a cockerel with a plume for the lid, in the centre of the table. I collected the vegetable tureens.
'Is that the experiment?' I asked and pointed at the cockerel, before the ritual question.
'Whose turn is it?' father said, first looking at me then at my mother. In unison we said 'Yours'.
'Oooh-ee' he said as he raised the lid, exposing a whole chicken glazed with flat mushrooms and bell peppers.
'Looks yummy' I said and bent forward to sniff the herby aroma.

My mother mimed to my father 'you carve first then scoop some of the couscous stuffing on each serving.' It was a serious tasting session with absolute silence.
'What's in the stuffing? It's delicious.' I said.
'It's couscous, fresh coriander, field mushrooms from Mr. Jenkins farm, lemon zest and a nip of ginger.' The rumblings in my stomach subsided quickly. Then, for no apparent reason and oblivious of timing, I blurted out.
'I've met an American guy in Salzburg.'
'Oh, yes' said my father, helping himself to more chicken . . . then asking if we would like some more. I went on.
'Actually, he's one of the sponsors - at least his bank is.' More silence! 'He was in London this weekend . . . well I thought it would be the weekend but he left to-day.' My mother looked up from her plate at my father but she didn't draw his attention.
'Were you disappointed?' she said.

'No, Mother, I was furious: not because he had changed his plan but he gave no reason, no tangible excuse. Just threw it at me like the tail end of a dead fish. And he was late for lunch too.'

My father put his knife and fork down.

'That's not a crime, Katrina, being late for lunch.'

'I know that. It was his flippant manner I found offensive - so I walked out of the restaurant.' I felt relief telling them, however petty it sounded.

My father was holding his glass, resting his arms on the wings of his rustic chair.

'What were you walking away from, my dear?'

A penetrating question forcing me to explain.

'As a start, he's self-sufficient, confident, erudite, clever, musical and unfortunately good-looking: enough to make anybody conceited. But unfortunately he's not.'

'Coo' Mummy said looking directly at my father, 'has he an older brother?'

'I hope he does,' Daddy said. 'That would be two women off my back.' I stroked my father's hair, confirming my affection.

'So he's different or difficult, Katrina?' he questioned.

'Both. One because he's distant, I am never sure if I am a convenience because we're working in tandem, or because I'm English and a relief from the Teutonic characters he deals with everyday, or from his head office who demand 150% commitment plus overtime, or if he remotely cares about me.'

'And two?' Mother said.

'To be exact, he didn't come to London for a weekend with me. Just extended a meeting in Cambridge, with a stay-over.'

I stopped talking and reflected on what I had said. 'The more I think about it, I know I was right to walk out.'

Yet it remained an unsolved emotional problem. Without sibling competition or collusion, my actions and reactions had been formulated by my parents' expectations: now, I am controlled by my own. If I daydream, reality will eventually catch up, testing my resourcefulness.

While my father left the table to put another log on the fire mother decided we'd have dessert on our laps in the drawing room. 'I can't manage dessert,' I said.

'It's only crème caramel - just a little one?' she said and tipped her head to one side in a pleading pose.
'All right, I'll have one as it's so tiny.'

The only sound in the drawing room was the splitting of the brittle caramel as we cracked the surface of our pudding and the crackling from the fire. Mother said: 'How old is this American man?'
'Somewhere between thirty-five and forty. I've forgotten if he ever told me. You will not believe this, he suggested I meet his mother in New York at Christmas, a bizarre invitation especially as his mother's called Vivacious?' Father thought it hilarious.
'Is that her character or a description?' He waited to hear more but I felt I'd said enough: so he took the initiative.
'Why don't you ask him here for Christmas?'

I was balancing a cup of coffee on the arm of my chair, looking into the flames, playing high and low.
'Daddy, as far as I'm concerned he can go home to his spirited mother for Christmas and go to the Boston tea party for New Year.' Mother immediately asked.
'Where will you spend Christmas darling?'
'Here, of course.' The tone of my voice closed the conversation for the evening.

I said goodnight to my parents as the grandfather clock in the hall struck ten thirty.

***

I wakened as the bells were ringing from Ellesborough church. Unlike the boom of Big Ben, these were a melodious tinkle.

Breakfast was always late on Sundays. Father suggested we go for a hike, although the clouds were heavy and an east wind blowing. We had "all weather" clothes: my oxblood hiking boots which I bought in Lillywhites, Wellingtons, my riding mac, my parents' waterproofs, an assortment of woolly hats, walking sticks and my father's old army fatigues. Soon after breakfast we were ready to go.

We always climbed the steep route to the Beacon, a high point in the Chiltern Hills near our house. Even when I was a small child I would scamper up the steep slope often on all fours, grabbing the chalky rocks, sliding backwards and having my bottom pushed by my mother. But on such a damp cold

December morning we drove round the Beacon, past the side gate to Chequers, the Prime Minister's country home, and parked the car in the woods.

We walked along the ridge, till we reached the summit. The panorama over the vale of Aylesbury was totally obliterated. We had to decide which route to take back to the car - the long or the short. Father said 'long,' I said 'short,' mother said, 'let's toss.' My father fished in his corduroy trousers for a coin.

'You call Cynthia - heads, long, tails, short. He flipped a penny so high he missed it on the way down and we had to rummage in the rough grass to find our fate.

'It's here,' I shouted, poking around for the brown coin.

'Don't touch it,' father said, 'it's vital evidence,' as we moved the spiky grasses covering its edge. 'Heads,' we all said. 'The long route.' I complained. I was ignored. Another ritual.

'Stamina, show a little stamina,' Daddy said. 'We'll take longer steps, it'll take half the time!' I looked at my father suspiciously. 'So that's how you fooled me all these years!'

A naughty smile crossed his face, and off we marched. My feet responded to the rhythm and became lighter. City worries distanced with each stride. We walked through dense dark woods, high trees blotting out the light, as we squelched along on a carpet of rotting leaves, discoloured yellows and browns, the remnants of a glorious past.

'No slacking now,' the gruff voice of authority said. 'One step per yard, one per yard, left right, left right,' as we swung our arms in unison.

Our cheeks were as red as our noses by the time we reached the car and time no longer mattered.

The weekend had passed too quickly. By evening sleet was falling and the garden was a shimmering white blanket as my father walked with me to the car.

'Drive carefully, my dear. Go slowly till the main road. It looks treacherous.'

LONDON
28

I had devised a circuitous route through Regent's Park from my house in Regent's Mews, a small cul-de-sac hiding between Baker Street and Camden Town. I chose the house for its simplicity. Its eclectic heritage appealed to my minimalist taste. My walks were programmed according to the season. In February the west side of the park has snowdrops and crocus, dancing in the grass, competing for space. This early spring carpet joyously appears, projecting thoughts of summer's warmth as velvet smooth petals suddenly erupt in a blaze of deep purple, citrus yellow, and shades of delicate mauve. My winter walk is past massive trees, oaks hundreds of years old, weeping willows that drape into the lake, umbrella pines, maple, birch, and giant horse chestnuts. Stark, solid trunks, with naked branches, forming abstract shapes against a grey marbled sky. They're waiting, still, silent, sleeping. Dark mottled barks shed their coats: squirrels rush between their boughs - halting - looking - pleading. There is friendliness in the park in winter: uncluttered communication between nature and the senses, allowing time to distil one's thoughts.

When I arrived at my office Sue didn't waste time. 'Are we working in my office or am I coming to yours?' I looked at the long telephone list on her desk.

'I'll stay here.' I pointed to the list. 'Shall we clear those first?'

'Jack Steinhart phoned three times. First at nine o'clock,' she looked up from the list, 'when we usually open up shop. Anton Hempf and Desmond Hegarty want you to call them.' She went on. 'The accountants want your tax return and Liberty's said your dress has arrived. Shall I call them in turn?'

'No, call Dr.Hempf first.'

'Then Steinhart?' Sue said.

'No - if he calls again, take a message.'

'I tried that, twice.'

Anton Hempf invited me to join him and Anna Frishman for lunch on Wednesday. Desmond wanted a floor plan of the R.A. and the accountant told me I was late with the 1970 figures. Sue called on the inter-com, 'Steinhart on the phone again, says it's important.' Without knowing if his call was personal or impersonal, I replied. 'Tell him I'm busy - I'll call later.' I wanted to make it clear my time could not to be filched at whim. At the same time I couldn't jeopardise the exhibition for selfish pride. Why was I playing games anyway? To make a statement? I had already done that when I walked out of the Rotunda. To make him feel guilty about being late for lunch? That was trivial: for pleading the Fifth Amendment? Or the real reason: commitment. I asked Sue to ring him.

'At last Katrina, I've been trying since nine to contact you.'

'I know, I've been busy.'

The conversation that followed, or more accurately, the one I listened to, left me shocked and bewildered. When I heard the telephone rest in its cradle, I sat forward, put my head in my hands and said "Bloody Hell".

My timetable was reduced to insignificance, and I sat quietly thinking about what I had been told and what I should do. I could hear Sue typing in her office and decided not to tell her. I rang Desmond.

'Are you friendly with Adrian Liston, The Times art critic?'

'No, Katrina. He hates my guts!'

'Shame, I need a contact. I'll call you later and explain.'

I rang The Times newsroom and asked to speak to Paul McKenzie, an investigative journalist who frequently hit the front page. I could hear the rap of typewriters and visualized hungry newsmen tapping out copy to shove at department heads, hoping the first draft would pass muster, so they wouldn't get sent back like errant schoolboys to re-write the crap into something literally plausible. After a few moments a gruff voice said 'McKenzie.' I gave him my name and a brief résumé of what I was doing. Then an outline of what I had heard from Austria. I told him, 'The incident happened over the week-end.'

'Where are you speaking from Miss Edan.' he said promptly.

'My office in Camden town.'

'What's the address?' I gave him the details.

'I'll be there in half an hour.'

Paul McKenzie was the archetypal hungry newsman: tall, wiry, mid-forties, slightly balding, with a loose tie hanging half-mast below his unbuttoned shirt collar. He threw a well-worn mackintosh over the back of the chair. He shook my hand with a moist palm and sat down heavily opposite me. He put a small Dictaphone on my desk, took a notepad from his pocket, and waited.

For a journalist the race against time is ongoing. Yesterday's news is the death knell for relegation to the back of nowhere. McKenzie didn't strike me as a has-been, more a stereotype of his profession. Like a hardened criminal all he wanted was the spoils. Paid snoops glean information in bars for men like McKenzie, waiting for a bragging slip of the tongue, a confidential tap on the side of the nose: a sign for a little "dropsy" to pass from one pocket to another. This is McKenzie's world: news that licks the presses and relegates the competition to scrape the barrel. If a scoop breaks on his front page, every other paper is only rushing for the crumbs. I was about to give an exclusive to Paul McKenzie.

He switched on the Dictaphone. 'You don't mind, do you?' giving me little alternative.

'I don't mind at all, as long as we get two things in place first. One: I want a copy of the tape you're recording, and two: your assurance that what I tell you will get headline coverage on the front page.'

McKenzie said, 'that's a tall order: I can punch your story into the editor's face but he'll decide where, when, and if it's included.'

'Also,' I added, 'I want everything we agree sent in writing to my lawyers, Peters, Gulick, Davidson. I'll call them now.' I said.

McKenzie hadn't expected this and fidgeted with arrogant impatience, but I knew from experience that journalists would sell their grandmothers in exchange for a front-page story, with a by-line. And why, I thought, should he be different?

Alan Gulick has been my lawyer for eight years. He is very short on words outside the law, which he knows without reference. I explained what I intended to do.

Gulick said, 'You can go ahead with the interview, Miss Edan, I'll write to Prickett to-day.'

McKenzie said coldly, 'Are you ready?'

I gave him precise details of what Jack Steinhart had told me

without revealing my source. I gave him the proposed exhibition date, October 1973, at the Royal Academy.
'How long have you been looking for stolen art?'
'Since late 69.'
'Has anything been in the press before?',
'In Austria there have been a few preliminary announcements and a mention in "Art Ahead" here. The information I'm giving you only surfaced last night. The Austrian police called Professor Frohmann at eight this morning and Austria called me at nine. When I eventually spoke at eleven to-day the police had not released the information but Professor Frohmann is too well known for this story to stay under wraps for long.'

He questioned me for almost an hour, delving for historic fact; evidence that my source was authentic. He switched off the Dictaphone and lit a cigarette without asking permission to smoke, adding more nicotine to his already stained fingers. McKenzie warned: 'Expect some repercussions when this story breaks.'
'What sort of repercussions?' I wanted to know.
'Never can tell. You'll probably get every hack in the business knocking on your lavatory door. Just be prepared.'

He stood up, put his raincoat over his arm, and the notepad in his coat pocket.
'Thank you. I'll be in touch. Can I have your home telephone number?'

In one impulsive moment he had it. Hell, I thought afterwards, you've just given your life away!

Sue came into the office. 'Who's he?' she said, as we heard the front door slam.
'An advertising contact,' I said casually. 'I've given him a résumé of the exhibition. He might get some free publicity. Anyway it was worth a try.'

Embarking on surreptitious behaviour was not my standard practice. I had never kept information from Sue nor engaged in devious activities relating to a project. But, by excluding her, any whiplash rested solely with me. Neither Sue, Desmond, Anton nor Jack knew I'd contacted The Times. If it went disastrously wrong, I'd take the flak. The exhibition was becoming a chronicle of disasters anyway – so why not heap the pile to its maximum and then set it alight?

At five past nine on Tuesday morning the office phone rang. I answered as Sue was collecting stationery and wouldn't be in till eleven. Paul McKenzie was on the line.

'The Times editor decided to print my article immediately: it's in this morning's edition. We want to get a jump on Reuters before they pick up the connection in Austria.'

'But you agreed I'd get a page proof?'

'I know, but we would have lost a day, and probably, the story.'

I didn't believe him.

'Which page is it on, Mr.McKenzie?'

'Front. It's not the splash, it's right, first column.'

I put the phone down, pulled my coat on, quickly locked the office and went to the newsagent in the market next to the Greek delicatessen. I bought four copies of The Times. As I walked back to the office I read the headline in bold black print.

SON ACCUSED OF ART THEFT FROM EX-NAZI FATHER

Desperate to read the full text of the story, I rushed back to the office. The phone was ringing as I opened the door. I threw a copy of The Times on Sue's desk and picked up the phone. It was The Times saying they were sending some copies of the newspaper to my office. I sat down and scanned every word Paul McKenzie had written.

SIXTY works of art, destined for an exhibition at the Royal Academy in London in October 1973, were stolen from the gallery of Professor Wilhelm Frohmann in Salzburg, during a weekend heist by the Professor's son, Kurt Frohmann. After a two-week search the pictures were discovered in Munich yesterday and included works by Cézanne, Renoir and Monet.

Katrina Edan, a British curator is working with Frohmann to uncover works of art stolen during the Nazi regime.

In Austria Frohmann is a media personality and a respected art historian. Between 1939-1945, he was the personal curator for Hermann Goering, and colluded in cultural genocide. Goering's haul of treasures from France alone filled eleven carriages of a train, mostly taken into "safe custody" by Wilhelm Frohmann. At the Nuremberg war trials, Frohmann showed no remorse, only pride in his effort to save works of art, destined for Adolf Hitler's

grand museum project in Linz. Frohmann denied secretly trading on the side for his own benefit. He was sentenced to three years.

Katrina Edan confirmed that many orphan works are hanging undetected in museums and private homes, too hot for sale on the open market and too incriminating for Governments to reveal. This has created a vast underground black market, a cash and carry trade for unscrupulous dealers to sell works of dubious provenance.

After twenty-five years dealing in loot is still rampant. Curators of museums worldwide have bought masterpieces with false documentation. These iniquitous spoils of war hang resplendently on their walls, admired and revered by an unsuspecting public.

Kurt Frohmann, the accused son of Professor Wilhelm Frohmann, will have more than larceny to answer for.

As expected, the phone started ringing. I was staring at The Times headline in disbelief waiting for the inevitable call from Austria. It was Desmond.

'You two timing, double crossing, daughter of a bitch.' Desmond said on the attack. 'I have just read the front page of The Times. Who are you trying to hood-wink?'

'Hey, hold on, I'm not up for insults this morning. Anyway, how do you find time to read the first edition? Why aren't you working?'

'You skinny cow - I read while I'm eating.'

I had forgotten breakfast hoping Sue would bring some carbohydrates in to keep us motoring.

'I've never lied to you, Desmond, so why are you so aggressive?'

'O.K. I'm aggressive. But is the story in The Times true?'

'Absolutely. Straight from the horse's mouth.'

'You may need protection, Katrina. I know a good agency, full of beefy muscle: hey, some even stay overnight.'

'Don't joke, Desmond. This theft could jeopardize two years' work.'

'No-way. It'll start a nice line in reportage, however derogatory. Dirt is the most saleable item for the press.'

'Thanks, pal.' I put the phone down. Before I had a chance to get the dialling tone it rang again.

'Hello? Miss Edan please.'

'Who's speaking?' I asked,

'The Evening Standard.'

'One minute.' I put my hand over the mouthpiece for a few seconds, then said, 'Miss Edan is out of the office. Would you call back?' Click, he was gone. Ding-ding, it was the Daily Telegraph. I gave them the same routine.

At last I heard the front door open, and I went into Sue's office before she saw the newspaper. She had a woollen scarf wrapped around her neck, a long black coat and was carrying a bag of office supplies and a Cullen's food bag.

'God, it's nippy out there,' she said as she wiped her nose on the back of her glove and put the bags in the kitchen.

'I hope you've bought some breakfast. I'm famished,' I said as I poked around in the carrier bag. Brown bread, cheese, tomatoes, olives, ham and croissants.

I held the flaky curled croissant and said, 'I'll have mine stuffed with everything.' The phone rang. 'I'll take it Sue'.

The voice said, 'Leigh Ramsey from the BBC newsroom.' I covered the mouthpiece and talked to myself for a second, then: 'Edan speaking.'

A quiet velvet toned voice spoke seductively.

'I was intrigued, Miss Edan, by The Times report this morning, and I think our listeners would like to know more about the exhibition you're curating.' This gentle approach did not hook me, as I'm not fooled by a softly-softly approach, even from the BBC.

'What would you like to know, Miss Ramsey?

'Could you possibly find a time to come to the studio for a short interview?' She quickened the pace, 'we'll send a car for you - it won't take long.'

I thought quickly, as I didn't want to infringe my arrangement with The Times, but no reference had been made to radio or television, so I felt free to accept. It could be a fortuitous bonus, as long as the questions followed her request: to talk about the forthcoming exhibition in 1973.

'When would you like to record, Miss Ramsey?'

'This afternoon around four, in time for the six o'clock news.' The rest was a formality.

Sue was standing in the doorway holding The Times as I put the phone down. 'Congratulations Katrina. Whose been licking whose arse to get this one?'

'Jack Steinhart told me yesterday.'
'Sneaky bastard. How does he get such hot gossip?'
'From Frohmann, and it isn't gossip!'
'So why didn't you tell me?'
'Because I didn't want to implicate anyone here. The article could be the kiss of Judas - you know the press as well as I do - mean, shabby, double crossers.'

Before Sue sat down I asked when breakfast would arrive.
'Oh - I forgot it - I've been reading the newspaper.'
'We're going to get a barrage of telephone calls. I don't want to speak to anyone unless they're one of the regulars - Hempf, Elizabeth, Steinhart - you know the crew, but most importantly whomever you speak to, you know absolutely nothing. Say anything, be the switchboard operator, a temp, anybody, as long as she's dumb.' Sue put on her basset dog face, head down eyes up and lids droopy.
'You mean take a "stumm powder"?' We ate our croissants re-reading McKenzie's article.

Fielding the phone satisfied Sue's expert skills. Warding off a news hungry press about a robbery in Austria, would not normally spirit its way onto the front page of The Times, but the human dimension - son stealing from Nazi father - set the green light of journalism in the go position. Once Reuters put the "kosher" stamp on the story, every newspaper worldwide would know the details.

The phone rang as we were putting the newspapers away. 'It's McKenzie,' Sue said, 'he's not on my crew list. Do you want to speak?' I gave the thumbs up.

I slipped a foot out of my shoe as it pinched my toe, and Sue closed my office door.

The guttural voice of McKenzie asked 'Are there any new developments in Austria?'
'No. I doubt if anyone could get through, the phone's been ringing like a fire engine.'
'Call Austria then,' McKenzie said. 'We need continuity to keep the story running . . . so far we're well ahead of the pack.'
'If I hear anything, you'll be the first to know.'

Immediately the line cleared, I phoned Jack. He'd heard nothing further but he had seen The Times morning edition.

'I suppose if you hadn't given the story, a local correspondent would have picked it up, so it's just as well it came from you.'
'Jack, why can't Frohmann bail his son out, if all the pictures are found and returned?'
'Not here, Katrina.' I heard a heavy sigh. 'Why do I have to give all the rotten news? Get a law book out of the library.'
'In German, Jack?'
'O.K. This is how it works. Frohmann has to sue, whether it's his son or his granny. It's the law here.'
'You mean he's legally bound to indict his own son?'
'Right, and give evidence and send him to jail if found guilty. Frohmann could get crucified by his own sperm.'

I slowly put the phone down aware this could be the death knell for Wilhelm Frohmann: his wife's death from alcoholism, defection by his daughter, and theft by his son. What, I asked myself, is there left for him to live for?'

Putting aside the Professor's motives, he had treated me with respect, albeit hard-won. Our mutual commitment to stimulate appreciation in the arts was a common denominator. By giving the article to McKenzie I hadn't condemned the Professor, only reported fact. But how he would react I had yet to find out. So I called him. Frau Stolz answered the phone.
'I'll ask the Professor if he will speak to you.' As if I were an unnecessary interruption.
The Professor's voice was thin. 'What can I do for you, Miss Edan?
'At the moment, you'll be pleased to know, nothing, I'm just phoning to ask how you are.'
'I'm weary and my eyes are sore and I have a cold,' he said.
'Why not rest at home?' I suggested.
'I have too much work. I am trying to select slides for my Rembrandt book, but they are poor quality, old and faded and it's difficult to distinguish accurate colours. I have one in front of me now. Jeremiah Lamenting the Destruction of Jerusalem. I can read the solitude of the old man but the detail on his brow, showing a flash of prophecy, looks like a folded wad of cotton wool. I can't possibly use it. And, I have another, a self-portrait, with one eye totally obscured.'

The Professor's frustration was compounded by the disintegration of his own family, and failing to find the sagacity of Rembrandt's Jeremiah within a slide, only hinted at his depth of disappointment. I made a suggestion.

'Maybe Anton has some better copies he could loan?'

Professor Frohmann's voice lifted as if some other, more important cause had come to his rescue.

LONDON

29

Shopping is my bête noir, a recalcitrant shopper, forced to apply myself for special occasions. This time it was my mother's birthday. At nine in the morning when the ladies who lunch, dine and club, were still tucked up somewhere, oblivious the next day had started, I was already in the perfume department at Harvey Nichols. To me the assistants look like wax models, preened to perfection, their faces talking advertisements, with designer bottles as their backdrop. One enterprising salesgirl asked if she could help me. Maybe she could.
'I'd like something new,' I challenged.
'Is it for you, madam?' said her perfectly outlined lips.
'No, but I'd like something zingy and not too floral?' She took a beautiful sculpted bottle from a glass shelf.
'You might like this?' she said as she squirted a puff onto my wrist. I sniffed. 'It's too sharp, too acid. Have you something more subtle?' She squeezed another whiff onto my other wrist.
'This is Yves Saint Laurent's latest, Opium,' she waved the bottle in reverence.
'Um, interesting,' I said 'definitely an evening perfume, I like it.'

The terracotta bottle was a squat oval shape, with a heavy glass stopper rimmed in gold on the top.
'Would you like it gift wrapped, madam?'
I said 'yes' although my mother had taught me how to fold tidy ends and crinkle paper bows.

Cynthia Edan is a smart woman, her taste a little "country", but very feminine and pretty. She met my father when he was sent on a training course from Sandhurst to Middle Wallop, where she lived. My grandmother occupied her time, as a social finder and fixer. At the time my mother was eighteen and wasn't looking for a "suitor" or a permanent boyfriend, intent on playing the field and finishing a cookery course. However, my grandmother regularly made discreet inquiries when the new arrivals of young officers came to Middle Wallop, no doubt with her daughters' future in mind. My mother was a tall slim blonde and had a twenty-one-inch waistline, before she had me, and a good bust line. In an aloof way, she was stunning and not unaware of her attractiveness. She told me how she first met my father.

"It was at a party in Ditchfield House, the home of one of my friends, Fiona Hackett. Her parents had converted the barn with its massive oak rafters and wooden floor, into a family space for parties and dances. Big sofas were scattered around the sides and a grand piano stood at one end. If she arranged a dance, the young officers on the training course at the local barracks were always invited and friends came from London, which made a good crowd.

Fiona, Denise Erickson and I always summed up the potential of the new officers. We'd get into a huddle and decide which one we were going to target. On one occasion I was a bit slow off the mark, but I didn't fancy any of them anyway, till your father arrived. That one, I said, with my hand over my mouth so only they could hear. The selection in place, the next move was the introductions. Fiona's mother swanned across the room - "Fiona darling, come and meet some visitors." Like cygnets we followed in line to meet this motley assortment of ex-sixth-formers, their new uniforms unconvincing. We were all madly in love, either with Tyrone Power, Clark Gable, or Cary Grant - real men who knew how to make a woman feel sensuous and wanted. Knew how to place their lips just a whisper away, lingering there, teasingly, and making one desperate for intimate contact. What did these recruits know about women - real women - like us? I shook hands with them in turn, not registering their names until I came to my target."

My mother, Cynthia had taught me how significant a handshake can be, that first moment of physical contact, a telling gesture giving insight into character. She explained the gesture of the diplomatic formal handshake, thumb on top, fingers lightly curled, the conceited grab, the domineering bone crusher, the wet fish handshake, reserved for wimps and bachelors. Her mouth curled into a grin as she remembered shaking hands with my father.

"Firm where the palms touch, staying an impish second longer than required, an unspoken message, Katrina, called technique, something you can't learn, only feel." For me it was a fairy tale romance. Sometimes mother and I would play handshake.

I'd shout, "wet fish", Mummy shouted "wimp", Daddy shouted "shut up".

***

Sue put the phone list on my desk. Instead of reading it, I looked at my watch. It was one-thirty. 'Have you had lunch Sue?'
'Nope, too busy Boss.'
'Let's shut up shop and go to the brasserie for lunch.'
'Who's paying?' Sue asked, while reaching for her coat.
'I am. I have a psychological aversion to sandwiches right now.'

The temperature was dropping and my thin mackintosh was no protection from the easterly wind. Sue offered me her scarf, which I quickly doubled round my neck.

I ordered a half bottle of red wine and we both ordered spaghetti carbonara. Sue then told me McKenzie had called twice and she'd managed to squeeze a message from him.
'He's talking to The Times lawyer here and their correspondent in Vienna is forecasting that Frohmann will put his son in the nick.'
'Anyone else call?'
'Steinhart,' she said.

My antennae told me that Sue was concealing something.
'Are you up to mischief?' I asked, as Sue's tongue licked a trickle of spaghetti from the corner of her mouth.
'Not yet.'
I raised my voice. 'Sue, what, or more accurately who, are you up to?'
'Do I have to tell you?'
'Of course not, as long as it's private and not business.'
'O.K. Boss, seeing as you're paying - Paul McKenzie asked me to have dinner with him to-night.'

I was careful not to respond hastily and hurt Sue's feelings, but this was typical sneaky press practice, so I asked her, 'what do you make of that?'

'Katrina, I'm really looking forward to dinner. You know I go for the rough scum. I find them exciting, especially literary minds with carnal expectations. Can't wait.'
'Is that all?' I shook some more Parmesan over my spaghetti.
'Well, if he thinks my mouthpiece is to feed and water, and fertilize his writing, he'll be helplessly disappointed.' She went

on . . . 'Do you remember when we organized the Cézanne exhibition and Gordon Summers from the Spectator, took me for dinner to get a behind-the-scenes exclusive?'
'Yes of course I remember.'
'But, do you remember I pushed him into the fountain at Trafalgar Square?'
Sue was laughing so much she could hardly continue. Then I infectiously laughed too.
Two men sitting at the next table asked. 'Private joke? Can we join in?'
We laughed even more.
'Well,' Sue said, 'when Gordon Summers stood up in his dripping clothes,' she covered her mouth with her arm, hooting with laughter, 'his tie over his shoulder, his hair in his mouth, I shouted at him: "If you wait all night the National Gallery opens at ten, they give information - free.'
Paul McKenzie had met his match with Sue Hepple.

Street markets grow in London on designated days. Uninteresting streets become bustling thoroughfares and a colourful part of London life. Sue and I stopped in Inverness Street, our local market, and bought some Cox's Orange Pippins, which we munched as dessert in the office.

First, I opened the letter with the RA monogram. The committee had agreed the dates, with a request that the catalogue and any publicity should credit them as the sponsors of the Private Rooms and ended with felicitations for the success of the exhibition.

Sue called on the inter-com, 'Steinhart on the line. Are you in?'

As he was my only source of further information, I took the call, hoping he had more news from the police. On the contrary, he said.
'I think you owe me an explanation. If you have a problem, tell me. Maybe I can solve it?'
'That is the problem Jack: you can solve everything. If it's money, you have it - if it's contacts, you know them, if there's gossip, you get it - and thank you, I'm grateful.'
'Katrina, stop playing games, or am I missing something here?'

'Yes . . . stop breezing into my life when and if it suits you.'
'Hang on Katrina. What the hell are you talking about?'
'You,' I said, 'I'm trying to get an exhibition up and running without your tendentious intervention. I need you like a fish needs a hairdryer.'

I heard him whistle in a descending cadence, then dead silence. I pictured Jack sitting at his desk selecting words to pacify me. After all, if I really analysed my emotions, he had only changed plans, which I had presumed were definite. But his autocratic Yankee manner, one click of the finger and that's it baby, is certainly not my style.
'I'm sorry, Katrina. You'll have to go with me on this one, but I would like to explain personally, if you'll give me the chance. I'll call you again.' He hung up.

Sue walked into my office to ask if she could leave at five. 'I want to put on my war paint!' she said.
'Need to borrow a spear?' I asked defensively.
'No Boss, I have my own.'

LONDON

30

To-day would be a difficult day for Anna Frishman. Anton Hempf and I knew she would need courage to implement the proposals we were about to make to her. We had carefully planned a fail-safe way for restitution, by confronting Otto Prantl with defrauding her of her inheritance.

Anna's father, mother and two sisters perished in the holocaust. If Prantl knew of a survivor, he would certainly not have allowed the paintings to be exhibited, and if Anna makes a claim, she would be metaphorically speaking from the grave.

Otto Prantl had waited twenty five years for the opportunity to officially launder important paintings, so he could legitimately sell them on the open market for millions more than could be hustled on the black one.

During her years as a refugee, Anna had fought loneliness and trauma, never coming to terms with the past. In spite of her classified work in London during the latter years of the war, and translating for the Foreign office - work that kept her occupied - the underlying grief relentlessly remained. Yet this proud, dignified lady always found time to give to others, even starting a charitable fund for mentally damaged survivors of the holocaust . . . and there were many.

The dining room in Anton's house was set for lunch. A distinct European atmosphere pervaded the space with heavy red velvet curtains draped at the Georgian windowpanes. On top of a sideboard on one side of the room was a photo of Anton's wife in a silver frame and a tiffany style lamp, and on the other side floor-to-ceiling mahogany bookshelves. A recording of Tchaikovsky's Violin concerto played softly in the background. Anna appeared calm and relaxed, her hair pulled back into a chignon, wearing a beige woollen two-piece suit with an insignia of the Red Cross on her lapel. Anton opened a bottle of Liebfraumilch and poured some for Anna.

'Just a little' she said, quickly, and held her fingers up to show the measure. 'You know I'm not a great drinker, I get silly.'

'Very well,' Anton said. 'I'll just pour a taster.' He held the bottle over my glass. 'You don't get silly' he said knowingly.

'Has Katrina told you the Royal Academy has agreed to host the exhibition?' he looked at me admiringly.
'Wonderful Katrina, congratulations. When will it open?'
'October 1973,' I told her.

A dish of white fish with a separate dish of chrane was on the table. I helped myself to black rye bread. Anton said to Anna.
'Everything is in place for you to make a claim on the paintings taken from your father's galerie, we just need a short note of confirmation from you.' Anna looked at Anton querulously. He continued, 'Otto Prantl has already sent the crates from Vienna to Salzburg, and Katrina will list them accurately to remind you of what was taken.' Anna sat bolt upright.
'I don't need a reminder - my memory's indelibly etched with the complete collection my father owned. I know every painting.'

We sat quietly for a moment to let Anna collect her thoughts and continue.
'I will not testify, if that's what you have in mind,' she said with strong conviction.

I looked at Anton without responding. We just waited, silently.
'I'm frightened,' Anna said. 'Something terrible could happen.'

A most ambiguous response, I thought and I asked. 'What do you think might happen, Anna?'
'When the Nazis know there's a living witness, they'll find me.'

For Anna, the past was becoming the present, and any assurances for her safety we could offer, would not alleviate her fear.

I tried. 'Anna, my friend, there are thousands of surviving refugees with recorded and witnessed testimonies, no one would dare remove personal evidence - that's tantamount to compounded fraud.' Anna was listening intently when Anton said.
'We understand it will be difficult, but Anna, your testimony will be of immense importance and an example for others. And I can assure you, you are absolutely safe.'

The housekeeper brought a tray of chicken portions in paprika sauce and a dish of rice, which she set in front of Anton. I changed the subject momentarily.
'I always get the wrong proportions of cayenne and paprika, and the chicken isn't red enough.'

Anna nodded. 'One day I'll show you. It's so simple.'
'And,' I said, 'I have a simple way for you to prepare a testimony: just write a list of every picture you remember. Then add the date you last saw them and where.'
'You said it was simple Katrina!'
'And you said you had an accurate mental picture, so it will be simple,' Anton said. We could see she was not convinced.
'If I put that in writing, will my name be on the testimony?'
'No Anna,' Anton replied, that will not be necessary. You can make a sworn declaration at my lawyers. Your list will only substantiate what you remember from 1939, without declaring your identity and Katrina will check exactly what is in the crates in Salzburg, before comparing her list with yours.'
Anna became very agitated and left the table.
'And what happens if they don't believe me?
Anton said 'Anna, *they* don't exist. We are talking about Katrina. She will decide if a claim is valid. And you have the Edvard Munch canvas Johannes removed from its stretcher, and your forged passport: enough to substantiate your identity.'

Anton's housekeeper collected the dishes and put an apple strudel in the centre of the table. I cut it into slices. Anna returned to the table as if she'd been defeated in some mind game and had no alternative but to capitulate.

Anton was less conciliatory. 'If you refuse it will negate everything Katrina's trying to achieve. She leaves for Salzburg on Monday and it's important your list is witnessed before then. What do you say, my dear?'

Quietly she said 'I'll do my best,' a word indicative of her character, best, her only criterion. But there were tears in her eyes. To reassure her I said.
'Your declaration will not be revealed till the exhibition closes. The forward in the catalogue explains that only written claims will be accepted, and all pictures will be shown for the full duration of the exhibition. No one except yourself, Anton and I and of course the lawyer, will even know your list exists - so relax my dear. You are absolutely safe.'

SALZBURG

31

The approach to Salzburg airport was hazardous at the best of times: in winter it was nothing less than dangerous. The Austrian Airlines fight was cruising at 33,000 ft above the Alps in bright sunlight. The world below was unpopulated and remote, a grandiose wild achievement of nature inaccessible to man, dangerously precipitous and getting nearer to us every minute. As the plane started to descend the mountains became threateningly close. We floated between soaring peaks above us on the approach to the runway. Snow was falling and within seconds we were in a white fog. Wind rocked us sideways and up, then dropped us into air pockets sending the small propeller jet lurching with fright at the onslaught. The air steward clung to the headrests as he checked our seat belts. Then an announcement came from the Captain telling us that we were unable to land in Salzburg because of the rough weather conditions but we would land in Munich, in about 45 minutes.

I looked out of the window: outside it was a total whiteout. I pressed the call button for the steward. I had to subdue my fear quickly before I became a shuddering nervous wreck.

'Yes madam,' he asked, clinging to the seat and desperately trying to stand still.

'How can the pilot see to turn in this narrow valley, with that blizzard blowing outside?'

'Don't worry madam,' he said, as if worry were connected to a switch, 'we don't turn in the valley; we climb above the cloud line then over the Alps into Munich. We'll be clear in a few minutes.'

Ha, I said to myself: keep the peasants happy or they'll have a revolution on their hands. The woman in the seat next to me spoke for the first time.

'I'm glad you asked that question: I was so petrified I couldn't speak. I've never flown before.'

Immediately I became very maternal, reassuring her that planes had instruments guiding their height and direction: ice breakers, warning lights, and airport communication.

'Planes are very sophisticated machines, absolutely nothing to worry about.'

I don't know if I helped her. I certainly helped myself, although I was not convinced until the clouds parted and we escaped into the void between heaven and earth.

'We'll land in a few minutes,' I said with relief, as my stomach returned to its normal resting place.

A thin layer of snow covered the runway as our luggage was carted off the plane and thrown into the belly of a coach waiting to shuttle us to Salzburg. I climbed aboard and sat in a seat by a window. I needn't have bothered. The snowstorm that had swirled around us at 20,000ft was driving horizontally across the ground, carpeting the landscape and reducing visibility to imagination.

Two hours later we were in Salzburg. It was cloaked in white like a Victorian Christmas card. Of course there weren't any taxis, and rather than stand in the bleak snowstorm, I boarded a tramcar, which stopped outside the Hotel Östereichisherhof. It had been a fractious journey. I was drained of energy, and not ready to concentrate.

I looked in the mirror: dark shadows had grown under my eyes. It was only five o'clock, but the tensions of the journey, the blinding snow, combined with my anxiety, were taking their toll.

I spoke briefly to Lisette Chenier, the Professor's secretary and arranged to be at the galerie by eight in the morning. I felt grateful for the comfort of the room, the bed with its big soft inviting duvet, the squashy velvet armchair, soft carpets, and the dish of Mozart Kugel. I called room service, ordered an omelette with salad, ate one "little Mozart" and went to bed.

By morning the storm had subsided. Snow blanketed the city, church spires became white virgin offerings to God, and snow hung heavily over roofs suspended in drapes and folds, too cold to move. From my window overlooking the river Salzach, I watched the sea gulls sliding from the sculpted irregular ice shapes on the banks of the frozen river, slipping like drunks towards the thin trickle of water in the middle of the river. I left the hotel wrapped in my sheepskin coat and hat; the flaps pulled firmly down, my high boots sank into the white powder. Road clearance teams had started to clear the bridges as I walked the short distance along the Giselakai to the galerie. The usual bustle of the morning was reduced to silence, the only sound the crunch of snow underfoot, and cars crawling slowly.

Professor Frohmann was already at the galerie when I arrived, but I was surprised to see Otto Prantl sitting with him in his office. The thought of Anna Frishman signing a document that would snare Prantl, gave me a vicarious uplift as I contemplated his entrapment. He was, after all, still a liar and a thief, perpetuating activities curtailed in 1945, and now attempting to legitimise the spoils of war. He was smoking a thin cigarillo, his shiny black hair oiled into place. It accentuated his taut owl like features, and dark recessed eyes.

'Please,' the Professor held a chair back for me. Herr Prantl nodded.

Prantl spoke first, 'Miss Edan, all the crates are here from my galerie. And the crates are also here from the galerie of Gerhard Hofer.' He knocked the ash from his cigarillo into an ornamental ashtray in the shape of edelweiss.

'Some of the crates are in a warehouse, as the Professor's galerie is full.'

'How many paintings do you estimate we have, Herr Prantl?'

'About a thousand. Would you agree Wilhelm?'

I flashed back to the Royal Academy walls and knew they couldn't show that number of paintings. I turned to Frohmann.

'Does that include the works collected in Badgastein?'

'No Miss Edan, They are still coming in.' he said conclusively.

'Have you any idea what the total number might be?'

Prantl answered. 'That will depend on when we close the checkpoint.'

Professor Frohmann added. 'We could receive double, it's impossible to guess.' The phone rang interrupting the dialogue. The cradle rocked as Frohmann put the phone down.' He said to Prantl. 'The police are here.'

I recognized the police officer as the man who had made the original report, close shaven, cool, and anxious to get his report finalized. The conversation was in German, and except for the occasional word from Frohmann, the officer did all the talking. Prantl was totally redundant.

After about ten minutes the officer left. He stopped at the doorway, turned, and saluted. Was it an act of solidarity? or a mark of respect for age and position? I doubt either: more likely an acknowledgment of power and influence. A few words passed between Prantl and Frohmann before he spoke to me.
'I shall explain briefly. It appears the police have recovered all the paintings taken from the galerie. They are being held in a police pound in the city: we can view them anytime.' He didn't mention his accused son Kurt Frohmann, but I needed to know the up-to-date situation so I could inform McKenzie. So I discreetly asked.
'And how is Kurt, Professor? It must be a distressing time for him.'
'He's on bail, I have given half a million schilling.' Frohmann said abruptly, before quickly addressing Prantl. 'I think we should look at the crated works, it will take a long time.'

We went to the rear galerie to start the task of listing. Pieter, Wilhelm Frohmann's driver was waiting, a lever at the ready. He was a rugged skinned man of peasant stock, with hands more useful than his brain. But then, no demands were made of him, other than driving and simple tasks. Stephan Moser had the lists. We started with the crates from Otto Prantl. I didn't know what they contained as I hadn't discussed the collection with Anna. But I knew her testimonial would have been completed and witnessed, and the listing I was preparing would hopefully tally with hers. It took three hours to list the contents marked "Prantl". At no point did I register any doubt about authenticity. When we finished I asked Otto Prantl to sign the document for the return of "his" paintings, which he'd agreed to loan. I had put red marks against paintings that I suspected of being fraudulent, either fakes outside the oeuvre of the artist, or obvious pastiches. When Prantl asked what the marks were for, I told him.
'I'm allocating them to rooms in the Academy. The marks are for the hanging crew.' I think he believed me.

We checked crates from museums in France, Liechtenstein, Holland, and Germany, stamped and numbered them and sealed them with wax. There were many more than I had expected. Duplication was rife during the nazi regime. Masterpieces from the Jeu de Paume, the Louvre, the great private collections of the Rothschild and Rosenberg families were taken on the orders of Goering and Hitler. Copies were made and passed to unscrupulous dealers like Karl Haberstock, who sold them through auction houses and international art dealers at high prices via an organized market place in "neutral" Switzerland. This scam generated millions in foreign currency for the coffers of the Third Reich and an impossible dichotomy of bureaucracy versus reason, when the Swiss prevaricated with countless promises to co-operate with the Allies, who were searching for masterpieces known to be in the hands of Swiss dealers, and constantly failing to respond.

***

It was a foggy morning and the snow was stacked by the roadside, grey and dirty, like industrial waste: the iridescent sparkle of yesterday's virgin snow had died.

I arrived at the police pound and gave my name to a policeman on duty. He opened a massive wrought iron gate with intricate emblems of past bishops woven into the ironwork. He directed me across the courtyard to vault three.

Wilhelm Frohmann was talking to a police officer. He acknowledged me briefly, nodding, and immediately told the officer to unlock the iron grid over a vaulted stone walled area and remove the first crate.

The Professor was anxious to start the painful identification of paintings, which could be worth millions, yet at the same time, it would be a sad emotional shredding of what remained of his family. It was apparent after the first crate had been opened that the thieves had handled the paintings with great care, confirming my suspicion they were taken "to order". Corrugated paper corners, and extra board carefully protected each work and runners had been inserted inside the crate: the work of a packer who knew the measurements well in advance?

Frohmann's face was taut with anguish. As the policeman pulled one of the paintings out of the crate, he screamed in German and English, 'Got in Himmel, you imbecile' he said, 'dat ist ein priceless work of art. You will never touch anything so valuable in your lifetime,' he repeated, 'ever in your lifetime. Do you understand me?' This explosion sent blood rushing to his face. The tension in the cold room suddenly rose and I could see Professor Frohmann was at breaking point.

So as not to exacerbate his distress, I made no comments. Slowly we worked through the crates until we came to a Cézanne landscape: Mont Sainte-Victoire, which I remembered seeing in a catalogue of the Lucerne auction in 1939. The painting was sold to an unnamed dealer in New York for 7,000 Swiss francs, £1750, then sold on to the Art Institute of Chicago for an undisclosed sum. Today it is worth in excess of twenty million pounds. Somewhere, I knew, there must be false accreditation, and one of the paintings, either the one in the crate or the one hanging on display in Chicago, was a fake. I held the painting up to my eye level and said to the Professor 'beautiful' at the same time I was looking at the brushwork, how the bristles on the brush spread into cubic forms, merging with Mediterranean earth colours on a dirty canvas. It had not been cleaned and my first impression was that it was a genuine Cézanne. So I presumed the Cézanne exhibited in Chicago, must be a fake?

Works by Matisse, Braque, Monet, Frans Hals, Chardin, Rembrandt and Vermeer, were slowly lifted from their protective wrapping.

It was cold in the police pound, but the sweat was building on Frohmann's face. He pursed his lips and licked the drops from the fringe of his grey moustache, his concentration ebbing as he struggled to keep his composure. Slowly, his skin turned from scarlet to sickly white. He held his head in his hands, turning from side to side trying to deny what blatantly affronted him: then telling me I would have to complete the listing of the works from Badgastein, alone.

This was the day of judgement for Professor Wilhelm Frohmann. His signature on the document of authenticity for the paintings we had viewed, would condemn Kurt Frohmann; the sacrificial lamb with the knife already at his throat. This time the hand of God would not intervene.

***

It was documented and used as evidence at his trial that Wilhelm Frohmann had made frequent visits to Paris in his capacity as curator for Hermann Goering, collecting major paintings to hang in Carinhall, Goering's palatial mansion on the scale of Versailles.

Many high profile art collectors and dealers desperately tried to move their collections south in the wake of the oncoming German army. Many were Jews. Paul Rosenberg's vast collection was sent to a bank vault in Bordeaux, others were stored in a rented chateau nearby, but some of the most important works were deposited in museums in and around Paris for "safe Keeping" and have never been recovered. Rosenberg fled via Lisbon to New York returning after the war to try and recover his dissipated collection.

When George Wildenstein fled to Aix-en-Provence he left 330 objects in the Banque de France and sent 82 paintings to the Louvre for "safe keeping". The contents of his home on the outskirts of Paris and his galerie remained but were looted by the German Art Brigade.

Miriam de Rothschild lost most of her collection, which she had buried in an unmarked sand dune near Dieppe. Nothing has ever been retrieved.

Peggy Guggenheim was fortuitously refused space in the Louvre for her collection: it was considered too avant-garde and not worth saving. Some of the greatest masterpieces of modern art this century, including major works by Braque, Picasso and Van Gogh, belonging to her, were at risk of confiscation as degenerate. To minimise detection she removed all the canvases from their stretchers, and sent them to Vichy France, to be hidden in a friend's barn.

Henry Matisse, another escapee from Paris, stayed with Rosenberg in Bordeaux until Rosenberg left for New York. Matisse then drove from town to town across southern France for two months, before settling in Vence.

George Braque was also on the move to Bordeaux, the temporary seat of French government, with as many paintings as his car would hold. On his arrival he deposited part of his collection and a Cranach portrait in the same bank as Rosenberg. This proved a dire error, as "unnamed friends" in Paris, disclosed the whereabouts of Rosenberg's collection to the Nazi. The Germans removed the Rosenberg paintings from the bank, and discovered and confiscated the Braque collection at the same time.

Georges Braque was an Aryan, so his collection was ostensibly "protected", except the Germans told him, if he did not sell the Cranach to them, they would not guarantee the survival of his personal collection, which under the label "degenerate" would have been sold or burned.

With the background history of looted and faked works of art exposed, museums and collectors, who had acquired pictures just before World War ll, or during the Nazi regime, were possibly holding fakes or loot. Galerie owners like Wilhelm Frohmann and Otto Prantl, would find it hard to escape public exposure a second time around. It was different for governments who were holding valuable art and antiques, knowing their value was increasing on the world market and knowing that within a further decade no one would be alive to accuse them. Paintings will just surface: found in the vaults of some remote castle, like a time warp, until the climate is politically clear and museums would not be accused of larceny.

When the allied restitution programme ceased in 1952 any unclaimed works were handed over to the German government and declared "heirless". Many claimants gave up trying to repossess their lost treasures, too disillusioned with the repressive claims procedure, which left a dearth of orphan paintings that were placed in public collections or held in permanent storage. By the nineteen-seventies these "heirless" works, had been consigned to oblivion.

SALZBURG

32

Frustration and anger prevented me from contacting Jack Steinhart. I had a gruelling schedule and his puerile stop-go attitude to my feelings only dissipated my resilience at a time when I needed unequivocal focus. He knew from Professor Frohmann that I had been in Salzburg for five days, but had not until to-day made any effort to reach me.

The cold persisted relentlessly and I cosseted myself in my invaluable lambskin coat. I felt confident, aloof and guarded from the whims of Jack's charm, as I went to the Goldener Hirsh to meet him for lunch. I deposited my coat, but kept on a black beret, pulled obliquely over one eye.

Jack was waiting at a table, and said simply 'Hello.'

I looked at the menu unnecessarily, recalling the mushrooms I had seen in the market square, and ordered the risotto of assorted wild fungi. I was busy watching a fat lady with large breasts sitting at an adjacent table, with a Pekinese dog on her lap, while Jack ordered. The dog looked like part of her anatomy, as its head protruded from between her vast breasts, like a meer cat, looking at her plate of suckling pig, waiting, its tongue flapping. A high-pitched, yap: again, yap, yap ... Shush, shush, Tiger" said the fat lady as she planted a dripping piece of meat into the dog's salivating mouth.

The waiter poured from a bottle of Grüner Veltliner. Jack said, 'cheers.' I didn't answer: indicating my continued hostility.

'I think we should try and sort out your problem, first.' He said.

'My problem!' I retorted, 'I think you're the one with the problem!' I said haughtily.

'Yes, I know you're angry and I know why,' he said confidently.

'Good,' I said. 'You can tell me in plain English.'

His eyes drifted away, past me, focusing somewhere in the distance, his lips quivered and hesitated before saying coldly,

'When you walked into my office and asked for over a million bucks, I must admit, my only concern was the company's money. Then, you dived totally unprepared into a hornet's nest, without netting or knowledge. O.K . . . so Dr. Hempf gave you introductions, but he didn't do what I stepped in to do,' he said with arrogance.

'You mean warning me I'm dealing with the Nazi: telling me I trod a dangerous path and to get out while I was still able? All negative clichés Jack, not what I call encouragement.'

'You see it one way, I another.'

His voice was brisk. 'I have tried in my own way to help you and it's only your irascible determination which convinced me you might make it.'

'Might' I said with contempt, 'means strength - not perhaps!'

Jack had a frown between his fair eyebrows, which deepened as he nodded. 'That's exactly what I mean. Anyway, it's no longer important because I'm quitting my job.'

If Jack thought I'd respond with emotional pleading he was sadly mistaken. I just said, 'When?' as if it didn't matter.

'This job is taking over my life,' he confessed,' I don't want to be a pawn in a system anymore, waiting for some smart-arse at head office to tell me I'm through.'

The waiter served from a side table. Jack waited, thinking.

'You ask when? That's the burning question. My bank contract is till December - then I want out. I would have broken the contract before if you hadn't walked into my life!' His eyes were icy cold and penetrating.

'What does "walk into my life" mean, Jack?'

He was looking at me intently, holding my attention with a glacial look, leaning across the table on his arms.

'I care about where you are and what is happening to you. Who you are with, and why. I know the danger you are in and what could happen when you're in Vienna. You tell me I have too many answers, but believe me I wouldn't survive in this job if I hadn't.'

I took a deep breath. Was this what I wanted to hear? Was I misinterpreting words? What is care anyway? The fat lady cared for her dog, the restaurant the food, the waiter the service, such a non-committal word, care, until he said.

'Do I stand a chance, Katrina, or have I really blown it?'

He confronted me with a loaded question I couldn't answer. I remembered my father's advice: "never respond to a question until you are sure you are giving the answer you want, not the

one someone wants to hear". I saw the Pekinese strutting contentedly, his low-slung body going paw by paw in front of his fat mistress and out of the restaurant. I thought of Desmond, his lack of sentiment and his advice about money. Jack's bank was still giving me money but if problems arose in Austria I would have no immediate back up. With this in mind I said.
'At least you're staying till Christmas, maybe I will have completed the search by then,' avoiding any personal reference, 'and life will become more normal?'
With nothing more to add, we left the restaurant.

I sat at the desk in my hotel room with what appeared an impossible situation. Jack's leaving would not help, but my immediate concern was the limited space allocated by the Royal Academy, enough for six hundred paintings, but to date 2000 were stored and more were waiting for listing. That figure could double by the end of the year. I telephoned Anton Hempf and explained the disparity between the space and the number of works we had received. It would be impossible to hang all the pictures at one time, and rotating 3000 or more, also impossible in four weeks. Although Anton was not an Academician he had friends who were. If Anton could persuade the Academy to loan The Diploma galleries - it would give me the extra space I needed. The only alternative would be to delay for one year, but then the sponsorship contracts would expire creating further problems.

I telephoned Anton and asked if he would speak to Sir Hugh Casson. I hesitated, knowing Anton disliked asking favours but this was much more.
'I have no alternative venue, and the difficulties are compounded if we don't keep to schedule. Paintings will disappear and I'll have no redress.'
'I understand the implications, Katrina, but the Royal Academy also has a schedule and a responsibility to their students' careers. The final year students' always have the Diploma galleries at that time of year.'
'So I'll do something to boost their careers,' I suggested. 'If the Academy will allow the students to give up two weeks in October, it would release enough space to show everything. In

return, I'll list their names in the catalogue and give the prizewinners special mention for their charity. The Times, will give them exposure outside anything they'd normally get as graduates.'

I didn't know if Paul McKenzie would write to order but I had to take a calculated risk.

Anton disliked long conversations on the phone and I heard him tapping his pencil. He said, 'I think you should speak to Sir Hugh yourself.'

'Anton, it's deadline time and it's running out fast.' I continued. 'If it's "no", I'll have to use encyclopaedic thought, but right now, I'd like to hang on to what we have - don't you agree?'

'I can't argue that point, I will call you later.'

I phoned Sue. Letters had arrived following my radio interview, mostly from refugees in Great Britain, but also from abroad, as the programme was relayed the same night on the World Service.

'Have you spoken to McKenzie because I have some information - not much - but enough to keep the story alive.'

'He's called a number of times,' Sue said. 'I told him you were abroad and there's nothing to report.'

'Sue, this is very important. Tell him this immediately. Frohmann has paid half a million schillings to bail his accused son, Kurt, following the theft. The works are now in a police pound in Salzburg. Tell him I estimate their value will run to millions. And don't forget the place and date of the exhibition.'

I heard the typewriter rattling fast, and visualized Sue with the telephone wrapped around her chin.

'Did you get it, Sue? I want to be sure the details are accurate. Try to get McKenzie to slip it into tomorrow's paper. Give him my telephone number here, if there's a problem.'

I wanted the story to circulate before Anton approached the Academy, making it more difficult for them to back down: I could always plead, "the Press is a law unto itself" if I were challenged. I told Sue we had overrun the hanging space and I was trying to get the Diploma Gallery and the Private Rooms. '

LONDON
33

My desk was clinically tidy. I sat with a mug of coffee thinking about what needed to be signed and sealed. Waiting to speak to Anton at ten seemed an eternity: I was at a standstill until I knew what he had arranged with the Royal Academy. Sue arrived shortly after nine looking like she'd been dragged through a hedge backwards. She showed me a copy of The Times with the article I had wanted Paul McKenzie to write.

It was what I expected . . . a terse unembellished headline followed by the facts.

AUSTRIAN PROFESSOR PAYS HALF MILLION SHILLINGS BAIL FOR HIS SON

Professor Wilhelm Frohmann and Katrina Edan, curator of an exhibition at the Royal Academy, valued paintings stolen by the Professors son, in excess of fifty million pounds. The paintings are being held in a police pound in Salzburg. They will be damming evidence at the forthcoming trial of Kurt Frohmann,

The article continued with the details I had given him.

'Good work Sue. Any repercussions?'

'Not yet'

'Has Hempf called?'

'Not so far.' Sue returned to her desk.

I started to write the proposal for the RA. I knew my idea for extra space was diabolical but I had nothing to lose and everything to gain. I called Anton Hempf and was told an appointment had been made for me to meet Sir Hugh.

'Did he respond to my suggestion?'

'Not directly. He's thinking about it.'

'Will you come with me, Anton?'

'I will come but my presence won't make the slightest difference to his decision.' I didn't labour the point.

The meeting with Sir Hugh Casson was short. Anton had certainly briefed him on the excessive number of paintings turned in. 'I hear you have over 2000 exhibits, Miss Edan, that's a sizable number considering the circumstances.'

'Yes Sir, it's a critical issue especially as so many masterpieces have been found.'

I was hoping he'd ask more, but he didn't. He was very brief.

'You can have the Diploma gallery, but I must ask you to pay for painting all the rooms, and the security costs including front entrance if you open outside of Academy hours. Do you have Government Indemnity?'

'I've applied but it's too early to estimate final figures. But I don't see a problem.'

He turned to Anton; 'You'll be here on Thursday for the dinner?'

Anton replied quietly. 'It's an evening I'd be reluctant to miss.'

'Good. And Miss Edan, you can have all the rooms in the Diplomas and the Private rooms, but I should be obliged if you would consult with my press secretary before giving any further information to the newspapers.'

'I apologise, Sir Hugh. The article was given over the phone from Austria. I never expected it to be printed so soon.' My fingers were crossed but my conscience clear: the cause as far as I was concerned, was greater than the deed.

I returned to the office relieved but not exuberant. Although the foundation for the exhibition was now in place a lot remained to be organized. I called Paul McKenzie at The Times. He took my call immediately. I heard the click of his lighter as he said 'McKenzie.'

The picture I projected of him standing with a cigarette dangling from his face, shirt-sleeves rolled, tie at half mast, the skin round his eyes embalmed with last nights alcohol, was remarkably nasty.

I looked at my watch, 'Do you have a lunch appointment?'

'No, it's chip butty day.'

'Could you possibly change that, I have an idea I'd like to put to you?'

It's not often the press turns down a free lunch but I wasn't sure about McKenzie. However, it didn't take long for the reply.

'What time and where?'

'Twelve thirty, the Wig and Pen. I'm not a member but I presume you are?'

'Right . . . Wig and Pen, twelve thirty.' The phone went down with a bang. I called Desmond Hegarty.

'How about buying me dinner? I purred.

'You scrounger. Is that all you called me for?'
'No. There's been an overrun on the number of exhibits by more than 2000. I have renegotiated the space.'
'O.K. Katrina, when and where do you want your free bash?'
'The Dorchester, Saturday' I said in an exaggerated upper class voice. 'It's so convenient, just down the road.'
'So is Asprey's and I don't shop there,' Desmond replied.
I waited. 'O.K, the Dorchester shall have the pleasure of our company . . . Saturday night? I'll collect you at eight.'

I threw my camel coat over my shoulders, pulled on a black beret from the cupboard and told Sue I was having lunch with Paul McKenzie.
'Whatever for?' she commented, her big eyes wide in amazement.
'I thought we hadn't time to be even moderately promiscuous.'

***

Fleet Street was buzzing as my taxi pulled up outside the Wig and Pen club, an establishment redolent with history easily recognizable from the Dickensian facade. Few examples of 16th century Tudor architecture are so well preserved as this building, owned originally by the Bishops of London until 1625 when it became a private home, the same year Charles 1 was losing his crown and eventually his head, and Guy Fawkes attempted to blow up the Houses of Parliament earlier, and was also beheaded.

Later the premises, at 230 Strand, became a commercial establishment, selling a penn'orth of meat and bread to the crowds who gathered to see the heads of traitors spiked on the Temple Gate opposite.

The building, now the home of the Wig and Pen club, is the only one in the Strand to survive the Great Fire of London, and the original suspended staircase, the only one of its kind remaining in the world.

To-day judges, barristers, jurists, and junior flotsam, laden with pink taped files, spill onto the pavement from the Law Courts, like the exodus from Noah's Ark, en route to watering holes in the Strand and Fleet Street.

Paul McKenzie was standing by the bar, a half empty scotch

glass in his hand. He wore a dark brown corduroy suit and a crocheted tie. It was noisy and the barman continually pushed a glass under one of the myriad upturned bottles slung across the wall behind him.

The robust atmosphere, thick with smoke and chatter, locked the 20th century firmly outside. Heavy draped curtains dressed the stained glass windows, the small lattice panes obscuring light and prying eyes.

I looked up above the bar to a painting of an ominous looking judge, draped in wig and robes.

'Bloody Judge Jeffries, the hanging judge,' McKenzie told me.

Around the picture were framed newspaper cuttings in no particular order of date or content.

'And those?' I asked, pointing to the wall.

'Front pages of exclusives sent in by editors, who renamed this bar, the Judge Jeffries/Front page bar!'

I nodded. 'So the rivalry between the law and the press has been resolved?'

'Never,' McKenzie said as he paid the barman and led me to the staircase. 'This place is hotter than MI5 headquarters for gossip, if you can stay sober long enough to get to a typewriter.'

Tables were jammed so close together, no wonder gossip was rife. I was relieved we had a corner table with a fraction more space.

'Scotch?' McKenzie asked. He beckoned the waiter.

'Same as usual, Mr McKenzie?' the red coated man asked.

He passed us two hand-written menus, with an impressive coat of arms on the top of the page. The alternatives. Pigs' Trotters, roast lamb, prime Angus beef, sausages and mash, steak and kidney pie, and roast chicken with trimmings. A very down to earth menu, pitched somewhere between school dinners and pretension. I ordered steak and kidney pie, McKenzie asked for prime Angus, another scotch, and a bottle of Brouilly. 'Make sure it's 69,' he told the waiter. Then he came straight to the point.

'Are you buying me lunch, Miss Edan, to keep the Frohmann story running?'

'No, I want to add a further dimension.' 'Go on' he said.

'I want the refugees from central Europe, to get the exhibition date well in advance, so they can get evidence to corroborate claims.'

McKenzie was drinking his scotch and looking down at the tablecloth, listening but not looking at me. 'You mean "Presents from the Past" sort of stuff?' he said.

'That's trivial. I was thinking more practically, as the "presents" will be 32 years late.'

'There is something you have obviously forgotten, Miss Edan.'

'What's that?' I asked.

'My column is not for advertising good causes, however justified. There's a separate page for that. The agony column.'

I found his remark offensive.

'Mr.McKenzie,' I said, in a formal tone, 'I can't be frivolous about this idea, nor will I pay for adverts: I'm giving you stories you couldn't get anywhere else, except second-hand. I expect a pay-off. There are souls out there still bleeding, and if I can make just one person happy through my efforts, that will be my present.'

It takes more than a declaration of altruism to move a hardened newspaperman of Paul McKenzie's ilk, and it wasn't my intention to try. His hand was resting on the stem of his glass, which he emptied hastily.

'I'll think about it and see if I get inspired.' McKenzie said.

'Is that the best you can do? I'd really like to have something on record before the country goes to sleep for the Easter holidays and wakes up for Christmas.'

'I agree, it's cosier to have something in the can, but it'll depend on what happens in the next few days. If there's an earthquake in Lewisham, it wouldn't get a quarter of an inch.'

I had pushed as far as I could, anything else would fall on deaf ears, so I asked him where he was spending Easter.

'Brighton,' he said, 'the Palace Hotel, feet up, late nights, late mornings, candy floss, peppermint rock and a copy of The Beano.'

I returned to my office sedated by scotch and wine to find Sue nodding on the telephone, yes, yes, she was saying - then.

She covered the mouthpiece with her hand and whispered 'it's the RA's press office.

I sat on her guest chair in front of the typewriter.

'We'll need a list of "grateful thanks" for the frontispiece of the catalogue: apart from the students at the RA - do you have a list?'

'No,' Sue said. 'I think we should wait. You might get a whopping benefactor when McKenzie writes your Easter message.'

I looked at Sue in astonishment. 'How do you know?'

'He called after lunch for the name of the lawyer in Austria - Daniel Clipstein.'

'Umm - I wonder why?'

It was four o'clock and I was no longer motivated. I said to Sue. 'Where are you spending Easter?'

'Brighton,' she said, as she continued typing.

After one scotch and half a bottle of wine, my head was crystal clear. 'The Palace Hotel?' I asked.

'Wouldn't stay anywhere else.' she replied.

I went to my office with a saucy contented smile. I know Sue would never compromise her integrity for a story or any other reason. Maybe, after all, Paul McKenzie had more than journalistic expertise and a penchant for tippling.

***

My first meeting after the Easter holiday brought me sharply into focus. I was at the National Gallery to prepare a document with Elizabeth Cuthbertson for the loan of Gustav Klimt's portrait of Hermine Gallia.

Elizabeth asked me if I had a good holiday. She sat rigidly upright at her desk, a draft copy of an agreement in front of her. I had presumed we'd discuss it in detail but she had already written a simply worded agreement, which covered the salient points.

I made sure the details were the same as previously discussed: that transit insurance would be the responsibility of the exhibition organizer: hanging time would be for the duration of the exhibition and the National gallery would store the painting in its vaults until the exhibition opened. But there was one clause missing, which was agreed between Gerhard Hofer and myself. That it must be specified in the catalogue that no claims would be considered. As we both knew the history of the painting, this addition didn't present a problem.

'Just one other thing,' Elizabeth said, taking another sheet of paper from her desk. 'Do you know when the painting will arrive here so I can get the first instalment authorised?'

I had no idea when we would start shipping.

'I can't give you a date yet,' I told her, 'as pictures are still being listed. Would a month in advance be acceptable?' Elizabeth agreed and as I left she said, 'Give my regards to Mr.Steinhart when you next see him.' she smiled.

***

Mail, which Sue was sorting, had accumulated during the Easter holiday. I collected the Tel Aviv file to study and asked her to book a flight within the next few days.

ISRAEL

34

The contrast between England and Israel in April is dramatic. Tall palm trees like sentinels surround Lod airport and deep purple fronds of Bougainvillea trail across the crusty concrete arrivals building, their perfume lost in the haze of heat and aircraft fumes. The light was intense. I felt the heat on my body as the sun's rays cut through the unimpeded atmosphere. A blue and white flag with the emblem of the Star of David hung limp in the still air: a symbol of Israel's short territorial history. Yet every passenger who walks through the guarded gates, and whatever their mission, is a pilgrim discovering the pages of the bible, a journey back, for a journey forward. To walk on this hallowed soil is an uplifting experience: an injection of hope and promise.

From the Sheraton hotel in Tel Aviv I phoned Elgin at the U.S. embassy and arranged to meet him and Bunny later, then I left immediately for my meeting with Dr.Chaim Levine at the Art Museum.

He was almost tripping over his words to tell me about his progress. For him, the combination of restitution and retribution was a mission, a driving force with no time for retrogression.

Dr.Levine showed me three newspapers Maariv and L'diot, with translations stapled to them, and a copy of the Jerusalem Post in English. His sharp, close eyes focused directly on me.

'I managed to get articles into our newspapers,' he said as a formality. But I knew it was a fait accompli. I looked at the translations that covered four columns.

'Perhaps I should read them later.'

'Certainly, Miss Edan, but you will see I have requested information about family paintings that were "sold" with receipts or looted without: any identifying details which could help establish ownership. I have asked for photographs that might have been seen reproduced somewhere, in an art book perhaps, anywhere any claimant last saw the painting.'

'Have you had any response to the articles Dr.Levine?'

'Letters have come to this office which are being translated as they arrive. Some are in German, some French, some Polish,

and of course Hebrew. Miss Edan, you will have a difficult task sifting the real from the imagined, the wishful from the fact.' He paused, sipped some water, and asked. 'How is the search going in Austria?'
'The checkpoint at Badgastein is still open. We have around two thousand items.'
'Are they being collated by country or by owner?'
'To be honest, I haven't even started collating.'

Dr.Levine appeared concerned. 'I think you should make it an urgent priority to get them listed by country. At least where they were found.'
'Most of the paintings, except those from museums, are given with a P.O.Box number. These come from the hopefuls who have no interest in art and are holding "hot" items. If they submit them to be included in the exhibition they have a chance of turning their loot into cash. It is a calculated gamble with no risk. But, if they hold on to them, their heirs will have a lot to prove, especially after the exhibition. The publicity will make museums, auction houses and dealers wary of handling works with dubious provenance.' Where will they sell?' I said.
He nodded in agreement. 'You are right, but hopefully some joy will eventually compensate the ill fated.

***

Elgin had left a message at the hotel. "Bunny and I will collect you at 7.45pm. Have concert tickets."

We went to the Mann Auditorium for a Beethoven concert. Bunny and Elgin held season tickets and were most enthusiastic about the quality and versatility of the orchestra.
'Sitting on that stage,' Elgin said, indicating the orchestra, 'are at least ten nationalities, with the common language of music. A real polyglot crew, who can shake the Gods with their vibrations.'

He was right: they thundered expressively, and the appreciative audience thundered their response.

After the concert we sat at a pavement cafe on Dizengoff Street for a sandwich. Bunny pecked at hers, as if her rose bud mouth pertly placed in her sun-tanned face, was not to be invaded. Elgin, white faced by comparison, had a cigarette on the go the whole time, taking it from his mouth occasionally to eat.

'Great to see you back on foreign soil,' he said, 'Dr.Levine's been hitting the headlines. We saw the translation from the text of an interview with him in the Jerusalem post. Did he get any results?'

'Yes, letters have been arriving at his office ever since. He's going to forward them to me. I'll try and co-ordinate descriptions with works I've collected.'

'How many paintings do you have Katrina?' said Bunny between nibbling.

'Around two thousand.'

Bunny looked quickly at Elgin. 'She can't possibly manage that amount alone?'

'How do you know? You're not a curator, Katrina knows exactly how to handle exhibits.'

I said to Elgin, 'I wish you were right. Professor Frohmann's son will be tried on the 10 July and whichever way the case goes, the emotional drain on Frohmann will be catastrophic. That leaves the slithering viper, Otto Prantl, and Stephan Moser, Frohmann's assistant who works at a snails pace, and myself.' A quick visual conversation passed between Elgin and Bunny.

'Are you thinking the same as me?' Bunny said. In unison they said, 'Myrtle.'

'You're losing me in this dialogue. Myrtle is an aromatic plant for perfume? What are you talking about?' I asked.

Elgin explained. 'Myrtle Shaw is Bunny's cousin. She's spending a year in Vienna researching social history for her Ph.D. She'd jump at the chance to help. It could give an extra dimension to her own research.'

'How old is Myrtle?' I asked Bunny.

Again she looked at Elgin. 'What would you say Elg? Twenty six or is she twenty seven?'

'Around about,' he said. 'I can tell you Katrina, she's very thorough and industrious. She could be a valuable help collating works for you.'

'Frankly Elgin, I'm on a tight budget, I'm not sure I can afford to pay anyone.' I said.

'Pity. I know she's paying her own expenses, as she's spent her

government allowance.'
Bunny said, 'Why don't you call her when you're in Vienna? Maybe you can come to some amicable arrangement. Anyway, I think you'll like her.' She wrote Myrtle's phone number on the back of the menu.'

As we left, Elgin said 'Please give Myrtle our love and tell her we expect to see her here before she leaves Europe.'
'Don't forget Jack. Give him our love too,' Bunny said. She gave me a firm hug. 'Good luck.'

SALZBURG

35

I was lucky. The skies were clear and the plane landed on schedule in Salzburg at noon. Jack was at the airport to collect me and we went straight to the courthouse to hear the case against Kurt Frohmann, for theft. He warned me the case might take a few days depending on the witness statements and also whether the plea was guilty or not guilty.

The courtroom was full. We sat near the back. I saw Daniel Clipstein a few rows in front of us with a woman.

'Who's she?' I asked Jack.

'Helena Rutter, a lawyer who worked with Clipstein on the indictment of Adolf Eichmann.'

Professor Frohmann was sitting with his own lawyer, the defence lawyer and a clerk. The courtroom was musty and too hot with a low hum from people talking. The legal teams chatted as if it were just another working day: much less formal than the pomp and pageantry of wigs and gowns, familiar in British courts.

Kurt Frohmann was led into a small-elevated box between two officials. When the presiding judge entered wearing a black robe and a white tie, everyone stood.

"Will the accused please identify himself? Are you Kurt Frohmann? Kurt nodded. "Will you state your full name and date of birth? Then the indictment was read out. "You are accused of theft, collusion with others to defraud, and illegal transportation of art between Austria and Germany". A few whispers trembled onto empty air. Kurt was standing looking at the judge. "How do you plead?" he was asked. A deathly silence hung over the courtroom waiting for the reply. With his chin held high, his hands resting on the sides of the box he said "Guilty."

I couldn't see Professor Frohmann's face, but I knew how he must feel. His son was not even attempting to absolve himself. He offered no defence with this plea, effectively implicating his father in setting up the heist.

The judge, a thin man, wearing rimless spectacles on a very thin beaky nose, asked the defence lawyer if there were any mitigating circumstances - suggesting blackmail or the threat of physical violence. He answered: "None". The judge asked if any damage had been caused to the stolen works. The defence lawyer said, "No." He then asked. "How many other people were involved in the robbery?' The defence lawyer said. "At the moment it is unknown." Someone in the court shouted. "That is a lie. That is a bloody lie. His father set him up." An orderly was called to the judge's bench and announced to the court. "Judge Ackermann will adjourn this case immediately if there are any further interruptions." After the court quietened, the judge continued.

"I repeat, were there any other persons involved in the robbery?"

This time the defence lawyer said. "Yes Sir, they are German citizens." I looked at Jack, mystified by what was going on around me.

Jack whispered 'I'll explain later.' I knew other people were involved. It was reported in the newspapers that a Munich galerie had the stolen paintings and that after the burglary, documents shown at the Austrian/German border stated they were en route to Hamburg. The judge asked the defence. "How many works were stolen?"

'Sixty.'

"And how many of those were found?"

"Sixty." There was total silence in the courtroom, the judge making notes and intermittently looking up at the defendant before passing a note to an orderly, who announced. "A custodial sentence will be determined at ten tomorrow morning." Kurt Frohmann was still on bail, at least for another day.

When Wilhelm Frohmann turned to leave the court on the arm by his lawyer, his head was bowed, averting the crushing gaze upon him, his back curled, the weight of the past and the present a wrenching upheaval.

From that moment all blood ties were severed and the words of James Joyce reverberated in my head:

All moanday, tearsday, wailsday
thumpsday, frightday, shatterday till
the fear of the Law.

Jack and I discussed the case at my hotel. I had set aside any personal animosity that could hinder my progress and Jack Steinhart was integral to that end. He knew the mechanics of Austrian law and he would share that with me. He was close to Frohmann and when the dust of this case had settled, Jack's position would remain intact. It would be reckless to put my heart where my head should be. Analysing his motive didn't matter. I had to keep every door open for the progress of the exhibition: anything else must become a sideline.

'I cannot understand why Kurt Frohmann didn't offer any defence,' I said, 'unless it was some form of retribution. Does the guilty plea imply the Frohmann Galerie could be involved in an insurance fraud?'

'Exactly,' Jack said. 'And Kurt wants it to appear he is protecting his father. It's a vindictive move by Kurt because he would have been found guilty anyway. He knew it, so by pleading guilty he dragged his father with him.'

'And the accomplices? Do they go Scot free?'

'No, they've been indicted for receiving stolen goods, not taking them: they'll be tried in Munich,' he said authoritatively. 'You're in a tight corner too, the court will decide when the paintings can be released: they're evidence, without them the trial would be null and void.'

I thought about the implications but with so many other crates to be listed first, it hardly mattered.

'I have over two thousand works which have to be listed for insurance before they can be shipped, so even if I get them next year, sixty paintings won't be a problem.'

'You'll be camping at Frohmann's galerie to list over a thousand paintings!'

'Hopefully not. I was talking with Bunny and Elgin - oh - they send their love to you,' I said hastily. 'Bunny's cousin, Myrtle is researching in Vienna and suggested I call her. Do you know her?'

'No, I've never met her. What is her subject?'

'Social history.'

'Sounds OK to me. At least she'd be working in your interest and will take some of the load off your back.'

'I've decided to wait. When Wilhelm's over the shock of this case, he'll still want to work. Actually Jack, it's essential for him, to keep his mind active and have something to motivate him.'
'What about the Rembrandt book?'
'He has that too. I've brought some quality slides from Anton Hempf, a tidbit in all this melancholy: but for me, time is creeping uncontrolled towards deadlines.'
'Are you going to call The Times, and give them an up-date?'
'No, I'll do that tomorrow after the sentence is given. Paul McKenzie wants hot news. Right now it's only on the boil.'

***

By 9.45.a.m. the courtroom was full. The press box was alive with journalists waiting to sprint to the telephone, where a junior was holding the line open to their news desk.

I looked around the court for Daniel Clipstein. He wasn't there. Nor, was Professor Wilhelm Frohmann. Jack joined me a few minutes before the Judge entered the court. The defendant was asked to rise. Kurt Frohmann's confidence had crumbled. He stood in the box, waiting for his sentence, with a look of resignation and disbelief. The full impact of his crime was upon him and any hint of schadenfreude gone. So too was impunity through nepotism.

The judge addressed the defence." Do you have anything further to add before I pass sentence?"
"No" came the reply.
Judge Ackermann swivelled his chair to face Kurt. 'I sentence you to three years in prison for premeditated burglary, with no remission. The sentence will run from to-day, 11 July 1971.'

A trickle of sound entered the courtroom as papers shuffled and the voice of the orderly said, "Rise." as the judge left the court,

Kurt was taken from the box and led away to serve his sentence: a carbon copy of the sentence his father received at Nuremberg for collaborating with the Nazis.

It was a dull heavy afternoon with ominous grey clouds. The spotlights were on full in the galerie and Stephan Moser was removing the remains of the last exhibition.

'Do you know when the Professor will arrive?'
'He's already here, Miss Edan, He's in his office.'
'Would you tell him I'm here.'
'I can't do that,' he said. 'The Professor has asked not to be disturbed.'
'Fine, I'll be in the galerie listing the works from Badgastein. Do you have an up-to-date list?' He handed me a folded paper.

All the crates from Museums were stamped and the contents listed. Fifteen crates were marked with Gerhard Hofer's name and I presumed it was the consignment from behind the Iron Curtain. I started to check the items one by one. I was half way through the first crate when Frohmann came into the galerie. 'Gut,' he said, 'I'm pleased you are here. Where's Pieter? He should be helping you.'

He picked up the phone on a small table. 'Moser, send Pieter in to help Miss Edan.' The Professor listened. 'Why is he out? Where is he?' I didn't hear the answer, but I heard the Professor say in a firm and commanding voice, 'Tell him I want him here, now.' Then he turned to me.
'Otto Prantl will be here tomorrow to help list the crates from Badgastein. It is too time consuming for me.'

He flipped open one of the boxes, forcing the lid back with a crack.

As soon as Pieter arrived to help me, the Professor left.

That evening I called Myrtle Shaw in Vienna. 'Hello' said a woman with a soft American accent.
'I am a friend of Bunny and Elgin. They asked me to call you.'
'It's great to hear an English voice. Nice of you to call.'
'Did Elgin tell you I might need some help with my work?'
'He did, but he didn't say how I might help.'

I gave her a quick précis of what I was attempting.
'The difficulty is you're working in Vienna and I need someone here in Salzburg.'
'That's not a problem Miss Edan: I have studies in most cities, including Germany and Holland but not exclusively capitals.'
'Could you come to Salzburg Miss Shaw?'
'Yes, I'd like to. But I'm leaving for the United States in two days for the summer. I'll be back in September. Is that too late?'

I gave her my London office number, and the telephone number of the Galerie Frohmann.
'We'll arrange a meeting when you return to Austria.'
'I look forward to meeting you Miss Edan.' she said.

***

Paul McKenzie had not printed the verdict of the trial in The Times, although four days had passed. I called him and asked why. He told me, 'It came on the ticker and I decided I wanted more colour: like what happened when Kurt Frohmann was sentenced.' he said. 'The father/son reaction, that sort of angle.'
'I have to disappoint you. Professor Frohmann wasn't in court for the verdict, only the guilty plea.'
'Great,' said McKenzie 'I can pull a good story out of that!'
'Like what, Mr.McKenzie?'
'Like father leaves son on the burning deck, or absent father rejects thieving son. I don't know what I'll write until it's written. Just give me some details to work on.'
'I gave McKenzie the scenario in the courtroom and the effect it had on the Professor.
'Got it,' he said. 'I'll keep it running.'

***

It had been a typical English summer, a washout, never two consecutive days of sunshine and for all but the hardy a cold bleak autumn seemed inevitable. September and October can compensate with an Indian summer. Not this year. High winds swept the landscape leaving the trees bereft of colour and the sodden earth waiting to freeze. Salzburg was equally dismal.

Myrtle Shaw returned to Vienna and we arranged to meet in Salzburg in the lobby of the hotel Östereichisherhof. I had no idea what she looked like. It was bizarre to imagine her from a voice at the end of a line, but I did. She sounded sweet and ineffectual on the phone, so I just kept my eyes on the revolving doors waiting for someone looking lost and waif-like to enter.

A small slim blonde about the same build as Bunny walked to the concierge's desk. She disappeared immediately. Another lone woman arrived in a heavy red jacket, but didn't give me a glance. Then a tall raven-haired woman, her hair sleeked back in a headband, a flawless white skin and seductive slanting eyes, was walking towards me confidently.

'Miss Edan,' she said, 'I'm Myrtle Shaw.' She shook my hand with a firm grip, her shoulder down, her chin high, and her eyes in direct contact with mine.

'Did you have a comfortable journey?' I said, as we went through the lobby, past a cascade of white lilies in an oriental vase, and down the wide stone stairs, to the hotel's Keller for lunch.

'Let me warn you in advance, never take the Orient Express unless you want to arrive smelling of stale garlic and stale sweat,' I said as we waited for the waiter to give us a table.

'Is it really that unpleasant? It's supposed to be romantic.' Myrtle Shaw said.

'Only in mystery stories,' I said with a smile.

We were seated in an alcove decorated with frescoes of hunting scenes, very quiet and very private. We both ordered Tagesuppe and goulash and a glass of red wine.

I certainly get my share of wolf whistles but Myrtle Shaw's looks demanded attention. Like Carmen in the opera, she was the type men have to pay homage. She was the archetypical trophy they couldn't live without. Her beauty needed mans' protection. So, I asked myself, why, with this model image does she want to list paintings in Salzburg? With that thought in mind I explained the purpose of the exhibition and what had to be completed.

'All the paintings are suspected loot or the property of museums who took them into care during the war. It's important that everything we list corresponds with the contents of the crates before they are re-sealed.'

'What will happen to unclaimed paintings?' she asked directly.

'They'll be returned to Salzburg for collection by number.'

Although Myrtle had been recommended by Elgin, I still wanted proof of her capabilities.

'Have you any knowledge of art, Miss Shaw?'

'Not practical, but part of my MA included art history, in the context of social history. So acquisitions, like paintings and antiques were important.'

'So you know the difference between a Manet and a Mantegna?'

'I'd feel ashamed if I didn't, Miss Edan.'

I then had to broach the subject of payment, remembering what Elgin had said. She certainly didn't look short of a schilling or two. She wore an expensive black ankle length coat over a mustard coloured hand knitted two-piece - not the uniform of an impoverished student.
'Firstly, Miss Shaw I must ask you if you'd like to do the work. Secondly, if you could work in Salzburg?'
'I really would like to help, but it all depends on how long it would take?'
'The exhibition opens in October 1973, so the paper work must be completed by January '73.' I said.

Myrtle Shaw was mentally counting the months. 'My problem, is not with time, it's with money. I would need to stay in Salzburg overnight or maybe weekends, and I really can't afford the expense as I've leased an apartment in Vienna till next September.'
'Miss Shaw, if I paid all your expenses plus an hourly fee, would that help? I then added, 'But before you decide I would like to show you the galerie where you'd be working.'

We walked along Giselakai towards the Frohmann Galerie. Miss Shaw commented on the uniqueness of the old city on the other side of the river.

Otto Prantl and Wilhelm Frohmann were in the galerie talking furiously.
'Ah, just at the right moment,' Frohmann said. 'We are just deciding when to close Badgastein.' He surveyed Miss Shaw.
'You've brought a friend?'
'Not exactly,' I said. I introduced her to the Professor and Prantl, 'Miss Shaw might be able to help with the listings when I'm not in Salzburg. She's living in Vienna and can work at week-ends so we can keep ahead.' I turned to the Professor. 'Would that be agreeable?'

Both Professor Frohmann and Otto Prantl looked at Myrtle Shaw. Prantl's stare was positively lascivious. Even in his darkest moments Wilhelm Frohmann still had an eye for a ravishing beauty. He gave an impeccable performance of a man in control of himself and in command. Quite different from the man who only two months earlier had left a courtroom devastated, with his family metaphorically exterminated and now running on the surface of life, while trapped in his own loneliness. It was a measure of his true character or his conscience that he would still help with the exhibition, and present such a cordial front.

I took Myrtle to the front galerie and introduced her to Stephan Moser. He responded in the same dour way he received me. But as the introduction was merely courtesy - it didn't matter.

'Would you call me at the hotel tomorrow with your decision, Miss Shaw.'

'That's not necessary. I can tell you now. I'd like to do the work. It will be an interesting challenge, and I'll do the best I can.'

'In that case, I'll make some enquiries about lodgings, and we'll talk tomorrow.' Prantl had followed us into the galerie.

He said, 'The Professor has a studio empty, Pieter has moved into the house opposite with his wife. Maybe it would suit your friend?'

I looked at Otto Prantl thinking this proposition should have come from Frohmann, not him, and dismissed the suggestion as unheard.

The court case left me detached yet concomitant, wondering what might have ensued between father and son, if my project had not intervened. I had decided whatever the domestic situation at Frohmann's home, Myrtle Shaw would not be staying there. I phoned Jack and explained the implications if she stayed in such close proximity to the Frohmann household. Apart from the obvious gossip it might be counter-productive and inhibiting for her. I asked if he had any suggestions.

'Do you remember going to Parsch for lunch? The Inn by the river,' he prompted.' I had remembered; in fact I had remembered everywhere we'd been together. But I quickly dismissed any past sentiment hovering in my thinking, freeing myself from intrusive memory. I listened to what he said.

'The Inn is owned by Frau Ettinger. Why don't you telephone? It's a very pleasant position.' He gave me the number.

I dialled the Parsch Inn immediately. Frau Ettinger answered. I told her Jack Steinhart had recommended me and a colleague wanted a room at weekends and occasional days during the week. It would be for about one year. She suggested that a room could be made available as long as one week's notice was given in advance. I couldn't believe the price she quoted per day. It was less than a train ticket from London to Birmingham. I told her I would confirm the reservation in writing. I then called Myrtle Shaw in Vienna.

'I've contacted an Inn at Parsch,' I told her. 'It's a village a short bus ride from Salzburg.' I explained the arrangements. 'Will that work with your research, Miss Shaw, or have you changed your mind?'

'Absolutely not,' she replied, 'it's an opportunity for me to be involved with paintings: something I might never do again in Europe. I have a question, Miss Edan? Will Professor Frohmann and Herr Prantl help for the first few visits? After that I'm sure I'll get on quickly.' I knew she would, too.

WENDOVER

36

The spectre of winter shrouded London like a winter cloak: deep heavy grey-black clouds swooped low over the city, muting the river Thames to murky mud, the city fretting for air. The glorious parks lay sallow, misty and bleak, their grasses nipped by frozen dew, and birds waiting at the edge of lakes, for charity.

My winter walk through Regents Park was brisk and fast. I felt guilty as I passed the swans and ducks racing towards the bank of the pond, looking for a morsel of bread. Squirrels pranced onto the footpath as my heels clicked along. The exotic perfume of summer regrettably replaced by a dank cloying smell from sodden earth, mould and aromatic whiffs of refined horse manure around tender plants. Defiant trees broke the skyline. Nature's sculptures, every one original and never conforming in shape. .

The phone in my office was quiet and apart from a few letters to answer, I considered the year's work over. Sue was shopping and arrived at noon. Tucked under her arm was a bottle of Nuit St.Georges and a carrier bag from Cullen's. After a quick sandwich, we closed the office until next year.

I was wrapping presents at home when Jack telephoned. On a business level our dialogue was ongoing always picking up just where we'd left it. He kept me up-to-date with anything relevant to the exhibition.

'The Frohmann case is still running,' he said. 'It's getting more coverage since the verdict: the story's really travelling. The psycho's are analysing, the politicians are debating the law, the medics are recommending, the banks are whinging, and the insurance companies are ready to go AWOL.'

'Whatever you tell me, Jack, there's nothing I can do. Kurt's jail sentence has no bearing on the exhibition.'

'You're wrong, Katrina, it has: the best publicity is scandal. On a scale from dodgy to downright filth, any fall from grace rates media attention, temporarily. So . . . sixty paintings, plus sixty million, plus son dumps dad, will be milked till it's dry. I figure it this way. What next? Suicide! Will the Professor kill himself? Will his son? The press is stabbing at possibilities.'

It hadn't occurred to me that suicide would ever be an option for the Professor it was too easy. His pride would intervene. Unexpectedly, Jack said, 'I'm coming to London for a few days over Christmas.' I waited for an explanation. Why? I thought. Has his mother abandoned him again, or is she in the process of another divorce?'

'Elgin and Bunny are returning from the States via London and we've arranged to meet.' Jack said.

Oh, dear! . . . I hesitated . . . Alone at Christmas! Where was my Christian charity? Impulsively I said, 'You're welcome to come to my parents' home if you haven't made any arrangements.' I tried to sound casual, as that was the way I felt: and I knew the ritual of our family Christmas couldn't and wouldn't change even with Jack Steinhart as a guest.

Extricating my mind from being so focused was a slow process. I had only one ambition, to get Christmas over as quickly as possible and complete the final phase of the project. I was pleased, even excited, at having time with my parents, and I intended to be polite to Jack - as a friend, but preserve my emotional energy for more productive pursuits.

By ten thirty my car boot was full of Christmas offerings and I was wrapped in my sheepskin coat and hat, prepared for anything winter might throw at me.

I stopped at the bakery in Finchley Road. There was a queue. Extra assistants were wrapping loaves as fast as they appeared on trays. The heat and smell of fresh baking condoned the waiting time. I doubled our usual order. Two cottage loaves, two tin loaves, two-dozen scones, and one sticky bun to eat on the way home.

The house was locked and a note on the kitchen table said. Mother shopping, Daddy collecting turkey. Help yourself to lunch - back soon xxxx

Peace, at last. No double-dealing, no crisis, no decisions, bliss.

I have concluded it's the familiarity that makes Christmas pleasurable and any deviation would leave something lacking - something lost. It's the boat that never rocks, it goes smoothly along, never changing route - returning, year after year, re-inventing itself in exactly the same pattern, unlike New Year, with its expectations and resolutions, the antidote for perhapsers, chancers and failures. Christmas is eternal.

When my father returned with the turkey, holding it limp by its feet, plucked of feathers except for a wispy few around its neck, I was making tea in the kitchen.
'Hello darling', he said. He held the bird up like a trophy. 'Just get this hung in the larder, won't be a tick'.
'Wait a minute, Daddy,' I said in earnest, 'I must feel his breast.' I poked the flesh with my finger. 'You're sure it's a cockerel?' I asked, repeating what my mother would have asked.
'Of course it is. Old gumboots wouldn't give me a broody hen for Christmas. Don't worry, my dear.'

I put another spoon of tea in the pot, just as the door opened and mother appeared laden with shopping bags, which she put on the kitchen table. She looked so young in dark brown slacks and a polo sweater: her blonde hair swept up into brown ribbon, tied with a bow, her casual sexual finesse still part of her attractiveness.
'Just what I needed,' she said as she fell into a chair. 'Every year I promise myself I'll shop in August for Christmas - and every year I fail.'

Mother was unpacking the homemade mincemeat that she had bought from her friend Caroline.
'I've made the pastry - only have to plonk some of this inside and pop them in the oven.' She showed us the jam jar with holly printed cotton tied around the lid, seasonally customizing a very ordinary jar and no doubt paying double for the privilege.

In the evening we decorated the tree and made silly comments about the contents of the gift boxes. Daddy pointed to one box: 'Cow pat pâté, from our very own garden.'
'You're disgusting Richard, especially in front of Katrina!'
I raised my arm, in school fashion, asking to speak.
'Better not, Katrina,' father said, stopping any vulgar repartee.
Then he announced in mock army fashion. 'Everyone must be assaulted by anticipation; Christmas is about excess, and there's no reason why we,' he winked at my mother, 'shouldn't comply.'

Mother set her coffee cup down, looked up and said. 'I think it's bedtime.' They had secret messages for foreclosing touchy or irritating conversation, but I never found the code!

Aunt Rose, Father's sister, and her husband are an odd couple. Nature made a mistake in drawing them together: they just didn't look comfortable aesthetically. Unlike my father, who is tall and robust and finely featured, his sister's face is sharp and angular and she is thin, not slim. Her career as a librarian had been dominant in her life because she loved books. In a quiet way she was knowledgeable. John, on the other hand, disliked engineering and wished he had opted for languages, so he could travel and unravel world problems. I suspected he also had a roving eye, but Rose didn't look, so the marriage stayed intact and on course for old age. They had one son, my cousin, James, a quantity surveyor working for a company in Singapore. He was two years older than me, and as a child was always in charge: reliable, very self-assured, he knew "things" I didn't. He'd promised to tell me these "things", but by the time I was ten and he was twelve, I made it quite clear that I knew babies didn't come from gooseberry bushes, so he'd better have something extraordinary to tell me or shut up. The question of superiority never arose again and we have been on level ground ever since.

A car door slammed in the driveway. I hastily pulled the curtain back from the kitchen window.

'Don't worry, Katrina, father's outside moving cars.'

My father and Jack came into the kitchen together.

'Cynthia, this is Jack, We're old friends, we've just walked the length of the garden together,' he said, putting us all at ease and negating formality. Jack handed my mother a bunch of pink roses, and me a single orchid. A simple gesture, which I appreciated: anything excessive would have been intimidating.

Mother was wearing a moss green dress with a pink scarf at the neck. 'How clever of you to choose pink,' she said, as she held the roses up to her face. 'Katrina, take Jack into the drawing room, I'll join you in a few minutes.'

A pungent mixture of turkey roasting and charcoal from the log fire filled the house with seasonal warmth.

'I'm absolutely, positively, ragingly thirsty. Any chance of a drink Daddy, or do we have to wait for the gong?' I turned to Jack. 'I'm sure you're ready for a drink.'

'A scotch and soda would be great.'

'Make that two,' I said, A car chugged into the drive-way.

'I'll go,' Cynthia shouted from the hall.

Noisy chatter came from the hall before Aunt Rose, Uncle John and James, who looked stunning in a Nehru cut Indian

jacket of dark blue worsted and matching narrow cut trousers, joined us in the drawing room. I introduced Jack as a colleague.
I immediately said. 'East meets west, who is the best?' and hugged James. My father opened the champagne and James suggested we wait till Boxing Day for the year's family saga, of opening presents, so Jack wouldn't get bored.

Conversation during lunch became intercontinental with Jack giving us the state of the Union and John castigating Labour Policy in Britain.

John said, 'Our Prime Minister, should be shipped to Australia as slave labour! I'll tell you Jack; he's turning us all into slaves in this country. We're the laughing stock of the world, ruled by strikes and the trade unions.'
'Both my father and John,' I said to Jack 'are staunch Tories. It happened when they were born and given lethal doses of conservatism.' Father vehemently disagreed. 'Katrina, that's an unacceptable exaggeration. You haven't been tar brushed with blue.'
My mother joined in. 'Your father would never have survived in the army if politics had motivated him.'

There was no argument only opinion but it was Jack who moved the conversation on. 'I'm a little confused, not about the blues and reds, but what is Boxing Day?'
I was about to explain, so was John, so was my mother. 'I think James should tell him,' I said.
'What's funny about Boxing day, Katrina?' Jack looked perplexed.
'Don't take too long,' mother said to James, 'the Queen's speech is on the radio in five minutes.'
'Boxing day, December 26, is historical,' James said, 'because boxes were placed in churches for donations to the poor. And Christmas boxes, we'd call them tips now, were also given to tradesmen and servants by the upper classes. Boxing matches used to be staged in the open, to entertain the working classes and in later years inside.'

My father added. 'Invariably it was professional pugilists first followed by a free for all punch-up by the audience.'
'I'm surprised,' Jack said, 'I didn't know it was so historic.'
James said 'Actually Jack, it's become an anachronism: most

people spend Boxing Day recovering from the excesses of the day before.'

After the Queen's speech the table groaned with the weight of the glazed turkey, lying resplendently on a Royal Worcester serving dish, which sees the light of day once a year. Tureens filled with crunchy roast potatoes with toasted almonds, sprouts with lemon zest, applesauce and brandy gravy. There were no restrictive covenants on the amount of food.

While my father was carving, some exterior force made the voices around the table distant. I felt I was floating away, going somewhere else, as the saliva rose in my mouth. I tried to swallow, but my throat closed and my head started to spin. I left the table. Hovering faintness possessed me. I don't know how I managed to get to my room. Menacing images came into focus as my head touched the pillow and I drifted away. I was in a concentration camp: rusted bars gripped the air vent. My eyes stung from looking nowhere. Pippa was there too, a skeleton with a bandage round her head, crying. I heard two shots. I held my stomach and screamed, as the bullet hit the air in my stomach. Give me a candle, please give me a candle, I pleaded. I held my hand high, waiting for a light to lead me to heaven, when another shot exploded hitting my wrist: my hand had gone.

My mother was holding a cold flannel across my forehead. The pictures were vivid in my mind, my wrist aching. I clasped my hands together, squeezing them tightly desperately trying to find reality. As tears started to roll and the images fade, Mother handed me her white handkerchief, embroidered with a butterfly at the corner, a graphic reminder of my own fragility: a combination of tension and exertion was asserting its potency, catching me unawares.

I didn't want to spoil the day for my parents. I knew how much time and effort they had spent. Mother was reluctant to leave but I insisted. I must have drifted into sleep again because when I eventually went downstairs lunch had finished and the family and Jack were having coffee in the drawing room.

Father said, 'I think a nice cup of good English tea is what you need, my girl,' and he was right. I stopped drifting like the steam on the teacup and wondered if Jack thought he caused my anxiety. He left soon after and practically no conversation had passed between us.

When Pippa's parents died, the roles in my family changed. I became possessive and demanding, at the same time as my parents were trying to make me independent. But their presence was the only steadfast anchor in my life and I feared that would be taken away. There were no parallels in Pippa's life and mine. She was sent away to school leaving everyone she knew, casting her security into future despair. I stayed at home. Slowly Pippa lost her confidence, as I gained mine. Then she lost her reason. The trauma of losing her parents didn't surface till she attempted suicide when she was fifteen. My parents tried to visit her in hospital but the psychiatrist explained to them that Pippa couldn't face what had been buried in her unconscious for so long: my parents and I were too close to the event which triggered her drastic action: we only exacerbated Pippa's loneliness. The enormity of facing the world alone, the psychiatrist said, made exit appear her only option.

***

I looked out of the kitchen window. It was a bright clear morning with blue sky and a hoar frost. A robin hopped onto the windowsill, its head turning quickly, looking for breadcrumbs for its tiny beak.

Aunt Rose and John decided to walk to Wendover village with my parents. James and I walked to Ellesborough Church. We climbed the steep incline to the small ancient building, stood in the last pew with our own thoughts until James said, 'The Prime Minister's not here, how disappointing.' But the dark green holly decorating the pews and a Christmas tree with coloured fairy lights, gave this bleak edifice seasonal warmth.

The temperature was dropping fast and although the sun had shone a mist hugged the valley, creeping slowly towards us. Storm clouds were behind as we walked quickly along the Icknield Way towards home.

'This road was built by the Romans.' I told James. He looked down. 'You are wrong. It was built on top of the old Roman Road,' emphasizing on top. You've forgotten Katrina, I went to school in England not Singapore.'

We arrived home freezing. We sat by the fire in the drawing room rubbing our hands together and toasting our feet. James threw a log into the simmering ashes.

'I'm starving' he said and pointed a finger at me. 'The service is getting slow around here to-day. Be a good girl and run into the kitchen and get something hot.'

'Sod off and get it yourself.' I retaliated. 'There's no clap hand coolie service in this neck of the woods.' We were playing our usual games and burst out laughing in unison.

Over soup in the kitchen we talked about Christmas day. I was curious to catch up on what I'd missed during lunch. 'Anything important happen while I was resting yesterday?' I said, trying to sound off-hand.

'We were talking about the weaknesses and strengths of the American policy in Europe, if you think that's important. But, I think you want to talk about Jack Steinhart.'

'So what's your opinion of Jack?'

James was economical with words. 'Clever, very clever.'

'What does that mean, clever smart or clever brains?'

'Both, Katrina. He's success in the making, but I'm not sure I'd trust him.'

'What makes you say that?'

'Well, he had a good rapport with your father, talking animatedly about banking, politics and war. He has considerable historical knowledge on the wars in Europe.'

'Umm - I didn't know.' I popped some bread in the toaster.

'Katrina, something about Jack doesn't quite fit. Maybe he had a rough ride as a kid, I don't know. He hasn't a chip on his wide shoulders that's for sure, but if you're asking me if you should get involved, I'll tell you; you could get your toes in deep water and your fingers burnt.'

'Anything else, James?'

'If you fancy him and vice-a-versa, you're a big girl, I think you could handle him, as long as you don't expect what he's incapable of giving.' James took a ham from the larder and sliced thick chunks off the bone.

'Katrina, it's glaringly obvious that something other than a wink is going on between you. Why don't you admit it, face it, and deal with it rationally. Tell me, do you like the guy? . . . That's a

silly question,' James corrected, 'of course you like the guy, or he wouldn't be here.'
I hedged, saying inanely, 'Daddy invited him.'
'Hey, Katrina, it's me James you're talking to, not some unsuspecting idiot.'
'Sorry James. You're right. My antennae told me some time ago something about Jack just doesn't add up. He's very courteous and concerned about the exhibition, and he's helped me overcome some tricky problems. But I still don't trust him.'
'On what level? Business or personal?'

I thought carefully. 'Personal, I suppose. We're working in the same arena, but he never moves any goal posts to be with me. He changes plans, makes excuses. When I confront him, he always has a glib excuse.'
'So, you're not hearing what you want, but what he says?'
'I have no proof that he's lied to me: only my intuition tells me he's holding something back, for whatever reason, I have no idea.'
'Maybe he's married.' James said simply. 'Maybe he left the States to get away from a whinging shrew. Whatever, it's unimportant. What matters is, do you care?' I took a beer from the fridge, not sure how to answer.
'James, for the first time in my life I really don't know. One thing I do know, I have an exhibition to complete and Jack Steinhart is on the front line with me, albeit in a passive capacity. Maybe I'll just have to do what he's asked and "go with him on this one" and see what happens.
'That's your best and only choice. As long as he's keeping to the contract, get the exhibition behind you first. You have other sponsors, just put him in perspective: if there's anything personal to salvage, you'll know after three years.'

LONDON
37

There was a note on the mat from Jack Steinhart. "Please ring Elgin and Bunny Brooks at Durrants Hotel. They leave January 1st. Jack." I picked up a few late Christmas cards off the floor and read them while I waited for the kettle to boil. Then I phoned Elgin. He was out. I left a message: set the thermostat on the boiler to high and whistled round the house with a duster.

When the phone rang I had already climbed into bed with a book about the power of Genghis Khan and the demise of the Mogul Empire.

'Katrina, it's Bunny.' Her effervescent voice trilled down the line. 'Jack has reserved a table at Quaglino's for New Year's. Are you fixed up, or can you join us?' I hadn't even thought about New Year's Eve until that moment.

'I'd love to join you. What time and where?'

'Durrants Hotel, around eight. We're looking forward to seeing you, Katrina.' I heard Elgin's voice in the background. 'Elg says hello.'

The panelled hotel foyer had a country house feel, ruby red velvet drapes and matching chairs and Georgian glass doors that led into the bar.

Bunny looked stunning, in a black flapper dress to her knees with a fringe at the hem of jet beads and seed pearls. Her blonde hair had been cut into a straight bob. Elgin wore a single-breasted steel grey suit and a grey tie. I had never seen him in a suit before: the climate in Israel doesn't call for such overdressing. His mousy hair was quite long for a diplomat, hanging lankly onto his collar. Bunny gave me a kiss, as though I was a long-lost friend, Elgin pecked my cheek.

'Katrina, you look lovely.' he said.

'Turn around' Bunny said, 'I want to get a good look at that dress.' I swivelled like a wound-up china doll in my royal blue satin, showing the simple lines of the short straight skirt with the top held up by two very thin shoe string straps.

'Honey, it's a stunner, especially with your red hair,' she said.

I knew it suited me. It was a perennial stand-by.

The Brooks' are an unlikely couple in any society. Elgin's southern drawl and laid-back manner however, were deceptive. This man was no cowpoke He was sharp witted and astute, with a diplomat's poise and training in the art of saying very little about a lot of subjects. On the other hand Bunny was a chatterer and a delight to watch, even if sometimes her comments were a little inane, they were never out of place.

Jack was waiting in the bar at Quaglino's and waved as we entered. The tables were set with all the paraphernalia of New Year's Eve. Jack laughed when he saw what was on the table. 'More crackers.' he said as he held one up.

'See this, Elgin. It's a lethal weapon designed by English back room boys to annihilate G.I.Joe.'

'Yeah, no kidding. Looks like twisted coloured paper to me.'

'Ah-ha . . . that,' said Jack, pointing to his shiny red cracker, 'is dynamite, right Katrina?'

'Dead right sir.'

The evening was off to a good start and progressed in facetious fashion. We had a team game with peas, the three Yanks versus one Brit. I reckoned I had the edge on them, knowing how to stab peas and not scoop them, the Yanks sending them rolling around the table and Bunny, shouting, 'Come here you green monster,' as the peas slid up the spaces in her fork.'

By eleven o'clock the restaurant was noisy: whistles were blowing, streamers darted from table to table and champagne corks popped. A farmer walked around the restaurant with a pig on a lead. Not that this in itself was so funny, but the pig was wearing a bowler hat. Elgin, Bunny and Jack were rolling with laughter.

'One up for the Brits,' Elgin said, waving his cracker, 'they certainly laugh at themselves.'

The minutes were ticking slowly towards New Year as the waiter put a dish of flaming crêpes suzettes on a griddle in the centre of our table, and the air filled with the aromatic fumes of brandy. The champagne glasses were waiting for the magic moment, when Big Ben strikes. The band stopped playing and through the speakers came the first boom. I stood up. Jack, Elgin and Bunny followed. As the chimes rang out we counted through to twelve. The band played Auld Lang Sine as we linked hands and made a raucous attempt at the words. Elgin lit a cigarette and accidentally set fire to his cracker, which exploded immediately. Bunny was in shock.' You idiot Elg, Jack said it was dynamite!'

'O.K. just testing,' he said with a slur, pushing a blower with a feather on the end into Bunny's face.

'Don't get suggestive, Brooks,' she sniggered, curling her tongue out with a come hither smile.

Our consumption of alcohol made everything funny, If Al Capone had walked in with artillery at his hip and demanded our money or our lives, we'd have laughed.

Jack was sitting next to me, and took my hand under the table. I took his hand, still holding mine and laid it on the cloth.

'Elgin,' I said in a voice that sounded miles away, 'would you please keep your friend Mr.Steinhart in check? He's making passes at me.' Elgin didn't answer - Bunny did.

'Honey, the guy's nuts about you - give him a break - he only wants to hold your hand!' I pouted, looked at Jack's hand and let go. What had Jack told them, my muddled mind wanted to know? If he were any sort of gentleman, I reasoned, he'd know the rules: he could ruin a girl's reputation.

We heard the notes of a lone piper as he slow marched into the room, resplendent in black watch tartan, and the traditional regalia of a Scotsman. Nothing moves me more than the haunting rasp of the pipes. This unique sound, heaving with nostalgia, made tears well into my eyes. I held my lips tight, biting into my lower lip, as he circled the tables before the sound faded into the distance, long after he'd left the room. Like the last post, a lone piper symbolizes the end, not the beginning. And although it was New Year, it ended one of the most extraordinary years in my life.

LONDON

38

'Good news' Sue said, and handed me a letter from the National Gallery in Oslo. It was everything I had hoped for and more. They had agreed to loan Edvard Munch's "The Scream," and to subsidize an edition of posters of the painting, with the proviso that the revenue went to a charity for the victims of racial persecution.

'Sue, ring Paul McKenzie. Send him a copy of the letter from Oslo and give him the title of the exhibition.

THE SCREAM: ORPHAN PAINTINGS LOOTED BY THE NAZIS.

He's reporting on the Frohmann trial, so this new information will keep the story moving. And we can write the catalogue and an up-dated press release, so McKenzie will have some follow-up. Will McKenzie give us any special consideration?'

'Doubt it,' Sue said.

'Couldn't you make it a personal request?'

'I could, but it wouldn't cut any ice.'

'Then you'll have to beg, cadge, grovel, if necessary, for free space Sue. Play one Newspaper against another: use all your native cunning. Make sure you tell the media this is more than an art exhibition, it's an exposure of the spoils of treachery.'

A shrill ring attacked the front door bell. Sue tumbled downstairs and came back with an express letter. I looked at the postmark. Badgastein, Austria. I ripped open the envelope. Inside was a typed letter.

Dear Madam,

On February 27 1972 I returned four signed paintings to the collection point at the Hotel Straubinger Badgastein. A German soldier who was billeted with us in 1944 left them at my home. When the Russians approached his company retreated into the woods and went west. He said he would return for his possessions. He did not. These pictures have been in our attic since he left.

The letter was unsigned and it appeared to me, suspicious. Why had they never looked at them before? What else had they kept in their attic? I immediately phoned Myrtle Shaw in Vienna. There was no reply. Then I phoned Parsch and was told she had been at the Inn for two days but was out at the moment. I telephoned the Frohmann Galerie. Stephan Moser answered. I didn't want to discuss the letter with the Professor or Prantl, nor did I want to discuss the details on their phone line. He put me through to Myrtle in the rear galerie.

'I'm calling to see how you're managing?' I said mendaciously.

'Fine, just fine.' she answered. 'I have Pieter here at the moment, opening and sealing, and Moser's been helping too. Still quite a way to go, but we're getting there.'

'Have you seen the Professor?'

'He was here Miss Edan, but left for Vienna with Herr Prantl.'

'I have a meeting in a few minutes,' I lied, 'could you call me at my home later from Parsch? Anytime before midnight, so we can keep up to date.'

At nine o'clock she called. I told her that a box had been received in Badgastein containing four important paintings: two Rembrandts, a Vermeer and a Durer.

'I want to be absolutely sure they arrive in Salzburg.'

'Is there any reason why they should not, Miss Edan?'

'Yes, Miss Shaw: theft.' I had made it clear to her when we first met that many dealers would try to legitimise their inventory at the exhibition, so pictures could be sold on the open market. But this didn't preclude theft and concealment of the very valuable pieces.

'So, you're telling me Miss Edan, once a thief always a thief. Or, more likely, a hopeful last chancer.'

'Absolutely. If the stakes are high enough, the risk is only pro-rata. Kurt Frohmann is a classic example.' Miss Shaw didn't comment.

'I don't want you to worry. If you see the box, call me, I'll fly over to assess them myself. I hope that puts your mind at rest.'

'Miss Edan, I'm not at all worried, I can only list what I see.'

'How long will you stay in Salzburg?'

'Till tomorrow evening, I'll return here in five days' time.'

As soon as the line disconnected I called Anton. We arranged to meet for coffee at his home the next day.

I was about to leave the office when Sue told me Jack Steinhart was calling from Chicago.

'I'm coming back via London on Saturday. Do you have anything planned or could we meet?'

He sounded tentative, probably expecting a negative response from me, which he didn't get. I needed Jack Steinhart. He was my only source of unexpurgated information in Austria, and that alone made him important. I told him to call me when he arrived.

***

When I saw Anton Hempf the following morning, I asked for a list of missing Rembrandt paintings.

'Why do you want a list?'

'Because two have been handed in at the collecting point.'

'I seem to remember,' Anton said, running his hand through his hair, 'that Kurt Frohmann stole a Rembrandt that had been handed in.'

'You're right, I also suspect that works that have been stored in monastries and castles are being picked over before I see them.'

'But you have seen some important works.'

'I know, but I think they're the sprats to keep me happy; considering the number of works handed in, the ratio is disproportionate.'

Anton did not react immediately. Then he said. 'I think I should prepare a list of missing works from the Borbone-Parma and the Finaly collections. The records are well documented and you might recognise a painting from the title.'

He smiled broadly: pleased that any snippet of information he gave me might lead to the discovery of a lost work of art.

***

Jack telephoned as promised. 'I've just arrived at Blades Hotel.' He said, 'I'm scruffy I need to clean up. Could you come here for dinner?' I agreed to meet him at eight.

I drove through Hyde Park to South Kensington. Blades is a small hotel frequented by pop stars and media people. An unusual choice I thought.

As I entered Blades the dramatic black and white marble foyer immediately struck me. A small discreet desk served as reception but there was no one there. I looked in the mirrored walls magnifying the space and noticed my hair looked redder than usual. It must be tinted glass I told myself, as my smiling reflection came back to me and my brown velvet suit turned to autumn rust. 'Can I help you madam?' A young Japanese boy with hair like an old-fashioned brylcream advert was standing by the desk.

'I'm meeting Mr.Steinhart,' I said. He pressed a button on a mini exchange.

When Jack came into the foyer, I knew immediately by his smile that he was in a good mood. This was confirmed by his first words to me. 'I'm celebrating, Katrina.'

We were walking downstairs towards the bar and restaurant.

'I've ordered a bottle of champagne and the Japanese menu for two,' he told me.

Round tables covered with white tablecloths were widely spaced, each with a lantern set in the centre, a touch of oriental charm. Stark black wrought iron chairs rested on a black marble floor, relieved dramatically by citron yellow upholstered seats.

Jack seemed genuinely concerned about my progress in Salzburg.

'How was the Professor? What's your new assistant like?'

'Slow down, please. One question at a time.'

He emptied his glass and beckoned the waiter immediately poured some more.

'Right,' Jack said, 'I'll ask questions in sequence. 'One how's Frohmann?'

'He's putting on a good front. I can't comment on his health. He's living on drugs and adrenaline, not a very sustaining cocktail.' The waiter put an assortment of tiny dishes on the table, which we picked at with our fingers.

'And your new assistant. How's she matching up?'

'O.K. so far, I think she's capable.' I told him about the letter I'd received from Badgastein. 'I've asked Myrtle Shaw to let me know if the box doesn't arrive in Salzburg.'

'Are you telling me you suspect someone's thieving?'

'I am, and Otto Prantl's name slides easily into place. Unfortunately so does Frohmann's.'
'Tricky situation. What happens if the box isn't found?'
'I'll deal with that if and when it happens.' Jack lapsed into silence pondering on what I had said, but moved the conversation back to himself.
'It's strange' he said, 'by next year my life will be entirely different. Where I go, where I work, where I play and with whom? Maybe I'll vegetate awhile. Wrong word, I should say, contemplate. Yes - I'll like that. I've quit, but I still have to work my year's notice.' Anxious to tell me what this potential freedom would mean to him, he said briskly.
'This will be the first time in eight years I'll be free of market forces: not having to calculate risk against gain, margins against profit, success or failure. Nor being in the hot seat in a cold war. Katrina, I don't want to die young. Investment banking is not toll free. It's the short route to early burnout and a ticket to nowhere.'
'So how do bank executives survive to grey-haired power?'
'Delegate, my dear Katrina . . . they delegate: slide like squirmy worms, eating at the guts of guys like me.' There was venom in his voice as he said. 'I'm tired of being motivated by the wrong people for the wrong reasons. Cold cash.' He repeated 'cold bloody cash.'
'Isn't that what makes the world go round?'
'Sure, from London to Frankfurt to Chicago - not the world. Your exhibition is about restitution in kind - not money. Money is only a short measure for justice.'
'Jack, you're forgetting, it's your bank's money and Samuel Hall's that made it all possible.'
'But it's not the cause, it's only the effect: the platform if you like.'

The waiter cleared the dishes and replaced them with another variety. The smile had gone from Jack's face, the muscles in his jaw line twitched. His eyes, glassy and cold, drifted far away.
I jolted him back.
'I thought you were celebrating?' Slowly he came back from the distance with a reluctant momentary smile.

'I am. I'll order another bottle. I remember telling you, Katrina, that I would explain that what appears to be secretive and bizarre behaviour to you, is normal for me.' Before I had a chance to speak, he said. 'I'm limited in what I can tell you. My business is confidential and banking is a sensitive exacting job, especially when a lot of other people's money is involved.'
'You've told me that before,' I said.
He ignored my remark. 'So I'll risk telling you my immediate assignment as I don't want this antagonism to go on. Money has come into branches of our bank with numbers corresponding to a heist of millions of pounds some years ago. I have been given the tacky job of finding its origin.'
'Isn't it paid into accounts?'
'Sure, but it's mixed with legal money and paid into banks worldwide including Laufenbankgeschaft. I have to trace cash accounts that are swelling too rapidly. It's tough.'
'So, it's tough, Jack. My job's tough too. I haven't a support system or a corporation backing me up, nor minions to help. I solicit every step, from inception to finish. Why should I sympathise with you?'
'Good question. My answer is I don't want your sympathy, just a little understanding. Is that unreasonable?'
'No, not at all, except to me it sounds like lies.'
Jack didn't take kindly to that remark.
'So, I'm a liar.' he said, looking vaguely around the room. 'It's been a natural habit since I was a child. Starting with my father, liars brought me up, so I'm well qualified. I knew my father for eight years, on and off between his absences from home. He left home when I was nine. He walked out of the door, waved and said he'd be back. I waited. And I waited. By the time I was ten, I knew he was a liar. The "Uncles" came and went from my mother's life, then a succession of husbands followed my stepfathers. My mother shipped me to school in Vermont. She told me it would be fun and it wasn't. I was in the way of her fun, but at the time I believed her, until I realized she was also a liar.'

Jack looked vulnerable. Reviving the insecurity of his childhood exposed his facade, that paper-thin veil of success, on show for acknowledgement by the outside world, when his inner world was a catalogue of unhappiness.

I challenged him. 'I cannot believe that you were so deprived that a simple country background in the Shires of England appears omnipotent?'

'I'm not comparing your background with mine. I did feel deprived but not materially: I just came from a self-centred couple whose destiny didn't include me. Maybe I was lucky. I could still be on a ranch in New Mexico pulling foals out of horses arses, watching my mom and dad get old, hating each other's guts and talking about the old country.'

'I'm a rootless American, Katrina. My father came from German stock and mother, Irish. I am a European on foreign soil. I'm a polygon, many sided, a speck of dust floating across continents, blown by insecurity.'

'Jack, are you telling me you'll disappear regularly to find your identity?'

'Not at all. I'll disappear to find a tangible commodity - money: when the job's done - I quit.'

'And?' I said, in psychotherapy style.

'I'll arrive first then I'll make my decisions.'

A wise conclusion I thought. Anticipation is a motivating thought; it is also destructive, depending on the way you think about the unknown future.

LONDON

39

Four weeks had passed before Myrtle phoned: the box containing the four paintings had not arrived. I pondered over the options. I could confront Professor Frohmann and Otto Prantl or I could bide my time and wait. If I confronted them, the unsigned letter would have to be shown, giving them time to cover their tracks: leaving it longer would delay recovery.

I decided on an anonymous advert. I called Jack in the hope he could enlist the help of Anton Kodech. He was sceptical.

'Whoa, this is sensitive. I'm not sure Kodech will touch it.'

'In that case I'll have to make it a public issue. Then the Collecting Point and all the ancillary services will become suspect, including Frohmann. Who is the thief, Kurt or his father?

'Maybe both,' Jack said, 'and Kurt Frohmann was the fall guy who got caught?'

'All I want is a few simple lines. "Four paintings. Two Rembrandts, one Vermeer and a Dürer have been mislaid." Simple, to the point, and not accusing.' Jack agreed to speak to Kodech.

My inner judgement concluded it would be printed. Not because of benevolence from the press but because Jack was on the other end of the phone.

My suspicions about Jack were increasing by the day: maybe he had paid Kodech to write in the Austrian press, but with whose money? Who was gaining what, and why?

Too many unanswered questions were scattered in my head, blowing like confetti, with nowhere to settle. Two weeks to the day on 1st April - fools' day - the advert appeared.

A box containing four paintings, two Rembrandts one Vermeer and one Dürer, destined for the exhibition at the Royal Academy in London arranged by curator Katrina Edan, has not reached its destination in Salzburg. The box was handed in at a Collecting Point in Badgastein. Anyone with any knowledge of its whereabouts is invited to return the box to Galerie Frohmann in Salzburg. Confidentiality will be respected.

In other words, no questions would be asked and a number would refer to the paintings: presuming the message had the desired outcome.

Sue called on the inter-com.' Jack Steinhart on the line from Vienna.' I looked at the clock it was 9.15.am.

'Good morning, how's the weather in London?' Funny question: since when has idle chatter warranted phone time?

'I met your assistant Myrtle Shaw last night.'

'Oh yes, and where did you meet her?'

'At the American Embassy's ex-pat party.' I anticipated the next remark. 'Quite a stunner, and a lot happening in that pretty head.'

'Good,' I remarked. 'I need a few thinkers around me for a change.'

'Katrina, she has a problem.'

'Why didn't she call me?'

'She did, and you weren't there.' Strange I thought, Sue didn't tell me she'd called.

'It appears that one of Prantl's crates has a painting missing.'

'How does she know?'

'Because you told her to check contents at random and this crate doesn't tally with the listing.'

'Do you know which painting is missing?'

'No, she didn't say, but she wants to know if she should discuss it with Prantl?'

This infuriated me. 'Jack, this is totally out of order. Why the hell is she talking to you about works of art that don't concern you? And how the hell did she know you were involved?'

'Hey - hold on a minute, I'll explain.' I waited for one of Jack's smooth plausible excuses.

'Frohmann and Prantl were in Vienna last week when Myrtle was in Salzburg. Frohmann gave her my name as a contact for emergencies. It was a coincidence we met at the embassy.'

'Even so,' I said 'she has no authority to discuss anything - and I mean anything - with you.'

'You're absolutely right, but at these embassy shindigs, everyone gossips about what they're up to and who! It's the ex-pat way of social circulation. We meet folks on our own wavelength.'

I didn't like what I was hearing. For information to be bandied

about the cocktail circuit could jeopardise both the exhibition and everything Anton and I had set up for Anna Frishman.
'Do you know where Myrtle is now?' I asked Jack.
'Yes, she's at her apartment waiting for you to call.'
'Before you go, Jack, I have a request.'
'What is it?'
'Keep your mouth shut, if it's possible. I don't want this information given to Prantl or Frohmann. Under any other circumstances I'd sack Myrtle immediately. It's one thing to have a thinking apparatus on your neck but useless if the gap in your face can't contain it.'
'Don't get so rough Katrina. Nothing ever gets outside of embassy doors, it's an unwritten rule.' I was not convinced.

Myrtle Shaw sounded apprehensive. 'I can't understand if it was my mistake or the crates were mixed? My burning question came first. 'Why did you discuss it with Jack Steinhart?'
She fumbled for a reply. 'Miss Edan, when I first went to the American embassy in Vienna, I was told that all conversations within the compound were confidential and not to be repeated outside, especially on ex-pat night.'
'Maybe I didn't make myself clear, but under no circumstances can you discuss the contents of the listings with anyone other than myself. And that includes Jack Steinhart and any other embassy flotsam. Have I made the point clear, Miss Shaw?'
'I'm sorry Miss Edan.'
'I don't want you to mention the discrepancy to Professor Frohmann or Otto Prantl, I shall deal with it personally and please in future if you find any abnormalities which you don't understand - tell me immediately.'
'I will' she said quickly, 'I really will.'

I could hear by the tone of her voice she was genuinely remorseful and I'm sure my admonition was clear.

On the 29th April Myrtle phoned. There had been no response to the advert in the paper and nothing had been received in Salzburg. It was impossible that Frohmann, Prantl and Gerhard Hofer had not read the advertisement. So, how many more paintings had they taken and where were they being stored? Questions I needed answers to immediately.

SALZBURG

40

In May I flew to Salzburg leaving a glorious scented leafy London with almond and cherry trees heavy with blossom.

In Austria, the waters of the Salzach River danced over rocks and stones, as the sunlight had teased away winters ice and snow. One hour after I arrived at the Hotel Elephant, Myrtle Shaw joined me in the hotel's stube to discuss the works she had listed. The total number, which had been photographed to date, was just under 3000. I noted there were crates from the Galerie Frohmann added at the end of the list without identification.

'When did these arrive, Miss Shaw?' I said as I ran my finger to the end of the page.

'I'm afraid I don't know. Stephan Moser added them to the list, I haven't seen the contents.'

We were both looking at the eclectic mix of works that had been listed, dating from 17th century to late 20th. Myrtle explained.

'The paintings marked with an asterisk were those I could not identify because the artist's name was missing.' She paused and shifted uneasily in her chair.

'I attempted to classify them by period, to save you time, but I'm not sure I if I got it right.' I was grateful for her initiative and expressed this to her.

'You have been as thorough as possible under the circumstances and I do appreciate your help. Miss Shaw have you seen Mr.Steinhart since I spoke to you?'

'No, I haven't. I've seen more of Herr Prantl, because when he's coming here from Vienna, we travel on the same train. He's been most helpful. He has given me some interesting insights on how the international art market works.'

'Like what, Miss Shaw?'

'Well, he told me how competitive the museums are and how they employ searchers and consultants worldwide to find works by all the great masters. Even one painting, if it's a good example of the artist's oeuvre, can increase the prestige of a museum.'

Her dark intense eyes, fringed with long dark lashes, flashed with excitement. 'Miss Edan, Herr Prantl told me even a small museum like the one in Albi, has become a major tourist attraction because of its association with Toulouse-Lautrec: tourism has changed the economy of this small market town.'

She was telling me what I already knew, but I was more interested in Prantl than a résumé of the commercial art market. I discreetly asked her if she liked his galerie in Vienna.

'I've only been once,' she said. 'He invited me for dinner and I met him there. He's very knowledgeable, Miss Edan.'

I replied with innocence. 'I really don't know him, we've only met a few times, and mostly to discuss works he's submitting to the exhibition.'

'He's invited me to his country home in Filzmoos,' Myrtle said: 'it's a tiny village somewhere in the mountains. I haven't had a chance to go yet, but I will.'

'Filzmoos . . . Filzmoos,' I repeated, searching for a connection. 'I've heard that name before, I can't recall who mentioned Filzmoos to me - but I remember someone told me it is charming, very rustic and gemütlichkeit.' As I was speaking, I remembered. Two years ago Jack had asked me to spend a weekend with him in Filzmoos. That recollection remained private.

It was hard to visualise the svelte Myrtle with her silky white skin, and full inviting red lips, with the slick, nervous persona of Prantl. She was certainly paddling in shark-infested waters: I hoped she wouldn't go in too deep.

'Miss Shaw, I have one last request. If you hear from any source the possible whereabouts of the missing box, I would appreciate your telling me. And only me,' I added.

'Of course I will, Miss Edan.'

LONDON

41

My desk was heaving with untouched paperwork waiting to be cleared but a call from the National Gallery diverted my priorities, even though the curator had become a friend. I rang Elizabeth to ask if it was urgent pleading, 'I'm snowed under with a backlog of correspondence.'

'Sorry, but it is. Could you come to the National this morning?'

'I could be there in about an hour, if that's O.K.' I hastily wrote a note for Sue, telling her where I would be.

Trafalgar Square was filling with tourists throwing seeds like planters in a field, encouraging the pigeons (Elizabeth's "dirty beasts") to foul the old stone arena and cause havoc to the adjacent buildings. This plebeian activity perpetuated throughout the year, was fast becoming an environmental hazard. Towering above the square, the statue of Lord Nelson looks into the distance, a tribute to the great battle of Trafalgar in 1805, a symbol of British naval supremacy. It was an ironic twist that the House of Rothschild financed the British fleet, while the House of Rothschild in Paris was simultaneously backing the French and Spanish. Brother against brother, or were they in league, banking on the winner and the loser, and coming out even?

Elizabeth looked tired. She had lost a considerable amount of weight and her bobbed hair accentuated her prominent cheekbones, previously hidden by a much fatter face. Her litheness made her look younger and more energetic.

'It's absolutely frantic here' she said. 'We're moving some of the early Renaissance collection and putting the Leonardo da Vinci Virgin of the Rocks, into its own niche.'

She showed me the plan before taking some papers from her desk. 'I'd like you to read this.' Elizabeth handed me a letter.

'You'll see the board have agreed to release the first payment for the Hermine Gallia on 30th September subject to delivery of the painting before that date.' Elizabeth registered my apprehension.

'Is there a problem?' she queried.

'Not exactly,' I said. 'Except we're dealing with a lump of sticky untrusting garbage. If the Klimt comes to London prior to the

other crates, Hofer's suspicious mind will immediately think we're going to default.'
'That's outrageous, Katrina. He's already had a deposit of £10,000 and we're going to transfer £163,000 immediately the painting arrives here. It's unthinkable the National would default. We're a National Institution.'
'I agree Elizabeth, but convincing Gerhard Hofer needs Freudian insight.'
Elizabeth looked perplexed.
'Maybe', I said, 'if I waved the cheque under his nose, he'd agree. I know it's unethical business practice, but I don't want any delays.'

Elizabeth was mulling over what I had said before suggesting:
'If Anderson at Samuel Hall's bank will agree, he could send a cheque to the Laufenbankgeschaft for your collection. But I must emphasize that it cannot be cashed till the end of September.'

VIENNA
42

Professor Frohmann had made arrangements for me to meet Hofer in his office. I left the Hotel Graben at eight and walked the familiar few hundred yards to Frohmann's galerie in the cavernous enclave behind the baroque facade of the Dorotheergasse. In two years, I had learned that no one admitted to being a member of the Nazi party, the past was relegated to history, and a surreptitious smouldering silence. Given the opportunity, the party would rise like a phoenix from the ashes, to avenge Adolf Hitler's dream of a supreme Aryan race. To deny the existence of pro-Nazi activity was naive and I was about to trade with two of its most skilled vendors.

Gerhard Hofer and the Professor were drinking tee mit rhum. I could smell the alcohol. The Professor stood and shook my hand. Hofer nodded and continued drinking tee, reluctant to accept my presence. In fact, this denial was an indictment of his own insecurity, unable to acknowledge me either as a curator or as a woman. As far as he was concerned, I was only a messenger for money. Any other talent I had was irrelevant and dispensable.

'Some tee Miss Edan?' the Professor offered.

'Thank you, Herr Professor but without the rhum.' I decided that alcohol for breakfast might have its medicinal value in winter, but could also enlist a recruit for Alcoholics Anonymous. Gerhard Hofer was, as I had expected suspicious of sending the Gustav Klimt painting to London before he'd received payment. I showed him the cheque for £163,000.

'This will be held at the Laufenbankgeschaft in Salzburg, and will be released to your account immediately the painting arrives at the National Gallery.'

He was disgruntled and sceptical, looking at the tealeaves inside his cup, pursing and stretching his lips alternately, in silent thought. It was only after the intervention of Professor Frohmann that he agreed.

'Gerhard,' Frohmann said, 'It's to your advantage. You will save a considerable amount of insurance and there is absolutely no doubt you'll get paid. It is a National Gallery, remember!'

Greed being Hofer's criterion prompted him to sign the agreement prepared by the National Gallery. Professor Frohmann witnessed his signature with an uncontrollably shaky hand and I counter-signed.

Gerhard Hofer tipped the teacup over and placed it rim down on the saucer. 'Vat vill you do about insurance Fraulein? I vant £500,000 insurance cover for theft, damage, gone missing, delay Everytink. You understand?'

'It will be insured for all contingencies, Herr Hofer.'

'Don't make no mistakes,' he said as a warning.

As he left Hofer touched his black beret to Frohmann and turned his back resentfully on me, a pathetic figure caught in his own distrust and insecurity.

'Another cup of tee, Miss Edan?' The Professor lit a cigarette and drew deeply on the tip before placing it into its holder. He opened the drawer of his desk and shuffled around before taking an envelope out which he handed to me. I opened the flap and looked at a series of Rembrandt photos. The Professor was squinting through his thick lenses, bending over his desk, towards me.

'Very nice,' I said.

'Yes, they are, but what do you think of the colours?'

I looked closely and placed one down in front of the Professor.

'Which colours do you mean?' I asked

'Any,' he said, pointing at a painted yellow satin cloak, draped over the shoulders of Bathsheba. 'This piece - around the chair, this green colour, is it too light?'

I looked at the picture again. A rich golden yellow, without a hint of green, shone clearly from the photo. I didn't answer immediately. I looked up at Wilhelm Frohmann. He handed me another picture. Again he had mis-read the shade and referred to Prussian blue when clearly it was Carmine. To minimise the shock and allow the lump in my throat to subside, I held the first picture up to the light, and turned it from angle to angle.

'It's more towards yellow than green Professor. The shadows in the folds give it a green appearance (which wasn't true) but I'd say it was more golden yellow.' I was holding the photo against a thin shaft of light coming through the narrow window by his desk. 'Yes' I repeated, 'I would definitely say yellow.'

'And this one?' The Professor handed me another slide: a scene from the Adoration of the Magi. Again I translated the colours. 'It is becoming increasingly difficult for me to distinguish the tones,' he said. 'My eyes aren't as good as they were.'

This was an understatement that saddened me. His eyes were deceiving him and he was left with an imagined reality, a world fast becoming shadows in his memory. To lose an arm, a leg, even a lung, would be a horrendous incapacity, but for him to go blind would be a living death.

LONDON

43

Gustav Klimt's painting of Hermine Gallia arrived at the National Gallery as arranged. Jack telephoned to say that Hofer had insisted the money was paid in pound notes. 'I told him the bank didn't hold that amount of cash and he'd have to wait till I could get it transferred. It's an unusual request for such a large sum, but Hofer's devious mind makes all transactions with him unpredictable. 'I'll give him the money personally, in Vienna'

'That's dangerous?' I said.

'Katrina, the cash doesn't go in the top of my sock. A courier will transfer it to an associate bank in Vienna. I'll go there to collect the receipt from Hofer.'

***

The crates from Salzburg were ready for shipping to London and would clear customs within three weeks. Confident all was now in place in Austria, I started to read the letters we had received in response to the advertisement, which had been syndicated in newspapers worldwide, for claimants to come forward

So many tragic stories were related in the letters we received, Sue had become embroiled in emotional turmoil. 'How can I answer these? It's a gravedigger's job. Anything I write is trivia compared to what is here.' She threw her hand from one side of her desk to the other, across a crowd of envelopes.

'Sue, Daniel Clipstein, the man with the staff of Moses has vetted all the letters. All you need to do is send a simple acknowledgement. I took a letter at random from her desk. It was headed.

SURVIVOR OF THE SHOAH

When I was eight I saw my home robbed, pillaged, then destroyed. I was rescued and brought up a Catholic by a family in Poland. My parents and my sister were beaten and taken away. This image will stay with me eternally. But another comes to mind. I used to sit with my father in front of two paintings, while he gave me English lessons. One picture I remember clearly. It had a shepherd with a crook in his hand. My father explained the difference between a shepherd's crook with a hooked end for reigning in the sheep

and a human crook, a thief who lives from crime. He also told me the story of Jezebel, the wife of King Ahab of Israel. My father taught me from books and pictures in our home. I always laughed at the shepherd in the picture because his hat was crooked. My father asked me why he was funny. I replied "Papa, you're a crook with a crooked picture of a shepherd wearing a crooked hat, herding sheep with a crook." This answer deserved one raspberry flavoured sweet in blue paper. The other painting I remember was just shapes. Triangles and squares with flowers on top in strong colours. This was the subject for my arithmetic lesson. These recollections may appear childish but I was a child when they were recorded. Aaron Kleinerman, New York.

He listed the sizes of the pictures he had described and asked where he could see a catalogue.

Similar stories were repeated, some more graphically than others, but overall they conveyed the urgency of getting the illustrated catalogue completed and distributed. All the letters we received were answered with the same simple request.

"We, the organisers of the exhibition of looted art, would be grateful if you would go to your Embassy (cultural attaché's office) or Consulate to identify any painting illustrated in the Catalogue. Each picture will have a number and colour. Please quote this and the date of your original letter, so we can sympathetically and honestly deal with your claim."

***

To have a dignitary open the exhibition became less attractive the more thought I gave the idea. For the refugees who would attend it would be insignificant words, however erudite. After all they were now the hunters, not the hunted, and the exhibition had a definite purpose; it was not a show. I knew from Anna that her cousin, Joseph Frishman had been sponsored to study in America and left England when he was eighteen. He spoke English, German and Hebrew. He had a master's degree in human relations and a PhD. in comparative theology. He was a Rabbi in Cincinnati. Before finishing the frontispiece of the catalogue I called him in the United States. He said it would be a privilege.

VIENNA

44

Filzmoos is not a name renowned as a holiday venue, nor is the village of Alt Aussee in the Salzkammergut (the salt estates). Both in diverse ways have become synonymous with changing the facts of history. At the end of the last century Alt Aussee attracted writers, musicians and thinkers. The tranquil waters of the lake and the remoteness of its geography, with its simple shacks and farmhouses were a magnet for creative people.

It is where Theodor Herzl formulated his ideas on Zionism and draughted his famous pamphlet "Der Judenstaat", proposing a Jewish national state. In this remote setting Hugo von Hoffmannstal the librettist wrote "Der Rosenkavlier","Ariadne and Naxos" and "Electra", and Richard Strauss, the composer, visited. Sigmund Freud and Arthur Schnitzler metaphorically dipped their quills into the water of the Alt Aussee.

Adolf Hitler designated this tranquil mountainous region for a more macabre purpose, when he ordered the salt mines to be extended and adapted as a repository for the largest collection for plundered art in history. This valuable horde included works by Rembrandt, Rubens, Michelangelo, Titian and the Rothschild and Rosenberg collections, all intended for installation in Hitler's dream Museum in Linz.

Joseph Goebbels lived at Alt Aussee from 1944 and Adolf Eichmann was in hiding in the dying days of the war before escaping to Argentina.

Filzmoos had a more recent history and it was not until a call from Jack, telling me it was important to go to Vienna as soon as possible, that I learned why.

Jack was at Vienna airport to meet me in a Mercedes Benz borrowed from a colleague. I had been delayed by an over attentive customs officer who had seen me struggling with my heavy suitcase: to his disappointment he didn't find any gold bars, just clothes and more clothes. Having my pants picked over by a bored customs man, whose vicarious pleasure was titillated by searching the luggage of attractive females, didn't sweeten my temper. As I arrived at the exit barrier I could see Jack was very edgy 'What kept you?' he said sharply.

'Knickers,' I answered . . . He looked at me in disbelief.
'That's not an admonition,' I said, 'it's a fact.'

During the drive into Vienna he told me he had spoken with Sue. 'She has booked a room for you at the Hotel Graben but I have changed your reservation: you're staying at the Hotel De France.'

'On whose authority?'

'Mine Katrina. It's not safe for you to stay at the Graben. I'll explain later.'

The hotel De France on the Schottenring is a small luxury hotel frequented by visitors who prefer the privacy of room service and a small bar exclusively for residents.

I immediately confronted Jack. 'I hope you have a good reason for bringing me here, or I'll check out as quickly as I checked in.'

'Where are you staying Jack?'

'Right here. I have the room next to yours. I want you to stay in your room and not go out till I return. Katrina, when will you ever trust me?' he said with frustration.

Shunted into a bizarre situation, with no agenda, I phoned Myrtle Shaw and invited her to the hotel for coffee. She arrived wearing a grey knitted dress with a huge shawl collar, a red beret matched her deep red lips and fingernails, and her mascara was so thick, it must have been there overnight. She was anxious to talk, as though I was a revered confidant, rather than an acquaintance that had given her casual employment, albeit fortuitous for us both.

'I don't quite know where to start,' she hesitated. 'Well,' . . . she put a finger up to her lips and removed a hair which had strayed. 'I told you Otto Prantl had invited me to Filzmoos. Well, I went for a long weekend. Miss Edan, he has the most extravagant chalet I've ever seen. A massive rustic building set on a mountainside.' Her eyes widened, 'and his art collection is priceless.'

I felt chilled. Whether it was her revelation or my racing mind, I don't know. I did know however, that what she said only confirmed that Prantl had already creamed the collections and no one would investigate him further. Myrtle said excitedly,

'There was a Brancusi bust in the entrance, a Bronzino Madonna, a Cézanne, a Jan Stein – Miss Edan, so many treasures. But one

was outstanding: a Michelangelo Buonarroti sculpture "Mask of a Fawn" and one of real interest to you, Sir Joshua Reynolds "Girl with Flowers". Actually the plaque said "Mädchen mit Blumen", but I reckon the translation was added.'
'Was it your first visit?'
'No. I stayed for a weekend a few weeks before. We drove from Salzburg. He is staying in Filzmoos for two weeks and wanted me to stay too, but I had to leave to complete the listing.'

So, now the bastard was Otto! I said to myself contemptuously; she had completed a tedious job and if she chose to fall into bed with the devil, I should wish her sweet dreams.

Not long after she left Jack knocked on the door, came into my room, loosened his tie, sat down, and like Myrtle said.
'I don't know where to start.' He took a letter from his briefcase and gave it to me. It was headed Bankhaus Schiller. I shook my head. 'I don't know them, Jack.'
'I'll explain,' he said. 'As you know the cheque arrived from the National Gallery in London to be held in my office. But Hofer asked for pound notes, so I forwarded the cheque to Credit Suisse in Zurich, as we do not keep that amount of foreign currency in Salzburg. A special courier delivered the money to the Bankhaus Schiller here in Vienna. Hofer signed the receipt for £163,333 cash, the first of the three instalments and I counter-signed, so did the official from the Bankhaus. As far as I'm concerned the deal was straight forward.'
'So what is the problem?'
'I think you should read the letter,' he said.

Dear Sir,
At our auction sale in the Dorotheum last week, Herr Gerhard Hofer bought a painting, at the hammer price of 1.450.000 Austrian schilling (£22,000 pounds) He paid in sterling notes, which we presented to our bank in Vienna. We were unable to convert the pound notes, as they were forgeries. We have contacted Herr Hofer, and he told us the notes came from your bank. Please advise us, by return, of the bank that supplied the notes to you and the sequence of numbers. The chief accountant of the Dorotheum signed the letter.

'I can't understand this, Jack. We know Hofer's a crook, but he's not an idiot. Surely he wouldn't use counterfeit money so close to home?'
'Exactly. That's what perplexes me. I'll have to sort this out quickly before Hofer gets his bullyboys lined up. It could get rough.'
'Jack if the notes you gave Hofer were genuine, why is he accusing the Laufenbankgeschaft of supplying counterfeit?'
'Because I handed them over believing the dud notes were genuine. And the payment to the Dorotheum was not the only payment he made. He put a cash deposit on a property in Grinzing and the agent has handed the notes to the police.'
'Woo-hoo, I bet Hofer's dripping blood.'
'He is, Katrina, and he's been arrested, but he'll be out on bail immediately. That's why I wanted you here: the security's better than the Graben.'
'At the prices they're charging, it should be. I still don't know why I had to come to Vienna.'
Jack shuffled the papers together on the table and took another out of his briefcase. It was from Daniel Clipstein. All it said was:

I **suggest Miss Edan calls at the Prantl Galerie as soon as possible. A box addressed to the Hotel Straubinger in Badgastein is waiting collection and authentication.**

'Why didn't Frohmann look at them?'
'Because he's at Baden-bei-Wein for a week's rest: he's not even accepting phone calls.'
'Unfortunately, I have a meeting this afternoon so I can't go with you. I have arranged for a young secretary from the American Embassy to accompany you. It's not advisable you go alone.'
'I think you're being ridiculously melodramatic. Of course I can go alone. I don't need a bodyguard. And if I did, what good is a secretary?'
'A presence,' Jack said, 'if nothing else. I'm not worried about Otto Prantl, but I am worried about Gerhard Hofer.'

He looked at an antique gold and silver timepiece on the mantelpiece over the unlit fire. 'Gus Plantini, is a nice guy, an

Italian American. He will collect you from here at 3.30. He's not a big talker, won't disturb you.'

Jack collected his briefcase and jacket and said before leaving. 'I shall be back in the hotel around sixish. I think you'll be ready for a strong drink.'

Reception called to say Mr.Plantini was waiting in the lobby. I thought junior secretaries were thin lithe youthful guys, recently graduated from law school or one of the Ivy League colleges. This guy was over six foot tall, beefy, obviously had to shave twice a day and was, as Jack told me, retiring with words. He politely shook my hand, said who he was, said the car was outside, all in a whisper and nothing more. Obviously this was outside his normal duties and I could only presume he was doing Jack a favour. Must have found him on ex-pat night at the American embassy, the sanctuary for unexpurgated gossip.

As we approached the Kartnerstrasse a crowd of people were gathered near the Galerie Prantl. 'I think you might have to get out here, Miss Edan, I can't go any further, there's a barrier.'

Bollards had been placed across the road and red and white tape tied to poles along the pavement. Gus Plantini parked his car and we walked the last few hundred yards towards the Galerie. As we came closer I could see a major catastrophe had happened. I thought there had been a fire, as large pieces of plate glass were strewn across the pavement, but as we neared the front of the building it became clear what had happened.

Swastikas, the ancient symbol of a Greek cross, adopted by the Nazis in 1933, were slashed across the building in red paint. Splintered glass clung precariously around spaces in the showcase windows. The door hung on tortured broken hinges, gouged from the doorframe and twisted into a surreal shape. As we approached I smelt the wet paint dripping from the swastikas, but we were stopped before we could get any nearer.

Gus Plantini spoke to a policeman in German who beckoned to an officer in a radio car. Gus Plantini spoke again in German. The officer asked me in English why I wanted entry. I told him I had been asked to identify a box of paintings for an exhibition in London. He called another officer. Plantini translated again.

'They have to telephone for permission to let you in. You can either wait or come back later.'

'I'll wait,' I said. 'Did the police say if anything had been taken?'
'No they didn't say, but it looks like a burglary to me.'
'A racist burglary, how rare! Or is there one every week?'
Plantini didn't answer. I looked at the empty easels that had recently displayed watercolours by Egon Schiele, oils by Kokoschka, flower paintings by Mignon. Now the easels were vacant, useless broken sticks of wood with no significance.

We stood silently with the gaping crowd until the police gave me permission to go into the galerie. Gus Plantini was told to wait outside. My fingers had started to go numb with the cold. I said to Plantini 'I don't know how long this will take, it seems pointless for you to stand here.'

On entering the building I was asked to put white rubber covers over my shoes and tie them at the ankles and a white overall and white rubber gloves. I had seen the experts dusting for fingerprints at the Galerie Frohmann in Salzburg, but not with this amount of fuss. One white-coated man was scrupulously dusting an empty picture frame, while the policeman beckoned me to follow him. I went down the stairs leading to the rooms where Otto Prantl stored the paintings pillaged from Anna Frishman's family. An arc light had been set up with its beam directed onto chalk markings on the sticky floor. The smell of rotting excreta was unbearable. I asked the police officer if we could go to another room.
'We could, but they're all the same.' he said. In the next room, blood was splattered across the walls dripping like a Jackson Pollock painting. I felt very sick and claustrophobic. The officer pointed to a crate in the centre of the room. ' I will leave you to do your work,' he said.

I was shaking as I looked at the top of the box. Boldly marked in blue dye was the Star of David. I closed my eyes; I didn't want to look inside. What would I see? Beauty? Is there beauty in things - these things? I was overcome by disgust and automated into action, doing what was familiar to me, without any gratification. I sat down on the box. The raw stink caught in my nostrils, in my head and for a flash my imagination ran riot. They would forget I was here. And then the thought came to me. Do I really matter? I am only a fragment in a collage of events, which will happen with or without me, I am dispensable. I started to sweat under the white overall, my hands clammy in rubber. I dragged myself from this internal monologue and opened the box. Two Rembrandts, one Vermeer and a Dürer. All their beauty was lost and all I could see was a surface, a deception to engage me in the painter's vision - a trick. I snapped the lid shut. It only took an instant but that instant told me that what I was looking at was not beauty, but tragedy.

I opened the door. A small man with wire-rimmed glasses was kneeling over the chalk lines, meticulously measuring. He looked up. His overall was stained with blood. He pointed to the door. 'Ausgang,' he said. I looked at the shape of the markings. 'Was someone injured?'

'Otto Prantl, the owner of the galerie: I don't know if he has gone to the hospital or the mortuary, I only measure.' I nodded acknowledgment and went upstairs.

It was dark outside and policemen were still on duty. I walked past the barriers looking for a taxi. Shops were closing and there was a light drizzle. I turned towards St.Stephen's cathedral. I felt a hand on my arm. I swung round in alarm. It was Plantini: God, I'm getting paranoid, I told myself.

The hotel was no consolation. The horrendous scene of horror left me shocked, numb and drained. At the reception desk, I was handed a note and a letter. The note was from Jack. "Waiting for you in my room". The other was a typed envelope. In the warmth of the lift my stomach started to heave. Saliva was seeping from my lips. I unlocked my door, threw off my hat, dropped my coat round my feet, getting to the bathroom seconds before I was violently sick. Everything forced itself out of my stomach and I crossed my arms over my ribs trying to stop the pain. When the tension eased I went into the bedroom and removed all my clothes and stuffed them into a laundry bag. An insidious stench, so strong, had invaded my whole body. I stood under the shower and let the soft water run down my hair and mix with my salty tears. I emptied a bottle of scented shampoo over me: it stung as it seeped into my eyes: I couldn't see beyond my own despair. The hotel's towelling bathrobe was small comfort. I phoned the housekeeper and gave her all my clothes including my camel coat and put my shoes outside the door for cleaning. I phoned Jack and told him I was tired. Then I climbed into bed and opened the letter. It was from Daniel Clipstein.

Dear Miss Edan,
I should appreciate if you would come to my office tomorrow morning at eleven o'clock. I have some information, which I think is important. I trust you are well.
Daniel Clipstein.

I was woken by a knock on my door; at the same time the telephone rang. I opened the door. Jack looked surprised to see me in a robe.
'It's 10.30 am, Katrina,' he said, with emphasis on the A.M.
'Isn't Clipstein expecting you?' The phone rang again. The operator said "Herr Hofer on the line, will you take the call madam?'
'No', I said emphatically. 'Tell him I'll call later.' I hastily put the phone down. 'That was our mutual friend Herr Hofer. I can guess what he wants. Blood.'

I was not aggressive towards Jack, quite the reverse, although I suspected some surreptitious activity was being kept from me, I wanted more than explanations I wanted justification.
'What happened to Prantl? Why didn't you tell me he'd been attacked before I went to the Galerie? You knew - that's why you sent Plantini to hold my hand. Why Jack? I need honest answers.'
'You're right Katrina. It must have been a shock to discover that Prantl had been murdered. I wish I could have warned you.'

The events of the previous day loomed in front of me: I felt my legs weakening, the room becoming distant as I tried to grasp the tailboard of the bed. I was floating into peaceful oblivion, away from trauma and tragedy. I don't know how long I was in my utopian paradise but a strange man leaning over me, with a stethoscope round his neck, interrupted it. It took some time before I realized where I was. Jack was standing at the other side of the bed reassuring me that nothing was going to happen.
'This is Dr.Hamilton, Katrina.'

He looked a kindly middle-aged man with a full head of dark hair, peppered with grey.

'Can you manage to sit up?' he said. I tried to sit up but I couldn't. 'Let me give you a hand,' he said with a distinctly English accent. With a gentle heave I was sitting up. He made little knocking sounds on my back. Then he pulled my lower lids down one at a time and peered into my eyes with a medical torch. 'When did you eat last, Miss Edan?' I looked first at Jack then the doctor.

'I must be honest, I can't remember.'

'Have you been vomiting?' I wanted to say no in case he asked why but I said, 'Yes.' in a clipped tone. I didn't want this man prying into my thoughts. I knew why I'd been sick: it was enough to unnerve anyone, and I didn't need some condescending doctor repeating the usual jargon. But he did.

'I want you to take two of these immediately and two every four hours for 24 hours.' He gave me the customary brown bottle. 'They will settle your stomach. Drink at least four pints of water a day because you are very dehydrated. And I suggest you eat some dry toast and tea now and stay in bed.' He patted my hand. 'You'll feel better by the morning. Nothing to worry about.'

Totally ill informed words, I had everything to worry about. As he went to the door with Jack he said, 'She'll be fine,'

'Thank you, Ted, for coming over, I wanted to be sure.'

'Goodbye, young lady' he said. I managed a petulant smile. Nice man, but his words were redundant.

'Where did you find him, Jack?'

'He's the doctor for the British and American embassies here. Very reliable guy.' Jack was dialling room service. I sipped some tea but I couldn't eat. Jack refused to discuss anything at all. 'You're going to take the Doc's tablets and go to sleep. I'll come and see how you're feeling later. And Katrina, I'm next door if you need me.'

I wasn't expecting yellow roses at my door the following morning, when I collected my shoes from the corridor. The flowers were standing resplendently in a yellow and white vase wrapped with yellow ribbon with a tiny envelope attached. Flowers evoke immediate joy: they are alive, seductive, sweet smelling ornaments, to be admired. Unlike words they have silent meaning. I read the brief message. Jack - next door.

My mirror image distressed me: pale and drawn, my skin lacking lustre. I attempted a quick rejuvenating programme; I splashed cold then warm water onto my face. I covered my eyes for ten minutes with cotton wool pads soaked in witch hazel. Then I applied a thicker layer of make-up than usual. When I felt moderately normal, I knocked on Jack's door. He was on the phone and beckoned me to sit down. It was impossible not to overhear the conversation.

'Do you think that's a wise move?' Jack said. 'Why can't we get a contract?' Silence while he listened. Jack mimicked words to me in the shape of "one minute."

'O.K. I'll be in the office by noon. Have the papers ready.' He hung up. The room, exactly the same as mine in reverse, had Empire furniture not Biedermeier.

'How are you this morning? You're looking so much better, fancy a little breakfast?' I didn't want any food, but agreed to tea and toast.

'Thank you for the flowers: They are beautiful. Thank God there is still some beauty in this world.'

Jack pulled on the knot of his tie. He was wearing black cords and a black shirt and a light tweed jacket, unaware of his own physical presence. A trolley arrived with breakfast. Jack took the initiative, saying, 'I guess you're waiting for some answers. So, I'll tell you as much as I can and as much as I know. Yes, I knew Prantl had been killed, but I don't know who took him out. His chalet in Filzmoos was also ransacked and most of his collection taken. The police aren't releasing any details - so everything I'm telling you is conjecture, but more importantly strictly confidential.'

I raised my eyebrows. 'You mean Paul McKenzie?'

'And Sue, and anyone else, including Hempf.'

'Tell me Jack, if the police didn't release information, how did you know Prantl was dead?'

'From Daniel Clipstein.'

'Daniel Clipstein!' I said with surprise. 'And how did he know?'

'I told you two years ago, if you remember, there isn't much, if anything, that Clipstein and his boss, Simon Wiesenthal, don't know. Especially here.'

'Talking of Daniel Clipstein, he asked me to go to his office.'

'But it's not safe for you to go out alone with Hofer prowling the streets especially as he knows where you're staying. Maybe Sue gave him a forwarding number. Have you spoken to her?'
'No, I haven't. And if I had, she has lips as tight as a miser.'

Jack poured two more cups of tea. 'Then there's only one answer. We were followed from the airport.'
'That doesn't put me in danger. Hermine Gallia is in the National's vault and as far as I'm concerned, the cheque was delivered.'
'I absolutely agree, except for one factor. You, and I repeat, you Katrina are the prime suspect for passing counterfeit money to Hofer. As far as he's concerned, you'll pay - and he's not thinking paper money.'
'That's absurd. I had nothing to do with the payment - it came from Elizabeth Cuthbertson at the National Gallery via Bernard Anderson at Samuel Hall.'
'Quite correct, and the money was delivered by courier to the Bankhaus Schiller from Switzerland. I'm still trying to unravel where and what went wrong. But I think you should know just a little more so you don't feel in the dark,' Jack said with concern.
'Because of its situation, Vienna is the centre for "switch dealers". It doesn't mean switching from legal to counterfeit, it's the name given to private bankers who unravel currency deals between East and West. In other words, they turn the iron curtain into a piece of flimsy netting. The switchers deal in "clearing dollars", not U.S. dollars but money units used for accounting purposes between banks. As the eastern block has virtually no hard currency, the switchers negotiate deals in non-convertible currency or barter. It's the barter trade which is the grey area and rife for illicit trading, mostly in armaments.'
'Why are you telling me this Jack? What has it to do with Hofer?'
'Plenty - because his galerie in Vienna and his art deals are only part of his multifarious activities. And he uses Bankhaus Schiller because they are switch dealers.'
'I still don't understand why he passed forged notes.'
'Well, I'll tell you, but not here.'
'Why not here, it's as good as my room.'

Jack was being evasive as usual, just when I thought I had his confidence, then without asking me he dialled Clipstein and arranged for him to collect me from the hotel lobby at 11.30.
'I'll see you later, perhaps you'll be ready for a light supper?' he said. 'And finish the pills.' he ordered, as if he were my keeper.

***

Grateful for my over packing I had a selection of warm sweaters, skirts and trousers. Frozen air stuck on the window. Dark heavy clouds curtained the city; a winter overture drifted in and the grey panorama predicted the cold to come.

As the lobby clock struck 11.30 Daniel Clipstein came through the door in a long black woollen coat almost to the ground and a thick fleece hat with earflaps. To me he looked similar to Toulouse Lautrec, or a civil servant in a Tolstoy novel, or an inquisitor in a play by Chekov.

He saw me immediately. We shook hands. 'You're feeling better? Mr Steinhart told me you had a disturbed night.'
'I'm feeling much better thank you.'
'It is extremely cold outside, do you have a coat?'
'Oh - I didn't know we were going out.'
'I think you would be wise to wrap up very well.'

I collected my coat, wrapped a Hermes scarf over my head, and asked Clipstein if we were going to his office.
'No - we're going to a friend's house for some coffee and a sandwich.' I didn't question him further but thought it rather odd.

We drove through the old city along narrow streets just wide enough for one car, then out onto the Burgringstrasse, then back into the old city. We were heading in the same direction as ten minutes before. Clipstein must have seen me looking back at the same street.
'Don't worry Miss Edan: I'm just making sure we're not being followed. Five more minutes and the car that has been tailing us will be stuck in the traffic.'

His car was an old black British Humber, a classic collector's dream, with an engine that shifted the bulky beast past its more modern counterparts, as we thundered along the open road. We crossed the Danube by the Floridsdorfer Brücke following a sign

to Mühlschüttel where Daniel Clipstein stopped the car in front of an apartment building.
'I am sorry to have taken so long Miss Edan,' he smiled, 'It was those irritating detours.'
'Not far,' Clipstein told me as we walked around a corner to a parallel street. All the apartment blocks were the same: rows of depressing grey concrete, examples of modern urban architecture, a pretentious failure, created as a working class paradise. After passing one block we entered the next building and climbed to the third floor. Clipstein had a key to a sparsely furnished bed-sitting room. A wooden table was pushed up against a wall with two chairs, which could have been retrieved from a skip. The fold-up bed was extended and covered with a grey blanket. A telephone and a radio completed the furnishings. The floor was bare concrete. As a saving grace, it was warm.
'Please, take off your coat and I'll make some coffee, or would you prefer tea?'
'Tea please, and may I have a glass of water?' I put my coat on the iron bed. There was no sign of Clipstein's friend and I was curious to know when he or she would arrive.

Clipstein set the teapot on the table with two mugs and took some sandwiches wrapped in a linen napkin from his leather satchel. He unfolded the napkin carefully, proudly displaying the sandwiches.
'My wife made these, egg and onion or cheese and chrane.' I took one of the small squares.
'I'm sorry for being so confusing. I told you we were meeting a friend. That's not the case. I had to say that as the car might have been bugged. This place is a safe house used by people willing to disclose information for our cause. It is regularly swept. I don't mean vacuumed - it's tested for listening devices.'

I looked around the room, amazed this information was divulged to me, an outsider. I was sympathetic to the cause of justice for the victims of persecution, but nervous of the cloak and dagger activity happening around me,
'Dr.Clipstein, could you tell me what is your actual role in all this intrigue?' Without hesitation he said.
'My job is to find Nazis who committed crimes against humanity

in the concentration camps, and bring them to trial. It's as simple as that.'
'Simple? Dr Clipstein, it can't be!'
'The Documentation Centre has far reaching tentacles, and we are fully operative worldwide, Miss Edan. Individuals are turning in paintings for your exhibition: in my organization, people are turned in. The older they get, the more frightened they are of being found and prosecuted. The balance of fear has shifted.'
'Are you saying they have to expurgate their guilt?'
'Certainly not. They consider themselves the victims, not the guilty. It is the witnesses who have seen the crimes perpetrated, who want to confess before they die. Even then, it takes subterranean investigations to get our prey. We must have invincible corroborated evidence before an arrest can be made.'

I took the last of my pills with a glass of water. 'Dr.Clipstein, you've been an invaluable help to me and I know from Jack Steinhart your organization helped fund my project, albeit without my knowledge. Why, Dr.Clipstein?'

'Miss Edan, I have a confession to make and I offer my apologies in advance. I know you will understand because you have proved you are beyond reproach in your dealings, courageous in your efforts and selfless in your aptitude. You have also been under the sword of Damocles. What I am about to tell you must never be repeated anywhere, to anyone.'

His tone was that of a man of law. 'I will go back a little, if you don't mind, in fact 35 years when Wilhelm Frohmann, Otto Prantl, Gerhard Hofer and Anton Hempf were students. You may or may not remember they started a magazine at Vienna University called "Revolt". Anton Hempf was the editor, Frohmann and Otto Prantl the writers and Gerhard Hofer the printer, as he had access to his father's press in Vienna. Frohmann told you he was jailed for 3 years for procuring stolen art for Herman Goering.'
'Yes, that's correct. But what did Otto Prantl do to underwrite his own murder?'
'His case was entirely different. Like Frohmann he was instrumental in wholesale theft.'

Clipstein wagged his forefinger knowingly. 'But, he commissioned forgers to copy masterpieces which he sold for vast sums to help finance the German war machine. When he was arrested he refused to give vital information about the treasures taken by the Russians or to reveal the whereabouts of fakes he gave to Swiss dealers. Museums and entrepreneurs worldwide were duped and bought forged art. Prantl was sentenced to five years. But, his forged "masterpieces" are still being innocently admired to-day.'

'And Gerhard Hofer?'

'He was tried for murdering Jews, but there was not enough evidence and he was acquitted. The Documentation Centre subsequently investigated. We uncovered evidence that Hofer had murdered Jews who were trying to escape from Burgenland to Trieste, but there were no witnesses. We hadn't enough evidence to execute justice until you came to Austria with your project.'

'Me?' I said in amazement.

'Yes Miss Edan. We have used you in a number of different ways because you held the trump card we needed to convict Hofer. It was difficult to know how or when we could use the card - excuse me - that is your alias, but we took a calculated risk and backed you.'

'Dr.Clipstein. What exactly did you do?'

'Apart from putting money into your fund we used you as bait to trap Gerhard Hofer.'

These revelations confused me. I couldn't understand why or how I had been so naive.

'I'll explain a little more.' Clipstein said. 'When Hofer offered the Gustav Klimt painting to you, someone filtered information to Hofer, that you had the right connections for a private treaty sale. He responded by offering you the painting. The subsequent sale by you, to your National Gallery, was a credit to your artistic and commercial ability and confirmed that we had found the right person. I hope I'm making this clear to you,'

'Not yet, Dr.Clipstein, but please go on.'

'Towards the end of the war, the American forces were advancing on Vienna. A directive was given by Adolf Hitler to blow up Mauthausen concentration camp, which is not far from here, and leave no trace of its existence and no witnesses. The rapid advance of the allies aborted the destruction before the button was pushed. Why Mauthausen, you might ask?. Why not Auschwitz or Buchenwald?' he said sharply. 'Because, Miss Edan, a vast printing works had been set up in the camp for the production of counterfeit money. The Nazi in charge of administration at Mauthausen was Werner Hofer, Gerhard's father. When the Americans entered the camp they found evidence that 43 million pounds sterling had been printed in forged bank notes.'

I felt I was being dragged somewhere I didn't want to go, a tense uncomfortable place, where I was out of control. Clipstein sensed my discomfort.

'I apologise for keeping you here – I have nearly finished, but these historical facts are important, so you'll understand why you are implicated. When the Americans liberated Mauthausen, soldiers who had seen violent military action openly cried. They were looking at the fleshless sticks that once had been men and women and were now starving moving skeletons. Many died. That was a certain freedom, but one survivor, Simon Wiesenthal, listed the names of 91 Nazi criminals for a war crimes unit: on that list was Werner Hofer. He was tried at Nuremberg and sentenced to death. But his son, Gerhard Hofer went free. It has taken us twenty years of relentless infiltration in the villages around Breck where Gerhard Hofer was stationed to uncover the truth and find witnesses prepared to speak. They were too frightened to come forward unless Hofer was held in custody. So, if we could get him jailed on any charge, we could then reveal our documents and witnesses would come forward. That process is now active. I must add, Miss Edan, this has only been achieved by the diligence and steadfast resolve of one man: Simon Wiesenthal, who pledged that Nazis would be hunted like animals, and dedicated his life at the Documentation Centre in Vienna to finding "vanished" war criminals and bringing them to justice.'

There must have been anger inside Clipstein's mind, but his control was enviable. He cast his eyes down in silent reflection.

'I must tell you.' he said. 'The money Gerhard Hofer received was counterfeit but it was not supplied by Credit Suisse. Their bank notes were genuine. A courier at the Austrian border switched the notes. When the notes were handed to Hofer by the Bankhaus Schiller in the presence of Jack Steinhart, they had no reason to suspect they were not genuine.'

'So, who ordered the border switch. Did you, Dr.Clipstein?'

'I will be absolutely honest with you. I did not. So you see, Miss Edan, you are in danger here as you are the prime suspect. Revenge killings in Vienna slip through police investigations like tea through a strainer, so you must be extremely careful.'

'May I ask you, does Jack Steinhart know what you have told me?'

'I am sorry, Miss Edan, I can't tell you what Mr.Steinhart knows. He is only our banker.'

This was an evasive reply and very far from the truth. A cliché, I'd heard Jack use. "I'm only his banker", he'd say of Frohmann, when trying to placate me.

Clipstein folded the linen napkin and put it in his satchel. He left the two mugs on the table - unwashed.

On the way back to the hotel Daniel Clipstein told me how pleased he was that the exhibition was so advanced. 'I would like to be there when it opens,' he said. 'Maybe I can bring my wife; she has never been to London.'

From the lobby he telephoned Jack's room. 'I'm returning Miss Edan, she's on her way to her room now.' He took off a black woollen glove and extended his hand. 'We'll speak again before you go home. Don't worry, you are perfectly safe in this hotel.'

I certainly didn't feel safe as I rode in the lift to the second floor.

It was teatime, but I'd had enough tea for one day. In times like these only one person is sensitive enough to set me on an even keel. I rang Desmond Hegarty in his safe haven in London hoping for a little comfort.

'You're home quickly.' Desmond said.

'I'm not home Desmond, I'm in Vienna.' I sighed before saying, 'unfortunately.'

'Are you O.K? You sound strange.'

'I'm physically and mentally spent. It's freezing, miserably grey, and the sooner I leave here the better.'

'Has something gone wrong, Katrina?'

'Not exactly wrong, just a series of confusing incidents.'

'So something is wrong. Care to talk?'
'No Desmond, just wanted to chat a little.'
'Well, I'll give you some good news. I've finished the Royal Festival Hall project. I won't get a knighthood for the work but I'm pleased. It's very harmonious, as I'd hoped. Katrina, there are some hilarious critiques. I'll keep them for you. One critic wanted to know what else the magnetic tags would pull. Frustrated bastard! He probably hoped he could undo every chicks zipper by some extraneous remote control.'

I started to laugh. As usual, Desmond had sparked my imagination, and I could visualize the chaos of confusion in the lobby of the Festival Hall, akin to a nineteenth century Thomas Rowlandson scene and now rollicking material for contemporary caricature.
'When are you leaving Vienna? I'll collect you from the airport.'
'I'll call you as soon as I know. Let's go to a nice soppy film with a happy ending.'
'And Katrina, cheer up: remember you always get low at the end of a project. Stop worrying - by next year you'll be begging me to design an exhibition for the world's duck population!'
'You're absolutely right,' I said grinning to myself. 'That's a wonderful idea. No one has ever curated an exhibition of the world's duck paintings. I'll see you in a few days.'

***

I knew I felt better as I fancied a scotch. I took a mini bottle from the fridge, tipped it into a tumbler and filled it with water.

Then the phone rang. I looked at the curled innocuous plastic instrument, not wanting to touch it, dreading Hofer might be at the other end. Even the phone looked dirty. It took me a few seconds to decide. Why should I be the target of verbal abuse and threats? I left it ringing . . . Shortly after, there was a knock on my door. I hesitated, 'You can open the door, Katrina, it's Jack.' I reluctantly let him in. I wanted time alone to assess the situation and decide how to move the exhibition forward, without the dramas of the last few days restraining me.
'Why didn't you answer the phone? Are you O.K?' Jack asked.
'I'm afraid my imagination is getting the better of me.'

'Don't worry, you've had a rough few days, and I bet Clipstein gave you something extra to think about!'
'Everyone's telling me not to worry: Clipstein, you, Desmond. I am bloody worried. And incidentally, how much do you know of what Clipstein told me?'
'Most,' he said calmly.
'Perhaps you can add to that,' I countered. He looked at my weak scotch. 'So you're feeling a little better. That's good. Maybe you would like to go out for a light supper?'
'Out! I cupped my head in my hands. I understood from both you and Clipstein that it's not safe for me to go out.'

Jack took a mini scotch from the fridge, and said, 'it will be all right; I know a small restaurant off the track. Could you be ready in fifteen minutes?'

Jack's car was waiting outside. The concierge had collected it from the garage. I hadn't bothered to change, just gave my face a cat's lick and a promise and some powder, just enough to leave my self esteem intact. We went around the Ringstrasse, slipping into narrow streets and out again, in exactly the same way as Clipstein drove.
'Are we being followed?' I asked in a knowing voice, turning to look out of the back window.
'No and we're not likely to be either.'

We pulled into a small street off Mariahilferstrasse. There were very few cars and no people. The door to the restaurant was so inconspicuous, if one didn't know it was there it could have been someone's front door. Inside, there were only six tables. A very robust man greeted us.
'Monsieur Steinhart,' he said as he wrapped his arms round Jack while patting his back at the same time 'Good to see you.'
He looked at me approvingly, 'Ah-ha, you have some pretty company' he said with a wink. I expected him to embrace me too but I was spared the familiarity.

'Mislav is Hungarian' Jack said. 'He escaped when the commuists invaded his country. He's a marvellous cook,' Jack added. 'But if your stomach is still a little queasy he'll prepare anything you want.' But my mind wasn't on food it was on answers. I wanted so many answers. I pushed the menu away.

'Katrina, you have to eat: you've had two quarters of a sandwich in twenty four hours.'
'Say that again! You're telling me Clipstein told you how many sandwiches I'd eaten. This is becoming a farce.'
'Katrina I asked him if you'd eaten, because the doctor said it was important.'
'But you're not my doctor, nor my keeper, nor a self anointed saint.'
'A sip of wine maybe?' Jack asked. I nodded. But he was right. After I'd eaten a light omelette and a little mashed potato, my stomach didn't complain and my nerve endings felt quieter and less taut. I was trying not to be belligerent, but was overwhelmed by so much clandestine activity. It was beyond my belief.

Pictures of Mauthausen kept flashing across my eyes that wouldn't go away. I'd seen them before - in books, on newsreels. But now those pictures were alive. I stood on the same ground that Daniel Lehner's parents scrubbed with toothbrushes: the sweat they left was still in my air.

Like Clipstein, Jack said, 'I'll have to give you some background history so you understand.' This soft glove approach was redundant. I understood too well that I'd been used, and was still being used. But to what end I wanted to know?

Jack spoke quietly, although the tables were so well spaced no one could have overheard.

'When the Russians were advancing on Berlin and Vienna, Otto Prantl negotiated with the Russians. He offered to sell art treasures to the West through his contacts in Switzerland. This would enable Russia to get valuable convertible currency to buy arms. Although jailed for war crimes, the KGB filed his name as a prospective operator. After Prantl's release in 1951, he started to re-establish the Prantl galerie and he was enlisted as a KGB agent.
'Why didn't the art investigators look in the galerie for loot?'
'They did - it was empty. Over the next ten years, till 1961, he traded in minor works of art. Gradually he introduced, piece-by-piece, paintings of high value. At that point the CIA became more interested in Prantl than Hofer. Hofer is a go-between in the hierarchy of international espionage, a porter, so to speak. Neither Hofer nor Prantl banked with me, but the bankers are a

clique, and we keep our eyes and ears open for each other, so no one gets caught by international fraudsters.' Jack asked for some coffee and a glass of water. 'You look very tired, Katrina. Would you prefer I leave the rest till tomorrow?'
'No no - go on.'
'The movement of looted art from Russia to the West was Hofer's responsibility before passing works on to Prantl. The salient point for investigation was the "empty" trucks going back to the USSR. The CIA, MI6, and MOSSAD were all monitoring Prantl's activities. They let the trucks "run" until they had all the information they needed. Then Prantl was "blown away".'
'Blown away!' I repeated, 'Murdered?'
'That's right,'
'Don't tell me you don't know who killed him?'
'I would be insulting your intelligence if I said I don't know. I'll give you the only answer I can. He could have been killed by any of the agencies, even his own, the KGB. Once an agent has been burned, he's no longer an asset. Hofer could even have killed him. The swastikas and the mayhem at Prantl's galerie were a smokescreen to make it look like a racist revenge. It wasn't.'

I took a deep breath. I had heard enough for one day and wanted more than anything to go home. My natural resilience was overloaded.

We hardly spoke on the way back to the hotel, although many questions remained unanswered. When we arrived at my room I asked Jack to come in for a minute. I took off my coat and asked him immediately. 'What was Prantl sending back to Russia in the "empty" trucks? And who put the missing box in his galerie?'
'Please Katrina I'm also tired. Can I tell you in the morning?'

Siberian winds had swept in throughout the night, and a haze of white icy gauze swirled around the city like a dust storm in the Sahara, constantly moving, never settling, and always threatening. I felt isolated from reason, like a survivor on Géricault's "Raft of Medusa" surrounded by corpses and sickness, rolling through a never ending thunderous storm.

Like Vincent van Gogh, I had been coerced into fear of being destroyed by my own rampant imagination. It was wild, ugly,

hard-edged and brutal, and regrettably, self-inflicted. I dressed with respect for the weather. A black skirt and heavy black sweater. When the phone rang I had to pick it up: I couldn't shirk answering again or let my imagination get the better of me. It was reception. 'Miss Edan, Herr Moser is in the foyer: he would like to speak to you. Can I put him through?'
'Miss Edan, I'm sorry to trouble you so early. I'm going to visit Professor Frohmann. He would like you to come with me.'
'When are you leaving, Stephan?'
'I would like to leave as soon as possible.'

It was a few minutes before nine. I told him I'd be in the lobby in thirty minutes. I hastily pulled on my black knee high boots and my faithful camel coat and I was ready to leave. I telephoned Jack's room before leaving but there was no reply.

The temperature had risen slightly and snow was settling on the taxi in large puffballs, resting on the fir trees, transforming the Vienna woods into white, like a veiled untouched virgin.

My thoughts took me back to the first time I visited Wilhelm Frohmann, over three years ago. I recalled the overwhelming attraction of this sophisticated raconteur, his wit, his controlling countenance, and his rakish appearance, which fitted more comfortably into the nineteenth century than the twentieth. Now, he was a disillusioned lonely man living out his final years grudgingly, waiting for the final call.

I had never found Stephan Moser to be talkative, only convivial. He ran the Galerie Frohmann in Salzburg efficiently, but as a job only, rather than a commitment to art per se. The overpowering presence of the Professor was only a contributing factor because Moser was destined to be a shadow. That was his capacity.

The Professor was in the salon drinking coffee, wrapped in a red velvet dressing gown. He stood for a moment when we went in, but the effort looked pained.
'You will have some coffee I'm sure, and maybe a slice of apfel strudel.' Marta, his maid was waiting for our reply.

The Professor asked Moser about the sale of a painting by Watenphul to a client in Italy, and then asked Moser to take some notes.

'I would like you to record this conversation as a witness.' He looked from Moser to me.
'Don't worry, Miss Edan. Anything I say, or do, is legal.'

I had not reacted with doubt, but the Professor must have had reasons of his own for speaking of legality.
'I'm going to give you this.' He handed me a long cream envelope sealed with red sealing wax. I want you to give the envelope to Dr.Anton Hempf in London. There are two copies, one with my lawyer, and another with my banker, Jack Steinhart. They must remain unopened until I die.' He coughed as this unfamiliar word caught in his throat. Regaining his authority, he said to Moser, 'Have you put that down?'

Again, my imagination took hold. Is he expecting the same fate as Otto Prantl? Is he planning suicide? To bring the conversation into reality I said.
'Professor Frohmann, I was hoping you would come to London and see the exhibition. Then you could deliver the letter personally.'

He gave a forced laugh. 'I've always been a poor traveller, Miss Edan, and it's too late now to even think about it.'

The coffee arrived and after the first sip realized I had missed breakfast. 'Have a little schnapps: it's essential in this weather,' Frohmann said. The bottle was on the tray with thimble glasses. As Wilhelm Frohmann lit a cigarette, he started to cough. He drank some schnapps before saying. 'I cannot understand why anyone would kill a galerie owner. After all, he went to prison, as I did, just for doing his job.'

Frohmann was talking to a fake audience, spilling his thoughts onto unresponsive ears. Neither Moser nor I commented. Frohmann gesticulated with his hands. 'Why should Jewish agitators keep regurgitating the past? It's gone - forgotten - never to return. Why force the past into the present? We can't change events. What is there to gain?'
'Retribution,' I said.

The Professor retaliated tersely, 'Call it what you like, retribution, revenge, it brings nothing back but bad memories.' He pulled deeply on his cigarette, 'I don't understand what is going on anymore.'

These were the words of a tired old man, reluctantly admitting defeat, as the past loomed nearer than the present.

My parting words to Professor Wilhelm Frohmann were genuinely felt. 'Without your help,' I said, 'I would never have organized this exhibition. In the beginning, you thought my chance of succeeding was unrealistic. Too young, too naive! But sometimes Professor, ignorance powers one past fear, and when I first met you, I could only see the goal not the route. You helped me cross the wasteland and for that I am truly grateful.

***

Back at the hotel I collected messages from Clipstein and Jack. I rang Jack first.' Where the hell have you been?' he shouted.

'I beg your pardon. Who the hell are you talking to?'

'Katrina, why didn't you leave a message? Both Clipstein and I have been trying to find you.'

'So, you've found me. What next?' I contested.

'Keep your coat on, we're going out. I'll give you ten minutes.'

Once again, Jack was taking over. On the way to his car, I said, 'I hope you have a good reason for dragging me around like a rag doll. Otherwise you'll have some very offensive words to unpack.'

I was sitting in Daniel Clipstein's office, feeling smug. I had actually gone out without permission and without a keeper, and surprisingly, returned. Jack pulled a sheaf of papers from his briefcase and dropped them on Clipstein's desk. 'Got em', he said. 'Every god dam piece of evidence you'll ever need.'

Clipstein, held the papers, rubbing his thumbs across them as though he was feeling precious metal.

'Jack, I think I should tell Miss Edan what has happened since last night,'

'Sure, Daniel, fire away,' Jack said, 'and don't hold back. Give her the whole shooting works.'

In the privacy of Clipstein's office I was about to be told why Otto Prantl had been murdered.

'Are we de-bugged Jack?'

'Absolutely, every louse has been swept out.'

'Miss Edan, I believe Jack told you Prantl had been recruited into the KGB? What Jack didn't tell you was that Prantl's activities extended way beyond his art interests. Like Hofer, he was selling looted art smuggled in from the East. But what was he giving them in exchange? It was Uranium, the most important component for the manufacture of the nuclear bomb. The consignments came from Afghanistan via Tehran. It was then smuggled into Vienna on the Orient Express from Turkey. The trucks which Gerhard Hofer brought into Vienna carrying art looted by the Russians returned east with hidden uranium.' At this point Jack interrupted.

'Unknown to Russian intelligence, Prantl's consignments were left to run by the British and American controllers in Vienna. When the USSR invaded Afghanistan it certainly was not for the carpets it was to rape the country of mineral deposits.'

'I don't understand. Why was Prantl killed? Why not Hofer?'

Clipstein answered. 'Because, if Hofer had been taken out, Prantl would have defected immediately, taking his sources and his secrets with him. But with Prantl dead, Hofer will certainly squeal to save his own skin. He might even know who is running the KGB desk in Vienna.' Clipstein was crouched over papers on his desk. He looked up at Jack. 'That will cost us more,' he said with a wry smile.

'So, Dr.Clipstein, everything you told me yesterday about the counterfeit money was false?' I said despondently.

'No, Miss Edan. Everything I told you was correct. You see, there was more than one reason why Hofer had to stay alive, and more than one reason why he must not. And, Miss Edan, he is accused of passing counterfeit money, not killing Jews.'

Jack said assuredly. 'That bastard is going away for a long time, whichever way he plays his cards.'

I said to Jack, 'Surely he has enough sense to leave if he is on bail.'

'Was on bail,' Jack said. 'He was re-arrested last night after his warehouse was raided and crates containing small arms and rifles were found. Part of his export business for the "empty" trucks.'

'Dr.Clipstein, why, if this border trade is known to you, isn't it known to the Austrian authorities?'

Jack spoke. 'You're right, of course they know. It's part of the Cold War: a Cold War getting dangerously hot. It could ignite anytime. The Austrians are not sure which side to back, so the bastards are playing both. Communists are on their borders in occupied Hungary, Czechoslovakia and Yugoslavia. Only five years ago in 1968, Dubček spoke out for autonomy for the Czechs: Moscow responded by sending 100,000 soviet troops and tanks to Prague to deliver their message. Believe me, Katrina, the West is as vulnerable now as when Hitler walked into Poland in 1939.' Jack elucidated further: 'Richard Nixon's drowning in Watergate, Edward Heath's saying goodbye to the British Empire, the USSR could open an offensive anytime. It's that close.'

A chill went through me at the thought of another predator licking at democracy. Nuclear war has no borders, no Maginot Line, no English Channel. The scale of destruction could end Western Civilization, akin to the fall of the Greek and Roman Empires. And the horrifying fact is, any megalomaniac in a country with nuclear capacity could push the fatal button.

Dr.Clipstein put Jack's papers in a filing cabinet and said to me. 'I'll have your four paintings delivered to your hotel tomorrow morning. They are packed in two boxes. They will be easier to transport.'

With the thought of nuclear war in my head, they hardly seemed to matter. I didn't even ask who found the missing box.

ISRAEL
45

A number of letters were waiting in London from Dr.Chaim Levine in Tel Aviv. Sue had scrutinized them and showed me some of particular importance. All related to claims from photographs reproduced in the exhibition catalogue. One letter described two of the paintings in the box found at Prantl's galerie but they had not appeared in the catalogue.

I decided to go to Israel. With four weeks before the opening of the exhibition, I asked Sue to book a flight for two days only. I called Dr.Levine and arranged a final meeting.

***

It was unusually hot in Tel Aviv for early October with temperatures in the nineties. I wore a black sleeveless shift dress and jacket and put another in white in my suitcase. I packed a cardigan for the return journey. As I disembarked from the plane, warm air hung like a blanket across the tarmac, an immovable heat in a windless vacuum.

I arrived at the Sheraton Hotel, at the same time as a tourist party was checking out, and in spite of the size of the lobby, it seemed crowded. A massive sculpture by the artist Agam covered one wall of the lounge with a long sofa in front and a vast array of armchairs and tables filled the space to capacity. I was given a room on the fourth floor overlooking the sea. The Sheraton had all the amenities of an American style hotel, without the glitz.

On Friday I met Dr.Levine in the busy lobby. Locals meeting friends, businessmen striking deals, hustlers and opportunists, floated about the lobby. Dr Levine moved quickly through the area as though no one existed to a quiet corner overlooking the electric blue water of the Mediterranean, where we could see the gentle surf silently lapping the shoreline.

He put a letter on the table. His first words to me were: 'If one crate went missing, how many more might have slipped through?'

'I don't know, Dr.Levine, I had to trust Frohmann and Prantl or at least appear to, to get anything.'

'I know: you would not have received 3000 works otherwise.' he said. He did not mention Prantl's early death, although he must have known, as it was reported in all the newspapers.

A bird with red feathers, set like a collar round its neck, flew onto the parapet. Dr Levine put a piece of cake by its webbed feet as the bird watched warily before taking a brave peck.

Chaim Levine came back from this momentary diversion and said. 'As your visit is short I have made an appointment to visit the claimant immediately: it is not far from here and I think the claim is genuine.'

The ride to Herzlia along the Tel Aviv-Haifa road took twenty minutes. The taxi driver, a recent immigrant, had difficulty finding the street, eventually resorting to a book of maps. We approached a decrepit apartment-block next to a building site. There were no high rise buildings, just uniform rows of three storey boxes, stacked one on top of the other, with no hint of aesthetics, a mass of old grey concrete, which people called home. On an empty lot next to the flats, gas canisters were strewn over the desert floor. Weeds and spiky sticks of grass poked between the debris. A building site in waiting . . .

Wild stealthy cats scampered about, rummaging in the rubble. Some crouched waiting to attack a rat or mouse, even each other. Others maundered around our feet menacingly, their bones protruding from mangy skin.

Dr.Levine pressed a bell with a name written in Hebrew. A window on the first floor opened and a woman peered out. We waited under the shade of a concrete canopy and walked with her up a dingy ill-kept staircase to her small apartment, crammed with heavy old German style furniture and knick-knacks in niches and cabinets. Rosenthal plates hung on the walls and embroidered lace curtains draped the windows.

Greta Livonovitch beckoned us to sit on a dark red velvet settee, a kindly looking plump woman, with reddish blonde hair, a light complexion and brown eyes, a very erect carriage, which made her appear taller than five foot. I tried to guess her age and concluded she was around seventy-two.

Dr. Levine asked her if she spoke English. 'Miss Edan is from London,' he said.

'My English is not good but I talk a little.'

'Then we'll speak in English' he said.' She smiled. Dr.Levine said. 'If there is anything that is not clear, please ask me in Hebrew or German - whichever you prefer. We have a few questions regarding your letter to my office.' He took the letter from his pocket and handed it to her. Mrs.Livonovitch became agitated, saying. 'Everything I write is true, you understand. I remember, I can remember,' she said.

'Of course,' Dr.Levine said. 'That is all we want you to do.'

She relaxed a little but was still nervous. She offered us some knipfel biscuits. She placed tea, milk and lemon on a Turkish style brass topped table.

'Just one or two explanations will make it easier for us to identify the two paintings you are claiming,' Levine said.

'Miss Edan, will you tell Mrs Livonovitch what you need to know?'

I asked, 'do you remember the address where you last saw your pictures?'.

'Yes, I do. In my first home in Dresden, then last in Vienna.'

'What year was that, Mrs Livonovitch?'

'That was in 1937. You see Miss,' she turned to Dr.Levine for my name. 'Edan,' he said.

'My father was professor of music at the Academy in Dresden, before he became lecturer in music at the Vienna Academy. That is when we moved. I was a small child. We inherited two Rembrandts, and a Dürer from my grandfather who was Dutch. It probably was a gift or an exchange. My grandfather was a lawyer and spoke five languages. Sometimes he would give his services for the price of a painting: once he received a new piano - which I remember, because he gave it to my father. She smiled. Greta gave us her last address in Vienna. Her description of the paintings concurred with works missing from Rembrandt's oeuvre but the Dürer was a little vague, and I became suspicious. She may have seen it in a book and imagined it was a family heirloom.

'She was nude, I remember,' Greta said, 'with a necklace, and trees in the background, spindly trees, very dark green.' She stopped speaking and re-filled our cups with tea.

'Do you remember if it was a small painting or a large one? And was it shiny or dull?' I looked at Mrs.Livonovitch waiting for an answer. She pointed to a landscape on her wall. 'It was about half the size of that.'

'Have you been back to Vienna since the end of the war?'

I had touched a raw nerve. She exploded.

'Never . . . never as long as I live will I set foot on Austrian or German soil. Never.' she repeated. Dr Levine defused her anger.

'I understand,' he said, 'please rest assured if your paintings are identified your claim will be submitted and you will be able to go to London to identify them.'

'To London?' she exclaimed, 'Oh my dear, I don't know.' Before she could say anymore Dr.Levine said, 'All expenses paid.' She was bewildered. The fear of leaving the security of Israel's borders was a daunting prospect, and her description of the Dürer, was unclear. I would need further documentary proof before I would be convinced that enough evidence had been given to make her claim conclusive.

Dr.Levine shook her hand and said 'Tsom Kal' have an easy fast. She replied, still holding his hand. 'There is nothing in this world that will give me greater pleasure than having my family's paintings returned.'

As we walked to the main street to hail a taxi Dr. Levine asked me a question. 'Do you think she knows how many millions her pictures are worth?' We both knew the answer. The price had no relevance.

I returned to the Sheraton Hotel. It was a very special night in the Jewish calendar: the evening before the Day of Atonement and the fast of Yom Kippur.

Dinner was served in the restaurant for residents only, and by sundown, the dining room closed. Breakfast was pre-packaged for guests not observing the fast, and set on a buffet table. An announcement board in the lobby told hotel guests that a service for Kol Nidre would be held in the hotel synagogue at sunset. The service on Saturday started at 9.30am.

I went to my room and called Bunny and Elgin. Bunny had 'flu and Elgin told me he was about to get it too. 'I'll call you on Sunday Katrina. One of us should be street worthy by then.'

'I'm leaving on Sunday at 5 p.m. I hope you'll both feel better so we can meet.'

The most solemn day in the Hebrew calendar closes the nation like a shutter on a high security prison. Streets empty of cars, public transport stops, radio stations close, newspapers stop printing and the only thing that moves are the waves along the seashore.

I dressed in my white cotton sleeveless dress and sandals and went downstairs to the breakfast room where hot water in large silver urns was available to make tea or coffee. The chanting from the synagogue was the only sound in the hotel. The front desk was closed and the usual hubbub silenced. I wandered along the cliffs to the Hilton Hotel and looked in an arcade of shuttered shops. I was admiring a tray of diamond rings when a young man standing next to me spoke in English. 'Exquisite, aren't they?' He was very tall with mousy hair and in his late twenties.

'I saw you in the lobby of the Sheraton Hotel. I'm staying there with my grandfather.' he said, as we looked in the window of an art gallery.

'How nice,' I said 'Are you on holiday?'

'Not exactly. My grandfather was stationed in Palestine in World War ll and wanted to return to see its progress. He's also Jewish, so this country has a special significance for him.' He spoke with detachment. 'I'm not Jewish. I'm not sure what I am.'

'What would you like to be?' I asked.

'Free of dogma. It puzzles me that blood can give one religion. I consider it's knowledge, experience and ultimately choice. I would ideally like to see everyman as a world brother, with all the Gods combining their wisdom for mankind.'

'Tall order,' I commented, 'what is your profession?'

'I'm an accountant - that means everything adds up on paper and nothing adds up in life!'

'Oh dear, you are cynical. I'm sure the balance will change with time.'

We walked along the waterfront before turning back along Hayarkon Street. There was an eerie silence - a foreboding emptiness, as if time had forgotten a day in the calendar and was waiting for a gong. We were nearing the hotel when I heard a siren.

'Must be a fire somewhere,' he said. But the wailing continued. It was the drone of an air-raid siren. 'Strange day to practice,' I said. Then, out of the silence . . . pandemonium. Like the flick of a lighter, trucks and cars were racing along the streets. Loud speakers on the roofs of cars were blaring in Hebrew. Young men were running along the pavement removing prayer shawls, others were stopping cars. Buses appeared and stopped at designated points, picking up the civilian army, their rifles and rucksacks slung across their shoulders.

When we arrived at the hotel, the radio in the lobby was on full volume - making the same repeated announcement in Hebrew, over and over. A coded call to arms.

Within the next few hours, I saw how a nation dealt with invasion: because the nation is the defence force. Every man up to fifty was a trained soldier, ready to be at the front line to defend his country. This was no Dad's Army. They all knew how to handle a gun, or drive a tank, man a cannon, or command an infantry unit. When God parted the waters of the Red Sea to take the Jews from slavery, He had no intention of abandoning them. Difficult reasoning for a holocaust survivor, 4000 years later, but in 1973 annihilation was imminent.

News was filtering through that the Egyptians in the South and the Syrians in the North had invaded Israel. The front desk of the hotel was crowded with bewildered tourists, desperate to leave. An announcement came on the hotel's public address system asking all guests to report to their respective Embassies the following morning. A further announcement followed, that airline offices would open in the evening for confirmation of flights.

I tried to call Elgin. It was impossible to get a line. I sat in the lobby and the real drama of what was happening around me struck. I watched as an Arab hotel worker stuck brown parcel tape across the glass windows. I had lived with taped windows before, for over five years, in my home, in my school, in the shops. It was no deterrent. Windows still shattered in the draught of a bomb explosion, to be replaced by boards, a depressing sight from both inside and out. I had never expected to see taped windows again. The young man I had met earlier was also in the lobby and invited me to have dinner with him and his grandfather. 'By the way, I didn't give you my name.' he said 'Jonathan Ridley and my grandfather's Sam Ridley.'

Dinner was only being served in the small restaurant next to the piano bar, on the lower ground floor. In emergencies, like the one we found ourselves in, relationships mature quickly. We arranged to go together to the Embassy to register our names and Sam Ridley suggested we also go to the British airways office to confirm our tickets. We became a unit with grandfather Ridley, with his mop of grey hair, in charge.

I had a sleepless night. The noise of warplanes and helicopters were hurling through the night sky incessantly. The city was in darkness and all guests were told to keep curtains drawn and only use bedside lamps. I was listening as the drone of aircraft passed overhead, desperate for the sound to weaken and pass away, as I had done so often as a child, waiting for the thud, then the explosion, pinching myself, to see if I was alive. The memories were vivid and wouldn't go away.

In the morning we walked along Hayarkon Street to the British Embassy expecting a queue. There was no queue: in fact the embassy was shut.

'I can't believe this,' Jonathan said, looking at the plaque on the door. Open ten to three. It was Sam Ridley who rationalized, 'Yes, but not on Saturday and Sunday.'

'Even in an emergency, like war?' I said in exasperation.

'Seems like it,' he said. We then went to the office of British Airways in the Hilton Hotel. It was impossible to get in the door. Hundreds of passengers were shouting and waving tickets. An office employee put a notice on the window. Only passengers with tickets for flights to London to-day would be admitted. Jonathan and Sam Ridley's flight was confirmed for 16.00hrs. My seat was confirmed on the next flight at 20.00hrs.

'Now,' he said confidently, 'everything's arranged so we can have a nice lunch.' Jonathan looked at me then at Sam Ridley. 'And where do you suggest grandpa, all the restaurants are closed!'

'The Hilton's open. We'll give it a try. That O.K. with you, Miss Edan?'

In the early evening I packed my small bag, paid my bill and tried to call London. There were no international lines available. Nor were there any internal lines, so I couldn't call Elgin.

Before I said goodbye to Jonathan and his grandfather, I gave them my parents' telephone number in Wendover and asked them to let them know I would arrive on a later flight.

Eventually, Elgin called. 'What a mess,' he said. 'The Israelis left their borders almost naked of troops for the High Holy days, now they're in big trouble.'

'What does big trouble mean, Elgin?'

'It means the Egyptian army are half way across the Sinai desert and the Israeli's are calling help. They don't know which border to load. They're really in trouble. Anyway, I wanted to know if you're O.K. It's impossible for me to leave the Embassy, and Bunny's running errands for the staff here.'

'Don't worry Elgin: I have a confirmed flight for this evening. I'll try and call you from London. Take care and give my love to Bunny.'

***

I left the hotel at 4.30 by taxi for the airport. The road from Tel Aviv to Lod heaved with military trucks. Convoys were slowing the traffic and the half hour journey took nearly two. Security personnel in khaki short-sleeved shirts and belts carrying every form of weapon: hand grenades, bayonets, and sheath knives wrapped around their bodies, like walking arsenals, guarded the airport entrance.

I could never have anticipated what happened in the next few hours. I struggled through a heaving mass of hysterical, crying, screaming people, all pushing their way towards the check-in desks. It was remarkably nasty. People were getting vicious, and the babble of languages couldn't hide the distraught feelings behind the threats and pleas. I saw a man sobbing. "Not again, not again", he screamed, his hands wrapped round his head, bowing and bowing as an announcement said the plane to Rome was full. For many of the travellers it was a re-enactment of a previous escape from Nazi Europe. They were terrified by their own thoughts and insecurity. A fight broke out between two men both claiming the last seat on a flight to Athens. It was hard for me to keep my moral compass and not join in the fray. I had a ticket, I had a confirmed seat, but I was refused a boarding pass. No explanation was given, only "full". By midnight it was impossible to get onto the airport concourse. The seething mass of humanity huddled in family bundles had destinations to nowhere.

Outside, in the fresh air, the temperature was dropping. I put my cardigan on and sat on a rock by a palm tree. A young couple were sitting on the grass nearby. I heard the strong Glaswegian accent. 'Did you have seats on the flight to London?' I asked.
'We did, and it didn't make a tinker of a difference.'
'How long have you been here?'
'We've been in Israel for three weeks and it seems like another three here.'
'What are our chances for the next flight?'
'What next flight? All flights have been cancelled,' the young man said knowingly.
'Are you sure?'
'Absolutely, because the airport's closed and to keep the mob from going berserk, they're announcing the planes are full.'

While I tried to digest this bizarre information, they were discussing what to do. There was no transport, no taxis, and the walk to Tel Aviv impossible. The young Scotsman said 'why don't we get our hire car back, and go back to Haifa?'
'Good idea,' his companion agreed. 'Where are you from?' she asked me.
'From London. I've been staying at the Sheraton in Tel Aviv.'
'We're getting a bit low on funds. If we get a car, we'll drop you at Tel Aviv if you'll contribute a bit to the detour.'
'Excellent idea,' I said as I picked up my travel bag. We trudged round the airport until we found a hire firm open. By one thirty we were on our way to Tel Aviv in total blackness, leaving behind a trapped human cargo, condemned to misery.

By two-thirty I was standing in the lobby of the Sheraton hotel in the dark. My eyes became accustomed to the darkness and I saw a glimmer of light from the far end of the lounge. It was coming towards me. A man holding a lantern asked what I was doing in the hotel. I told him I was a guest and gave him my room number.
'And who are you?' I wanted to know.
'I am the night porter. There is no one else on duty.' he said.

The top two floors of the hotel were closed and he didn't have keys to any other rooms. The lantern was near my face and he must have seen how tired I was.
'Don't worry,' he said, 'You can sleep here.' He pointed to the sofa under the Agam sculpture that was long enough to seat twenty people. 'I'll find you a blanket.' He returned with a blanket and a kettle of tea and left his lantern to keep me company.'

A skeleton staff arrived at 8 am. I explained the situation to a young receptionist and was given a room on the side of the hotel. All rooms overlooking the sea were occupied. I later learned they were kept empty for the army, in the event of an invasion from the sea.

I called Dr.Levine's office and was told he was "on duty". No explanation, just "on duty".

I tried to call London without success. The exhibition was at the last crucial stage and I was utterly impotent. I walked along Dizengoff Street. All the shops were closed with the exception of a few run by ancient wizened old men and women, selling newspapers I couldn't read and dried fruits and unappetising sleepy nuts.

By ten I was at the British Embassy to register. It was locked. I was disgusted: no wonder the British Empire was in decline. Two Englishmen were sitting at a pavement cafe a few hundred yards from the Embassy building and I asked them if they knew when it would open. One man put his coffee cup down. 'Yes madam, when we've finished our breakfast.' Both men had white short-sleeved shirts and beige cotton trousers, were absolutely nonplussed by the situation and considered me an interruption.
'This is my second unsuccessful attempt to register my name with the Embassy. I have two questions I'd like answered.'
'Fire away,' one said as they continued eating.
'What will happen to the British tourists if the airport doesn't open?'
'Nothing. Just don't worry. We have a cruiser waiting off the coast if there's an emergency. Just pop round from time to time.'
I looked out to sea: not one ship in sight as far as the horizon.
'And your other question? Madam.'

'Did you go to public school?' They looked across the table one to the other, surprised by my question.
'Because I suggest your parents get a refund. They obviously didn't teach you any manners!' I waggled my behind as I stalked off, giving them something extra to remember.

***

Memory is a torment when it revives trapped unexorcised thoughts, too distant to act upon, too deep to unravel. In my isolation in the Sheraton hotel, this negativity sapped my energy, leaving the only option available . . . wait.

By noon the hotel lobby was filling with journalists. The world press had descended on Israel. Foreign correspondents were drafted from neighbouring countries, some by air from Cyprus, others direct from London. They waited for an official from the Israeli government for a news briefing. I sat in the lounge, watching cameramen haul equipment into corners, then join their colleagues . . . waiting. There was a noticeable silence when a bald headed man in a khaki shirt, and trousers tucked into heavy black laced boots, walked through the doors with two hefty olive skinned bodyguards in full battle dress, the iron ware around their waists bulging prominently. All seats were quickly filled, so many of the press corps squatted on the floor, note-books on their knees. The few guests in the lounge were not asked to leave. The information about to be given was for world publication anyway.

Daniel Dorfman introduced himself in English from the centre of a circle that had formed around him. 'Gentlemen as you know, the Israeli nation has been invaded. A premeditated incursion started on our borders on Saturday 6 October, developing within hours into full-scale war. We are fighting with every available man and machine at our disposal, but we are outnumbered by a thousand to one. The Egyptians have crossed the Sinai desert and are nearing Beersheva. On our Northern border the Syrians have crossed the Golan Heights and are approaching Tiberius. Gentlemen, the situation is very serious for Israel: without help we may not survive. My government urges men and women, ex-army personnel, Israelis abroad, to return home immediately. We also need doctors and trained nurses and anyone with hospital

experience. Every effort will be made to expedite transportation and no time will be wasted in getting volunteers to places where they are needed.' Daniel Dorfman then asked 'Are there any questions?' A number of hands went up.
'Yes,' he said to a man sitting in an armchair.
'Peter Chaffey, London Daily Telegraph. How will the volunteers get here, and who will pick up the bill?'
'El Al planes will be flying in and out of Lod between the hours of midnight and 3 a.m. Details will be given to Israeli Embassies worldwide. All personnel coming to Israel must come on a voluntary basis. Next question.'
'Do we have carte blanche to travel anywhere?'
'Of course, but I urge you all to carry your press credentials and photos and authorization from your newspapers. You will not get to the frontlines without. Anymore?' Another hand went up.
'Is there a hot line for the press?'
'Yes, all Embassy lines are cleared and from to-day there will be press lines also.' Daniel Dorfman looked around the room. Men were making notes, ready to wire their story, before setting off to the frontline to tell the world, at first hand, the intimate bloody details of men killing each other.
'Thank you gentleman, shalom.' And Dorfman was gone.

I went to the bar, ordered a double scotch and sat at an empty table. It wasn't long before the bar filled with the press, not on a drinking spree but taking a quick nip before deciding which front to cover.

I felt invisible among this brave breed of war correspondents about to risk their lives to keep the world supplied with "news".

The phone rang on the bar. The barman, a man in his late sixties, one of the replacement staff, called "Miss Edan." I didn't react.
Another call. "Is Miss Katrina Edan in the bar?"
'Here' I put my hand up like a schoolgirl, as I hastened to the phone. It was my mother.
'At last I have found you. We have been trying to phone you since Saturday night, we're so worried. How are you?'
'Mummy, it's wonderful to hear you. I'm fine, you needn't worry.'

'Jonathan Ridley called yesterday and told us you would be returning on Sunday night. What happened?' I told my Mother.
'How dreadful. We're getting frightful news here. I hope you're being careful. Is there anything I can do to help, Katrina?'

In a situation like this no one would be more adaptable and conscientious than Sue. But the volume of detailed work, combined with interviews and claims, was more than any one person could handle.

'Mother, could you go to my office and man the phone, so Sue can do my outside work? Sue will give you the low-down on what's urgent. Could you do that?'

'Of course I will. Anything else?'

'Yes - I love you and please don't worry.'

'Don't go, Katrina, Daddy wants to talk to you.' To hear my father on the phone was the most reassuring asset right now. Calm and forward thinking, a soldier's clinical mind, always anticipating what might become imminent.

'Katrina I'll take Cynthia to your office, she'll hold the fort. Who else needs help?'

'Sue and Desmond Hegarty will be trying to cope with everything. Desmond will hang the exhibition, but could you help at the warehouse, maybe oversee the transport to the Royal Academy. Sue has the listings and Desmond has the plan, but I want to make sure nothing goes missing.'

'Of course I can darling. I'll try and call you again tomorrow around mid-day and let you know everything's in order. Remember we love you.'

Speaking to my parents lifted my nagging desolation, and I knew that once Sue had given my father a résumé of what was needed at the warehouse, every employee under his command would respect his authority and work for him and with him. No fag in the face foreman waiting for a tea break: my father was a man of action and this word worked unequivocally for him. No action - no progress. No action - no results. No action - stalemate. No action - regret.

I felt more secure now after speaking with him and remembering these words. The party sitting at the next table heard me speaking in English. 'Don't sit there alone, come and join us,' a woman said. 'What are you drinking?'

'Scotch, please.' I said to an attractive rather dishevelled woman. She was with three men and another women. They were a motley assortment, difficult to categorize.
'You here alone?' she asked as the barman put a Scotch in front of me.
'I am.' I slipped my black and white cotton jacket off as the Scotch started its journey round my veins. She introduced the group round the table. 'Tim, Gregoire, Timu, Alison, and I'm Deborah. We know who you are we heard the bar call. You don't look like a tourist! What's keeping you here?'
'Simple, I can't get out . . . and you?'

She told me they were part of the film crew making Joseph and the Brothers. 'Alison's continuity, I'm costume design, Tim's lighting and Gregoire and Timu are assistant directors to Zakis.' She turned and looked around. 'He should be joining us. He's trying to get a replacement crew. All our technicians left on the first blast of the siren when we were in the desert half way through a take.' She finished her gin and tonic and ordered another.

Tim chipped in. 'Fat chance of getting another crew. If we do they'll turn up in discarded chariots from "The Last Crusade," and that film was made thirty years ago.'
'Don't be so pessimistic,' one of the Greeks yawned. 'I think we should take a siesta for the duration of the war, it could be over in a couple of days.' But Deborah could not be cajoled. She was a feisty, frizzed blonde, about my age; with I suspect a promiscuous pedigree.
'Actually, Katrina we're in a fucking mess. The lead actor brought his wife out for a holiday and they're worried about their kids in London. Zakis is losing money by the hour and even if we opted to fold, we can't. We can't work and we can't leave. So we're in the shit. What about you?' I told her my situation.
'Christ, you're in bigger fucking shit than we are. Two weeks to curtain-up and you're stuck in a fucking war.'

I thanked Deborah for the drink.
'We're going to a Turkish restaurant to-night,' she said 'you're welcome to join us. Drinks here at eight.' I decided to walk on the beach. I reckoned quite a lot of time might have to be spent

underground, so while it was still hot and the skies powder blue, I should take advantage.

It was not a relaxing walk. Red Cross hospital planes and helicopters were ferrying wounded soldiers from the front in a constant stream. As one plane disappeared and the engine noise subsided, another came low over the water's edge with its flaps down ready to land and take off again for another mercy mission.

I held my shoes in my hand and kept walking. My dress felt sticky, and I considered buying another. The white dress was no longer white and the black dress hid the number of times it had been worn. I returned to the hotel and decided to ring Elgin's home number. Bunny answered. 'Hi Katrina. Elgin told me you had called from London. How are you?'

'Bunny, I'm still in Tel Aviv. I couldn't get through to you before.'

'What happened? I thought you had a ticket.'

'I have, but British Airways aren't flying, so I'm stuck.'

'Hell Katrina. What will happen with your exhibition?'

'I refuse to think about it. I'm going to the airways office later to see if the situation has changed.'

'I would come over immediately, but Elgin's at the Embassy and we have to keep our home line manned. Elg's been working night and day, but tomorrow he's off at eleven. We'll come straight to your hotel. Keep your chin up pal. This war might have finished by then.'

I doubted it. I washed my white dress and hung it on a hanger in the sun. I borrowed an iron and board. The dress was ready, and so was I. Ready to join Joseph and the Brothers and leave caution to the wind. As I went down the stairs from the lobby to the bar, I heard the piano playing, "You must remember this, a kiss is just a kiss, a sigh is just a sigh." Time was going by fast for the young couples holding hands, sipping a last drink together. Young boys of eighteen and nineteen in full battle dress, ready to join their units. For me it was a film reel viewed from the safety of a seat, a long way from the action. I had seen Pippa's father going to war. That was real. I had seen him leave and never come back.

Blue smoke filled the bar. All the round glass topped tables were surrounded by families: lovers embracing: the last kiss, the last moment they might ever have together. Yet, the sound of laughter drowned this emotive atmosphere. A group of young Israeli girls with soldiers joined hands in a circle and swayed to the music, smiling and singing a song of joy and togetherness, a marriage of hope, not an end.

Deborah waved from a table in the middle of the room and beckoned me to go round the crush. Two tables were pulled together. I counted fourteen people.

'Join the club' she said. 'This is Katrina everyone. She's in double shit, so treat her gently.' I can only describe the scene as dedicated alcoholic. I joined in. Keith, one of the actors stood up and in a lilting, punctuated, cockney dialect said.

'Liedies and gents. We're about to depart for a litil eastern promise. We 'ave free, number free, not buckshee chariots wiv four wheels, waiting in the forecourt. He paused and waved his arm across his body in a Shakespearean flourish, 'I urge you to put your bums in place and we'll start to roll.'

Amid hoots of laughter from adjoining tables we trooped out to yoo-hoos and a voice from the bar shouting. 'The barmy Brits are back,' and I think if we had sung Onward Christian Soldiers, it would only have generated more laughter.

***

Oh, my God we're being bombed. I could hear the bells ringing for evacuation. I stuffed my head under the pillow. The bell didn't stop. I fumbled for the light - good - electricity, not a direct hit. I tried putting my feet on the ground but they floated up to meet me. Shit, I said to myself, it's the phone. I picked it up. 'What?'

'Katrina, is that you?' I looked down at my naked body.

'It was me when I put it to bed, I think.'

A distant voice, somewhere from another planet was trying to invade my world. 'Who are you?'

'It's Jack, I've been trying to speak to you since Saturday.'

'Jack, ah, I remember, Jack, but which Jack?'

'Katrina, are you being funny?'

I giggled 'Yes, isn't it great to be funny? Are you a funny Jack?'

No, I decided he's a miserable old bugger playing air raids. 'Fuck off, I'm waiting for the siren and we'll all go to the bar and have another little drinkie.'
'All right, Katrina. So you've had the lid off the bottle. I guess I'll try again.'
'Do that Jack,' I said. 'Try again. And how's Jill?'

At 6.30 the phone rang again. Ouch, my head. That rattling ring, like a chain saw was cutting though the membranes of my existence. I picked it up quickly to stop the torment.
'Katrina, it's Jack.'
'It's six thirty Jack, I'm a bit woozy. Have you tried to call before?'
'Yes I have. Are you O.K? Have you seen Bunny and Elgin?'
'No, I'm seeing them later to-day. They thought I'd left.'
'I spoke with your father last night, and he told me that he and Cynthia are going to help Sue in London.'
'I know. Because there's absolutely nothing I can do from here.'
'Myrtle Shaw has offered to stop over in London and help. She's on her way back to the States. She could be a useful hand.'

Myrtle could help hang the exhibition. She'd be invaluable for Desmond. She knew the breakdown of crates from Museums, castles, collections and private individuals. I asked Jack to call Sue and tell her.
'Sure Katrina, when do you think you'll get out?'
'No idea. The airport is full of stranded tourists and even the chief rabbi of Britain can't get a seat. What chance do I have?'
'You'll make it Katrina, and with time to spare. I miss you. I'll speak to you again in a few days. Don't worry.'

I put the phone down. I miss you too, Jack. I didn't go downstairs for breakfast. Instead I soaked in a deep bath, washed the smell of stale cigarettes from my hair and by eleven I was waiting in the lobby for Bunny and Elgin.

In spite of my effort to look sprightly, I looked dire. My eyes were red, with a deep band of blue immediately below, and every movement was an effort.

As Elgin and Bunny came into the lobby, it was Elgin who spoke first. 'Katrina, are you developing delinquent habits? You look bushed.'
'Hung over is the right word Elgin.'

'Never mind' he said as he gave me a kiss on the cheek. Bunny said. 'You're fine Katrina. Some good coffee in the fresh air, and you will look a million dollars.'

We walked to Hayarkon Street past the British Embassy to a small café and I told them what happened when I tried to register.

'I guess we're all taking a beating. One American woman who said she knows the President, is going to report Elg and get him sacked!'

'That's right, Katrina.' Elgin said. 'What she doesn't know is that Richard Nixon is drowning in Watergate and his name will be dirtier than mine by the time she gets home.'

We ordered pita bread and hummus and chopped salad and coffee. Once I started eating the gremlins in my body calmed down and were gradually being ousted.

Both Elgin and Bunny looked tired. Elgin told me 'since last Saturday every official has been on call 24 hours. We have thousands of tourists running out of dollars and hotels want to know who's picking up the tab. There are still no public lines out from here and only a few lines in at restricted times. It's a real headache.'

Bunny said to Elgin in a strong voice, 'Let's face it honey, the Americans are getting hysterical, they've never been in a war situation. Our wars are on television.'

'What about Pearl Harbour? Wasn't that a war?'

This time Bunny had the last word. 'That was on television too, in Technicolor.'

The conversation was going nowhere except into exasperation, so I asked Elgin. 'Are American Airlines flying into Lod?'

'No, the only airline flying is El Al for security reasons.'

'Why?' I wanted to know.

'Because some hot-head might fly in with a bomb and disembark leaving the plane to blow up.'

'So,' Bunny said, 'one U.S. plane goes fuzz.'

'Bunny,' Elgin said, 'you don't understand. The runway would be blown up with it.' While we dipped pita bread into the swirl of olive oil and hummus there was silence. Bunny looked worried and put her hand on mine.

'I feel upset for you Katrina. After four years' work you're really being cheated. Have you spoken to Dr.Levine?'
'I tried - he's "on duty."'
'Oh, that,' Elgin said, 'means he's probably a reserve general.'
'That won't help Katrina, Elgin. Can't you find a flight for her?'
'It's not that easy. Only priority passengers are leaving.'
'Sure, but that includes large tourist groups that Israel want out fast. You could rifle a seat from someone.'

Elgin looked at me with real concern. 'Personally, I think you're a priority, and all I can say is I'll do my best - but I'm not in charge. If I manage anything, it will be at very short notice - like a couple of hours, and then you may have to go via New York.'

I clasped my hands together in prayer fashion.
'Elgin, any route anytime, via anywhere. I'll be waiting.' I turned to Bunny. 'Your cousin Myrtle Shaw was a good recommendation. She's going to stop over in London en route home and lend a hand.'

Bunny's eyes sparkled for the first time. 'There you are Elgin - I told you she would be right for the job.'
Elgin said 'Jack phoned this morning - he sounded pretty uptight. He's going to London tomorrow to see the sponsors, so I guess they'll keep everything afloat.'

Four days later a call came from Elgin. 'Katrina there's a flight leaving for London at 1 a.m. this morning, you're on. Take your British Airways ticket to the El Al Desk at the airport and give them this number: 01198260. The flight is to New York with a stopover in London.' I looked at the clock in the hotel lobby. It was 9.p.m. Four hours and I'd be on my way home.
'Elgin, I am really grateful.'
'Katrina, I spoke to Jack before he left London, He's called your parents with the flight departure time. It should take about five and a half hours if you get off on time.'
'Give my love to Bunny, and I'll speak to you from London next time, not Tel Aviv.'

I was so excited I rushed down to the bar to tell Alison and Deborah and the film crew that I was going home in four hours.
'I have come to say goodbye, and thank you for your support.' There was a chorus of voices: "Good luck with the exhibition".

Without them I might have broken down, felt cheated and sorry for myself. But they were a stalwart bunch and in their profession delays are only par for the course and if a shoot actually finished on time, it was nothing less than a miracle.
'Any messages to take home?'
'Paper' Alison said, 'anyone with a notebook?' Deborah pulled a notepad from her beaded Yemeni sack and passed it around.
'Keith's wife asked me to call her parents in Hampshire where their children were staying.'
'What would you like me say?'
'Just tell them we're alright and we'll be home soon, and I'll bring Emma and Gerry a stuffed camel.'
Tim said, 'Where the hell are you going to find a stuffed camel?'
'Anymore?' I collected little pieces of paper with numbers and messages and promised they would be the first calls I made.

Within an hour I had checked out of the hotel and was en route to the airport. The taxi was stopped at three checkpoints before being allowed to enter the perimeter of the airport. I remember the pandemonium when I was there before. But the paranoia had subsided and an overall resignation hung over the waiting crowd. Pilgrims, families with children, clerics, rabbis, were still waiting and being told flights were full.

The El Al desk gave me a boarding pass but no seat number. When the flight was called there was a stampede of American men and women that made the all blacks rugby team look like an infants' outing. One woman screaming "Harry, Harry, I'm over here, come on" as she held her full girth in front of the steps to the plane.

The shock of entering a jumbo jet for the first time nearly sent me to the nearest exit. Its massive interior, more like a flying dance hall than a plane, was filling with noisy New Yorkers shouting from one side to the other. The airhostesses were offhand and harassed. I sat in an aisle seat near the front. As the engines started to warm, all the lights went out. A voice came over the system, first in Hebrew then in English. "All lights will be turned off until we have passed over Israeli territory. Please do not smoke, use matches or torches until we give permission. Please stay in your seats with the belts fastened." Then we took off. The great giant rocked from side to side as it climbed into the blackness. I could see flashes of light around the wings. I thought it was lightning or maybe gunfire. My imagination was in overdrive fuelled by the hysteria around me. Women started to scream and shout 'We're going down, we're crashing.' Another scream, 'turn back, turn back.' I gripped the arms of my seat, closed my eyes, and listened to the words in my head: we're still flying, we're still in the sky, but the crying and prayers echoing through the cabin around me drowned my thoughts. I felt the plane's slow effort to climb and then its wings tipped to the right and we changed direction. This rocking and swinging and moving from left to right lasted about half an hour but it seemed like forever. Not until we were above the clouds did the crying and praying stop.

There was no clapping when we landed in London unlike arrival in Israel, when spontaneous applause erupts. For Christians, landing in the Holy Land symbolizes the return of the Prodigal Son, for Jews, arrival in the Promised Land and for many others, a spiritual beginning.

At London airport only three passengers disembarked. I pulled my cardigan close round my neck, and marched towards the departure gate.

LONDON

46

Few people were at London airport on this cold October morning, and with only hand luggage I avoided any waiting time. At the exit barrier I saw my mother and father waving frantically. Within seconds, four arms enveloped me at once and the embrace smothered me. First, mother looked at me in my scruffy black cotton dress and sandals in horror. 'Darling, you'll freeze to death. Haven't you anything else to wear?' She didn't realize these were my comfort clothes: they had suffered with me, knew how I felt, I had an empathy with them. Anyway I was wearing a cardigan. Then it was my father's turn.

I could see a slight tear in the corner of his eye as he hugged me for several seconds. 'Welcome home. You will not believe this; I have two blankets in the car, one for your legs, and the other for the rest of you. Let's have a coffee first.'

I felt so disorientated, still rocking with the plane, unfocused but wildly excited. I told my parents my experience on the flight, when I thought we were being shot out of the sky. 'It was really frightening. I will never fly on one of those fairground machines again. They're suicidal.' I said.

My parents looked at each other without making any remarks.

'I suggest,' my father said, 'Katrina gets her breath back and tells us in her own time about what happened. We can tell her how well everything has been going here.'

Mother conceded, 'Of course. You're absolutely right Richard. We must give her the good news first.'

'Is there bad news?' I had to know immediately.

'No darling, Sue's supervision has been exemplary. Your exhibition is on course, on time and only needs your finishing touches.'

'That means signing cheques, I presume.'

I was anxious to leave the airport and get home. White-faced businessmen, in their uniform of dark overcoats, briefcases in tow scurried about. Announcements every few minutes exacerbated my tension and ravaged my fragile nerves.

It was 9.a.m when we arrived at my house. My parents had been sleeping in my room and I insisted they stayed there. 'I'll sleep on the sofa tonight, but right now I want a bath, some clean clothes and a couple of hours sleep before I go to the office.' Then I remembered. 'Oh! I must make some important phone calls first.'

'Darling surely they can wait.'

'Not these Mother.' I hastily found the papers I had collected in the bar at the Sheraton and rang them each in turn.

'Now what are the finishing touches I have to deal with?'

'Katrina, slowdown, they're only ticks and dots and those can wait till tomorrow,' my father said. 'Have a rest my dear, you have had an exhausting time, you'll feel much better after forty winks.'

It must have been like the Charge of the Light Brigade when Richard and Cynthia Edan arrived in my office during my absence. It was unmentionably tidy. Sue was in high spirits, although she looked exhausted.

'Welcome home Katrina. I couldn't find a George medal, so I bought you some flowers.' She handed me a bunch of white calla lilies, which must have cost her a fortune. I looked inside the voluptuous curve of white velveteen petals with thick yellow stamens tucked inside.

'Thank you, Sue, they're lovely.' She knew how much I admired the painting "Flower Day" by Diego Rivera of a woman kneeling in reverence like a black Madonna carrying a basket high on her back crammed with calla lilies, forming a halo around her head.

I said to Sue. 'My parents told me you have practically made me obsolete.' Sue looked surprised. I was expecting some smart repartee, but instead she said. 'No, boss I only carried on where you left off.'

'Well you've done a great job and everything's running on time.'

'Absolutely right boss, but it's going to cost yer!'

My parents were in my office, waiting for instructions. Sue said. 'Could you arrange for Cynthia and Richard to man the office so we can go to the Royal Academy?' I noted with interest how quickly she'd handed authority back to me.

In the taxi to the Academy Sue told me how well my father and Myrtle Shaw managed the checking at the warehouse. 'She has a memory like a mirror, and your father should be permanently enlisted.'

We went straight to the Diploma Gallery where Desmond was focusing lights. He came down from a scaffold in paint-splattered trousers and a raggedy old shirt. 'At last, the heroine returns.' A big hug, a kiss and he stretched both arms wide. 'Do you like it, Katrina?'

I looked at the pastel walls with the paintings hung evenly, all numbered and labelled, some with titles, and others listed "title unknown." Partitions linked blue rooms to green and then on to yellow then pastel orange. It was difficult to acknowledge that these works of art displayed so serenely on these walls were the spoils of war. It would be a dereliction of truth to view them any other way. But I was satisfied, even pleased with the result. I had attempted in my own way to give back a visual remnant, something of beauty for those refugees who snatched life from the brink of extermination. Seeing the paintings on the walls of the Royal Academy satisfied my belief that everything is possible.

Sue and I returned to the office before my parents had left, and I received instructions not to work too late. Sue had compiled a list of people who had called.

'They all said it was urgent! But they always do,' Sue said with resignation. 'I've inserted the dates so you can decide.' She gave me her "A" list. Elizabeth Cuthbertson, Myrtle Shaw, Dr.Anton Hempf, Jack Steinhart, Paul McKenzie, the Evening News, the News of the World, the BBC and Austrian Television,

Without referring to Sue's involvement with McKenzie, I guessed she knew want he wanted.

'She handed me a cutting from The Times. McKenzie had run a story dramatizing my enforced stay in Israel.

BRITISH ART HISTORIAN TRAPPED IN ISRAELI WAR

Katrina Edan, the curator of the exhibition of looted Nazi art due to open at the Royal Academy in Piccadilly on the 24 October, is caught in the firing line following the invasion of Israel. She was visiting Dr.Chaim Levine, the director of the Museum of Tel Aviv to confirm a claim for masterpieces with an estimated value in the

region of five million pounds. With only two weeks to the opening date, Edan's London team is completing the final touches, so the exhibition will open on time. Any claimants planning to come to London should advise the exhibition office and bring copies of their filed claim. Rabbi Dr. Josef Frishman from New York will give an opening address.

'Good work Sue. I hope the press doesn't grill me on the Israeli/Arab conflict. I'll have to admit I spent most of the time getting plastered.'
'I knew you wanted the story to run, so I told Paul it was an opportunity not to be missed.'
'Do I need to call him or is that it?'
'Make it the last call.' she said knowingly.

My concern about the Gustav Klimt painting and the disasters that could ensue had to be exorcised. I was grateful the schedule was running smoothly, but I had lost continuity and needed firm confirmation that promises were being adhered to. When I spoke with Elizabeth Cuthbertson, she was very consoling and assured me the Klimt was in the vaults of the National Gallery and would be hung two days before the opening. But it was the revelation that followed that amazed me.
'While you were away, I was searching in the archives for the provenances of pictures received between the dates you listed on the museum circular, and I found three paintings which are extremely obscure. One you mentioned to me some time ago, a Frans Hals that you had heard about in a letter from a refugee. The other two are a complete mystery. They are both listed as private loans to the Museum: a Hans Memling Portrait of a Young Man, received in 1939, the other by Jean Honoré Fragonard, Three Men and a Boy beneath a Sacrificial Altar, received in 1941. Is it too late to include them in the exhibition?'
'Are they photographed, Elizabeth?'
'Every item in the collection is photographed, including Hermine Gallia.'

I told Elizabeth the catalogues had been distributed but late arrivals would appear in the addendum.

Sue was sitting opposite me ticking off the telephone list and taking notes. After only two hours sleep in twenty-four I was

losing concentration and physically beginning to wilt. I asked Sue to call Myrtle and Steinhart to say I was home and tell them I would call in the morning. 'Where is Steinhart, by the way?'
'In Vienna, I believe. He had a meeting here with Bernard Anderson and Elizabeth Cuthbertson, then he took off.'

***

I smelt cottage pie as I opened my front door, and although I was too tired to eat, mother insisted. After supper was cleared, I fell asleep on my sofa, which now had crisp inviting sheets and a big soft pillow. My father turned the phone off so I wouldn't be disturbed. As the light went out my mind switched off too.

In the morning, my parents were waiting for their orders. It now became a joke. 'Daddy, I can manage. Sue will be in the office, I'll be floating, Desmond's at the exhibition. Really, you've both done so much, you're due for a rest.'
Mother took over. 'All right my dear, we'll stay here and look after you.' My father said. 'At this stage Katrina, with the exceptional circumstances, it might be as well to have some "incase" back up, even if we are due for retirement.
'Don't mis-understand Daddy, I do appreciate everything you've done, but we really can manage.'

LONDON

47

The last few days before an exhibition opens are always a whirlwind but this one presented extra special demands, making the final hurdle threaten my flagging energy.

Sue handed me her progress list:

Anna Frishman collecting Joseph Frishman from airport.

Dr.Levine and Greta Livonovitch arrive from Tel Aviv together.

Daniel Clipstein arriving with his wife.

Personal invites sent to: - Dr.Anton Hempf, Anna Frishman Daniel Lerhmann, Bernard Anderson and the board of Samuel Hall. Jack Steinhart and board of Imperial Chicago, Elizabeth Cuthbertson and the trustees of the National Gallery, Corinne Rothschild, Sir Hugh Casson, Myrtle Shaw, Elgin and Bunny Brooks and your parents.

'I put the Brooks in because they helped you out of Israel, and your parents because - well - you always invite your parents, and anyway, they're staff now,' she grinned.

I should have relaxed and let the exhibition generate its own outcome. This was impossible. A list of timed interviews at the Royal Academy, starting the following day looked awesome. Every fifteen minutes from nine till eleven was booked. Sue rushed out of the office.

'Can't stay, have to make urgent call.'

I signed the cheques on my desk then I called Anton Hempf.

I had received two letters from Jack by express. One was for Anton Hempf the other for Elizabeth. Surprisingly when I told Elizabeth on the phone I had a letter from Jack for her, she said.

'Can I come to your office this afternoon to collect it?'

I had suspected for some time that Elizabeth and Jack were meeting, but to find a common denominator was difficult. And sending a letter via me, seemed bizarre. My priorities excluded thinking about it anymore.

Sue was all smiles when she returned. 'You look worn out Katrina, are you all right?'

'It was a difficult trip' I said conservatively: even then it was an understatement, harrowing was more accurate. I picked up the progress list. 'Anything more to add to this, Sue?'

'Yes, McKenzie will interview Dr.Levine and Greta Livonovitch at the airport and print the next day. Do you have any last minute revelations for him?'

I had enough for a journalistic picnic in fact, but nothing I could tell McKenzie.

'Is Myrtle Shaw still in London?'

'I really don't know,' Sue said. 'She hasn't answered her invitation.' Compared to me Sue looked radiant. Her hair shone, her white angora sweater looked teasingly strokable: her skirt was short and she wore fine black nylons with high-heeled shoes.

I took a mirror from my handbag and surveyed the wreck. My red hair was dull and lank: my eyes were nearly the same colour. I snapped the mirror shut.

The events of the last three years had dug deep into my psyche with cumulative effect. In this state it was difficult to have optimism, although I argued in my head that neither good nor evil are forever: we're programmed into complex emotional patterns with overriding powers that dominate and motivate us, throwing us alternately into turmoil and chaos, success and elation: tossing us into love which disrupts and blinds and then slides away. This internal dialogue was becoming inhibiting.

On my way out I told Sue. 'I'm going to the hairdresser; I'll be back before two. Elizabeth Cuthbertson is due at 2.30.

***

This particular visit to the hairdresser was an event. I wanted the intrusive images focusing in my head eradicated: taken by the roots so my thinking could come back into perspective. I floated in my own fantasies until the stylist at Vidal's said: 'And how would you like to look to-day, Miss Edan?'

I answered with one word . . . 'Civilized.'

He snipped and primped and glossed and goaded over his creation: my hair was on lease with me the onlooker. I left with a sharp shining mane resting on my shoulders, hair I could toss about in abandon yet totally controlled by the stylist's scissors.

I arrived back in my office five minutes before Elizabeth. Her slim black skirt and long black jacket must have been at least a size smaller than when I last saw her. She put a box of Fortnum's chocolates on my desk. 'Just a little treat for you,' and said I looked good in turquoise.

I looked down at my old Chanel boucle suit then handed her Jack's letter. She slit the envelope and pulled out the contents. I tried not to look, but my curiosity didn't allow it. Elizabeth gave a big sigh and put the papers on the table.

'You must be wondering why Steinhart sent his letter to your office.'

'Not really, I lied.' Elizabeth obviously didn't believe me. 'He wants me to read it in front of you.'

She was holding the letter scanning it, taking her time. 'Jack Steinhart says in his letter that Gerhard Hofer is in jail on a fraud charge and further charges are pending. He has also enclosed a cheque for £163.333, my original cheque to Samuel Hall for the first instalment for the Gustav Klimt portrait.'

'Are you telling me, Elizabeth, that Bernard Anderson didn't forward the money?'

'Not precisely. He forwarded the cheque to Jack Steinhart, who held it at his bank. Both Bernard Anderson and I knew this would be the procedure. An identical amount, £163.333, was collected by courier from a numbered bank account in Switzerland.'

'Wait a minute, Elizabeth. Whose account in Switzerland?'

'I can't answer, because I don't know. I do know that the money was switched to counterfeit at the border and the genuine notes returned to the Swiss account holder.'

'And what else do you know, Elizabeth?' My tone was accusing.

'I can't say I've enjoyed these clandestine activities Katrina, but when I explain further, I hope you'll understand and forgive me.'

'I'm not at all sure I'm prepared to forgive anyone about anything at anytime,' I replied.

'I can understand your reaction. But there were extenuating circumstances. If you remember, I met Anton Hempf and Jack Steinhart at a dinner at your house. Some weeks later, Anton Hempf called and invited me to his home. We had a very relaxed evening and discussed a number of mutual interests, including the portrait of Hermine Gallia. He told me how delighted he was the painting was coming to London. Then he said something very obscure. "I feel the picture has followed me".

'Naturally I asked him why. Katrina, he told me how Gerhard Hofer had "bought" the painting in exchange for a visa.' Elizabeth put her elbows on the desk with her hands clasped in front. 'I cannot tell you, how shocked I was. My mind was all over the place. You sold the painting to me with an impeccable provenance. The board has no idea of its full history.'

She was correct, but at the time I sold the painting, I didn't know it had a tainted history either.

'So what did you do, Elizabeth?'

'The following day I sat in my office and tried to ascertain the repercussions. There were so many. I decided, rightly or wrongly to discuss the purchase with Bernard Anderson. Jack Steinhart came to London at Anderson's request. During that meeting Steinhart resolved how we would "buy" the painting and not disclose that anything was amiss, especially to you Katrina. Jack Steinhart was very confident and said he would be personally responsible for your safety.'

'So you set a trap to get Hofer and the painting as well?'

'No, Katrina, I had no part in setting the trap. I only agreed to pay for the painting and go along with the ruse. Morally I had no choice. If I'd refused, all the information we had released about the first showing of the Klimt painting at the Academy, would have been null and void: something to be avoided before such a controversial exhibition. If I had bought it knowing its provenance the National Gallery would be implicated in a fraudulent conspiracy. So, Anderson and Steinhart agreed to return my cheque.'

'And what do they intend to do now?'

'I can only tell you that Bernard Anderson has not reported anything to his board. Nor for that matter have I. But something must be resolved between you and me because the National Gallery is holding a painting it no longer owns, contrary to all the advertising.'

'Just a minute, Elizabeth.' I dialled Sue on the intercom.

'Did Jack Steinhart say what time he is arriving?'

'No Katrina, it was just a brief telephone message.'

'Try getting him on the phone, it's urgent.'

Within minutes Jack was on the line. 'Steinhart,' he said

'Jack, I have Elizabeth Cuthbertson in my office. I don't need to tell you why. I must know exactly what the Austrian press has released so I can call Paul McKenzie.'
'The only information circulating here is that Hofer's in jail for paying the Dorotheum Auction house in counterfeit pounds. You can give him that information but I suggest you discuss it first with Elizabeth Cuthbertson. I'll be at the Cumberland Hotel, Marble Arch, to-night. I might have more information by then.'

I called Sue and asked her to make us some coffee. 'I presume you still drink or have you given up eating and drinking?' I said to Elizabeth as I opened the chocolates and offered them to her.

Then I said. 'This is what I intend to do. To-night I shall tell Anton Hempf that Hofer's in jail on fraud charges and the National Gallery will not purchase the painting. I'm sure he'll be very sceptical and reticent. But, if I show him this cheque,' I picked up the returned cheque from Jack 'it might convince Anton of his responsibility to the National Gallery, and to set an example for others to come forward and make a claim. But I need you to collude with me and I shall explain why.'
'Katrina, I can't make a habit of this, I could lose my job and my reputation.'
'You won't because what I intend to do will give the National Gallery a benevolent image. I want you to give a statement to The Times telling them it has come to your notice that the painting being shown at the "Scream" exhibition was obtained illegally by the Austrian owner in 1938. The National Gallery has agreed to leave the painting on show, hoping an owner or relative will come forward with a claim.'

Elizabeth looked at me in amazement. 'And then.' I said. 'I will ask Anton to make a claim. But whatever the outcome I want your assurance that you will offer the painting to Anton, at the end of the exhibition.'
'Katrina, I understand the morals behind what you're saying but I'm not in a position to give away a picture worth half a million pounds.'
'You can give it away because you don't own it. When Hofer's tried you'll be just another of his victims. Retrospective blackmail from any source is unthinkable and in the case of the

Klimt painting, we know the provenance was doctored and you were misled.'

'I'm not happy about your proposal. I would prefer the whole episode remained low key, but if you insist I speak to the press, I will.'

I called Sue into my office. She smiled politely at Elizabeth.

'I want Paul McKenzie in this office within half an hour.'

'You want what?'

'Paul McKenzie,' I repeated, 'of The Times, here - pronto.'

She gave me a very suspicious what-are-you-up to look.

McKenzie arrived forty-five minutes later. Elizabeth told him almost verbatim what I'd asked her to say. I gave him the counterfeit story: 'I want it blown across the front page in **big black bold**. Get the splash it's worth it. And don't forget Mr.McKenzie to quote the Hermine Gallia painting is being shown at the Royal Academy.'

'At last,' he said, 'something nice and sinister.'

The morning before the exhibition opened we had front-page coverage with an extended story on the National Gallery's purchase of a £500,000 painting of dubious provenance.

As usual Paul McKenzie's article had an eye-catching headline.

NAZI WAR CRIMINAL SELLS
STOLEN PAINTING TO THE NATIONAL GALLERY

Fortunately, I had seen Anton Hempf the night before the article was printed, to give him the letter from Professor Frohmann. When I told him the Professor had asked that Anton should not open the letter till after Frohmann's death, Anton hastily shut the envelope in a drawer with a bang, as if it didn't exist.

Anton Hempf was a victim like all the other refugees and he reluctantly agreed to make a claim, more as an example than for reward. 'The paintings in the exhibition are not trophies to be carried away,' Anton said to me emotively. 'They are only the remnants of our shattered past.'

LONDON

48

On the morning the exhibition opened I was up at six. I washed my hair, stuffed a couple of rollers in the top for lift and looked in the wardrobe for something suitable. It was important that my sombre mood was disguised, so I selected a Black Watch tartan skirt that I bought in Leith because I liked the colours, a white shirt and a navy blazer. Before putting them on I held them against me and looked in the mirror. Yes, I said to myself, that's camera friendly. I was in my office by eight, ready for the barrage of telephone calls, which always preceded an opening.

The phone was ringing as I opened the front door. Paul McKenzie's voice almost broke the sound barrier. 'Have you seen the morning papers?' he shouted.

'No, I don't read the morning papers, Mr.McKenzie.'

'Well you'd better listen to this. The Daily Sketch has latched onto you with some libellous column inches. I want to know Miss Edan how much is true?'

'Until I see the paper, Mr.McKenzie, I can't tell you.'

'I'll read it to you,' he said. 'This is the headline.'

HOLOCAUST SURVIVORS QUEUE FOR MEMENTOES WORTH MILLIONS.

'Is there a queue Mr.McKenzie?'

'Not yet, it's 9 a.m. and The Sketch doesn't care one way or the other. There's no photograph, so who knows?'

'So what is the problem, Mr.McKenzie?' I was opening letters while I was listening.

'I'll read the problem to you.' he said.

"Katrina Edan, curator of The Scream exhibition opening to-day at the Royal Academy, will reveal how she was subjected to threats of violence during her attempt to put together the exhibition of looted art. Edan uncovered a trail of unprecedented deception on a scale worthy of an MI6 agent. Was her role as curator a cover for more covert activities?

Over 3000 works of art have been unearthed. Edan said it is only a prelude to a cover-up of international proportions; museums

worldwide will eventually be exposed, including the National Gallery and the Tate in London, for harbouring art acquired from dubious sources and records that defy scrutiny.

I could have thrown the phone down the line if technology had advanced so far. But before I could even question McKenzie he said. 'What the hell are you holding back? Give me the facts from the horse's mouth, Miss Edan, yours; or has the Sketch got a lead on something I haven't?'

'I'm sorry Mr.McKenzie I have nothing to add. I have given you facts not speculation. If your newspaper wants to upstage the Sketch or any other paper, it's not my concern. If I have anymore facts, you'll be the first to know.' I put the phone down abruptly.

Whatever was printed now had no relevance to the exhibition. Even disgusting lewd supposition, would only fire the imagination of the public and hopefully prod the consciences of curators knowingly holding stolen art in their museums, under the guise of custodians for their countries' artistic heritage.

The BBC was filming paintings when I entered the Diploma Gallery and cameras were being set up by Austrian and German television crews.

My first interview with a dowdy middle-aged woman from the London Illustrated News lasted fifteen minutes. Then the BBC placed me in front of the Gustav Klimt painting, while a girl with a giant powder puff took the shine off my nose, before the interviewer, a serious thin young man, stood with his microphone at the ready.

McKenzie was right. The BBC interviewer had read the early editions. "In your opinion Miss Edan, do you believe our national institutions are involved in corrupt dealings."

I answered negatively. 'You'll have to put that question to the curators of the museums. I'm only the curator of this exhibition.'

"Do you know what the value of the paintings on show amounts to?"

'That's an irrelevant question.' I answered. 'This exhibition has nothing to do with value; it's to do with justice.'

This line of questioning followed from one interviewer to the next until the Austrian television interviewer asked:

"One of Austria's most respected galerie owners, who helped you set up this exhibit was murdered. You were in Vienna at the time, can you comment on your position?"
The camera was rolling. I smiled. 'Certainly. If the Austrian police want to interview me, I'm available anytime.'

Joseph and Anna Frishman were due to arrive at the Royal Academy at 1.45. I waited in the foyer to greet them.

Joseph Frishman shook my hand with a firm grip. 'My cousin has written to me during the last few years, and I know how dedicated you have been to this exhibition.'
'Rabbi Frishman' I said, 'if it weren't for Anna, this exhibition might never have happened.'

I took them up the wide main staircase with large urns on either side filled with exotic flowers that had been donated by London florists. The pace was slow as people stopped to admire the flowers and smell the pungent perfume.

I felt the imposing presence of Joseph Frishman by my side. He was a tall-dignified man, and in spite of the circumstances that brought him to London, held his head high with pride and confidence. Although he was forty-five, ten years younger than Anna, his black hair, now streaked grey, and his stubble style beard, aged him. He wore a dark grey suit with a white shirt and a white tie. Anna, on the other hand, looked tense and nervous, clutching a silk scarf at her neck as if it were a comforter.

A small platform with a microphone had been placed in the centre of the first gallery. The room was gradually filling with men and women: tight groups speaking German, Hungarian, Polish, Dutch, French and English.

When the room was filled to capacity Joseph Frishman mounted the dais. He stood silently waiting for the cacophony of voices to abate to a whisper.

I was standing with Anna Frishman and Anton Hempf, an insignificant bystander in the drama of events, which created this exhibition: never having experienced the suffering of the people surrounding me. I wondered if paint on canvas could be any recompense for their losses. I wondered if I had achieved anything other than reviving suppressed misery. Holding a catalogue in his hand, his head bowed in contemplation or perhaps prayer, Joseph Frishman raised his head high and spoke.

'Ladies and gentlemen, welcome. It is normal, when opening an exhibition to say' . . . He hesitated . . . looked around at the silent audience . . . 'that it is my pleasure . . . Ladies and gentleman, pleasure is not a word I can use here - gratitude, yes - and that gratitude I must address to Miss Katrina Edan, for her exemplary dedication to finding and showing, in this illustrious venue, the paintings hanging here to-day.' He paused . . . 'I should like to share with you a few of my recollections - some will be similar to your own - others will not. Because, my friends, experience is personal, and only memory can be shared. The pictures hanging here to-day have a different meaning for every individual, and a different meaning from anything that ever hung on these walls before. They are the signature of our lost childhood, our lost youth, and the most hurtful of all - lost love. We, the survivors, were deprived of this most essential lesson in life, the love of family. As a child when I was afraid and alone, I would pretend I was a bird, flying around the world, collecting all the lonely isolated people who felt like me, a castaway in a foreign land. Rabbi Frishman was silent for a few moments before saying. 'My friends, I know now, I was not alone, God was with me. And to-day, God has brought us together. Only our faith and His power could have chosen us, from the millions who were sacrificed, to testify to the theft of our liberty and the attempted annihilation of our heritage.' Holding the microphone Rabbi Frishman said; 'I should like you to reflect silently for a few moments and give thanks for our survival, and ask God to renew our strength.' With head bowed he said, 'Amen.'

I shall never forget the haunting silence as Joseph Frishman stepped down from the podium: unlike the moments at birth when a baby cries and life starts, a moment of joy, this silence was not broken and as the crowd moved slowly into the adjoining rooms not a whisper could be heard.

Sue was standing with Paul McKenzie, both visibly moved and silent. My parents came across the room: stood with me, but said nothing. I saw Jack and the Clipstein's walking towards me. Jack introduced them to Anna and Joseph Frishman and my parents. Clipstein said to the Frishman's.

'I must thank you both for the support you have given Miss Edan. She has told me often this exhibition would never have been realized without you.'

Anna had a questioning expression. 'Really, I haven't done a thing, except complain.' she said.

Clipstein turned to me. 'Miss Edan, you haven't met my wife.' I shook hands with a short raven haired woman dressed in a black suit and sensible shoes.' She smiled and her dark soulful eyes relayed genuine appreciation.

'I must congratulate you,' she said. 'It must have been so difficult to put this all together.' Then, to my surprise, Jack said to Anna and Joseph, 'Could we have a few moments together before you see the exhibition?' Anna tensed, looking first at me then at Joseph.

'Don't worry Miss Frishman, Jack said, 'I only have good news.'

'In that case I'll join you,' I said.

'Of course, Katrina. Is anything private from you?'

What an enigma! Ever since I've known Jack, the truth has been manipulated to suit his own ends.

Few people were in the cafeteria. Jack spoke quietly and selected his words carefully - so I guessed he would tell Anna what had happened in Vienna. When she heard that Prantl had died in unnatural circumstances, she looked mystified.

'Mr.Steinhart, when did Prantl die?'

'The actual date of death has not been announced, even if it's known.' Jack said. 'Katrina, maybe you can explain a little more?' Anna, surprised by the conversation, said.

'If you knew, Katrina, why didn't you tell me?'

'Because I didn't know how or why Prantl died. Anyway Anna, it's irrelevant: your claim cannot be disputed now Prantl is dead, and even if he were living your claim would still be irrevocable.'

Jack explained to Joseph, 'The Prantl Galerie in Vienna will also become your property after the lawyers have substantiated your claim.'

There was no visible sign of pleasure, relief maybe, even gratitude. Anna was unmoved by what she was hearing, as if it no longer mattered. However Joseph said to me, 'If you need any verification for the procedures, I will support Anna's claim.'

We left the cafe and joined the mass of people studying the paintings in the crowded rooms. Anna stayed close to Joseph as they viewed the exhibits.

A woman in her mid-fifties in a black coat and a scarf over her head was standing in front of a small painting by Frans Hals. I noticed her because she was standing so close to the picture, I thought she had difficulty seeing. I went into the next room where the expressionist paintings were hung. It was so crowded I retreated back to the room with the Dutch paintings. The woman was still standing in front of the Frans Hals. I stood beside her and asked

'Do you know the painting?'

She moved her gaze and looked directly at me. 'Oh, yes,' she said, as her voice cracked, 'I know the painting.'

I waited a moment thinking she might explain why she knew it. Instead she said 'I wrote a letter to an office in Vienna but I didn't give my address. You see I have no proof, only memory.'

'But most of the people here to-day have only memories,' I said.

She was staring at the painting. 'I know every brush stroke on that canvas because I have studied it at the National Gallery.'

'But why did you study that particular painting?'

'Because it lined my suitcase when I came to England with Kindertransport in 1939.' It suddenly dawned on me I had read her letter. Clipstein had sent it to me from Vienna, but I couldn't remember her name. We moved slightly to one side so other people could view the painting.

I introduced myself and asked her name. 'Ester Rosenbaum,' she said, as her voice trembled with emotion.

'Miss Rosenbaum, you should make a claim. That's why these paintings are being shown.' She turned her head away from me as the tears flooded her eyes and choked her throat.'

'Claim, I can't claim. What is left to claim?'

'Please,' I said, 'I will help you.' I took her arm and led her from the gallery.

LONDON

49

Attendances at the exhibition were record breaking and claims were arriving at my office and Clipstein's office in Vienna, daily. Sue had given McKenzie the details of Prantl's death, which he splashed across The Times front page. The story was picked up in various forms by all the newspapers, rendering their own translations of events with countless unanswered questions. "Who was Otto Prantl?" "Why was he murdered?" "Is the British art curator, Katrina Edan involved?" "Is she a double agent?"

I called Sue into my office. She burst out laughing when I handed one of the papers to her. I looked over the top of the page I was reading straight into Sue's big wet brown eyes.

'Am I missing something, Sue? I can't see one funny line in any of these papers.'

'Because, Katrina, there aren't any. They're all embellished second hand tosh: some editor trying to salvage publicity for his paper so Joe Public doesn't say he read it in The Times.'

I noted that Sue had become very au fait with the mechanics of journalism.

'Something Paul told you I presume?' She was fumbling in her notebook and pulled a card from between the pages of its spiral binder and put it front of me. I read:

You are invited to attend Marylebone Registry Office
At 12.30.p.m on the 19 December 1973
To celebrate the marriage of
Sue Hepple and Paul McKenzie
Lunch at the Wig and Pen Club

'You're not serious? You're getting MARRIED?'

For once I was speechless. Hastily I corrected my astonished reaction.

'Congratulations. That announcement deserves a drink.'

I took a bottle of Scotch from the cabinet and poured two large doubles. 'Do we have any ice in the box Sue?'

'Of course. Remember I'm marrying Paul! What would life be like without ice in the fridge?'

The thought of Sue leaving would leave a void in my working life. What would I do? She's irreplaceable I thought irrationally.
'Where will you and Paul live after the wedding?'
'Paul's moving to my flat, then we'll look for a small house somewhere.' I couldn't wait a moment longer and I had to ask.
'Will you be leaving Sue?'
'You can't be serious Katrina. On Paul's salary? Anyway, he knows I'm not the stay-at-home wifely type.'
'Great,' I said with relief. 'I'll drink to that. Where's the honeymoon? Brighton?'
'Most certainly not,' she said with hauteur. 'I have reluctantly agreed to go to another resort starting with B. Barbados!'

***

The exhibition was into its third week when Jack called from the London office of Imperial Chicago bank. 'I've just arrived from Chicago' he said. 'Could I come to your home later, around fiveish?'

By four o'clock London is dark, so walking home isn't an option: it is cold and often wet and I tend to bridge the gap between office and home the quickest way possible.

Jack arrived soon after me at 5.30. with a streaming cold, and sucking eucalyptus tablets so strong their fumes invaded the room every time he coughed. In between coughing and sneezing he said, 'I don't know where to start?'
'Let me help you,' I said. 'From the beginning might be easiest.'

He looked rather helpless as he held a big white handkerchief for comfort and started to speak, but lost his voice. He coughed to clear his throat.
'Do you have a lemon Katrina? I could kill a steaming hot lemon juice with honey.'

He was in luck. My mother had told me when I left home that I should keep a lemon in the house for gin and tonic and colds, and honey because it gives energy.

Jack settled back in the striped armchair, his hands wrapped around the mug I had given him.
'Do you have an aspirin?' he asked.

As I left the room, I looked back over my shoulder. 'Will you be alive when I get back?'

I handed him the packet of aspirin and blurted out 'Sue's getting married in two weeks to Paul McKenzie. She told me to-day.'

Jack took a gulp of lemon juice while throwing a tablet down his throat. 'Great combination. I wouldn't bet on who'd win in the verbal abuse stakes, but if I had to, Sue has the edge.' Then he said, 'Is she leaving?'

'Nope, she's with me for life.'

'And what about your life, Katrina?'

I replied with a rhetorical question. 'What about my life? It feels pretty intact to me. Maybe yours Jack, is need of surveillance.'

He stood up and walked towards the window and looked up at the evening star, holding his mug of lemon and honey.

'You have no idea of the meaning of what you have just said.'

'Of course I have. I'm telling you Jack, look at yourself. Look into what's important in your life and where you want to be. So, you're fed up with banking . . . so what, who's not fed up with their job from time to time? That's no reason to quit.' Jack took a cough drop out of a packet and popped it into his mouth.

'I'm not fed up with banking Katrina: I'm fed up with living a double life. I'm fed up with lying, sacrificing relationships, ours, if we ever had one. The whole goddam shooting match of the Central Intelligence Agency.'

I was about to speak, but he didn't give me time.

'I'll give it to you straight. I've been an agent since I was recruited at Harvard eleven years ago. Believe me, I am telling you the truth.'

'At last' I said.

He blew his nose on the white hankie, put his mug down and said in a croaky voice.

'I am a trained operative within the CIA. I am trained to live a double life. I am trained to keep my mouth shut except to other members of the agency. I'm trained to kill if I have to.'

Jack stopped speaking for a moment, recognising my disbelief.

'I'm not a killer, Katrina. Corporate enterprise in banking is my apparatus. I am a non-official agent operating outside the station, living under cover of my job.'

'Why then,' I wanted to know 'were you recruited if you're so against the CIA? What was wrong with no thank you.'

'Because, at the time, the USSR was a real threat to world peace,

and the CIA recruiting officer told me I had the right skills to serve my country. I spoke fluent German, and I had studied European law.'
'And you're a good liar.' I said with conviction.
'No, that's one of the skills I learned. Another is to use everything and everyone to achieve a successful conclusion. I'm skilled in tradecraft, Katrina, passing letter drops via cutout agents, planting chemicals for invisible writing. I have a Minox camera. I'm a flaps and seals expert. But my main task is putting money into foreign ventures to bolster the US presence in Europe. All the activities of an outside agent in peacetime: very different skills from those used during war. Lying is a self-made trap. I know how to manipulate the truth to make it plausible. That's a skill.'

Since being told by Daniel Clipstein I had been used to snare Gerhard Hofer, I knew now that Jack had used me too. I tipped some Scotch down my throat and poured one for Jack. I said to him with disdain, 'So I was a tool and a fool in your scheme Jack?'
'Yup, that's the rub. But I've quit the agency for the only plausible reason that makes sense to me.'

Jack waited for me to ask what reason. I didn't ask.
'I would have quit sooner,' he said, 'but I wanted to stay close to you, because I didn't want you to get hurt. Believe me Katrina, I quit because I love you and I don't want to lie to you.' He gave a giant sneeze into his handkerchief and held out his glass for another Scotch. 'Please' he said.
'Is that a command?' I said as a gibe.

I wanted him to leave. I didn't want to hear anymore until I felt more at ease and less intimidated. I still distrusted him and this revelation of his activities outside of what I knew made me even more suspicious. But I did ask one last question while I poured myself another Scotch.
'Did you see Myrtle Shaw when you were in the States?'
'Who?' he asked, as if he'd never heard of her.
'Is that an excuse for an answer or do you have more to add?'
'Now I remember who you're talking about: the good-looking broad with black shiny hair and white shiny teeth: the one who

helped you out of trouble. HER. Sure I know her, she's a colleague.'
'A colleague?' I repeated, as I tossed a cushion to the end of the couch and put my feet up.
'Right,' Jack said 'A colleague.'
'In banking or spying? And you haven't answered my question. Did you see her in the States?'
'How could I, she doesn't exist and even if she does I don't know who she is or where she comes from. I know she's been burned now that her specific assignment is concluded: so she's been put to bed until her special expertise is needed again.'
'And what is her expertise, apart from being a good liar?'
'Katrina she's a trained CIA agent and was planted to catch Prantl. Her job was very dangerous. She went right into the hornets' nest, under your cover. Both Frohmann and Prantl were completely taken in by her.'
'So was I. Oh my God, how naive I have been! It's all falling into place. Bunny and Elgin set me up to install Myrtle, their long-lost cousin.' I said to Jack, 'so I'm on track if I say Bunny and Elgin are also CIA agents? If my father had known he was entertaining the CIA he would have invited the SAS to keep you company. I can't wait to tell him.'
'Katrina, I've spoken to you in complete confidence and told you some of the reasons why I acted the way I did. I've also broken the code of silence. But I hope you're wise enough to stay absolutely mute on what I've told you to-day. There are agents still working who could get hurt if the KGB gets a lead. I don't even know if my replacement at the Laufenbankgeschaft in Salzburg is in the service. If you tell any one, anything, you could be responsible for murder and I could be the corpse.'
He put his glass down, and coughed into his handkerchief. 'Would you call a taxi, Katrina. I'm going to bed with a bottle of Scotch.'

LONDON

50

The exhibition generated a vast amount of media space, as I had predicted. Journalists from radio, television, the press, delved into as many personal stories as they could elicit from anxious claimants. Some proved to be false.

Daniel Clipstein, however, had made sure that every claim was checked, erring towards leniency before sending back an application as unsubstantiated.

In spite of the publicity, only eighty-five of the paintings exhibited found owners. Those unclaimed were returned to museums and the orphan paintings were offered for sale to the sponsors. The rest were returned to Salzburg for collection by numbered receipt.

Gerhard Hofer's collection was confiscated and sold at auction in London. The money realized from the sale was donated for distribution to refugees returning to Vienna.

Anna Frishman's claim was fully acknowledged and all the works submitted by Otto Prantl were legally hers. That left the unclaimed paintings belonging to the Galerie Frohmann to be returned.

This did not happen. Three days before the close of the exhibition, I received an announcement.

PROFESSOR WILHELM FROHMANN
It is with deep regret we announce the death of
Wilhelm Frohmann
The funeral will take place at Anif
on December 7 1973.

Inside the envelope addressed to me was a note from Erich Baumrich. He wrote. I am Professor Frohmann's solicitor and I am forwarding the enclosed letter, according to the late Professor Frohmann's wishes.

Dear Miss Edan,
I have known for some time that my days were ending. It is my personal request to you that you are present when Anton Hempf

opens the letter you delivered to him from me. I have put in place legally, my last wishes. A copy of my will is with my solicitor and a further copy with Jack Steinhart. I trust Miss Edan that you will receive the acknowledgement you so well deserve.
I recall what Thomas Mann wrote in Der Zauberberg (The Magic Mountain, 1924):

"It is a fact that a man's dying is more the survivors' affair than his own."

True, except I have no survivors. Wilhelm Frohmann

The Professor's health had deteriorated over the past year and I should have been prepared. Somehow I wasn't.

My loyalty to exposing stolen art had not waned during the years I'd worked with him, yet at no time had I given him my complete trust. He was, after all, a Nazi, albeit a past Nazi. As I held the letter, I found myself bereft of a friend. In spite of his past, he had been a friend to me. I chose not to look at his motivations nor be his judge: I had curated and exposed the spoils of war, and he was the vehicle that helped me along. I did not feel sadness, just loss. I recalled the shine on his pearl tiepin, the velvet slippers, the twinkling eyes that could no longer see, and the slender fingers that held a Rembrandt slide as if it were a priceless gem.

Anton Hempf opened the letter from Wilhelm Frohmann in my presence. He read it first then handed it to me.

Dear Anton,
As a measure of my respect for you, it is my wish that the paintings exhibited in London from my galerie, should remain with you. It is my wish, dear friend, that the paintings in my homes in Vienna and Anif should also become yours. I respectfully ask you to finish editing my book on Rembrandt, and I respectfully understand why you do not wish to have your name associated. Our lives have taken very different directions, ultimately towards the same conclusion: that art will survive us all. Unfortunately, we were unable to go to that boundary together. Wilhelm.

***

Jack Steinhart, Elizabeth Cuthbertson, Sue Hepple, Paul McKenzie and Desmond Hegarty were at the Royal Academy on the final day of the exhibition. Paul said it was a wake, Desmond said it was a hassle. Elizabeth said, 'well done.' Sue said, 'what next? And Jack said, 'your money's run out.'

By 2 o'clock the doors closed and with it an exhibition which would have no sequel. Unlike anything else I had ever done, this was unique, a one-off time that I would never repeat. While I knew that countless masterpieces still remained undisclosed, festering on the walls behind the Iron Curtain, there was no more I could do except wait. Some time, in the not too distant future they will surface. What I had shown in this exhibition was only a soupçon of what will transpire later. My exhibition will be insignificant when the magnitude of deceit is unveiled, and great paintings still knowingly held illegally by museums around the world are exposed.

I went down the steps of the Royal Academy with Jack, through the revolving door to the courtyard and into Piccadilly. I gazed at the garlanded lampposts, interlaced with red and green. I looked up at the mythical figure of Father Christmas riding in an illuminated sleigh surrounded by a galaxy of winged angels.

The festive season had come relentlessly into focus: a stark contrast to the sombre mood in the rooms at the Royal Academy. We went towards Piccadilly Circus, our thoughts private, unshared. The statue of Eros, son of Aphrodite, the goddess of love, is poised on a plinth, high above the admiring crowd, a winged messenger with an arrow, waiting mischievously.

Jack broke the silence when he asked, 'Are you going to Wendover for Christmas?'

'Of course,' I said, resigned to the omnipresent ritual. 'And you?'

'I was thinking about Wendover too.' he said.

In the season of good will to all men and my liberated soul, and in the presence of Eros, I impulsively said to Jack. 'Why not invite Vivacious and your current stepfather. We could play Happy Families.'

***

Anton Hempf was named in the New Year's honours list and subsequently knighted by the Queen, in recognition of his outstanding contribution to the understanding and appreciation of art.

In 2002 The Bank of England confirmed that counterfeit notes were printed at Mauthausen during World War ll.

The Germans used these forged notes for purchases from neutral countries, to pay agents abroad and in occupied countries, and for disruptive economic warfare. Switzerland and Liechtenstein were used as clearinghouses, and as a depository by the hierarchy of the SS, for covert transactions and for personal gain.

Of the £516 million pounds allegedly printed, it was not until 1959, fourteen years after the end of the war, that printing presses and sodden wads of notes, estimated at a value of 3 million, were recovered from Lake Toplitz, in Austria.

Counterfeit money was circulating during the Cold War from 1945 and as late as 1989 when the Berlin Wall was removed. It is a fact that forged notes still surface for conversion to legal tender to-day.

Acknowledgements

I am indebted to Julia Casterton for her advice and encouragement and her unfailing belief in my manuscript during its progress. I am grateful to Marette Crescenzi and William Atkinson for their editing and invaluable comments. I must thank the following authors and their books: Derrick Byatt, *Promises to Pay;* Abba Eban, *Heritage;* Lynn H. Nicholas, *The Rape of Europa;* Yigal Lossin, *Pillars of Fire;* Russell Chamberlin, *Loot!* My thanks to The Wiener Library, The British Museum Library, The Royal Academy, and Yad Vachem, Jerusalem. I am indebted to Sara Levijan for her support and research in Tel Aviv and to Ann Friedman in Chicago. I should also like to thank Bertha Leverton of Kindertransport.